Hidden by Fire

Maggie Sloan Thriller Book 3

Judith A. Barrett

WOBBLY CREEK

ALSO BY JUDITH A. BARRETT

MAGGIE SLOAN THRILLER SERIES
RILEY MALLOY MYSTERY SERIES
GRID DOWN SURVIVAL SERIES
DONUT LADY COZY MYSTERY SERIES
WREN AND RASCAL MYSTERY SERIES
JENNA ROSS MYSTERY SERIES

HIDDEN BY FIRE

MAGGIE SLOAN THRILLER, BOOK 3

Published in the United States of America by Wobbly Creek, LLC

2020 Georgia

wobblycreek.com

Cover by Wobbly Creek, LLC

ISBN 978-1-7331241-8-8 eBook

ISBN 978-1-7331241-9-5 Paperback

DEDICATION

HIDDEN BY FIRE is dedicated to the colors red and emerald green and to first responders and health professionals, especially those in my family.

PREVIOUSLY

PREVIOUSLY...

My name is Maggie Sloan, and I always wanted to be a spy. However, sometimes life has its twists; I couldn't turn down a full scholarship, and a librarian would be an excellent cover for a spy, right? I never knew it was dangerous to be a librarian until the library explosion tossed me across the front lawn and almost to the parking lot. According to my doctor, the force of the blast left me "a mess" of broken bones.

Luckily, my imaginary men, Palace Guard and Spike, helped me with physical therapy. I didn't expect them to stick around, but they did. After a heart-wrenching murder, my best friend and FBI agent, Kate, and my imaginary men toughened me up and taught me some pretty cool shooting and fighting skills.

You might have noticed I mentioned "imaginary men." There's a long story behind that, but the short version is when I was in the hospital, Palace Guard helped me to stand when it appeared that I'd never stand or walk again, and Spike toughened me up, so that I could tackle the three stair steps that were between me and being released from the hospital.

Did I mention all the murders? Evidently, a librarian with the soul of a spy is a murder magnet. Police Officer Ewing, his actual name is Kevin, I eventually learned, and my imaginary men stuck with me in my tangles with killers. I dubbed Kevin "Larry" because he was undercover, and no one told me his name. I was surprised a simple nickname was such a sore point between us, so I lied about it. He adjusted to the nickname, but he still calls me out on any lies.

Kate asked me to do a little sleuthing for her in Galveston, Texas, and arranged for Larry to work with me. Larry's smart and a dang good partner most of the time, except he's competitive and has an annoying streak of not minding his own business.

I can't imagine being without Larry, Palace Guard, and Spike; when it was time to return from Galveston, Larry and I talked it over: things would be different at home because we wouldn't be as close. We'll adjust.

CHAPTER ONE

I leaned forward in my porch rocker and sharpened my knife while my old brown dog, Lucy, roamed the fenced-in yard. My small, pale-blue cottage out in the country, with a horse farm on one side and a goat farm on the other, suited Lucy, me, and the two imaginary men.

The familiar odor of the neighbor's goat farm drifted in with the south wind, and my eyes watered. I had set my phone on the porch, and it danced as it buzzed. I raised my eyebrows as I answered the phone. "Jennifer?"

"I don't have much time, Maggie. I never made this call. Got that? Kate will come see you in the morning. She'll ask you to work with Glenn. Don't let on that I told you and don't say yes until we talk. Come to my house for lunch tomorrow and bring Lucy and your men if you want." She hung up.

Spike cocked his head, and I shrugged. "It was Kate's mother. She was mysterious, which is out of character for her, but we're invited to her house for lunch tomorrow, so maybe we'll find out what's going on."

Palace Guard stood near the back fence. He pointed to the three-foot square bulls-eye target then raised his eyebrows.

I pushed the stray hair away from my face. "Yes, my knife is sharpened now, but Lucy enjoys the yard."

Spike rocked on his back-porch chair next to me. When he raised his hand, Lucy trotted to him and flopped next to his chair.

"Traitor," I mumbled as I trudged down the porch steps.

Palace Guard faced the target and pulled his arm back then simulated a knife throw in a smooth arc.

I copied him, and my knife left my hand in a perfect arc then spiraled down. My throw buried my knife's tip into the lower quarter of the target, but I had hit the target.

"At least I hit it." I turned to Spike to gloat, but he shook his head and waved circles with his hand.

"What do you mean, *again*? That was a near-perfect strike," I snarled.

He shrugged and repeated his *again* motion.

"You are infuriating." I faced the target and prepared to throw then narrowed my eyes as Palace Guard repeated his slow-motion arc and ended with his arm straight and his index finger pointed at the target.

"I see now. I stopped my arc too early and lost momentum. Rookie mistake. I'm lucky the tip stuck into the wood at all."

Palace Guard pointed to a car on the road north of us as it sped past the neighbor's horse farm. Palace Guard held up his forefinger and blew. *Smoking gun.*

I smiled. "Larry's here. Maybe he's finished up his special assignment and will be around. I've missed him." I rushed around the house to the driveway and waved.

He parked and approached the house with his head down.

"Were you waiting for me? Did Kate already tell you?" he asked. "Let's go inside."

I opened the front door. "Tell me what? I haven't seen you in three and a half months. I've received only seventeen texts from you and no phone calls, and the first thing you say is did Kate already tell me? How about hello?"

Palace Guard and Spike stood at the kitchen table with their arms crossed. Spike scowled at Larry.

"Hello, guys." Larry bit his lip then sat on the sofa.

Palace Guard and Spike maintained their stance, and I copied them.

Larry frowned. "You three make me nervous. Please sit down, Maggie."

"What's going on?" I narrowed my eyes.

"My special assignment hasn't been with the Harperville police department like I kind of said."

"Oh. I thought it was something bad." I flopped onto the sofa next to him. "You were on loan to Kate and the FBI again, weren't you? Of course, that's why you couldn't call. I knew that. When do you think you'll be back at your regular job?"

Larry stared at the floor. "I won't be coming back to the police department. I've been in training for the Georgia Bureau of Investigation at the training center north of Macon."

I raised my eyebrows. "Why didn't you tell me about this earlier?"

"I was afraid I'd wash out or that you'd be mad."

"Well, you're wrong on both counts. No way would you wash out because you are a talented law enforcement officer, and I'm not mad because I don't care. Must be good for your career. Nice of you to drop by."

I stomped to my bedroom and slammed the door.

"Maggie?" Larry tapped on the door. "I wasn't ready to tell anybody quite yet, but I needed to see you. You said I'm talented. Did you mean it? Maggie?"

"Goodbye. Let yourself out."

I held my breath as his footsteps headed to the front door. I leaned with my ear against the bedroom door.

He said, "Later, Palace Guard. See ya, Spike."

The front door clicked as it closed. When his car pulled out of the driveway, I slumped against the door then rushed to peek out my bedroom window as he drove north to the main road.

I strode to the living room and glared. "Did everybody know about this except me?"

Palace Guard turned away, and Spike shrugged. I stomped out to the back porch, and Lucy followed me. I slammed the door behind her, but when I turned, Palace Guard sat on the steps.

I flounced to my rocker. "First Parker left me when he died then Larry applied for a new job and didn't tell me. He'll go off to who knows where, and I'll never see him again. I guess I'm supposed to be alone."

Palace Guard rolled his eyes and laid the back of his hand on his forehead.

"I am not being dramatic," I growled as my tears dripped onto the porch.

After I wiped my runny nose on my shirtsleeve, then stomped to the door and twisted the doorknob, I pulled and tugged at the door. When it wouldn't open, I dropped to the floor and sobbed. "I've locked myself out."

Palace Guard reached over me and pushed open the door then smirked.

I glared then my mouth quivered into a smile. "I need to remember which way a door opens the next time I throw a fit."

The next morning, I rocked on the porch and sipped my coffee as the sky lightened. The low morning fog hung over the field behind my house, and the grass was damp from dew. Lucy stood at the edge of the porch and sniffed the air.

My phone buzzed with a text. Palace Guard and Spike peered over my shoulder as I read the message from Kate Coyle, FBI team leader and my friend. "Got coffee? Be there ten min."

As I pulled down a cup, Kate whipped open the front door and glided in. She had pulled her long brown hair on top of her head in a floppy version of a ponytail. She was tall, slender, and moved with the grace of a ballerina. "I forgot to tell you I was coming. Who's cooking breakfast, you or me?"

She stopped and grinned. "Hey, Spike. Great to see you. Palace Guard here?"

Spike held an imaginary rifle as he marched stiff-legged across the room in his impression of a Buckingham Palace Guard. Kate and I laughed, and Palace Guard narrowed his eyes.

"Must mean yes." Kate wiped her eyes. "I'd sure like to know why I see Spike, but not Palace Guard."

"I already told you. You aren't immature enough. Why didn't you tell me about Larry?" I mixed the batter for blueberry pancakes, my new specialty.

"Not my place. I only knew about his new job in my official capacity. Guess he told you. Good." Kate pulled out her mother's sausage patties.

"Feed your freezer," Jennifer had said when she delivered the sausage.

I smiled as I remembered Jennifer's kindness.

Kate dropped the patties into a skillet and turned up the heat then gulped down her coffee. "Can't talk about Larry. Hand me your griddle. I'll heat it up for you after the sausage is done. Here's the deal. The county changed your disability status. Your folder was marked *temporary*, and when they reviewed it last week, the county deemed your disability had ended. Case closed."

"That's great news, but I saw my file when I tried to fight it after the hospital released me. It was labeled *permanent*." I raised my eyebrows. "Magical change? That's excellent."

"Isn't it, though? But the reason I'm here is to tell you I need you for spy stuff. Actually, Dad does. His detective agency won the contract for the case assigned to Rosa before she died, but let's talk after we eat."

Kate placed the hot, browned sausages on the plate I'd covered with a paper towel.

I put my hands on my hips. "I adore Glenn, but I'm not interested."

Kate opened the refrigerator and handed me the blueberries then pointed to my mixing bowl. I folded the blueberries into the batter.

She refilled our coffee cups and set the silverware and maple syrup on the table then settled into her seat. "Dad needs somebody to do his legwork. That's where you come in now that you're eligible for employment."

She sipped her coffee. "This is excellent. Just like I taught you." She grinned. "Dad also forgot to tell Mom he has two contracts, and she got mad and quit the Coyle Detective Agency. Now he needs somebody to replace Mom."

Kate jumped up and pulled out the butter. "You know anybody else who needs a job? Mom said she'd be happy to train her replacement as long as she didn't have to work with Dad in the office. *That man's office* is what she said. I've never seen her so angry."

I plated Kate's pancakes and set them in front of her. "Another reason for me not to get involved. I don't want Jennifer mad at me."

Kate buttered her pancakes, and as the butter oozed down the side, she poured on the syrup. "We have a new potential recruit that needs an independent field evaluation. Dad's first contract is to interview the candidate. The second contract is to analyze some data. Did you know Dad re-injured his leg? Dad's doctor ordered him to stay off his feet and give his leg a chance to heal."

I narrowed my eyes. "I don't see where Glenn needs any help to analyze data. I'm not interested."

Kate shrugged. "Might require some travel. What do you think about Mobile, Alabama?"

"Now that's tempting. At the truck stop diner we liked? Will I fry fish or be the breakfast cook?"

Kate poked holes in her pancakes with her fork then poured more syrup. "Lucy can stay with Mom and Dad if you go out of town. Just two weeks. If you don't love the job, you can come home."

Kate cut her pancakes then swallowed her first bite. "Mmm. Good." She wiped the dripping syrup off her hand.

I scowled. "You said that before too. Two weeks and the come home part."

She snickered. "Don't burn your pancakes."

I rescued my pancakes and joined Kate at the table. After I'd eaten half of my two pancakes, I scooted back my chair. "More coffee? I should have made only one for myself. I'm stuffed."

"Lightweight." Kate cleared the table except for our cups. "I'll do the dishes. You cooked."

While she filled the sink with hot, soapy water, Kate said, "Your hair needs a touch up. You going gray this time or red?"

"I was looking at my roots the other day. I like my natural color."

Kate rinsed the griddle and examined my hair. "Might be interesting. You could cut your hair extra-short. Call your mother."

"She'd hang up on me and schedule an appointment."

"Yep, she would." Kate tossed the dish towel to the sink.

I pouted. "I could ask Larry if he was here."

"I gotta go. You never saw me."

Kate strode to the door. "Text him." She waved to Spike then slammed the door.

"Have you ever noticed Kate was never here? And Jennifer never called me," I said, and Spike did his wacky dance.

Palace Guard bounced on his toes and stretched. He wore his running shoes, shorts, and shirt.

"Good idea." I rushed to my bedroom and changed then hurried to the front porch to stretch.

"Horses or goats?" I asked.

Palace Guard leapt off the porch and headed south.

"Goats it is," I shouted with glee as I chased him down the road.

Palace Guard stopped at the goat farm and leaned on the fence. When I joined him, he pointed to the new babies' shed where triplets gamboled under their mother's watchful eye.

"Thanks. I needed to see cuteness." I kicked at the bottom of the sturdy fence post.

"Before we left Galveston, I told Larry I was terrified something would happen to him." I sniffed back my unwelcome tears. "I didn't give him a chance to talk at all yesterday, did I?"

Palace Guard shook his head and patted my shoulder then jogged toward the house until I raced past him. Palace Guard caught up with me in two strides. When we reached the end of the goat farm fence, he dove headfirst into the field next to my small cottage, and I plunged into the tall grass with him.

I kept my head down and listened. *A car speeding toward my house from the north.*

Palace Guard peered over the grass then blew on his finger. *Smoking gun.*

We rose, and he waited while I brushed the dried grass and dirt off my clothes.

Larry pulled into my driveway and stepped out of his car as Spike and Lucy bounded out of the house. Palace Guard waved, and I raced to Larry as he held out his arms for my finish line. I crashed into him, and he wrapped his arms around me.

We laughed, and he held onto me. I leaned against him. *This is nice.*

"Maggie, I signed the final papers at the police department and am on my way out of town. I have two more weeks of training left. Eleven days. I don't know..." He swallowed hard and glanced at Palace Guard who nodded.

I leaned back and met Larry's gaze as he searched my face. Spike tapped his foot in impatience.

"I don't know where I'll be going, but I want you with me wherever it is. Will you think about it?"

My eyes widened. "I was cranky and not nice at all yesterday. Does this mean you aren't mad at me?"

"Here. Keep this for me." He handed me his new Texas Tech ball cap then stroked my cheek with his fingertips as he kissed my gaping mouth with a soft kiss.

"Yes, I'm not mad at you." He released me and chuckled.

Palace Guard held up his hand, and Larry smacked a high-five then kissed me lightly again.

"Two weeks." He waved as he drove away.

"Two weeks," I mumbled as I touched my lips with my fingertips then returned his wave.

As I walked into the house, I asked, "Did you two know about this?"

Spike grinned and nodded, and Palace Guard smiled.

I grabbed my phone. "I have two weeks, but now I don't know what to think about Larry, and I still don't know what to do about my hair. Ella is a neutral party. I'll call her."

Ella picked up right away. "That you, Maggie? How did you know I needed to talk to you?"

"Are you okay?"

"I'm fine." She sighed. "Maybe I'm not; I was laid off and have until noon to pick up my things from the warehouse. I picked up my phone to call you, then it rang. Are you busy?"

"Not at all. We can talk on the way there."

"I'm downtown having my nails done. I'll pick you up in thirty minutes. You still at your little house out in the country?"

"Sure am. See you soon."

Spike held his nose and waved his hand in front of his face.

"I planned to shower, Spike. Don't be such a nag."

I showered then, after I dressed, Palace Guard, Spike, and I waited for Ella on the front porch while Lucy investigated the front yard.

"I met Ella before the explosion. I told you about her pie shirt. It said *pi Fixes Everything*, pi like 3.14."

Spike stuck out his tongue and fake-coughed in an exaggerated gag, and I snorted.

"You're just irritated because you didn't think of it first."

I called Jennifer. "I have a friend who might be looking for a job."

"Bring her with you for lunch," Jennifer whispered then hung up.

After Ella pulled into the driveway, I opened the passenger's door and glanced at the backseat. "Are those new seat covers, Ella? That pale cream color is beautiful."

She beamed. "Not too new. I had the car reupholstered when I got it last year. It's a reliable car, but the seats were ripped."

"Will we have time to pick up your things then come back here to pick up Lucy? We've all been invited to lunch."

"More than enough. Jump in." Ella's dark-brown eyes twinkled, and her round chocolate-cream face dimpled as she smiled.

"Tell me about this layoff," I said as she pulled out of the driveway.

"It's technically a furlough, not a layoff, because we can be recalled, but furlough sounds too much like a vacation to me. The company's new second warehouse at the other end of town burned down two weeks ago. Did you hear about it?"

I shuddered at the memory of the intense fire at Diane's Diner in Texas. "I hadn't heard about it. Was anyone hurt?"

"The fire was during the night shift, but everyone got out safely. We're convinced it was arson, but the fire marshal hasn't completed his investigation. The company can't afford to rebuild for a while, so they shuffled people around. The company furloughed over half of the mid-management staff at my facility. Can you believe I'm mid-management?" Ella chuckled.

"I'm not surprised. You're amazing."

"I don't have much to pick up because I don't keep personal items at work like most people do: you know, pictures and stuff. I have my favorite pens and my lamp from home. Everything else stays. I just needed the moral support. I understand the circumstances, but I still have a deflated ego. That's why I called you. Or almost called you. You're a great confidence-booster." Ella patted my hand. "Now, what do you have for me?"

"I'm interested in your thoughts about my hair. I've got options. I could go all gray again, go red again, or cut it all off and let it be my natural whatever color it is, light brown, I guess."

"What do you want to do?"

I stared at her. *If I knew that, why would I ask?*

"Gotcha." She laughed. "You just think about that."

Palace Guard reached from the back and patted her shoulder.

"Thanks," she said. "Maggie, did you know I have a guardian angel when you're around? She just patted me on the shoulder."

I'd be in big trouble if I repeated Ella called Palace Guard "she."

I glanced at Palace Guard, and he shook his finger at me.

When I smiled my sweet *I'd never do that* smile, he glared.

Ella pulled into the warehouse parking lot, waved to the security guard, and parked at the front door. "I'll leave you here with the engine running. You're my excuse to run in and back out. Look like my pitiful friend or something." She guffawed as she grabbed her shopping bag and climbed out.

I pulled down the visor and practiced pitiful looks in the mirror while Palace Guard's shoulders shook in laughter. When I realized the security guard was laughing too, I pretended to check my nonexistent makeup. I flipped up the visor when Ella came outside with her bag.

"What were you doing? The security guard was laughing at my car when I came out." Ella peered at me.

"Being pitiful. Did you get everything you wanted?"

"Sure did. Including some information. Will we investigate the fire? Because one of my night shift friends saw a man with a gas can run away from the warehouse right before the fire alarm went off. My money's on the fire marshal finding evidence of an accelerant."

"I hope we won't, but I do have more that I forgot to tell you. My disability was temporary after all, and it expired."

"That's great news. We're both out of work. That means we can open our own business. I'm a good marketer. I'll get us a contract. What do we call our new company? *Magella?* That has a nice ring."

While we sat at the red light, she tapped the steering wheel and furrowed her brow. "Do we have a retirement plan?"

When I laughed, she winked. "Not everybody gets my humor."

I wiped my eyes. "How's your daughter doing in DC?"

"She loves the big city. I told her I don't know whose child she is. I couldn't tolerate the traffic, but she's young and lives close to work. She has friends, and that's important. So, where will we go for lunch?"

"Jennifer Coyle invited us. We'll go to her house. She might know about a job opportunity."

"Oh good. We can write this off as a business expense. You ask Mrs. Coyle for a receipt." Ella snickered.

I smiled. "You just keep calling her Mrs. Coyle."

"Sounds like you're trying to get me into trouble," Ella said as she pulled into my driveway. I let Lucy out of the house, and after the five of us piled into my car, I headed to the Coyles' house.

Glenn's truck was in the driveway. When Lucy yipped, Jennifer rushed out of the house. She was short, not as short as I am, but short by Coyle standards. She was slender, and her short blond hair had a halo of silver around her face. Spike opened the car door for Lucy, and she bounded to Jennifer. Jennifer sat on the porch steps and hugged Lucy and cooed.

"Jennifer, this is Ella. Ella, Jennifer." *Mother would be proud of my manners.*

"Come on in." Jennifer rose and opened the front door. Lucy scrambled to get inside the house.

"Maggie, I wanted you to talk to Glenn before you committed to working with him. He's here," Jennifer whispered. "He has to stay home now, but I can tolerate that. My turf." She wiggled her eyebrows, and I snorted.

Jennifer peered at Ella. "You look familiar, Ella. Weren't you a library volunteer at the middle school?"

"I didn't think you'd remember, Mrs. Coyle. You must have had a hundred volunteers to schedule."

"It's so nice to see you." Jennifer hurried down the steps and linked her arm into Ella's. "Call me Jennifer. Do you remember the time..."

My imaginary men gaped, and I stared as the two women chatted as they strolled into the house.

"Guess we can go in too," I said. Spike shrugged, and Palace Guard nodded.

When we entered the den, Glenn sat in his chair with his leg propped up. He smiled while he massaged Lucy's neck and shoulders. "Hi, Maggie. Men with you?"

I dropped onto the sofa. "Sure are. So, what secret do you have that I can't tell anybody because they already know?"

He laughed. "You've been talking to the Coyle women. That's too subtle for me. I'm what you call transparent."

"Simple. I call you simple," Jennifer called from the kitchen.

"She's not as mad as she was yesterday when she called me a cicada," Glenn whispered.

I snickered then told him about Larry.

He examined my face. "Two weeks isn't long. What will you tell him?"

Spike sat on the floor in front of me, propped up his face with his hands, and fluttered his eyelashes.

"Cut it out, Spike. We're having a serious discussion. I don't know, Glenn. I can't bear to be away from him, and I worry about him all the time, but I don't know."

"Sorry I can't see the men," Glenn said. "Can Larry?"

When I nodded, he whistled. "Impressive. Well, we've got two weeks to figure this out."

"Kate said you need help, and she mentioned Mobile, Alabama."

"I have two contracts, but I don't know anything about Mobile. The first contract is easy. I'm supposed to interview and evaluate a potential recruit. The interview should be less than an hour then I'll spend a couple of hours on the evaluation. The second one is less well-defined. I'm supposed to receive some documents from a courier. I'm not clear on the type of data; maybe it needs interpretation more than analysis. I know it's not much to go on, but what do you think?"

"It wouldn't hurt to have something to keep me busy."

"I love it. Your brains, and my years of experience and bumbling. Unbeatable combination." Glenn chuckled. "Let's start tomorrow morning. We need to get you a laptop so you'll have tools when we're strategizing. Otherwise, the office will give you more space and a better set up. Laptop, anything else?"

"I'll bring my laptop tomorrow. That may be all I need."

Jennifer appeared in the doorway. "Lunch is ready. We can eat on the patio if you like."

"Sounds great," Glenn said.

"We'll wheel you out." Jennifer rolled a wheelchair into the den and locked the wheels. Glenn eased into the seat, and she pushed him to the patio door. Ella slipped into the den, and Jennifer introduced her to Glenn.

"Surprise," Jennifer said as she opened the sliding glass patio door. "I built a ramp yesterday so you can wheel in and out without someone pushing you."

Glenn laughed. "You are one amazing woman."

"First smart thing you've said in weeks." Jennifer's blue eyes twinkled. "Y'all head out. I've already set the patio table. I'll bring out sandwiches."

I headed to the kitchen. "I'll pour drinks."

"I'll help you carry them," Ella said. She followed me into the kitchen. "Maggie, Jennifer hired me to manage the office. She'll work with me the rest of the week to get me started."

We trooped out to the patio. After we had our fill of chicken salad sandwiches and fresh carrot and cucumber sticks with Jennifer's spicy jalapeno dip, Jennifer asked, "You're going to work with Glenn, right? I'll feed you breakfast if you're here by seven. Ella and I will meet at the office at eight."

"I'll be here," I said.

"Glenn, we're all set for tomorrow. You want to relax out here or in the air conditioning?"

I rose. "I'll clear the table and do the dishes then we'll go so you can rest, Glenn."

"I'll let you clear the table for me, but I'm particular about how my dishwasher is loaded," Jennifer said. "Glenn, see if the ramp works for you."

On our way to my house, Ella asked, "Did you decide about your hair?"

"Maybe my natural color. I'm still thinking."

After Ella left, I cleaned the bathrooms and changed the sheets on my bed. As I swept the great room, Spike fake-sneezed.

I glared. "If the dust bothers you, go outside. Sometimes I need actual sweeping to clear the cobwebs out of my head, so I can think."

When I swept the broom over his feet, he fell to the floor in a swoon and grinned up at me, and I chuckled. "You're not helping, but that was funny."

When my phone rang, I dashed to pick it up, then frowned. *Why did I think it would be Larry?*

"Hello, Mother. I was thinking about you earlier."

"Hello, Margaret. Big D and I would like to invite you to dinner tonight. You aren't seeing anybody are you? Big D's nephew is in town and will meet us at Vecchia Nonna. He's a bigshot lawyer in Atlanta. We'll pick you up at six. You were thinking about me? That's nice."

"I need to do something with my hair. Do you think your stylist can work me in?"

Mother hung up.

I stared at the phone, and Palace Guard smiled.

"You'd think I'd get used to it. My theory is her hearing aids have a built-in delay, but I'm not sure how a delay explains why she still never says goodbye."

I poured a glass of sweet tea and sat at the kitchen table. Palace Guard sat with me, and we stared at my phone. Before I emptied my glass, Mother called back.

"Margaret, your appointment with Doris is in thirty minutes. Color and cut." *Click.*

After my quick shower, Palace Guard and I left Spike and Lucy snoozing on the sofa. When we entered the shop, Doris greeted me at the door. She was the same age as Mother, but her swollen ankles told of the years she'd carried her extra weight and the long hours she'd spent on her feet. Her hair was dyed boot-black, and her wispy, pale eyebrows were defined with a fine black penciled-in arch that gave her a permanently surprised look.

"Cut and color, right? Did you have anything in mind?"

"Not short. I think I'd like something close to my natural hair color. Light brown?"

Doris waved toward her chair. "You still have a lot of red streaks. I think we can work that. Did you know your mother would love for you to be blond again?"

"I'm not surprised."

After I sat in the chair, she floated the cape around me and fastened it in the back then lifted sections of my hair and examined all the layers. "With your Texas tan and your green eyes, we can go with just about any color you like. You have a natural red in your hair, and your soft curls help me work in highlights. Let's go with shoulder length."

Doris combed out my tangles then snipped away under Palace Guard's watchful eye. She positioned herself in front of me and pulled down on the front side sections of my hair. When Doris was satisfied the sides were even, she said, "Now to mix. Be right back."

CHAPTER TWO

Palace Guard raised his eyebrows when Doris returned. When I swiveled the chair to look, I stared. She had four small bowls on a tray. She turned me away from the mirror then placed her tray on her work stand.

"This will be perfect for you," she said as she sectioned my hair. I closed my eyes and breathed in through my nose and out through my pursed lips to calm the looming panic.

Doris placed a plastic cap that reminded me of a shower cap over my head. "Okay, Maggie. Let's get you under the hair dryer for a bit." After I was seated, she pulled down the large silver dome and turned it on. The roar of the dryer drowned out all the surrounding sounds. I checked my phone. *Nothing.*

Palace Guard sat at the dryer seat next to me and peered at my phone. He blew on his finger.

"What do I say?" I mumbled then chewed on my thumbnail before I tapped. "Getting my hair cut and colored. Ready for a surprise?"

Palace Guard grinned and held up his hand. I smacked a high-five as the dryer cut off. When Doris raised her eyebrows, I brushed away the imaginary pesky fly, and Palace Guard smirked.

"Let's give you a rinse then I'll blow dry, and we'll see what we have." Doris pointed to the shampoo bowl.

I leaned back and enjoyed the warm water. When Doris turned off the water, she wrapped my head with a towel then the three of us trooped to her stylist's station. She whirled me to face away from the mirror, towel-dried my hair, and hummed as she eased the comb through my curls. Palace Guard cocked his head and peered as she worked.

She turned on her portable hair dryer and attacked my hair with a bristly brush. When she turned off the dryer, she whipped the chair around. "What do you think?"

"Beautiful work, Doris," a stylist said as she came closer to examine my hair.

Doris peered at me. "You like it?"

I turned my head from side to side. My hair was pale blond with copper red and dark blond and dark red streaks. "Looks like I spend all my time on the beach. I didn't expect this much red."

"Sun-kissed. That's exactly the look I was going for." Doris beamed. "Here's a mirror. Check the back." She twirled the chair, and I held up the mirror.

"Doesn't look like me." I furrowed my brow as I squinted at the back.

Doris guffawed. "Said the girl who dyed her platinum blond hair black then gray before she went to all red."

Palace Guard nodded.

"It'll grow on ya. Tell your mother hi for me. She already paid me and gave me a nice tip. Off you go." Doris whipped away my cape with a flourish, and I rose in a daze then squinted at the mirror again before I headed to the door.

When I climbed into the car, my phone buzzed.

Larry: "Will I like it?"

Palace Guard leaned over the back seat and read. He smiled and shook his head then winked.

"Good idea. I don't know if this counts as getting even or not, but I like it."

I tapped. "PG says no."

On our way home, I said, "If we were in Galveston, I'd stop for a taco to celebrate. Let's go for a long run."

I pulled into the driveway and parked then we hurried inside to change to running clothes. I checked in the backyard for Spike and Lucy and rushed back inside. "I can't find Lucy."

Palace Guard pointed south.

"Goat farm? I'll bet they're checking out the babies. I'll change."

When we dashed out the door, Spike and Lucy sauntered up the driveway. Spike froze.

"Do you think Larry will like it?" I asked.

Spike rolled his eyes.

"You think so?" I frowned as I patted my hair.

Lucy stopped for me to scratch her ears before they went inside.

Palace Guard trotted down the driveway, and I chased him. After we ran past the goat farm and around the corner, we continued to the next farm before we looped back to return. I ran as fast as I could when we continued north past the horse farm to the highway. We wheeled around and sprinted home. When we ran inside, I collapsed on the sofa. "Good run."

Spike pointed to my phone. I had a text.

Jennifer: "Blueberry pancakes or cinnamon rolls?"

I smiled as I tapped. "Cinnamon rolls."

My phone rang. *I'm a regular social butterfly.*

"Hello, Mother."

"Doris called me. She said your hair is stunning and that I'll love it. Do you love it? I forgot to remind you that Vecchia Nonna is a fancy restaurant. Wear something nice. See you at six."

I stared at my phone. "Now, what does that mean? What do I have that is nice?"

I hurried to my bedroom and frowned at the clothes in my closet. *Black pants, my red boots, and what?* I flipped through my running shirts until I reached the pale green blouse that Jennifer bought me. *Perfect. Disaster averted.*

I spent the rest of the afternoon on my computer researching less-common types of crimes for a quick refresher. At five-thirty, I showered, then dressed. As I examined my hair in the mirror, Spike pointed to the drawer where I had dumped the makeup I never used.

"What the heck. I have five minutes. Were you teasing me about my hair color?" I applied the pale rose lipstick and stared at my face. "Not too clownish, right?"

Spike held up his two thumbs, and I turned away from the mirror before I scrubbed away any signs of the lipstick.

Sergeant Arrington pulled into my driveway right at six o'clock, and Mother waved as I locked the door. "Come on, Margaret. We're ready to go."

When I reached the car, Palace Guard was in the back seat in his dress uniform. As I slid into the back seat, I smiled and whispered, "Thank you."

"You're welcome, Maggie," Sergeant Arrington said. "It's nice to see you."

"My Duane hasn't seen his nephew since Christopher was a child, but now he's a lawyer in Atlanta, an up-and-comer, as they say. What does that even mean? Christopher has a meeting in the morning. I didn't catch who the meeting was with. I was paying attention to Franklin. I would have brought my sweet cat along because I know you love him so much, Margaret, but Big D said Franklin would be more comfortable at home where he could roam and stretch out. Your hair is stunning. Isn't it, Big D? Doris was right. Did you know..."

I leaned back and listened to the lilt in Mother's voice. Her red hair glistened in the light, and her green eyes sparkled when she glanced at Sarge. She wore her favorite pink, blue, and bright green tropical blouse, and Sarge wore a crisp, white shirt with a blue tie that matched Mother's cornflower blue slacks. I snickered. *I wear black pants; Mother wears cornflower slacks.*

When we reached the restaurant on the outskirts of town, Sarge parked at the front entrance and opened Mother's door then mine. Palace Guard put his hand on his heart, and I nodded. *Vecchia Nonna Ristorante* was lettered in gold Old World script on the bright red canopy that protected the entryway from sun or rain.

While we waited for Sarge, Mother said, "We found this restaurant not long after it opened. Big D proposed to me here. Very romantic."

We strolled inside the fancy, romantic restaurant. I inhaled the aromas of garlic, herbs, and warm, fresh bread and stared at the high, domed ceiling. The paintings on the wall were reminiscent of the Baroque flamboyance, and the ornate crystal chandelier and amber lighting added to the ambiance of an Old-World banquet room. The soft background music was classical violin, and the lush, pale orange carpeting and white tablecloths muffled the clinks of dishes and the conversations. All the servers wore black pants, white shirts, and bow ties. The host rushed to greet us. He wore a black vest with *Maurice* embroidered on the pocket. "Sergeant, your table is ready. Follow me, please."

Maurice led us to a table for six. "You'll be more comfortable here. More elbow room," he said.

I glanced at Palace Guard as Sarge pulled out Mother's chair, and Maurice pulled out mine. When Palace Guard wiggled his eyebrows, I cleared my throat behind my hand to hide my snicker. I picked up the oversized menu, and Palace Guard peered over my shoulder.

A thought drifted through my mind. *Where are the tacos?* I pursed my lips then peeked at Palace Guard, and he winked.

I glanced at the ceiling. *It's going to be a long night.*

Our server appeared at our table and placed glasses of iced water and sweet tea in front of each of us. She was as short as me, but a little heavier. The purple streaks in her dark-brown hair and her lip ring left no doubt of her individuality and set her apart from the rest of the staff. She grinned. "Shall we start with an appetizer?"

"Our usual, please," Sarge said.

Our server hurried to put in the order.

"What do you think, Margaret? Isn't this nice?" Mother peered at me.

"It's definitely upscale for Harperville, Mother."

"That's the perfect word. Upscale. We have news. You tell her, Big D. It's your news."

Sarge patted Mother's hand. "My retirement was approved, and I retire at the end of this month. We purchased an RV and will tour the US."

"I'm so excited," Mother said. "We've talked about nothing but where we will travel. It's our time to see sights and wander."

"No schedule," Sarge said.

"Except for meals," Mother said. "We won't miss any meals."

A young man in a gray suit strode to our table. He was shorter and stockier than Sarge. *He looks nothing like Sarge. Must resemble his mother's side of the family.*

"Uncle Duane?" the young man asked.

Sarge and his nephew shook hands then Sarge said, "Come meet my wife and her daughter."

After the introductions, Christopher sat in the chair Mother had insisted we leave for him between Sarge and me.

"I understand you're a librarian," Christopher said after the server brought his water, tea, and appetizer plate.

Sarge snorted, and Mother beamed.

"I am. Well, I was," I said. *Please don't tell me you went into a library once.*

"I visited the New York City Library once..."

My eyes widened, Palace Guard's mouth opened, and Sarge's eyes narrowed.

"I just said something dumb, didn't I? Let me start over." He frowned at his plate then rose and strode to the front door then went outside.

Mother's hand flew over her mouth. "Did you say something that upset him, Margaret? He didn't go outside to cry, did he? Does Big D need to go find him? I think I have tissues." She opened her purse and rummaged for her packet of tissues.

Sarge patted Mother's hand. "They're fine. It's how young people get acquainted these days."

"I didn't know that. You are so smart."

Sarge smiled. "Let's step outside for a minute. The sunset should be glorious."

Sarge offered his arm then they strolled to the restaurant patio as Mother talked and waved her free hand and Sarge nodded.

Christopher returned to his seat. "Hi, Maggie. I think I need to start over."

I smiled. "Tell me what you do. I was told you are a lawyer."

"Much better way to start," he said. "I passed the Georgia bar exam and landed a job, and now I'm in training."

"Congratulations. I was a librarian until I was injured. I will start a new job next week. More data-related than strictly librarian."

"For the record, I was totally intimidated by the New York Library. What kind of data are you interested in?"

"Mostly demographics."

"We may have something in common after all," he said as he placed his napkin on his lap. "I know what demographics means."

As we laughed, Sarge and Mother returned.

"Oh good," Mother said. "You made up. We won't have an awkward dinner after all. Can we order now?"

Our server appeared as though she'd been summoned, and I stared at my menu.

Christopher held up his menu and whispered. "I hear the rustic linguini is the best."

"Rustic linguini," I said.

"Same for me," Christopher said.

After we ordered, Mother said, "I'd never been on the patio before. I was transported to Italy."

"Shall we?" Christopher asked.

When we rose, Palace Guard narrowed his eyes. As we strolled to the patio, Palace Guard crowded me to walk between us.

"It is comfortable out here," Christopher said when we stepped out onto the patio. "I expected flies."

"It's the breeze," I said. "When it stops, the gnats swarm."

"Just like Atlanta," he said. "Have you always lived in Harperville?"

"I have. I've traveled some, but I always come back. What about you?"

"I grew up in Atlanta. I'm not sure if I've ever been in a small town before. Have you known my uncle long?"

How did he know about the rustic linguini? I smiled. "Seems like I've known him forever. He and Mother are perfect for each other."

"I remembered him as a gruff cop."

"That was my first impression too."

Palace Guard tapped me on the shoulder and pointed to our table.

"Mother and Sarge must have looked at the artwork. She's always been involved with the arts. They're returning, and our food is on the table," I said. "Time to go inside."

"Why don't we have them bring it out here?" Christopher rubbed his hand across the tiled mosaic table. "Seems more authentic."

"You do that. I'm eating where I don't have to depend on a fickle breeze." Palace Guard and I headed inside. Palace Guard scowled as Christopher shrugged and followed us.

"Shall we lock him outside?" I whispered after I closed the door. Palace Guard grinned at my wicked smile and nodded.

When we had finished eating, Mother frowned at her purse. ""Excuse me. My phone's been buzzing. I need to peek."

She rose with her purse and headed to the women's restroom. I grabbed mine and followed her.

When we were in the fancy foyer, she pulled out her phone. "Oh, no." She dropped onto the loveseat.

"What's wrong, Mother?" I moved to her side and peered over her shoulder. "Uh oh. You double-booked."

"It's a big reception in recognition of Harriet's sales. She reached some milestone. A million dollars in sales or something. I can't miss that. I've got thirty minutes to get there. Go with us. You like Harriet. There will be lots of people there."

"I'm sorry, but I can't. Ella and I have plans for this evening. She can pick me up here."

"I remember Ella. She's been your friend since before the explosion." She rose, but paused when she reached the door. "Wait. What do we do about Christopher?"

"Easy. Invite him to go along. He can follow you. Lawyers need to network. This is perfect for him."

When Mother opened the door, two women came in. After they continued on to the restroom, Mother said, "You are always thinking, Margaret. It's a great networking opportunity."

"I'll be right there, Mother." After she left, I sat on the fancy loveseat and called Ella.

"Can you pick me up at the new Italian restaurant, Vecchia Nonna, outside of town?"

"Sure. When?"

"Fifteen minutes?"

"I'll be there right away. What's wrong? Shall I call nine-one-one?"

"No. I'm fine. I came to dinner with Mother and Sarge, but Mother remembered another commitment and has to leave."

"Harriet's fancy reception? And you didn't want to go? Imagine that." She chuckled. "Sure, I'll be there in ten minutes. What are we going to do? Go for ice cream or plaster the warehouse with toilet paper?"

I snickered. "We can decide. See you soon."

Before I left the foyer, the server came in. "The sergeant paid the bill then he and your mother left. I think they were in a rush. That stranger who joined your table is waiting by the door. Do you need a ride?"

"Thank you. A friend is coming to pick me up." I peered at her nametag. *Sierra.*

"If you're sure. There's something about him that set me on edge. He's nice enough and not crude, like the guy from Atlanta who came in yesterday with his big city attitude, but he's hiding something. My gut feeling." She shrugged.

"Good insight. I'll wait close to the host station for my friend."

"I'll have your back," she said.

Small towns in Georgia. Everybody's nice. I brushed away a tear. *I'm getting sentimental.*

After I left the restroom, I scanned the restaurant. Christopher scrolled through his phone as he sat on the bench. *Can't pass this up.*

I raised my phone and snapped a quick picture. He glanced up, but Sierra stepped in front of me and smiled. "Good idea."

Maurice was in conversation at a table. He glanced up and glared when I snapped the photo. He strode to his stand, and his smile didn't reach his eyes as I neared him. "Did you enjoy the rustic linguine? The young man asked me what was best, and I told him my favorite was the rustic linguine."

"It was delicious. Thank you for the recommendation."

He smirked as he stacked the menus.

When I approached Christopher's bench, I asked, "You're not going to the reception?"

"Uncle Duane gave me good directions. I'll wait with you until your ride shows up."

While I stood near the door, Christopher scrolled on his phone but scanned the room without lifting his head.

Two weeks. Then what? Another kiss? I smiled.

When Ella stopped at the entrance, I said, "Here she is. It was nice to meet you. I know you'll enjoy Harriet's reception."

He frowned as he glanced up. "Yeah."

I hurried to Ella's car, and Palace Guard and I climbed inside. "Thanks, Ella."

"Love your hair. Ice cream emergency?" she asked as she sped to the highway.

"Absolutely."

We stood in front of the glass case. "We need to press our noses against the glass," Ella said.

"You wouldn't be the first," the ice cream clerk said.

I read the board. "I'll have the toffee crunch. Two scoops in a waffle cone."

"Same for me," Ella said.

We carried our cones out to the patio table. "Ready? Go," Ella said.

We bit the bottoms off the cones and attacked our ice cream. Ice cream dripped down my hand, and I licked my fingers then bit the bottom of the cone a second time.

Ella grabbed her forehead. "Dang. Brain freeze. Gets me every time."

I was close to winning our ice cream competition when Ella shoved her remaining ice cream and cone into her mouth.

"You are such a cheater." I slammed my hand on the wrought-iron table. "That's not allowed in the rules."

"Another one of your made-up-after-the-fact rules? You are still a terrible loser." Ella grinned. "So, what's up with Larry?"

I caught her up except for one little detail.

"Ha. He kissed you, didn't he? About time."

"That's why it's so easy for you to cheat. You have ESP."

I flipped my hair, headed to the car, and waited with my arms crossed. When Ella unlocked the doors, I said, "Ella's Super Powers."

Ella guffawed. "Proud of yourself? Should be. My ESP failed, and I didn't see that coming."

"We've got a big day tomorrow. Ready to drop me off?" I yawned.

"Sure am, Party Animal. As long as you don't tell anyone we called it a night at eight-thirty."

After Ella dropped us off at my house, Palace Guard and I waved as she sped north.

"She loves to go fast," I said. When we went inside the house, Spike wiggled his eyebrows and held his hands behind his ears.

"Let's sit on the porch while Lucy patrols the yard."

I told Spike about the fancy restaurant, Christopher, the party for Harriet, and calling Ella. By the time I finished, all three of us were yawning, and Lucy had fallen asleep on the porch.

"Time to go to bed, Lucy," I said. Spike stroked her back, and she opened her eyes then plodded to the door. As I climbed into bed, my phone buzzed.

Larry: "Good night. Miss you. Tell PG thanks for the warning."

I chuckled then replied, "Two weeks."

I set my alarm for six, but Lucy's click-clicks as she trotted into my room woke me at five-thirty. I let her out back, made a cup of coffee, and stepped out onto the porch. The cicadas buzzed the warning of rain for the day, and the thick, humid air frizzed my hair.

"Ready for breakfast, girl?"

Lucy trotted to the porch and nosed the door. While she ate, I dressed for work then sent Larry a text. "Ten days."

Before I left, I jammed on Larry's Texas Tech ball cap. Fog covered the roadway, and when I reached the Coyles', the light raindrops sparkled on the lawn grass and created tiny diamonds. I parked in front of the house and knocked on the door.

Jennifer opened the door and grinned. "Ella called from the office a few minutes ago. I'd given her a key, and she's already organized the files. Why didn't we bring her in earlier? How do you want your eggs?"

"One egg, over medium. Ella's a force."

Jennifer chuckled. "That's for sure. There's a surprise for you on the patio. Ella will be here in a few minutes to pick me up. After we go over her list of supplies and do a few things at the office, we plan to go shopping."

"Good, you're here," Glenn said, as I followed Jennifer into the dining room. "Enjoy your breakfast. I have all my notes ready for you to review." Glenn wheeled away from the table and headed to the patio.

"Ella's here. See you later," Jennifer said.

After I ate, I carried out a fresh pot of coffee and two cups with me to the patio. On my way, my phone buzzed. After I poured our coffee, I checked.

Larry: "Too long."

I gazed at my phone then sighed as I slipped it into my backpack.

Glenn pointed to the patio table. "Jennifer made business cards for both of us. Here are yours."

I smiled as I read, "Coyle Detective Agency. Maggie Sloan. It even has my phone number. I'm official."

Glenn chuckled and handed me his notes. "This is the list of questions for the evaluation and some potential topics to cover. I want you to go over the data from the courier whatever it is and whenever we get it."

When someone knocked at the front door, Glenn asked, "Do you mind getting that? And drop the folder into the top drawer in my computer desk?" He slipped his notes back into the file folder and handed it to me.

When I went into his office, I scanned the room then placed the folder into the top drawer. I locked the door as I left. *No sense in making it easy.*

Before I opened the front door, Palace Guard motioned me to the window. I peeked at the dark blue car in the driveway then raised my eyebrows at the man in a gray suit at the door. *Christopher?*

I opened the door, and Christopher said, "Maggie?" The rain had intensified, and thunder rumbled in the distance.

"You here to see Glenn? He's on the patio. Follow me."

"Is Kate here?" he asked.

"No, just Glenn and me. Did you expect Kate?"

"No. Just thought."

I stopped in the kitchen. "You want coffee?"

"Sure. I heard Glenn was injured. Are you his health care worker? I like your truck."

I turned away and reached for a cup in a cabinet as I frowned. "Oh no. Just a friend of the family here to help." *Short-term memory problem, Bub?*

He peered past me. "I'm supposed to see Glenn." He clutched his briefcase.

"Patio's this way," I said.

Christopher hurried to open the sliding door for me, and Palace Guard rolled his eyes.

I stepped onto the patio. "Christopher Arrington's here. I met him last night when I had dinner with Mother and Sergeant Arrington." I chuckled. "He thought I was your home healthcare worker."

Glenn matched my chuckle as he examined my face.

While Christopher closed the patio door, I mouthed, "Family friend," and Glenn nodded.

"How's your coffee? More?" I asked.

Glenn raised his cup. "Sounds good."

Christopher strode to Glenn and stuck out his hand. "Christopher Arrington. I understand you know my uncle."

Glenn shook his hand. "Good man. Known him for years. Care to sit?" Glenn pointed to the chairs around the patio table. "So what brought you here? You here for the evaluation?"

"Evaluation?" Christopher hesitated. "Sure. Well, maybe. I brought some documents for you to evaluate too."

I grabbed the top paperback novel from Glenn's stash that he kept on his side table and sat on the wicker chair that was in the corner of the patio. Christopher selected a chair that faced Glenn with his back toward me.

Perfect. I'm officially invisible.

"So, what did you bring me?" Glenn asked.

Christopher set his briefcase on the table and opened it. The top blocked Glenn's view, but I had a perfect view of a pistol with a folder under it. When Christopher reached in, I reached for my knife in my leg holster, but relaxed as he pulled out the thick folder and handed it to Glenn. Palace Guard leaned over as Christopher reached inside his briefcase and pulled out a small object. While Glenn flipped through the papers, Christopher ran his hand along the underside of the patio table. Palace Guard raised his eyebrows and tapped his ear.

I narrowed my eyes. *What's your game, Christopher?*

"Wow. There's a lot here." Glenn glanced toward the patio door, and I slipped to the door and slid it open.

"There you are, Maggie. Would you mind copying this for me?" Glenn asked.

Christopher slammed his briefcase shut and rose. "I'm not sure it's okay to copy..."

Glenn waved his hand in a downward motion. "Sit, sit. Go ahead, Maggie. My copy machine is secure."

Christopher glared as he resumed his seat. I snatched the papers and bustled out of the room. "On it."

"While she does that, Christopher, why don't you give me a summary?" Glenn picked up his pen and spiral note pad.

I unlocked Glenn's office and ran the pages through his copier then saved the copies to my cloud storage. I snapped pictures of each page with my phone then returned the pages to the folder.

After I locked the office door, I returned to the patio. Glenn set the folder on the patio table while I picked up the coffee pot and cups and carried them into the kitchen.

I eased into the den as Christopher said, "I guess that's all I have for now. I'll see myself out."

"Don't forget your folder," Glenn said. "Are you available tomorrow afternoon? I'd like to get back together at two o'clock."

"Oh, okay."

I hurried to the kitchen door then walked into the den with a dishtowel in my hand. "Done so soon?" I asked when Christopher closed the patio door.

"Didn't know you were still here."

I chuckled. "Jennifer left me in charge to be sure Glenn didn't overdo."

"Yeah. All done. I'll let myself out." Christopher headed to the hall.

"Wrong way. Front door's this way."

"Thought I'd visit the head real quick."

I smiled as I pointed to the half bath. "This way. It's off the kitchen. It's easy to get turned around in this house."

Christopher frowned as he glanced down the hall then came into the kitchen and went into the half bath. After the toilet flushed, he came out with his phone in his hand.

As I followed him to the door, I asked, "How was the reception?"

Palace Guard tapped his ear.

I raised my eyebrows. *I meant Harriet's reception, but he was checking the bug reception, wasn't he?*

Palace Guard nodded.

"The reception? Why? Oh, last night. It was good." He left, and his tires squealed as he peeled out.

CHAPTER THREE

I returned to the patio and held my fingers over my lips, "You ready for a nap?"

I nodded.

"Sure. I'll pick up my books and notes and be right in," Glenn said.

I held up my hand then hurried to the half bath. After I slid my hand under the sink and checked around the toilet but didn't find anything, I returned to the patio and closed the door behind me.

Palace Guard tapped the patio table. I ran my finger along the underside where Christopher sat and found the bug. I tapped my ear and pointed.

Glenn nodded and wrote. "Go out to your car and text Kate. I'll go into the den and wait."

"Will you be okay if I run to the store while you nap?" I asked.

"Sure will. Thanks."

Palace Guard rode with me as I pulled away from the house and drove around the block then parked at the convenience store.

"This is a mess," I said as I texted Kate. "Call me. Elec bug at your folks' house."

My phone rang.

"Are Dad and Mom okay? Talk."

"Everybody's okay. Jennifer is at the office with Ella. Your dad is at the house. I'm around the corner. I don't know what's going on, but Christopher Arrington met with your dad and left an electronic bug under the patio table."

"You and Dad go to the office and stay there. I'm out of state. Dang it. I'll call Moe at the Harperville Police Department. Are you sure he's the real Christopher Arrington? Anything stolen?"

"I don't think so. The only time he was out of my sight was when he was with your dad or in the bathroom."

"Check with Dad to see if this Christopher slipped out of his sight for a minute or two."

Kate hung up, and I hurried inside the store and bought a half-gallon of milk. Before I reached the driveway, the rain had stopped. I opened the front door and called out. "It's me. I have the milk. Jennifer called and needs you to help with some decisions at the office."

As I opened the refrigerator and put away the milk, Glenn said, "My cane's next to the front door; I'm ready."

After I helped him into my car, we were on our way. "I'm not impressed by Christopher," I said. "Kate wants to know if he was out of your sight at all when I went into the house."

"No. He stayed with me and talked. He had me fooled. I still wasn't clear if he was the potential recruit or the courier, but I was ready to write him a glowing evaluation on the spot, and then I was confused."

"What did he say?"

"When he described the document as a white paper that analyzed suspicious activity and claimed he was the primary author, I thought the document was a sample of his work. When he switched to his story to the document was his first delivery as a courier, I was back to confused. In retrospect, he didn't say much at all that was clear other than he supported his mother while he attended law school by working nights at a pizza parlor. So, what do we have?"

"Shall I print the documents he brought for you to read?"

"You can do that?" He chuckled. "Of course you can."

I smiled. "I saved them on my private cloud."

When I pulled up to the office, Jennifer and Ella rushed to the car and helped Glenn as he eased out of the car. I parked then went inside.

"You've changed around the office," I said.

"Ella and I did that this morning. She said we needed to be more customer-friendly, and Glenn would need more room to maneuver. Kate said we need to stay here and that you'd explain."

"First, I need help with something in my car. Ella, do you mind?"

When Ella and I reached my car, she asked, "What's going on?"

"I found an electronic bug at the Coyles' house. Kate's having the house swept by experts. When you moved around the furniture, did you find anything?"

Ella chuckled. "That's why I rearranged the office. We even pulled out drawers and dusted them. Do you know how much grief my CIA daughter would give me if there was a bug at the office? She's as paranoid as you are."

"She'd tell you it's not paranoia if it's true. I didn't know if it was okay to talk in the office."

"We don't have to talk code, but we shouldn't announce our passwords either," she said as we strolled back inside. "The key Jennifer gave me doesn't work very well. Could you look at it later? Maybe it's just me."

"You got everything straight?" Glenn asked.

"Yes. No surprise that Ella and Jennifer's cleaning was thorough. No need for an exterminator."

"That's good news. We can work online while we're here. Our internet is secure, but I'm not so sure about the printer," Glenn said.

"I'll check it." I found the printer with an unsecured wi-fi connection. "You're right. I'll fix it. You okay with reading the documents on your tablet? I can pull up the files for you."

"That will work."

"We'll need lunch, but first, I need to know what's going on," Jennifer said.

I filled in Jennifer and Ella about the bug at the house and Christopher Arrington.

Jennifer nodded. "We're becoming a real detective agency. I might need some new sunglasses and a detective hat. You too, Glenn."

"We need a bottle of whiskey in the bottom file cabinet drawer," Ella said.

Glenn chuckled. "Add some cigars, and we'd be authentic, wouldn't we?"

Ella and I giggled.

"Lunch. Everybody okay with whatever we get?" Jennifer asked. "I'm going to call in an order for pickup."

After Jennifer and Ella left, Glenn read, and I removed the printer from the network then turned it off. When I turned the printer back on, I redirected it to the correct connection.

"Maggie, look at this."

I joined Glenn at his desk.

He handed me his tablet. "What do you see?"

I sat in his visitor's chair and read the first six pages. I cocked my head then reread the last three. "It's gibberish. After a paragraph or two, it jumps to an unrelated topic for half a page then to another for a paragraph or two. I recognized snippets of fiction and agriculture extension service pamphlets on gardening and pigs, and on page four I found a section of algebra textbook problems."

"Sure explains why he didn't want me to copy it, but now I don't understand why he gave it to me." Glenn leaned back in his chair. "I have my notes from his summary. You might as well scan them, so you can read those too."

"That's confusing. Why did he claim authorship, or maybe he didn't think you'd read it?" I frowned. "Our imposter Christopher might be expendable, especially if he didn't accomplish his goal at your house, whatever that goal was. I'll scan everything you've got."

"I'm calling Sergeant Arrington to ask him about his nephew."

Glenn picked up his phone, and when Sarge answered, I smiled. *No need to switch the phone to speaker.*

"Sarge, it's Glenn. Christopher Arrington came to see me this morning, and something was off."

Glenn held his breath, and so did I.

Sarge spoke in his normal bellowing voice. "Thought the same thing last night, Glenn. I called my brother in Atlanta early this morning and left a voice mail. When he calls back, I'll ask about his family. We haven't talked in at least a month. We all get busy, don't we?"

"That's the truth. I'm interested in the whereabouts of Christopher and what he's doing these days."

"So am I. I'll call you after I hear from Delbert."

After he hung up, Glenn glanced at me.

"I heard it all," I said. "How does claiming to be related to Sarge fit in with being evaluated by you for Kate or whatever he was doing?"

When Glenn's phone rang, he stared at it. "I don't know this number. It's a Virginia area code."

When Palace Guard nodded, I said, "It's okay to answer the call."

He shrugged then his eyes widened as he listened. "Three-thirty tomorrow for your interview? That's fine. Come to my office. You know where that is?"

After he hung up, he said, "I should have done this earlier, but my brain cells were too cranky to think straight. I need to ask Kate the name of her recruit and for a picture. Not sure if she'll give me a picture of the courier too, but I'll ask."

He grunted as he poked at his phone then handed it to me. "Can you text her for me? Jennifer manages our communication stuff, and I'm out of practice."

I cleaned up a few typos and finished his text. He read the screen and nodded, and I tapped send.

Glenn frowned. "If it weren't for you, Maggie, the imposter would have gotten away with whatever it was he was supposed to do. Now, I'm nervous, and I think I understand Larry better. How much longer is his training?"

"Ten days."

He nodded. "When Ella and Jennifer get back, I need to know where my contracts are so you can read them with me. For the first contract, we only need to deliver an evaluation for the potential recruit. I had thought we'd do that first then focus on the second contract." He narrowed his eyes. "Except you'll want to solve the puzzle of why a phony showed up, won't you?"

Palace Guard held up his hand.

"Hold up your hand, Glenn. Palace Guard wants to high-five."

Glenn held up his hand, and Palace Guard grinned and smacked it.

"Thanks, Palace Guard." Glenn stared at his hand, and I snickered.

Jennifer and Ella returned with food and drinks.

"Ham and swiss sub roll sandwiches cut in half, large salads, and sweet tea," Ella placed the sacks on Glenn's desk.

"Where are the contracts?" Glenn asked.

"In the file cabinet," Ella said. "Want me to get them?"

"Obvious. I should have thought of that. I'll get them after I eat. A few steps won't hurt me."

"Second drawer from the top." Ella opened the sacks and placed sandwiches and drinks around the table.

Glenn reached for his tea.

Jennifer slammed down her cup. "You'll do no such thing." She stomped to the filing cabinet and pulled out a folder then slapped it onto his desk. She glared at him as she bit into her sandwich.

After we ate, Jennifer said, "We've been operating too barebones around here. We need to beef up the breakroom so we can fix lunch here without wasting the time and money to order and pick up food. Ella and I are going shopping. We'll be back."

"I've found my leader." Ella grinned as she followed Jennifer out the door.

"As long as we don't turn into a spa," Glenn mumbled.

"Kate mentioned a missing spy when she asked me to help you." I drummed my fingers on my cell phone. "Your spa comment reminded me of something that was out of character for our impostor. Our Christopher Arrington was personable and even likeable at times, but then he shifted to a different personality like he remembered what he was supposed to be doing. Sneaky, almost incompetent, bad guy. It makes sense if he's new at undercover."

Glenn frowned. "Nobody's good all the time or evil all the time, but it's time to talk to Kate."

I sent a text to Kate. "Was our phony Christopher supposed to deliver documents? Do I still go to Mobile?"

"She's not going to answer, is she?" Glenn asked. "Let's read the contracts."

I sat on the other side of his desk while he opened the folder. We started with the first contract.

"Evaluate prospective candidate and submit written evaluation using the following criteria: self-starter, emotional intelligence, skill level, and aptitude," Glenn read aloud. "Open-ended, but clear enough. What do you think?"

My phone buzzed.

Kate: "No. My bad joke about Mobile backfired."

"What the heck, Kate?" I frowned. "She was teasing me about Mobile?"

I showed my phone to Glenn, and he shook his head. "Her version of an apology."

I smiled. "I have a follow-up."

I showed Glenn my phone then tapped send. "Who is our Christopher Arrington? The courier, job applicant, or bad guy?"

When my phone buzzed, Glenn said, "I think you got her attention."

Kate: "Need picture."

"I snapped a photo but never checked it." I held my phone so Glenn could see. "It's a little blurred, and his head is down."

"Not bad," Glenn said.

I sent the photo to Kate then said, "Maybe it's good enough for..."

I was interrupted by Glenn's ringing phone.

Glenn glanced at his phone. "It's Detective Ross. Kate said you call him Moe." Glenn answered then listened.

After he hung up, he said, "The transmitter for the electronic bug was cheap and had a short range of only to the street. However, his team found a GPS tracker on the back bumper of my truck."

""I'll check my car." I grabbed my flashlight from my purse on my way to the door. I ran my hand under both bumpers then knelt to get a better look underneath. *Nothing.*

I went inside. "My car's clean."

Glenn rubbed his chin. "If there was a GPS on my truck, Christopher or his boss didn't know about my injury. Not sure what that means. Here's the second contract."

"Christopher told me he'd heard you were injured and mentioned he liked my truck. I wonder if he thought your truck was mine? None of this makes sense because he asked if I was your health care worker. I chalked it up to his obvious lack of critical thinking." I frowned then paced as I read the three-page document before I handed it back to Glenn.

"Doesn't say much, does it? But there is a clause that gives you the right to cancel at any time."

"On the first page, the assignment is to provide services for a courier, not very specific, is it? The rest of the contract is *forthwith* and *wherefore*," Glenn said. "Not much to go on. My notes are from a conversation with Kate. Let's look at those again."

He squinted as he read the last page of his notes. "I'd forgotten she mentioned my contact might be in danger."

"I'll scan all your notes and documents we have to my cloud so I can focus on them after I get home, but if anyone is in danger, it's our Christopher."

My phone buzzed a text.

Kate: "Still verifying."

"What is she verifying? That he's a good guy that might have gone bad?" I handed my phone to Glenn.

Glenn frowned. "Or the picture wasn't clear enough to identify him, but it looked good enough to me." Glenn leaned back in his chair. "Don't tell Jennifer, but I'm exhausted. Would you mind taking me home? I think a nap will rejuvenate me. After you scan what we have, I'll call Jennifer and let her know we've done all we can here for now."

I scanned all Glenn's notes and documents, then saved the files to my cloud. While Glenn talked to Jennifer, I put the folder and his notes away and locked the file cabinet. After he finished his conversation, we locked the office.

"Jennifer said for you to come for breakfast again in the morning. She knows me too well. She said we can decide in the morning if I'll work at the house or the office."

I helped Glenn into the house then to his recliner. He was asleep before I reached the door. I locked it behind me.

When I pulled into our driveway, Spike and Lucy were waiting on the porch. Before we went inside, I asked, "Anybody been around, Spike?"

He shook his head, and I sighed in relief. As I stepped onto the porch, I dropped my keys. When I bent down to pick them up, Palace Guard knocked me to the ground, and a bullet zinged over my head. Spike and Lucy dashed to the left, and I rolled to the right. A man crashed through the field on the other side of the road as he ran north. I pulled my gun from my belt, but the shooter was out of range then disappeared. Palace Guard raced after the man, and I jumped into my car and headed north. When I reached the highway, Palace Guard stood on the side of the road and shook his head. I stopped, and he jumped into the car then I turned back to the house.

"A driver and car must have been waiting for him. Don't you think that's the only way he could have disappeared so fast?" I asked.

Palace Guard nodded.

When we pulled into the driveway, Spike and Lucy stood by the door.

"No luck," I said. "We know two things: he's a pretty good shot and a fast runner."

When we went inside the house, Lucy jumped onto the sofa and closed her eyes. I poured a tall glass of sweet tea and headed to the back porch. Palace Guard and Spike accompanied me.

I rocked in the light breeze and gulped down my tea. I set my glass on the porch, closed my eyes, and listened to the pleasant melodies of the bird songs and the drone of the buzzing cicadas.

I awoke with a start when my phone rang. *Glenn.*

"I hope I didn't wake you from a nap like Sarge did when he called me. Christopher Arrington is in court all this week with his first prosecution of a murder. Sarge said it's all over the Atlanta news, but isn't quite sensational enough to be on the news this far south. He's going to send me a link to the article. He said it includes a picture of his nephew. There's no way his nephew could have been here last night or this morning. Kate sent me the potential recruit's resume. His name is Dylan, not Christopher, and he's from the Bahamas. We'll meet him tomorrow, and I'll ask for his ID. Kate said sorry for the delay. Do you suppose that was a phony Kate?"

I chuckled. "I haven't heard from her yet. Can you go back to your nap?"

"No. I have a resume to read, and Jennifer just pulled into the garage. I can't sleep while she's cooking because all I dream about is food. See you in the morning."

After I hung up, I stared at my phone. "I need to go to Vecchia Nonna to talk to Sierra. I could order an appetizer and that could be my supper, right?"

Palace Guard nodded.

When we entered the restaurant, Maurice greeted me. "Good evening, Ms. Sloan. Are you meeting someone?"

"No, I enjoyed the patio so much last night that I thought it would be relaxing to have an appetizer there."

He nodded. "Rough day? Would you like Sierra as your server? Sarge always asks for her."

"That would be nice." We followed him to the patio, and he seated me at a prime table that caught the breeze but was in the shade. "She'll be right out."

The music on the patio was as relaxing and romantic as it was last night. I expected an Italian prince to leap over the wall with a sword. Palace Guard jumped up and assumed a fencing position. I giggled.

Sierra came out to the patio. "Nice to see you again. Morrie said you asked for me. Thank you. I brought you a nonalcoholic version of a Sicilian Sunset."

"Thanks. It's beautiful. Who's Morrie?"

Sierra chuckled. "That was a slip. Maurice. He hates it when someone calls him Morrie. His real name is Morris. Shall I give you a minute with your menu? Or would you care for the salami and fig crostini with ricotta or an arugula salad with prosciutto and oyster mushrooms?"

"Which do you recommend?" Sierra pointed to the crostini, and I nodded. "I wanted to ask you about the rude guy from Atlanta. Can you describe him?"

"Better than that. I'm an artist. I sketched him when I got home because he had a distinctive scar from his mouth to his ear. I can send you a copy after I get home this evening. What's your cell number? I'll text it to you."

I handed her my new card from the Coyle Detective Agency with my phone number on it. "My new job. I just started today, but they had business cards already made up for me."

"That's exciting. I'll put in your order and send you the sketch later." Sierra stuck the card into her front pants pocket.

Thank you for your efficiency, Jennifer.

I sipped my drink, munched on my appetizer, and gazed at the western sky as it changed colors from pale blue to pink to blaze orange. *Larry will like it here.* Palace Guard nodded.

I finished my drink and ate half of my appetizer. "Another drink?" Sierra asked. "It's my variation of an old favorite."

"It was wonderful, but I have work to catch up on."

"I'll box up your appetizer. Scramble an egg in the morning, and you have an Italian breakfast. I'll text you the sketch as soon as I get home."

Sierra brought me my box. "The chef added a small serving of the arugula salad. He wants you to try it." Sierra winked. "I think you have another fan too. Maurice asked me questions about you."

When I rose to leave, Sierra met me at the patio door. "A busboy, Toby, told me a man at the bar watched you. Toby wants to walk you to your car." She peered at my face. "He has special needs, but he's the best-hearted and most loyal man I know. You'll be safe with him. I'll send you a sketch of the man too."

A stocky young man with an old-fashioned bowl haircut and a big grin met me at the restaurant door. "I'll walk with you, Ms. Maggie. We want you to be safe."

"This is a wonderful restaurant," I said as we strolled to my car.

"Yes, ma'am. People are nice to me."

"Thank you for walking me to my car, Toby." I unlocked my door and climbed in.

The young man stood in the parking lot with his arms crossed while I drove away. *Nice people everywhere, and not one of them shot at me tonight.*

Palace Guard shook his head.

"You're right. That is kind of pitiful."

When we climbed out of the car at my cottage, Spike swept his arms wide to let us know the house was safe.

Larry texted me: "Need a fast forward. Time drags. You okay?"

Me: "Miss you."

Larry: "What's going on?"

I showed my phone to Palace Guard and Spike. "What did I say that made him think something was going on?"

Palace Guard raised his eyebrows and pointed to my last text. Spike did his wacky dance.

Me: "You have a suspicious mind."

Larry: "Will call on Saturday."

I downloaded all of Glenn's documents and saved them in a folder on my computer.

"I'm going to start with phony Christopher's document. There has to be a pattern I've missed."

Palace Guard read over my shoulder, and Spike and Lucy wandered outside until Spike coaxed Lucy inside then they relaxed on the sofa.

After two hours, my eyebrows raised. "Ah ha. Look at this." I pointed to the first page then the second page. "See the pattern?" I asked.

Palace Guard grinned, and we smacked a high five.

"It's too late to call Glenn, isn't it? Let's compare what we found with Glenn's notes from the impostor's summary."

My phone buzzed a text from an unknown caller then a second buzz. *Two sketches from Sierra.* I texted a thanks and added her to my contact list.

"She was right about the man from Atlanta's distinctive scar from the edge of his mouth to his ear. I don't recognize the other man." After I forwarded them to Kate, I sent her an email that explained each sketch.

Text from Kate: "When does Larry return?"

"Ten days."

"You are capable of getting into deep trouble in ten days. Don't."

I stared at Palace Guard. "Kate's worried."

I sat at my computer and read the impostor's document again. "This reads like historical fiction," I yawned. "Why all the secrecy about a short story? Maybe it will make more sense in the morning."

CHAPTER FOUR

At five-thirty, my phone buzzed a text.

Larry: "R U OK?"

I stretched. *What happened to good morning?*

I stumbled into the kitchen and started a pot of coffee. Palace Guard scowled as he pointed to my phone.

"I don't know what to say," I grumbled then tapped, "Barely awake."

Larry: "Good. Was worried."

I poured my coffee and opened the back door for Lucy. I rocked while Lucy inspected the yard.

When Palace Guard joined me, I asked, "Why do I get so annoyed when he says he was worried about me when I worry about him all the time?"

Palace Guard pointed to my phone, and I texted Larry. "I worry about you all the time."

I went inside and refilled my cup. When I returned to the porch, I had a text.

Larry: "You worry me more."

Spike did his wacky dance, and I laughed. "We're having a worry competition."

I downed my coffee and poured another cup then turned on my computer. My fingers flew across the keys, and when I highlighted sections of Christopher's document on the screen, Palace Guard nodded and grinned. After a few more searches, I turned off my computer and hurried to dress for breakfast and work. On my way out, I picked up my purse and Larry's ball cap then slung my backpack over my shoulder. Before I backed out of my driveway, I texted Larry, "You win."

Palace Guard read over my shoulder.

"I thought that would confuse him. What do you think?"

Palace Guard gave me a thumbs-up.

I parked across the street in front of the neighbor's house, so I wouldn't block in Jennifer. When I opened the Coyles' front door, the aroma of baking cinnamon rolls and the sound of sizzling sausage reminded me of Reggie's Diner and when Parker introduced me to Kate. *I'll always remember Parker.*

Palace Guard nodded and blew on his finger.

"You're right. Larry's amazing."

"Good morning, Maggie," Jennifer said. "Glad you're here early. Ella and I have a few things to do before the furniture we ordered is delivered at the office at ten. One egg, sausage, and one cinnamon roll coming up in a second. Glenn's on the patio. He says he's addicted to fresh air. I think he's found his private sanctuary. See if he needs a refill on his coffee."

Glenn smiled when I slid the patio door open and waved the coffee pot at him. "Maggie, I was up early this morning reading the Christopher document. It makes no sense at all to me."

"We can talk after I have breakfast. Kate always had a rule at Reggie's that if you don't eat your food while it's hot, she'd toss it and cook a fresh plate."

Glenn chuckled. "You're smart. She got that from her mom."

While I ate, Jennifer said, "I packed all our lunches this morning. There are sandwiches in the refrigerator. I made a fresh cherry pie last night, and there's ice cream in the freezer. All good brain food. What do you hear from Larry? How much longer is he in training?"

"Nine days," I said.

"Seems like an eternity?" she asked. "That's how I felt when Glenn was at the police academy. I packed my tent and sleeping bag to live on the grounds outside his barracks, but Mama said there was nowhere to brush my teeth or use the bathroom."

She scrubbed and rinsed the baking pan then dried her hands. "Dad and I hiked and camped when I was three years old, but Mama never went along. She was horrified when I said I'd pee in the woods. I don't know which shocked her more: that I said the word pee or that I wasn't worried about brushing my teeth. She always told me how relieved she was when Glenn graduated. Let me know if you decide to go camping, and I'll go with you."

I laughed along with her then wiped my eyes. "I'll keep that in mind."

"I like Larry, you know. I need to run. Ella and I are going to the range. Today's her first lesson, and we'll start with gun safety."

I stared at Jennifer. *I have her approval.*

Jennifer grabbed her purse and the lunches and drinks she'd packed for the office and rushed to her car. I hurried to the patio.

Glenn glanced up from his reading as I closed the sliding door. "I've read the impostor's documents twice this morning."

I sat at the patio table with him. "Read the odd paragraphs on the odd pages and the even paragraphs on the even pages."

After he finished, he dropped the pages on the table. "This is about the museum art robbery in Boston in 1990. As far as I know, still unsolved, right? There have been a variety of rumors about where the art is. One rumor says the thirteen masterpieces are in Ireland; another claims they are still in the Boston area; and I've even heard they are in Los Angeles or Las Vegas. The suspects have ranged from the on-duty security guards, rock musicians, members of the Boston Mafia, high-rolling gamblers, movie stars, and the Irish Republican Army."

"That sure narrows it down, doesn't it?" I snickered. "I verified everything in the impostor's document except the claim that two of the pieces were recovered and are in a private collection. Do you know if that's true?"

"There was a rumor about a private collection a few years ago, but then nothing more after the initial flurry. What about the pages of math equations? They don't make any sense at all."

"If you solve the equations, the answers are the dimensions of the paintings. Isn't that bizarre?"

"If I solved the equations, my answers would be wrong." Glenn chuckled. "Now what?"

Palace Guard shrugged.

"I have no idea, and neither does Palace Guard." I rose and stared at the gathering clouds. "Do you think we'll get rain? Will you be okay by yourself for thirty minutes or so? I need to go for a run to clear my head."

I hurried to the guest bathroom down the hall to change. I left my clothes, backpack, and purse in the bathtub and pulled the shower curtain so the room wouldn't look cluttered. When I came out wearing my running shirt, shorts, and shoes, Palace Guard and I bolted out the front door and ran four blocks then continued as we raced a large square around the Coyles' house. When we approached Glenn's house, we slowed then stopped.

"Is that Christopher's dark blue car in the driveway?"

Palace Guard narrowed his eyes, and I pulled my cell out of my bra and called Glenn.

"Hi! Just checking up on you. Anything I can bring you?"

"Ice cream sounds good. It got too hot for me on the patio. I moved to the front room to relax. See you when you get off work, honey."

He set his phone down but didn't hang up, so I put my phone on mute.

"My wife. She won't be here until later this afternoon. Suppose you could lower your gun? You're making me nervous."

I disconnected.

"Do you think you could check on Glenn? I'll loop back to the alley and meet you behind the house."

Palace Guard nodded, and I trotted to the alley.

I waited for Palace Guard behind the neighbor's house. When he joined me, he held up one finger.

"One man. Is it Christopher?"

He shook his head.

"A man with a gun. Is Glenn okay?"

Palace Guard dropped to the dirt and rubbed his cheek.

"Glenn's on the floor, and his face is injured?"

Palace Guard nodded.

"If I climb into a bedroom window and sneak down the hall, could I surprise the man?"

Palace Guard nodded then disappeared. I smiled as a bedroom window raised without a sound and made my way to the backyard then flipped over a large pot and rolled it to the window. I turned it upside down and stepped on it to climb into the bedroom. After I was inside, I pulled my pistol out of my waistband and my knife out of its ankle holster. I eased down the hallway. Palace Guard stood in the living room and motioned for me to continue to the corner.

I held up three fingers for a countdown. Three. Two fingers. One finger.

As I leapt into the living room, Palace Guard pushed over a lamp, and the intruder turned his head toward the lamp and away from me.

"Drop it," I growled in the warrior tone I learned from Kate.

He spun toward me and when he lifted his gun to aim, I threw my knife in a perfect arc and nailed his wrist. He screamed and fell to the floor as his gun skidded toward Glenn.

Glenn scooped up the gun and called nine-one-one.

I strode to the man and aimed my gun at his groin. "Give me a reason." I shared my best lioness smile.

The intruder cringed then his gaze focused on my pistol, and he didn't move.

I recognize that scar.

The sound of sirens came from all directions. I holstered my gun. "Mr. Coyle still has you covered, but I can draw as fast as I can throw a knife."

"Don't test her, fella," Glenn said.

I checked the den. Glenn's attacker had tossed the sofa and chair cushions to the floor, overturned chairs, and pulled out drawers. When the front door burst open, Moe rushed in with three uniformed police officers behind him.

"You okay, Glenn?" Moe asked.

"I think I re-injured my leg, but I'm okay."

Moe peered at Glenn. "Your face is messed up too."

Moe scanned the room then scowled at me.

"Maggie. Maggie Sloan," Glenn said.

"Are you sure? What happened to her hair? Does Kevin know?"

Glenn chuckled, Moe smirked, and Palace Guard smiled.

I narrowed my eyes. *Was that a joke? Who's Kevin?*

Palace Guard held up his smoking gun finger and blew.

I forgot Larry's alias. I still don't see what's funny, though.

"What about me?" the intruder cried. "She tried to kill me."

"Nope," Moe said. "She didn't try to kill you: if she'd tried, you'd be dead, but I can hear you talking."

"He broke in then knocked me down and searched the den," Glenn said. "I don't know what he was looking for."

"Ambulance is here." Moe waved to one of the officers. "Get his statement and ride with him to the hospital. Be sure to tag the knife as evidence and keep it in your sight. Guess you'll have to get a new knife, Maggie. Be awhile before you get this one back."

"One of the few things Maggie would look forward to buying; although, you know she has spares." Glenn smiled.

"You need help up, Glenn?" I asked.

"I'll help," one of the officers said.

I replaced the sofa cushions as two officers helped Glenn. While they moved him to the sofa, I hurried to the kitchen for ice.

"Where?" I asked. "Knee or ankle?"

"Let's do both. I twisted my ankle as I went down, and I heard my knee pop."

"I'm sorry, Glenn." I turned to Moe. "We need a second ambulance for Glenn."

"I agree." Moe nodded at the officer who stood next to him. "While we wait, can you tell us what happened, Glenn?"

Glenn leaned back while I placed ice on his knee. "Jennifer is at the office, and Maggie went for a run. I was on the patio when I heard the knock. I looked out the window and thought I recognized the car. When I opened the door, he pushed his way in. He asked where *it* was but wouldn't tell me what he was talking about. That was when he pushed me down. He opened drawers and tossed cushions around then my phone rang. It was Maggie, and I didn't mention anyone was here. Maggie can tell you the rest."

"I saw the car in the driveway and called Glenn. When he didn't mention anyone being here, I went around back and climbed in a window. I slipped down the hall and heard the man's voice. I surprised him and threw my knife at his hand. He dropped his gun, and Glenn called you. You got here quickly."

"Maggie, would you call Jennifer?" Glenn handed me his phone.

"Sure, but I'll use my phone so she doesn't start off with a panic."

I pulled my phone out of my bra, and Moe snorted. "Yep, you're Maggie."

When Glenn raised his eyebrows, Moe said, "I'll tell you later."

I turned my back to both of them. "Jennifer, a man broke in while I was on a run. He pushed Glenn down. The fall re-injured Glenn's knee, and he twisted his ankle. The police called an ambulance to transport him to the hospital to have it checked out."

"I'm on my way." Jennifer hung up.

"She'll beat the ambulance here," Glenn said.

When the crime scene technician bustled into the house, Moe pointed to the specific snapshots that he wanted then a police officer helped place numbered markers.

"I do have one more thing," I said. "Glenn's attacker was at Vecchia Nonna earlier this week. A server, Sierra, sent me a sketch."

Moe's eyes narrowed. "Why?"

"She mentioned a rude man had been there, and I asked her if she could describe him. She told me she had sketched him because of his face and sent me the sketch."

When I showed Moe the sketch, he showed the crime tech.

"Wow. Sierra is talented," she said. "We need a good sketch artist."

"Want to go to dinner tonight with my work wife and me? You can talk to Sierra without appearing to be out with some old man."

Moe's married?

The tech laughed. "I'll see if Heather's available."

Joke? I glanced at Palace Guard who nodded.

"Detective Ross," Jennifer called from the front door. "Would you please tell this kind, efficient police officer to let me come in?"

"Careful, detective," Glenn whispered. "She's being polite."

I snickered, and Moe sauntered to the door to talk to Jennifer.

"What's going on?" Glenn tried to raise himself far enough off the sofa to see.

I peeked out the window. "You won't believe this. Moe and Jennifer are headed to the shade."

"You're kidding," Glenn said.

"Nope, and now they're talking." I shifted to see better. "Whoa. Moe is smiling, and Jennifer's laughing." I narrowed my eyes. "I'm not sure I've ever seen Moe smile before."

The tech snorted then her face reddened. "Excuse me. Allergies."

"Jennifer's car is parked on the lawn, and Ella's guarding it," I said. "I almost forgot the ice for your ankle."

"Thanks, Maggie," Glenn said. "I'm enjoying the Jennifer and Moe saga."

After I placed the ice on his ankle, I returned to the window. "Moe's talking, and Jennifer is nodding and smiling. I never would have thought Moe had an ounce of charming in him."

I peered at the road. "Aww. Here's the ambulance."

"That's too bad," Glenn said. "We're back to reality now, aren't we?"

Palace Guard and the technician nodded.

"Moe's returning to the house, and Jennifer has her arms crossed. Yep, reality."

After Glenn was loaded into the ambulance, a police officer held the passenger door open for Jennifer, and she climbed in. Ella headed to the hospital in Jennifer's car.

"Can I pick up my things from the bathroom and leave now?" I asked.

Moe narrowed his eyes. "Officer, collect Ms. Sloan's things and check them. Then accompany her to her car."

Palace Guard smiled, and I nodded. *There's our Moe.*

The uniformed officer came out of the bathroom a few minutes later with my bag and purse, and we strolled to my car. He had brown-black eyes and pale brown skin and was slender and five inches taller than me. His short-clipped, black hair had the hint of slicked-down curls. I peered at his nametag. *Perry.*

"Wish I could have seen that knife throw." His professional demeanor vanished when he grinned. "You're a legend, Ms. Sloan. Detective Ewing must be proud of you."

Palace Guard raised his eyebrows.

Oops. I better text Larry.

"Thanks. I don't feel like a legend."

After I climbed into my car, I picked up my phone and tapped in a text. "Bad guy broke into Glenn's house while I was on a run. Glenn's knee hurt. I'm ok."

My phone rang before I reached the end of the block, and I pulled over.

"I already heard. I need details."

Still no good morning.

After fifteen minutes of describing the events, I said, "Jennifer rode with Glenn to the hospital, and Ella drove Jennifer's car. I could have told you all of this in five minutes if you hadn't interrupted."

Larry snorted. "You would have skipped the best parts. Wish I could have seen Moe smiling. I can't stand being away from you, but I'm glad Palace Guard was there. Nine days."

"I miss you. Nine days." I bit my lip to hold back the tears.

My phone rang again before I could turn on my engine. *Ella.*

"My turn." She chuckled. "Can you pick me up at the hospital? Jennifer's released me."

"I'll be right there."

I sat for a minute and glared at my phone. "Anybody else?"

I started my car and eased away from the curb then headed to the hospital. Ella waited for me at the patient drop off and pick up canopy.

When she hopped in, she said, "We're supposed to eat the lunches at the office. Are you hungry? I'm starving."

After we parked in front of the office, Ella stuck her key in the lock, but it didn't turn. "My key is cantankerous. It was fine for a while. I need another one. Let's use yours."

I unlocked the door, and while we relaxed in the breakroom, someone tapped on the front door. I slurped my tea then rounded the corner to see who was there, and my eyes widened.

"Phony Christopher's at the door," I whispered.

"I don't have a gun yet, but I'm a force in a takedown," Ella said. "I've got your back."

I grabbed my phone and texted Kate. "Phony Christopher at Det Agency"

When I opened the door, he flinched then stepped inside.

"I'm Maggie," I said. "You are?"

"Where's Glenn? I need to talk to him." He glanced around then pointed to the office. "Is he in there? It's important."

"Glenn's in the hospital. He was attacked at home earlier today. You know anything about it?"

"What? No." He stepped back then dropped into the visitor's chair. "Who was it?"

"He didn't tell me his name. Just like you."

My phone buzzed a text.

Kate. "Call me after he's gone. We need to talk."

"I need a name. I can't keep calling you Phony Christopher."

He snorted. "I'm a lawyer."

"Let's go into the office and sit."

As he followed me into the office, Ella asked, "Lawyer, have you eaten lunch?"

He shook his head, and Ella gathered up the food and her purse and carried them into the office. "Don't have any tea for you, but here's water." She spread the food out on the desk. "Eat as much as you want."

"First, your name or whatever you want me to call you," I said.

"Curtis. I'm kind of a contractor with the FBI. I work for different agencies and worked with the FBI once. My assignment..."

"Hold on," Ella said. "I'll eat my lunch in the other room, so I can answer the phone and keep an eye on the front door. Maggie, you can tell me what I need to know later." Ella picked up her lunch and sweet tea then closed the door behind her.

Curtis opened his bottle of water and gulped half the bottle then grabbed a sandwich and unwrapped it.

He bit into his sandwich and closed his eyes as he chewed. "Sorry. I was starving."

I slid a bag of chips across the desk, and he shook half the bag onto his napkin and the desk.

"My assignment is to audit art galleries and compare their physical inventory against their inventory records and certificates of authenticity. After I document any discrepancies, my findings are sent on to another analyst who digs into the underlying reasons for the inconsistencies. I minored in art history before I attended law school and have continued my art studies as a hobby. I'm considered an expert, but this undercover stuff is not one of my strengths."

I blinked. *No kidding.*

Palace Guard smiled.

He polished off his lunch, and I pointed to the remaining sandwich.

"Thanks. A former classmate of mine is the director of a museum in Mobile, Alabama. She told me a colleague of hers had an important document that needed to go to the FBI. She gave me her colleague's number to call for more information."

He unwrapped the last sandwich and chomped into it. "I didn't want to say no because I was..." He popped chips into his mouth.

Because you wanted to be a big shot?

He reached across the table and grabbed a napkin then wiped his mouth. "Because I was flattered."

I nodded. "Where was her colleague?"

"My classmate said Athens. When I called the number, no one answered, so I left a voicemail. I got a return call from a mechanical voice. You know, the kind that distorts the voice or something to make it different. The mechanical voice told me where to pick up the folder in Athens. When I picked up the folder, there was a note on it that said I needed to be careful about letting anyone know I had the folder, but the folder contained the five hundred dollars travel money, at least that's what the mechanical voice called it, so I thought it meant the money. The more I thought about the whole thing on my drive back to Atlanta, the more I worried. After I was home, I searched for FBI agents based in Georgia and found Kate Coyle in Harperville."

"What did the mechanical voice sound like?"

"You know, mechanical. Muffled like an old lady talking through a handkerchief to disguise her voice."

After he polished off the chips, he glanced at the empty sack. "I guess that will hold me until dinner. Thanks."

He crumpled his trash and placed it in the sack.

Bonus points for that.

"I called a buddy of mine. He told me Glenn Coyle had the contract for the delivery of some documents. Sounded like he was a key point of contact, so I drove to Harperville to talk to him."

He rose and peeked out the window then listened at the door. "Did you hear something?"

I narrowed my eyes. "Like what?"

"I thought I heard someone talking." He rubbed his hand through his hair. "On my way to Harperville, my friend in Mobile called me. She was in a panic. She said she got a call that she was in danger and was going to her sister's in Kansas or somewhere like that. My friend hung up before I could get the story straight."

This is a long story.

Palace Guard nodded.

"What about the bug you left at Glenn's house? And the tracker on the truck? And why did you pretend to be Sarge's nephew?"

"The folder had the gadget in it. I was supposed to leave it when I dropped off the document. I didn't know what it was. After I got to Harperville, I got a call at the hotel. A man said he knew I was going to see you at the Coyles' house, and he left an item in my room that I had to put on your vehicle if I wanted to return to Atlanta in one piece. I didn't know what it was. I followed orders and left it on the bumper of your truck like he said."

This time, you weren't flattered. Palace Guard smirked.

"Christopher Arrington attended an art history class that I taught, and I knew his uncle was with the police department in Harperville. When I arranged to meet Sergeant Arrington, I had thoughts of asking for help, but I found a note under my plate warning me to keep my mouth shut."

He fumbled in his pocket and pulled out a piece of paper then dropped it on the desk. He checked the window again then scooted his chair to a corner away from the window and door.

I picked up the note and read. "Say nothing. We are watching." *This convoluted story just got interesting.*

"So, why are you here?"

"I got another call after I met with Glenn. The man told me to leave the document I showed to Glenn in my room. When he asked if there were any copies, I told him only one, but I didn't have it. I hung up and checked out, but when I got to the parking lot, my car was gone. I knew that was a warning. Then I got a call saying I better get the document, or I'd never make it home. I called a taxi and went to Coyle's house, but no one was there, so I came to his office. Is the document here? Kate said I'm supposed to do whatever the man says."

When did you talk to Kate? I stared at him. "Let me check. I'll be right back."

I left the office and closed the door then called Sarge. Ella grabbed my arm and pulled me into the breakroom and closed the door.

"Are you okay?" he asked in his booming voice.

"I'm fine. Phony Christopher is here with me at the Coyle Detective Agency. I think he needs police protection."

"Detective Ross will be right there." Sarge hung up.

Ella said, "The vent between the office and the outer desk needs to be closed off. I heard everything, and in my professional opinion, his story is as phony as he is. Oh, and I recorded all of it. Am I fired?"

"Probably not."

A thud came from the office.

"What was that?" Ella asked.

"I'll check."

When I rushed into Glenn's office, the window was open, and Curtis was gone. I dashed to the window and Palace Guard was sprinting to the alley across the street.

"Maybe I can catch him."

I raced out the front door, dashed down the street, and turned at the alley. Palace Guard stood in the middle of the alley with his arms crossed. When I reached Palace Guard, he pointed. Curtis's body was crumpled near the dumpster.

"Dead?" I asked as I approached the body. Palace Guard nodded and stopped me.

"You're right. No reason to compromise the scene." I pulled my phone out of my bra and called Sarge.

"You in danger?" he growled.

"No. I'm fine, but Phony Christopher ran away from the office, and I found him in the alley next to a dumpster. He's dead. There's blood everywhere. I'm at the alley north of Glenn's office."

"Stay there," he growled and hung up.

"I guess we'll be seeing Moe pretty soon."

Palace Guard nodded.

While I waited in the alley, I called Ella. "You okay?"

"Yes. What about you?"

"I'll be there in a bit to catch you up. Meanwhile, secure the office and lock yourself in. Press your car fob's panic button if you need help. I found our visitor dead in the alley."

"Whoa. Will do. So far, this is the most exciting job I've ever had."

CHAPTER FIVE

I texted Larry. "I'm okay. Details later."

Palace Guard frowned.

"I know. Lame. Only nine more days."

A cruiser rounded the corner and screeched to a stop. Moe stepped out of the passenger's side and strode to where I stood.

"Where's the body, Maggie?"

I pointed to the dumpster. "On the other side."

"Stay here."

Another cruiser blocked the other end of the alley.

"Would you like to sit in the air conditioning, Ms. Sloan?" Moe's driver asked.

"No, but I do think I'll move to the shade. Thank you."

I sat on a stack of pallets that was shaded by a building's awning. More cruisers showed up at both ends of the alley, and officers rushed past me.

I feel invisible. It's kind of nice.

Palace Guard smiled as he joined me on the pallets.

Moe strode to the cruiser, and the young officer pointed to my shady spot.

Moe scowled. "I know you have more, Maggie."

I shrugged. "I had a long conversation with phony Christopher. He said his name was Curtis, before he bailed out the office window. My friend Ella is still at the office. She recorded the conversation."

Moe's eyes widened then his face resumed its scowl. "Let's go see your friend. Okay if we walk?"

I nodded, and as we headed toward the office, Moe said, "Tell me how you found the body."

"Phony Christopher and I were in Glenn's office. I left for a few minutes, and when I returned to the office, the window was open. I ran to the alley to look for him and found the body, so I called Sarge." When we reached the office, Ella unlocked the door.

"Ella, this is Detective..."

She peered at his nametag. "Ross."

"Somewhere the two of us can sit and talk?" Moe asked.

Ella led the way to the breakroom, and Moe closed the door behind them. I listened as Ella played her recording, but couldn't understand the words with the door closed. The female voice had a lilt like Mother's. *Is that what I sound like?*

I glanced above the door. "We need a vent for the breakroom."

Palace Guard snorted, and I paced then jumped when my phone rang. *Kate.*

"You okay? You need to talk to Larry. He wants to quit and return to Harperville this afternoon. I talked to Mom. We're going to find a bored, retired FBI agent to help her with the business. Mom said to tell you to go camping. Do you know what she's talking about? You don't know this, but your phony Christopher is also phony FBI. Remember Techie Maggie? She's still working on exactly who he was. Your turn. Tell."

"Before he bailed, phony Christopher told me a long story, and Ella recorded all of it. Moe is with Ella in the breakroom and is listening to the conversation."

"Ha. Mom said Ella was a keeper." Kate hung up.

I texted Larry. "Call?"

My phone rang.

"You aren't talking me out of this. I'm leaving at the end of the day," Larry said.

I breathed in, slow and deep then exhaled as I went into the office and closed the door. "Don't do it. I'll camp in the field at the training center until you graduate. This is the job you wanted. Only nine days. That's all. Then I'll shower."

Larry laughed. "You'll what? That's crazy. Not that I think for a second you won't do it."

I sat in the chair behind the desk and listened to the silence on the phone.

Larry sighed. "You win, Crazy Lady. You don't have to come here with a tent. We may get at least part of Sunday off, though. Maybe I can come..."

"I could come up Saturday and leave Monday."

"You'd do that? Even better. As soon as I know, I'll make you a reservation at a hotel near the training center. Don't bring a tent." He chuckled.

"It's nice to hear you laugh." My voice cracked.

"I gotta talk to the training officer. I can't wait to see you."

I smiled as we hung up. "We have weekend plans."

Palace Guard exhaled.

"Tell me about it; I was worried too. I'll have to thank Jennifer for telling me about camping."

Ella and Moe came out of the breakroom, and I joined them in the front office.

"All done," Ella said. "Detective Ross sent the recording to his phone, so I won't have to give up mine. Smart."

I stared when Moe's face reddened. *Since when does Moe smile and blush? Do we have a Moe impersonator? I need to talk to Kate.*

Moe's phone rang, and he frowned. "Excuse me. I need to answer this."

"Thanks," he said. "Maybe we can still go. I might have another option."

After he hung up, he peered at Ella then cleared his throat. "Ella, I'm going to the new Italian restaurant, along with our crime scene technician. The other officer we'd planned to go along with me wasn't available. Would you care to join me for dinner?"

Ella giggled. "I'd love to! Shall I meet you there? What time?"

"I'm not taking an official vehicle. Why don't I pick you up? Six-thirty okay?" He tapped his notebook and smiled. "I have your address."

"Yes, you do." Ella fluttered her eyelashes. "Six-thirty is fine."

Palace Guard mimicked Spike's gagging routine, and I coughed into my elbow to hide my snicker.

"Good. I'll see you then. I need to get back to the scene." Moe strutted out the door and down the street.

Ella patted her hair. "He's a nice man, don't you think? What do I wear?"

"Mother told me to wear something nice when we went. I wore a green blouse Jennifer bought me and black pants. Mother wore her tropical shirt and blue slacks."

"Thanks. I need to get my nails done. Do you need me for anything? Is it okay if I leave?"

"That's fine with me, and I don't think Jennifer will mind."

Ella rushed to Glenn's office for her purse then paused at the front door. "I'll be here in the morning at eight. Call me if you need me here earlier."

I secured the window then locked up.

As we climbed into my car, I said, "Let's go by the hospital before we go home."

I parked then waited at the Information Desk. The clerk hung up the phone and smiled. "Can I help you?"

"Glenn Coyle?"

She typed in his name then peered at her computer screen. "Can I see your ID?"

I showed her my driver's license.

She scrolled then said, "Here you are. Maggie Sloan. He's in recovery. The recovery waiting room is on the second floor."

When the elevator doors closed behind me, I snickered as I remembered the pharmacist and the rebel smuggling forces in the hospital in Texas.

Jennifer was flipping through a magazine, but set it down and rushed to hug me. "I'm glad to see you. Kate said you got into trouble again. Are you okay?"

"I'm fine. How's Glenn?"

"Still in recovery, but he's going to be a handful after he wakes up. He fractured his ankle; the bones were displaced and extended into the joint. Doc said it was a mess. He may need a knee replacement later. What about your man? How's Larry?"

"He wanted to walk away from his training when he heard what happened today. I told him to stay. It's only nine days, and I'd camp on the training field until he graduated. Thank you for the idea."

Jennifer chuckled. "What did he say to that?"

"He laughed and called me crazy lady, but he's staying. He may get this Sunday afternoon off. If he does, I'll go visit him. He specified *no tent*."

Jennifer and I laughed until the tears ran.

"I have a favor to ask," Jennifer said. "Would you mind if Lucy came to stay with us for a while? I think she'll be good for Glenn, and she'll keep him company while I'm at the office. The imaginary men are welcome too. Kate told me Lucy is particularly fond of Spike."

"I'll talk to Spike and Palace Guard and let you know. When do you expect Glenn to come home?"

"The surgeon told me maybe Friday. Did Kate tell you she's looking for a retired FBI agent or police detective to fill in for Glenn?"

"Yes. Ella and I plan to be at the office tomorrow. Anything special you want us to do?"

"I'm sure there's something, but I need to think about it. I can let you or Ella know later."

"That's great. Ella loves working at the detective agency, by the way."

"I'm relieved. After he heals a bit, Glenn has physical therapy and follow up doctor appointments ahead of him, but I don't plan to mention that to him."

A nurse opened the door. "Mrs. Coyle? Ready to see your husband?"

"I'm ready."

We hugged then she left with the nurse.

As Palace Guard and I waited for the elevator, I asked, "What do you think about Lucy staying with Glenn for a while?"

Palace Guard frowned then shook his head.

I smacked my forehead. "I just remembered Glenn was going to evaluate the real FBI candidate today. As soon as we get home, I'll text Kate to see if there's something we need to do."

When I pulled into the driveway, Spike and Lucy trotted from the backyard to meet us.

"We have a lot to tell you, Spike, but first, I need to text Kate."

We went inside, and Spike sat on the sofa then Lucy jumped up with him.

I sent the text to Kate then joined Lucy and Spike on the sofa.

"Spike, a man broke into Glenn's house and knocked Glenn down. Glenn twisted his bad knee and broke bones in his ankle. He's going to be out of commission for a while. Jennifer asked if Lucy could stay with them and keep Glenn company."

Lucy nuzzled Spike's hand, and he rubbed her face. He scowled then shook his head.

"I agree it's better if we stayed together, but I have a compromise. I might visit Larry this weekend and will leave on Saturday then be back on Monday. If you want to stay with Lucy, Jennifer included you in her invitation. What do you think about going to Glenn's when he gets out of the hospital and then coming home on Monday?"

Spike nodded, and Palace Guard held up his hand for a high-five.

"I'll call Jennifer."

When Jennifer answered, I said, "It's me. I'm going to visit Larry this weekend. Lucy and Spike can spend the weekend with you and Glenn to help Glenn adjust, but I'll come pick them up when I get back on Monday. I hope that will help."

"It will. I'll admit I'm not surprised. Y'all are a team."

"Thanks, we are."

I set down my phone. "She understood."

A text from Kate. "Interview changed. Dad not needed. Thanks."

I wiggled my eyebrows. "Kate's slipping. She was polite."

I poured a glass of tea, and we all trooped to the back porch. I settled in my rocker while Lucy prowled the backyard, and the birds serenaded us. When the horses whinnied for Lucy, Spike accompanied her to the fence that separated the cottage property from the horse farm. Lucy trotted along the fence, and one of the older mares joined her. They pranced then slowed their pace like two old friends out for a stroll. They touched noses through the fence then the old mare ambled to her barn.

"I miss Larry."

Palace Guard nodded.

A car pulled into our driveway, and Spike rounded the corner of the house to look. He danced his wacky dance then swept his hair away from his face, put the back of his hand on his forehead, and swayed in an exaggerated swoon.

"Officer Heather's here?"

Spike tried to turn a cartwheel, but he collapsed in the grass, and I laughed as I dashed to the front door.

I threw open the front door and squealed, "Heather!"

She grinned as she climbed out of her car with a white paper sack, a brown grocery sack, and her backpack slung over her shoulder. "I've brought dinner. Courtesy of Larry."

She wore a tight black leather skirt, red high heels, and a low-cut white blouse. Her long brown hair was in a single braid over her shoulder.

"Come inside. Shall I pour sweet tea?"

"Would Larry want us to toast him with a glass of sissy tea?" She handed me the brown sack.

When I peered inside, I said, "It's our favorite beer."

"Cold," we said in unison and laughed.

"Never gets old," Heather said as we went inside. Spike followed her so closely that he almost bumped into her. When I glared, he backed off.

I set two beers on the table then put the rest into the fridge.

"Don't open my beer," Heather said. "Even though I just finished a shift, I'm still on duty, but I can toast Larry with a capped beer. Pour me some of that sissy tea while I change."

I chuckled and poured her a glass of tea and set silverware and plates on the table then opened my bottle.

Heather came out of my bathroom in jeans, a white shirt with pockets, and black sneakers. Her braid was wrapped around her head.

She raised her unopened beer. "Here's to Larry."

We clinked our bottles and gulped our drinks. Heather grabbed a large bowl and two small ones out of the cabinet.

"Peek in the sack," she said.

"Tacos! I can't believe you brought tacos. Where did you find them?"

"I didn't. Larry ordered them. Sure am glad they had a drive-up window. Can you imagine if I'd pranced into that family restaurant dressed in my *tart* uniform?" She grinned as she poured tortilla chips into the bowl. She reached into her backpack and pulled out a jar of our favorite salsa then poured it into the bowls.

I spooned salsa on my taco. When I bit into the crunchy shell, I grabbed a paper towel to wipe my chin where salsa had leaked out of my mouth.

Heather held up her phone. "Let's send a photo to Larry."

I held my beer in a toast and a taco next to my face and put on my cheesy photo smile. Spike stood behind Heather, cocked his head close to hers, and fluttered his eyelashes. Palace Guard and I laughed, and Heather snapped the picture.

"This is perfect," she said as she tapped send.

My phone buzzed.

Larry: "You are gorgeous. p.s. I promise tacos wherever we go."

I sniffed back sneaky tears, with no success. Palace Guard put his hand on his heart, and Spike danced.

"What's wrong?" Heather asked as she snatched my phone then read the screen. "This is the most romantic text I've ever read. Keeper, right?"

"I think you're right."

"Of course I am." She grinned as she bit into her taco.

After we ate our fill, I packaged the leftovers and put them in the fridge.

"Want to sit on the porch? More tea?" I asked.

She peered at her empty glass. "I'm thirsty after all the salty chips. Sounds good."

I poured two glasses, and Heather grabbed the bowl of chips as we went outside and settled into the rockers.

"Are your real imaginary men still around?" Heather asked.

I nodded as I grabbed another handful of chips.

"Fascinating. I wonder..."

Heather was interrupted by her buzzing phone. She glanced at the screen. "Gotta go. Thanks for the break."

She dashed to the driveway and called out, "Bye, imaginary men."

Spike waved then pouted after she left.

I rocked and gazed at the dark clouds that rolled in from the south. The breeze became a brisk wind, and the temperature dropped.

"Might be a storm coming. Come on, Lucy, let's check the yard before the rain hits."

While Lucy explored the yard, I called Jennifer.

"How's Glenn, and how are you?" I asked.

Lucy trotted to the porch at the sound of distant, low rumbles.

"We're fine. He claims he can heal best on the patio. He wants to go home in the morning, but we'll see. Funny you called," she said. "I just got off the phone with Ella. She asked if we minded if she and Detective Ross went to the office to pick up the copy we have of the document after they eat. Glenn said it was okay with him, and I'm happy to have it gone. Doctor just came in. Talk to you later."

The wind picked up even more, and fat raindrops smacked the porch. Lucy moved to the door.

"I agree, girl. Let's go inside."

While rain slammed the side of the house, and the wind rattled the windows, I reviewed Glenn's notes from his meeting with Christopher then searched for art museums in Mobile, Alabama.

"This is interesting," I said. "Christopher said his classmate who called him about delivering a document to the FBI was the director at an art museum in Mobile and referred to the art director as *she*. I can't find any art museum in Mobile with a director who is female or any museum that has a vacancy in its art director position. What I don't understand is what was he hiding?"

The wind stopped, and I peeked outside. "The rain's almost gone."

"I can't verify anything that Christopher-Curtis said, and every time he opened his mouth, he contradicted himself. I'm going to shift to the document and see if I can confirm two pieces of art were found in a private collection. I need an artist." I smacked my forehead. "Sierra. She may know or be able to recommend an art historian or expert."

Palace Guard frowned then pointed to my car keys. "I should go to Vecchia Nonna?"

He shook his head and pointed to the document on my screen.

"The office?"

He nodded and hurried to the door. His face was tense as I headed to the highway, and I sped up. Before I turned the corner to the office, he pointed to the alley, and I pulled in. We strode to the corner, and Palace Guard put up his hand to stop me then peered around the corner. He held up two fingers then put his hands at the nine o'clock and three o'clock positions and imitated the motion of a child steering a car. *Two cars. Friend or foe?*

Palace Guard raised one finger and put his hand on his heart then raised a finger and held up his fists in a fighting position. I followed him to the street side of the cars. We crept along from the first car to the second then he motioned for me to stay low.

He disappeared. When he returned, he held up two fingers and put his hand on his heart then two fingers and raised his fists. *Two friends; two bad guys.*

He nodded. I shifted my knife to my left hand and flipped open the snap on my gun's holster. Palace Guard pushed the door, and it swung open. The sounds of scraping furniture, crashing drawers, and grunting came from Glenn's office. Moe and Ella were on the floor near the receptionist's desk. He had a laceration on his forehead, and Ella's bottom lip was swollen and bleeding. Moe's eyes widened, and Ella's eyes twinkled. Their hands and feet were bound, and duct tape was across their mouths. I sliced Moe's zip ties, and he pulled the tape off his mouth. He pulled a gun out of his boot while I cut the ties on Ella's hands and feet. Palace Guard tugged on Ella's sleeve, and she crawled to the breakroom door.

Moe pointed to the office. We crept to the door then stood on opposite sides. Moe put his hand on the knob. Palace Guard held up his hand to indicate stop, and I copied him. Palace Guard pointed to Ella. She had a large flowerpot in her hand. Moe followed my gaze and grinned. He held up three fingers then did a countdown: two, one. Ella dropped the pot on the floor, and the two men barreled out of the office.

Moe caught the first man with a solid kick to the kneecap then grabbed his arm and tossed him to the floor. I flipped the second man and put my knife at his throat.

Ella scrambled for her phone and called nine-one-one. "Two men broke into the Coyle Agency office and assaulted me and Detective Ross. The men are subdued. Detective Ross is requesting backup."

"Perfect, Ella," Moe said.

"Thank you, Lester." Ella's chocolate brown skin developed a pinkish tinge that rose from her neck to her cheeks.

Lester? Moe is Les?

I glowered at the man on the floor to keep from laughing.

"I'm not moving," he said.

"Smart man," Moe said.

The sound of sirens came from two directions. Officer Heather burst into the office. She raised her eyebrows then stepped outside and cleared her throat. When the first two cruisers pulled up, she barked orders. "Cuff the two assailants."

The two officers rushed in and read the two men their rights then placed handcuffs on them and guided them to their cruisers.

"I'll get the document." Ella went into the breakroom and returned with a white notebook labeled *Recipes*. She flipped through the clear plastic document sleeves until she came to the document. She clicked the binder open and handed the pages to Moe.

He chuckled. "You told me you were worried about the file cabinet being too obvious, but you definitely found a unique hiding place. You are brilliant."

"You need medical?" Heather stood in the doorway.

"I'm fine." Ella peered at Moe. "You've got a cut on your forehead, but it doesn't look stitch-worthy."

Moe patted his forehead then examined the sticky, red dampness on his fingers. "I'm fine. I could use a battle scar to counter my good looks."

He snickered, Ella giggled, and Heather rolled her eyes.

I stared as Moe and Ella strolled out arm in arm. "I guess I'm locking up."

"We need to photograph and document the scene first. You don't have to hang around, though. We'll secure the office before we leave," Heather said. "What's your theory?"

I rubbed my forehead. "The document is sprinkled with just enough factual information to make it believable, but much of it is padding. I think it's bait. Nothing else makes sense to me, but I don't know who it's supposed to catch or why. Or maybe it's a distraction from the genuine document."

Heather gazed at me. "Sleight of hand?"

"Makes sense. It's captured not only our attention but the attention of the entire population of the criminal element in Georgia."

Heather chuckled. "Sure seems like it, doesn't it?"

As two police officers and the crime scene tech entered the office, I said, "You don't need me here. I'm going home."

Heather frowned, and I said, "My car's around the corner in the alley."

She cleared her throat and raised an eyebrow, and a police officer said, "I'll walk you to your car."

Officer Perry was the same officer who had walked me to my car at Glenn's house. On the way to the alley, he said, "You know there's no way to beat this department in getting the word to Detective Ewing that you saved Detective Ross and his friend, don't you?" His face dimpled with his big grin.

My phone buzzed. I glanced at the text then showed Palace Guard and Officer Perry.

Larry: "Dang it, Maggie."

Palace Guard grinned, I smiled, and Officer Perry laughed.

"You want me to follow you home in the cruiser?"

"I'll be fine. Thanks for the offer."

I climbed into the car and started the engine, and he remained in the alley with his hand on his belt near his holster until I turned the corner to head home.

Palace Guard poked me in the back, and when I glanced at him in the rearview mirror, he fluttered his eyelashes, Spike-style.

"Oh, cut it out. He's just a nice guy who is serious about his responsibilities."

When we got home, Lucy was asleep on the sofa next to Spike. He raised his eyebrows.

"Bad guys at the office had tied up Ella and Moe. They're fine now. Not the bad guys. They went to jail."

Spike blew on his finger.

"And Larry's mad."

Spike nodded.

I showered then sent Larry a text. "Nine days."

I turned off the lights then collapsed in bed. *No way can I sleep tonight.*

CHAPTER SIX

Lucy nudged me at six, and I dragged myself out of bed. I started a pot of coffee before we stepped outside. She trotted to the back fence then dropped her nose to the ground to find the scent of any intruders. When she was satisfied that the yard was safe, she relieved herself and pranced to the porch.

I texted Larry. "Eight days."

Larry: "See you in three. Don't find any more bad guys. TIA."

Palace Guard frowned and pointed to the text.

"TIA? It means Thanks in advance."

Palace Guard smiled, and Spike danced his wacky dance. I shrugged and joined in the dance.

After I fed Lucy, I poured a cup of coffee and popped a taco into the oven to warm then cracked an egg into the skillet. When it was soft scrambled, I dumped the taco contents and scrambled them in while the taco shell crisped up.

Palace Guard wrinkled his nose.

"Not very pretty, is it? But it will be tasty." I plated my breakfast and poured more coffee.

I cut my scrambled concoction into bite-sized pieces with my fork then ate my first bite. "Not bad. It could be a new creation at Reggie's Diner if Kate decides to rebuild."

Spike stuck his face near my plate.

"Don't mess with me, Spike," I growled.

He stepped back and pointed to the coffee pot.

"You're right. I need more coffee."

I washed my plate and drank another cup then dressed for work. When I stepped onto the front porch, the sun was bright, and the sky was cloudless. I put on my sunglasses with my Texas Tech ball cap. *My new uniform.*

Palace Guard grinned.

When I reached the office, I expected to see crime scene tape and officers at the door, but the office had no visible signs of any police activity. I unlocked the door, and Palace Guard and I stepped inside. Chairs were turned over, and zip ties and tape were on the floor.

"I didn't know it was this much of a mess."

After I straightened up the front office, I opened Glenn's office door. The floor was littered with empty folders and papers, and the drawers for the wooden four-drawer file cabinet were broken.

"I don't think the file cabinet is salvageable."

I found a box in the alley then tossed in the splintered wood. Two of the desk drawers with locks were damaged from being jimmied. Glenn kept loose coins in his middle drawer, and all the money was gone.

"Talk about petty thieves."

I cleaned the top of the desk then stacked all the papers in the middle.

"Ella can organize these better than I can." I glanced at the clock. "It's almost eight. She'll be here soon."

A sound came from the front door. Palace Guard checked then held his hand on his heart.

"Ella?"

He nodded.

I rushed to the front door. Ella held her purse open as she rummaged through it. She wore a slim navy skirt, a white blouse, and a silky, navy scarf around her neck that she had arranged in some special fashion style that I could never duplicate. I glanced at her feet. She wore white socks and white gym shoes.

Whew. For a minute there, I thought she'd lost her mind.

She glowered at her purse then closed it. "I can't find my office key. It was on a yellow hibiscus keyring that Jennifer gave me. She said it stood for friendship. Isn't that sweet?" She scanned the room as she came inside. "It's a lot cleaner in here than I remembered. Have you already cleaned up?"

"Just in here. The drawers for Glenn's file cabinet were smashed, and papers were scattered all over the floor. I've picked up all the papers. I thought you wouldn't mind organizing them."

"Show me the drawers. Maybe they can be fixed," she said.

"Out here." I led the way to the alley.

Ella sorted through the wood. "We need a fireplace." She chortled, and I snickered.

"Does Jennifer know about the trouble here last night?" she asked.

"Oh no. I forgot," I said. "When I came in, my first thought was to clean up the mess."

She smiled as we went back inside. "I'll call her then I'll work on the papers."

"Thanks. I'll finish pulling Glenn's office together. What about the file cabinet?"

"I'll measure it for new drawers."

Ella strode to the breakroom and made a pot of coffee. She brought me a cup and then called Jennifer.

I swept the office then turned on Glenn's computer and relaxed after it booted up without any errors.

Ella came into the office. "Looks much better. Glenn's doctor will release him later this morning, and Jennifer will come to the office after she gets him settled at home. I have a tape measure in my car. I'll call folks to see if anyone's available to make new drawers."

"I'll find a locksmith and have a copy made of my office key for you. Your key might work better over time when you find it, but if we can get a quick fix, it will be more convenient. I'll swing by the Coyles' house too, just to check it. Will you be okay here by yourself?"

She snorted. "According to Lester, you're the one that finds trouble. I'll be fine."

Palace Guard nodded, and I flounced to my car.

"Locksmith first. There's a shop near the car dealership."

I entered the locksmith shop, and a customer leaned on the counter and chatted with the locksmith who operated the key duplicating machine. The whine of the machine drowned out the customer's words, and I smiled at the locksmith's occasional nods. As I waited, the scarred man came into the shop. I put on my sunglasses, pulled down my ball cap's bill, and wandered to the far corner of the shop to peer at the security items in the display case.

The first customer left, and scar man rushed to the counter.

"There's someone ahead of you," the locksmith said.

I leaned on the display case with my back to the men and waved "go ahead" as I craned my neck for a better look at an item in the far corner.

"Boss said he needs to know what type of key this is." He slammed a key down on the glass.

The locksmith examined the key. "It has rough edges. Looks like a copy of a copy, but not a very good one. It's a door key, but I don't think it works very well."

"What kind of door?" scar man growled. "Can you make a copy?"

"Maybe a business, but I'll need the original key to make another copy."

"If I had that, I wouldn't be here, would I?" Scar man stomped out of the shop.

I strolled to the counter and pointed to the key on the glass. "He left his key."

The locksmith smiled. "He'll come back with the original when he calms down. They always do. Now, what can I do for you?"

"I need a copy made of a key. I have a copy that works."

He chuckled as I handed him my key then frowned as he examined it. "What's this the key to?"

"My office. Coyle Detective Agency."

"You got anything that shows that's where you work?"

I cocked my head then pulled out one of the business cards Jennifer had made for me.

"Maggie Sloan. You have any ID?" he asked.

I raised my eyebrows and showed him my driver's license.

He grunted and put my key next to scar man's. "These two keys are identical. You know that guy? Why would he have a key to your office?"

My eyes narrowed. "Someone got into the office last night and assaulted my coworker and a police officer. My stepfather is Sergeant Arrington. I'll call him."

"Sarge is your stepfather? One of the best men I've ever had the pleasure of knowing. I'll get your copy made."

I called Sarge. "I'm at the locksmith. The man who assaulted Glenn was here with a copy of a key to the Coyle Detective Agency office."

After I hung up, I said, "Sarge is sending someone here."

Why did scar man have a copy of the office key?

"I'm not trying to make myself extra work, but Glenn needs to change his locks. He's an old friend of mine. Should I call him?"

"He's recuperating in the hospital from some injuries. I'm sure he'd like a call, but I'll ask Jennifer about the locks. Is that something you'd have time to do today?"

"I'll make time."

"Thanks." I called Jennifer. "I came to the locksmith's to make a copy of my key for Ella because she lost hers. He suggested we change the locks at the office. Is that okay with you?'

"I should have thought of that. That's an outstanding idea. Tell him to go ahead and bill us."

"Jennifer said to change the locks and bill the office. A police officer should be here soon. I'll wait."

My wait was brief. The shop bell jingled, and Moe strode inside.

Bad guys and Moe. Seems like that's all I see.

Palace Guard rolled his eyes.

Moe glanced at me and shook his head. "Now what, Maggie?"

"The man who attacked Glenn brought a key here to be copied," I said.

The locksmith raised his eyebrows then cleared his throat. "It had enough defects that I couldn't make a copy, and he was angry when I told him I needed the original. He left the key behind, and when Ms. Sloan gave me the key that she wanted copied, I noticed the similarities then confirmed they were the same key."

"What does your key unlock, Maggie?" Moe asked.

"The Coyle Detective Agency office."

"I'm changing the locks today," the locksmith said. "I'll print you a report of my comparison."

Moe furrowed his brow. "Thanks. That will be helpful, and I'll snap a picture of the two keys."

Moe left with the defective key and the printout.

As I headed to the door, the locksmith said, "I'll be at the Coyle Agency in an hour."

"I'll be there. Thank you."

When we entered the agency, Ella sat at the desk. She had dumped out her purse and was sifting through the contents.

"I have officially lost my mind, Maggie. Now I can't find my pocketknife. Want some tea?" She swept the contents she had spread on the table into her purse. "It must have fallen out somewhere."

While we sipped our tea, I told Ella about the events at the locksmith shop.

"I wonder if Curtis stole my key and my knife?" she asked. "I can see why he'd steal the key if he planned to come back later, but why steal the knife? "

"If he had your key, then somebody stole it from him, but the knife...I don't know." I frowned. "I'm going for a walk, but won't be long."

Ella nodded. "I think better when I move around too."

Palace Guard and I sauntered around the corner to the back of the shop. We searched around the window then headed to the alley with our heads down. We slowed our pace as we moved down the dusty, unpaved alley. After we passed the first two businesses, we reached the dumpster in the alley where we had found Curtis. My eyes watered at the stench of the old garbage steaming in the hot Georgia sun. As I searched around it, I put my hand on the side then jerked it back.

"Ow. Hot." I waved my hand to cool it.

I stood on my tiptoes but was too short to peer inside. As I scanned the area for something to stand on, Palace Guard climbed into the dumpster. I cringed as he stirred up more stink, then leaped out.

I held my breath as he came close with his clenched hands extended to me.

"No way am I going to touch whatever is in your hands."

He grinned then opened his right hand to show me the pocketknife he'd found. I shuddered then held out my hand for the dripping knife.

"Ugh. Thank you."

He pointed to his left hand, and I winced then held out my hand.

"For the record, you are no longer in my will."

Palace Guard smirked then dropped the item in my hand.

"Ella's yellow hibiscus keyring!" I squealed. "You're back in the will."

As we strolled back to the office, I said, "Now I want to know how they got into the dumpster. I expected to find the pocketknife on the ground. Unless Curtis tossed it away because it's broken." I shook my head. "Wasn't he running away from someone? I'll clean it up then we'll see what kind of shape it's in. Ella's going to be thrilled over her keyring."

Ella wrinkled her nose when I went into the office. "Did you find my knife? Why do you smell so bad?"

She followed me into the breakroom. I dropped the knife into the sink and ran hot water over it.

Ella picked the knife up and opened it. "This isn't my knife. Besides, it's broken."

I shrugged. "Which is why it was thrown away."

Ella hung her head as she turned to leave.

"Wait. I have one more thing." I opened my hand with the keyring.

Ella snatched it from me and clutched it to her chest. Tears slipped down her cheeks. "My keyring. Thank you for finding my keyring."

She hugged me then laughed. "Ew. You still stink."

I smiled. *Thanks for looking.*

Palace Guard nodded.

My phone rang. *Jennifer.*

"I've put you on speakerphone so Ella can hear too."

"Good. The doctor discharged Glenn from the hospital. All the paperwork is signed, and someone from transport will be here soon to wheel him out. We'll have lunch at home then I'll come to the office. Everything okay?"

Ella rolled her eyes and snorted.

I snickered. "We're fine. See you later."

"I'll order lunch," Ella said. "What do you want?"

"Whatever sounds good to you."

Ella's phone rang, and she answered. She giggled and wandered to the outer office.

Moe.

I wiped off the counter and straightened the chairs around the table. I scanned the floor. *Should I sweep?* My eyes widened at the pocketknife under the table, and I pointed it out to Palace Guard.

"I am so sorry you went to so much trouble. I didn't even think about looking in the office."

Palace Guard smiled and patted my shoulder.

"Thanks."

Ella hurried into the breakroom; her face was flushed. "That was Lester. He'll pick up lunch for us. He has some things to go over with you. I didn't expect to see him until this evening. Do I look all right?"

"You always look amazing."

She snickered. "An unbiased opinion. Come with me to Glenn's office. I need to talk to you about the file cabinet before Jennifer gets here."

"First, look under the table."

Ella peered under the table then picked up the knife. "It's mine. It must have dropped out of my purse. I'm so sorry about the dumpster."

"The good news is that we have one less puzzle to solve."

She led the way to Glenn's office. "I've received the quotes for the drawers. Each drawer has to be custom made because they are all different, so it's cheaper to get a new cabinet."

She patted the file cabinet. "However, I could install sturdy shelves and fashion a door then we could use it for supplies in the outer office. It will be a beautiful piece of furniture when I'm done. What do you think? Should I suggest it to Jennifer?"

"Of course. I can't wait to see it."

"Thanks. With it empty, I can move it by myself. Of course, a two-person lift would be easier." She chuckled. "I know you're a person, but you and I aren't exactly the same height."

She crouched. "I'd have to carry my end like this."

She lost her balance and fell on the floor as Moe came into the office.

She rose and brushed off her skirt. "Hello, Lester. Maggie's teaching me how to fall."

He chuckled. "You did it very well, Ella. You're a natural."

Ella laughed, and I stared at them then headed to the breakroom and sent Larry a text.

"Eight days. Sure I can't camp on the training grounds?"

Larry: "You okay?"

"No. Ella and Moe are annoying."

Larry: "Ella and Moe? Can't wait to hear. Three more days."

Larry: "Still no to camping."

I smiled. *He understands.*

Ella and Moe came into the breakroom. Moe set sacks on the table, and Ella giggled.

"You'll never guess what Lester got us for lunch." She set the individual to-go boxes, plastic ware, and napkins on the table while Moe pulled out the large cups of sweet tea.

I peeked inside my food box. "It's been ages since I've had chicken livers."

"It needs to be the signature celebratory lunch of the Coyle Detective Agency," Ella said as we dug in.

"What are we celebrating?" I dipped my roll into the gravy.

"Thursday." Ella grinned, and her dimples deepened.

Moe guffawed. "Ella, you are so funny."

Ella smacked his arm with a playful touch. "Oh, you."

I furrowed my brow and stared at my plate. *Excuse me. I'm eating here.*

Palace Guard covered his eyes with his hands then peeked at me, and I snickered.

I cleared my throat. "I don't understand the point of the low-range listening device that Curtis planted at Glenn's house.

It's almost like you'd have to be inside the house to pick up its signal."

Moe chuckled. "The criminal element is having quality problems just like the rest of us. We've heard a number of complaints through the grapevine about bad equipment. My team wanted to set up a hotline for crooks to report problems. The chief laughed when I suggested it then said he'd check with the District Attorney."

"You are a wonderful leader, Les." Ella fluttered her eyelashes, and after I mimicked her, she glared.

After we ate, Moe said, "Maggie, Kate found her courier. He's in a coma in a hospital's critical care unit. He was badly beaten and left for dead, but a homeless man found him in an alley. The homeless guy had trouble finding anyone who would listen to him, and then an elderly woman called for an ambulance because she misunderstood and thought he was ill." He rubbed the back of his neck. "That man is a hero. He saved the courier's life."

A tear rolled down Ella's cheek, and she brushed it away. "I'm afraid I would have ignored him and hurried away. Bless that woman for her willingness to help and that dear man for being persistent."

Moe nodded. "When the ambulance crew approached their patient, they found the courier's empty briefcase next to him. Kate said he carried the original document that was intended for Glenn. She hopes he had time to do something with the original when he realized he was in danger, but so far, no one knows what it is or where it might be. She's sure the bad guys think you have it." Moe gazed at me. "Be careful."

"Where was the courier attacked?" I asked.

Moe frowned. "Kate said he was on his way here from Mobile but was run off the road then beaten after he crashed."

Ella narrowed her eyes and glanced at me. "Lester, how can I help?"

"Your instincts are good. Trust them." Moe rose.

After he left, Ella said, "I'm going to recheck my measurements for the shelves."

The locksmith tapped on the door. "Ready for new locks? Let's see what we have here." While he inspected the back door, Jennifer came into the shop.

"Glenn's in the den. He wanted to sit on the patio, but it's too hot. I left after we ate lunch. Maybe he'll nap." She grinned.

The locksmith came out of the back room.

"How's Glenn?" he asked.

"Home and resting. Maggie said you'd change our locks."

"That's what I'm here for. How many keys do you want? The keys are in a pack of ten, and I'll set all the door and deadbolt locks to a single key."

"Ten keys are plenty," she said.

"I'll get to work," he said.

Ella stood in the doorway of Glenn's office. "Jennifer, can I talk to you about the file cabinet? I have an idea I want to discuss with you."

After a few minutes, Jennifer walked out of Glenn's office. "Where were you thinking the cabinet could go?" Jennifer scanned the room. "I never noticed how large this room is. We could set up a small waiting area near the front door, couldn't we? There's no reason for this desk to face the door. But I'm getting ahead of myself. First, we need another file cabinet. Maybe two."

"I glanced through the papers," I said. "It might be worth reviewing them more closely. Ella or I could scan and save them on the computer then you could review the documents to see which originals you need to keep on hand or if an electronic copy would be satisfactory. Ella could organize the computer files so each document would be faster to find."

"Good idea. We can stack them on the breakroom table and sort there. Ella, we have some open cases that need to be wrapped up. Let's go over those first to prioritize and close what we can."

"I'll select the papers to be scanned," I said.

I spent the rest of the afternoon in the breakroom as I read the papers from the file cabinet and placed the ones I thought could be scanned in a pile. Jennifer and Ella worked at the front office desk. While Jennifer reviewed each contract to determine what needed to be done, Ella made phone calls.

At four-thirty, Jennifer rose from her chair and stretched. "Let's call it a day and start fresh in the morning. Maggie, if you'll come here before you go to the house, we can go over the documents then you could stop at the post office and check our box for mail. I don't think I've checked it in two weeks."

On the way to my car, my phone buzzed a text.

Sierra: "I have an interview at the HPD tomorrow at ten! Call?"

When she picked up the phone, she said, "I'm excited and in a panic at the same time. What should I wear?"

I laughed. "I'm the worst person in the world to give you fashion advice, but when I was interviewing after I finished college, I wore what Mother called business professional. Think boring."

She chuckled. "That helps. Want to have lunch tomorrow to debrief or celebrate? I haven't been this nervous since senior prom."

"Sounds great. Text me after your interview, and we'll meet somewhere."

As we headed home, I said, "I hadn't thought about it until I talked to Sierra. What do I wear this weekend?"

Palace Guard stared at me, and I shrugged. "Who else could I ask? Ella would tell me to get my nails done, and Jennifer would buy me a whole new wardrobe."

I snickered, and Palace Guard grinned.

I woke the next morning at four and stumbled into the kitchen. "Too early for coffee or to send Larry a text."

I sat on the sofa to read a book then put up my feet. Lucy nudged me, and I woke with a start. "Six o'clock? I closed my eyes just for a second. Thanks, Lucy."

I started a pot of coffee then Lucy, Spike, and I went outside. The morning dew still clung to the grass where the sunbeams hadn't hit, and the clear sky foretold of a hot, sunny day.

I sent Larry a text. "Good morning! Two days."

Larry: "Found a bed-and-breakfast close to the center. I'll send you the address."

I whooped, and Lucy and Spike raced to my side. Palace Guard dashed to the back from the front of the house.

"I'm sorry." I rubbed Lucy's face, and she rolled to her back for her belly rub. I set the phone on the porch where the men could see it. Spike danced his wacky dance, and Palace Guard smiled.

When I went inside, Lucy followed me, and I fed her then showered and dressed for work.

I drummed my fingers on the steering wheel on the way to the detective agency. "I've never been to a bed-and-breakfast. Now I don't know what to wear for sure."

As I headed to the back lot, I noticed Jennifer's car was parked in front. I parked in my favorite spot, and Ella pulled in behind me. Ella opened her trunk and lifted out boards. I peered into the trunk. "Does this cardboard box go inside?"

"Sure does. It's my stain and all the supplies. I thought I'd get on it while you and Jennifer go over the documents."

She carried the boards, and I carried the box into the shop.

Jennifer smiled as we set our loads on the floor next to the front desk.

"Where do you want the file cabinet, Jennifer?" Ella asked. "I can stain the boards in the storage room this morning then install them this afternoon after they dry. It will be easier to move the file cabinet now rather than after the shelves are in."

Jennifer stood in the middle of the room then waved her hand away from the breakroom. "I think we should set up this whole side for you. We have the breakroom, bathroom, and storage room all on the other side. When we're big time, we can put another desk in the middle of the room for the receptionist."

"I love big goals." Ella grinned as she pointed. "We could put the file cabinet against the wall then set the desk so that my back is to the file cabinet. Glenn's office has that small printer. We may want a printer out here too. We'll need a table."

"That's easy," Jennifer said. "I can always find an extra table to bring in. Do you think you and I could move the file cabinet?"

"I brought a dolly to move it. I'll need you to guide me." Ella hurried out to her car then rolled a dolly into the office.

Ella pushed the dolly and led the way into Glenn's office. "I'll slip the dolly under the cabinet on this side then you two can push it toward me, and I'll ease it over."

I stood next to the wall, and Jennifer stood next to me.

Ella slipped the dolly into place. "Okay, I'll use leverage to tip it my way, and you push. Ready? Push."

The file cabinet leaned against the dolly then Ella balanced it and rolled it to the door. Jennifer steadied the cabinet as it went through the doorway.

I glanced at the floor where the cabinet had been and spotted something. *A key?* I stuck it into my pocket and hurried to help guide Ella.

Ella eased the cabinet into the spot she had picked then Jennifer and I steadied it as Ella lowered it toward us and into place.

"That was much easier than I expected," Jennifer said.

"Right tools for the job is the only way to go every time." Ella rolled her dolly out to her car.

Jennifer and I sat in the breakroom with the papers while Ella swept Glenn's office then sanded and stained shelves.

CHAPTER SEVEN

"I thought we could scan then shred this first stack," I said. "When you get Ella's printer, get a good shredder too."

Jennifer nodded. "We have one, but it's old and needs to be replaced."

I pointed to the table. "These papers are duplicates or old versions. They are candidates to shred but not scan. We'll go over them after you've looked at the rest." I patted the third stack. "I think you'll want these in the file cabinet. I'd still scan them though."

"You made this easy." Jennifer leaned back in her chair. "What time are you leaving tomorrow? Do you know where you'll stay?"

"It's about three hours away. I thought I'd leave right after lunch. Larry said he made a reservation for me at a bed and breakfast. He'll send me the address later, and I'll get it to you."

"A cozy bed and breakfast is perfect. What clothes are you packing for the weekend?"

My eyes widened, and she patted my hand. "I'll pick up a few things for you. You'll want your running clothes because that's what you do, and you'll also want jeans and boots for hiking. I'm guessing you're going out to lunch and dinner on Sunday. We'll see if they have a pool. I would guess they don't." She smiled. "Usually you're the organizer. Thanks for letting me help you for a change."

I relaxed as my tension slid away. "Thank you. I'm looking forward to seeing Larry, but I was anxious about what to wear."

"We're finished, right? I'll give you the key to the post office box. You can pick up the mail then go to the house. We'll let Glenn go through the mail. He's happy the surgery is over, and he's even happier to be home."

I followed the signs at the post office and found the mailbox for Coyle Detective Agency on the third row from the top. I smiled. *If the mailbox were on the top row, I wouldn't be able to pick up the mail.*

A man loitered near the end of the main aisle. I emptied the box that was stuffed with envelopes and cards then hurried to my car. *All junk.* The man hurried out behind me, but I climbed into my car and locked the door then glared at him as he strode toward my car then met my gaze and changed direction. I headed toward the detective agency then swerved down an alley to divert to Glenn's house. When I reached the house, the door was unlocked, and I locked it behind me.

"Glenn, I'm here." I called out.

"Good to see you, Maggie." Glenn beamed when I strolled into the den.

"I picked up the mail, but I didn't check it." I handed the mail to Glenn and sat next to him while he shuffled through it. The last two pieces were an oversized, colorful card advertising new cars and a six by nine envelope addressed to Kate Coyle with a return address in Mobile, Alabama.

"This is odd." He set the junk mail to the side as he examined the envelope.

I handed him his letter opener, and he slit open the envelope. A Georgia map and an art brochure for the Isabelle Stewart Gardner Museum in Boston fell out.

Glenn opened the brochure then shook it. "Nothing else in here. This is a brochure about the art stolen from the museum. Did I tell you there's speculation the art is in the regions of Philadelphia or Connecticut?" He chuckled. "Wouldn't want to work that door-to-door hunt." He glanced at my blank face. "That's a joke, Maggie. That would be impossible."

I furrowed my brow. *Why is that funny?*

Palace Guard rolled his eyes.

Sarcasm?

He nodded.

I cleared my throat. "There was a rumor that the FBI solved the case and knew who the thieves were, but that was a few years ago, right? What's interesting is that on the FBI website, there's a list of the top ten art crimes, but the list has only nine, and the Gardner Museum is missing. A more recent rumor is that three pieces of art were sold to a private buyer who lives in the South somewhere."

"Didn't Curtis say two? Although when it comes to believing Curtis or some unfounded rumor, put me down on the rumor's side. Do you get the feeling everyone is in on the art heist conspiracy except us?" Glenn unfolded the map and shook it then snorted. "I don't know what I expected to fall out."

I studied the museum's brochure. "The reward for information leading to the art pieces' return is ten million dollars."

Glenn whistled. "Sounds like a reason somebody doesn't want us to find the art before they do."

I smoothed out the map on the coffee table. "Athens is circled and so is a bank advertisement."

Glenn opened the envelope as wide as he could and shook it. "That's it. Why is Kate's name on it?"

"I'll check the return address." I frowned at the screen. "It's the FBI field office in Mobile."

"Do you think Kate stole the art? Never mind. She was in elementary school back then." Glenn chuckled. "Want some tea? Jennifer has some in the refrigerator, and it's too early for beer."

"There's a list of your medications on the counter," I said as I poured our tea. "Have you had your morning medicine?"

"No, I don't need it. I feel fine," Glenn grumbled. "Jennifer's nagging me by proxy now."

Before I returned to the kitchen for the list, I said, "The courier. He used the FBI address in Mobile as the return address and sent it addressed to Kate at your office."

"Sounds plausible to me," he said.

I handed Glenn his pills. "I'll scan the note and the map where it's circled."

Glenn grumbled then swallowed his pills. "What were we going to do this morning? The mail distracted me."

"Has Kate sent you any resumes of detectives to help you?"

"I haven't checked my email. Would you bring me my laptop?"

After he was set up with his laptop, I said, "Before I forget, I'm having lunch with a friend. Jennifer left sandwiches and salads in the refrigerator. I'll serve your lunch before I leave then I'll be back this afternoon at least for a while."

Palace Guard peered over Glenn's shoulder while I returned his medication to the kitchen. When I returned, Glenn said, "She sent me three. I printed them."

I picked up the papers from the printer and read. "Do you know any of these men?"

"Two of them were old when I started the Police Academy."

"These two?" I asked.

"Right. How did you know?"

"The latest date either of them mentions on the resume is fifteen years ago, and their cover letters don't mention any recent activities either. What about the third one?"

"Paul Vargas resigned from the Georgia state police ten years ago to avoid being fired. Nothing was proven, and he was never charged, but we all knew he was involved in a drug ring. See how many jobs he's held in the past ten years?"

I counted. "Six. Two mall security jobs, and the rest are retail sales."

Glenn nodded. "I'll bet what Kate had in mind was to give him a chance, and I would if he showed more stability. I'm not into charity cases, although he didn't try to hide his job-hopping. What do you think?"

"You could phone screen him first, but I think a face to face where you ask him hard questions about his past and his job history would be the way to go."

"We could do that." Glenn rubbed his chin. "Want to be my home health care person? Your observation skills are phenomenal."

I smiled. "It was funny how I was on the patio with you, and Curtis never noticed me."

"The invisible Gray Lady. Out of sight; out of mind." Glenn held up his hand.

Palace Guard smiled then smacked Glenn's hand, and Glenn laughed.

"Thanks, Palace Guard. Am I right?" he asked.

I stared. "You are."

"I'll call him." Glenn beamed as he picked up his phone.

As I carried our glasses to the kitchen, Larry texted the address of the bed-and-breakfast. When I checked it out, I smiled. *In the country surrounded by trees. It's beautiful.* I sent Larry a text. "B&B is gorgeous. Can't wait to see you."

Larry: "Better than camping?"

Palace Guard peered over my shoulder, and I grinned. "Even I get that."

Me: "Camping got nudged out."

When I returned to the den, Glenn asked, "Did you hear from Larry?"

"He sent me the address of the bed-and-breakfast where I'm staying this weekend." I handed him my phone.

He scrolled through the pictures. "Beautiful property. Perfect country retreat. I had a good chat with Paul. He's off until Monday and can come here this afternoon at two. Will that work for you? I do want you here, especially seeing as how I'm recovering and all." He wiggled his eyebrows, and I snickered.

I texted the address to Jennifer, and she called me. "Ella and I looked it up. What a gorgeous place. I did a little shopping this morning. What time are you leaving?"

"I'll leave tomorrow after lunch."

"Good. I'll have time to finish up my shopping after lunch then we'll wash the sizing out of your new clothes."

After we hung up, I said, "store cooties."

"What?" Glenn asked.

I snickered. "It was an ongoing argument between Kate and me. She said we washed out sizing, and I said store cooties. I'd forgotten about it until Jennifer said we'd wash out sizing."

Glenn laughed. "I'm taking your side."

My phone rang. "Maggie, it was a fantastic interview! Meet me at the pizza place down the street from the police department?"

"Be there in twenty minutes."

"Is it too early for your lunch, Glenn?"

"Why don't you give me half of my lunch now, and the rest after you get back? Then you won't be rushed."

I put a brownie from the freezer and half a sandwich on a plate and carried his plate and glass of tea into the den. "Here you go." I set his lunch on his tray next to his chair. "What else can I do?"

"Enjoy your lunch." Glenn reached for his sandwich.

When I reached the door, I glanced back at Palace Guard. "You going or staying?"

He pointed to Glenn.

"What did he say?" Glenn asked.

"He's staying with you."

Glenn's eyes widened. "Thanks, Palace Guard."

When I approached the pizza place, nostalgia and then loneliness tugged at me. *This is where Larry and I picked up pizza the first time we were hiding out from the bad guys.*

After I parked, I snapped a quick photo and sent it to Larry with the message, "Remember this?"

Larry: "Do I ever! Maggie pizza. Coming home NOW."

Me: "Camping."

Larry: "You win. Two days!"

Me: "Easy win. You stepped into my trap."

Larry: "Hilarious. That's sarcasm."

I snickered and headed into the pizza parlor.

"Hey, Maggie. Right on time," Sierra said. She wore her black work slacks, heels, and a purple shirt that gave her blue eyes a hint of lavender.

After we were seated in a booth and ordered, I said, "I want to hear everything."

"When I opened the door and stepped inside, I had such a horrible case of nerves that I almost walked out. Then this super cute police officer asked if he could help me. When I asked for Detective Ross, he told me I had the interview in the bag. He said everybody was pulling for me. Is that how the police department is?" Sierra's cheeks reddened.

I chuckled. "That's exactly how it is. Everybody knows everybody's business."

"The cute guy walked me to the detective's office. The crime tech that talked to me at the restaurant, DeeDee, was there too. Officer Ross didn't stay long. DeeDee and I chatted then we went to her office."

She gulped her tea. "DeeDee called her team into her office, and we drank coffee and munched on cinnamon rolls that one of the guys made this morning in my honor. I was impressed. They mostly told gruesome stories then gave me a grand tour of the crime lab. DeeDee's team is quite strange. My kind of people."

I smiled. "When do you start?"

"DeeDee said I'd get a formal letter on Monday with a start date on the following Monday. I'll give notice this afternoon. I'm excited. Can you believe I'll get benefits and everything?"

"That's outstanding."

She smiled. "You remember Toby, right? He's my brother. It's just the two of us now. Now that I have a regular job, he can quit too. He's a talented mechanic; he just needs the training then he's got a job waiting for him. The service manager at the car dealership has been after him to get his certification."

"Best news I've heard in ages."

After our server brought the pizza, we dug in. Sierra repeated some of the gory stories as we ate, and we giggled at crime lab humor.

The server dropped the bill on our table, and I snatched it up. "It's a tradition. I'm buying lunch to celebrate."

"Thank you. I'll call you when I get my first paycheck." Sierra grinned.

I parked in the driveway then bounded to the door. When I went inside, Glenn said, "You look refreshed. Good lunch?"

"It was. My friend Sierra interviewed at the police department. She's a talented sketch artist."

"They've been searching for a reliable artist for a year. Did they hire her? Did she talk to DeeDee? DeeDee is a force, and her team is very particular. Hard to work with, I understand."

"That wasn't the impression I got from Sierra. She loved the team."

Glenn snorted. "Your Sierra has unusual taste. Did they try to gross her out? That's how they screen candidates."

"She told me some of their stories, and they were hysterical."

"That's great news. Sounds like a perfect fit."

I hurried to the kitchen and pulled together his second lunch. When I placed it on his tray, he said, "Thanks. I jotted down some of my questions for Paul." He handed me his notes. "Can you think of anything else?"

"These are good. I can think of only two additional questions. The first is why did he stay in Harperville, and the second is would he go back to the state police?"

"Excellent." Glenn finished his sandwich. "I need another brownie."

Palace Guard pointed to the patio. The door was open. *Glenn went to the patio?*

Palace Guard grinned.

"It's ten minutes 'til two. Would you rather interview him on the patio?"

"Good idea." Glenn narrowed his eyes. "Was I busted?"

"What are you talking about? I'll get your wheelchair."

I rolled the wheelchair to Glenn's side, and he scooted forward in his recliner then swung himself into the seat. His brow was damp as he rolled himself to the patio.

"That was great. I'll gather his resume and your notes for you." I flipped on the ceiling fan before I headed to the den and kitchen and returned with a large pitcher of iced tea, two glasses, and Glenn's brownie.

"Thanks, Maggie. Jennifer would be proud of you." Glenn poured a glass of tea.

After I set his papers on the patio table, Palace Guard pointed to the front door.

"He's here," I said. "Right on time."

I answered the door. "Mr. Vargas?"

The muscular man at the door was tall, but not as tall as Glenn. He wore a long-sleeved blue shirt that complemented his pale brown skin, dark eyes, and black hair. His blue striped tie was in a full Windsor knot, and his khaki pants were pressed. His back was straight, his chin was high, and his shoulders were back. *Cop.*

"I'm here to see Glenn." When he smiled, his eyes crinkled.

"He's right this way. On the patio," I said.

"You're not Kate," he said.

"No, I'm Maggie."

His brow furrowed.

Running through your memory bank?

Before we reached the den, he said, "Librarian. I'm so sorry for your loss. Parker was a good man."

I paused and met his gaze. "Yes, he was. Thank you."

When we reached the den, I said, "Glenn, Mr. Vargas remembered me."

"Still keeping up, are you, Paul? Good to see you."

"I heard you were injured." Paul reached out his hand, and they shook. "Good to see they can't keep a good man down."

"Have a seat, Paul. I've got some questions for you. Maggie's here to listen."

Paul nodded and smiled.

I glanced at Glenn and smiled my Kate tiger smile as Paul sat.

Glenn ducked his face into his elbow and coughed. "Help yourself to a glass of sweet tea, Paul."

"Thank you." Paul remained relaxed and still in his seat.

Glenn peered at Paul's resume. "Go through your employment record since you left the state."

"I can summarize for you. My wife is an accountant, and she said I had to help pay the bills. I'm certain she insisted for my mental health, and she was right. As you can tell from my resume, I accepted whatever was offered. I thought the first security job would be a good fit, but I came across some questionable bookkeeping and was fired before I collected any hard evidence. The second security job was my favorite until the company was sold to a group that dismissed the existing employees and brought in their own. I slipped into a depression, but my wife and her lawyer friend from college traced the true owners to a criminal element. I snapped right out of it when she told me."

"She's a good woman," Glenn said.

"She's fierce." Paul smiled. "After that, I steered away from security. The rest of the jobs were...someone would find out I was a former cop and complain to management that I made them nervous, and it wasn't long until management sent me on my way. My wife reminded me I had the soul of a cop, and the problem was theirs, not mine. She was right, but we didn't have the resources to fight them. I'd accept the next job and keep my head down until someone was offended because I was there."

"The rumor was you left the state before you were fired because you were involved with a drug ring." Glenn's jaw was tight, and Paul met his gaze.

"I know, and I actually can't talk about that. I can tell you it wasn't true, but I know that's what anyone would say." He furrowed his brow and glanced away.

"Would you go back if circumstances changed?"

"I'd like to, but even after the truth comes out, the whispers will never stop."

Glenn narrowed his eyes. "Doesn't sound like you could ever be licensed as a private investigator then."

Paul's laugh was hollow. "They left that door open. The state gave me a license as a concession, I guess, and I've kept it up."

"Does Kate know any of this?" Glenn frowned.

Paul's face tightened. "I don't know what you're talking about."

Glenn kept his gaze on Paul. "What about you, Maggie? You have any questions?"

Where's my spray to clear out all the testosterone in this room?

I nodded, and when Paul shifted his gaze to me, his face softened.

"Anything else you'd like to say?" I asked.

He smiled and turned back to Glenn. "We're cut from the same cloth. Stubborn or pigheaded, as my wife says. We'll probably clash, but we'll work it out. I think your agency will be unbeatable with the two of us working together. Thank you for the chance,

Glenn." He rose and turned to me. "It was nice to meet you, Maggie. If there's nothing else, I'll go. Glenn, you know how to reach me."

I followed him to the door and locked it after he left.

"Well?" I asked when I returned to the patio.

"He's the man I remember, but when I asked if Kate knew about his past, he clammed up. Why do you suppose he shut down the conversation when I mentioned Kate? What do you think?"

"I don't know. I thought you asked him because Kate recommended him, but you obviously hit a nerve. I wonder if the investigation he couldn't talk about involved the FBI? That's a good Kate question. Do you know Mrs. Vargas?"

He laughed. "I do. She's your size, soft-spoken, and a veritable force. She's the only one who could have snapped him out of a depression and kept him going."

"I think he's a cop with integrity. I'd have him interview with Jennifer and Ella. Meanwhile, you need to talk to Kate."

Glenn raised his eyebrows. "If he can get past those two, he's perfect."

He reached for his phone and called Jennifer while I returned the pitcher and the clean glass to the kitchen.

"Are you ready to go back into the den?" I asked when I returned.

"Good idea. Jennifer is calling him to see if he'll swing by the agency. Now I feel sorry for him." Glenn smiled and wheeled himself back to his recliner. After he locked the wheels, he swung himself into his chair.

"My physical therapist would approve the workout." He leaned back. "Jennifer wants you to pick up your new clothes so you can pack for your weekend. I'll send a text for Kate to call me."

Glenn's phone buzzed a text. "Jennifer says he's on his way. Do you suppose we could mosey on over to the office and eavesdrop? Better him than me." He smirked and rubbed his hands together.

"You are terrible. Is there anything else I can do?"

"I have a home health care aide scheduled in fifteen minutes."

"I have a few things to do before I leave. I can stick around."

Glenn closed his eyes. "I'll enjoy some downtime and relax."

I straightened the patio and turned off the fan as I slid the door closed.

Palace Guard pointed to the door.

"Your home health aide is here."

When I opened the door, a wizened woman who wore a set of gray scrubs two sizes too big stood on the porch. "I'm Alma," she said as she strolled inside and glanced around. "Where's my victim?" She cackled. "Home health care humor. You are?"

I grinned. "Maggie. I'm a friend of the family. Glenn's in here." I led the way to the den.

"Alma, this is Glenn. Glenn, Alma."

"Hello, sweetheart. Ready to get nekkid for your bath?" Alma asked.

Glenn's eyes widened, and she chortled. "Just checking your hearing, dearie. We'll do a sponge bath later."

"See you later, Glenn." I scooted out of the house and found Palace Guard waiting in the car for me.

"She's unique, isn't she?"

Palace Guard rolled his eyes.

My hand brushed my pocket as I reached for my door to close it. *Key.*

"I've got time." I drove to the locksmith's shop.

When I opened the door, the locksmith was grinding keys. He nodded and smiled. After he finished the keys, he removed his goggles and ear protection and wiped his hands.

"What can I do for you today?" he asked.

"I found a key behind the file cabinet in our office. I wondered if you could look at it and tell me what it might open."

He held out his hand. "Let's see what you've got."

I pulled the key out of my pocket and gave it to him.

"This is easy. It's a bank safe deposit key. See this? One-eight-two. That's the number of the safe deposit box. I can't tell you which bank, though. Do you know who it belongs to? Even if you knew which bank, only the owner can open it, and the owner has to have identification. You'd need proof from the owner that you have the rights to open the box or else a court order. Not simple. Anything else I can do for you?"

"Wow. Thanks for the information. It's not as easy as I thought."

"Nothing is in your business, is it?" He turned back to his grinder.

On my way to the office, I asked, "Do you think Curtis left the key and grabbed Ella's key as a decoy in case anyone stole the safe deposit key from him? I don't think he's that smart. Do you think the bank on the brochure is where the safe deposit box is? Is this all completely unrelated?"

Palace Guard raised his eyebrows and peered at me.

After I parked, I said, "I could hand this off to Glenn, especially if he hires Paul. Then I won't stew about it all weekend. I'll visit him in the morning before I leave."

When I strolled inside the office, Jennifer and Ella were huddled over the printer near Ella's desk.

"Hi, Maggie." Jennifer stretched her back. "We're putting Ella's new printer through the paces. We finished scanning all the important documents and are working on the scan and file documents now. Ella set up a cloud for the agency for our document folders. We'll get a shredder next week. Paul said he met you when he talked to Glenn."

"What did you think of him?" I asked.

Ella grinned. "I was ready to give him the third degree, but Jennifer beat me to it."

"I just asked him if he could deal with orders from two bossy women," Jennifer said.

"What did he say?"

"He laughed and said he'd do as well as Glenn does," Jennifer said.

Ella nodded. "Best answer ever. Then we just chatted. He'll do just fine."

"I've got your new clothes in Glenn's office, Maggie. Did you say you were leaving tomorrow after lunch? Why don't you have lunch with us?"

"That would be perfect. I have a couple of things to go over with Glenn before I leave town. Speaking of Glenn, his home health care aide came to the house as I was leaving. How often will she visit him?"

"She's scheduled for three days a week, but the agency said we could schedule more or less, depending on how much care Glenn needs. I might be able to tend to him later, but right now my time's too tight."

A middle-aged man dressed in jeans and a plain orange T-shirt opened the office door. He carried a vase with an enormous bouquet of lilies. "Excuse me. Is this the Coyle Detective Agency?"

"Sure is," Jennifer said.

"Mrs. Coyle? I've rented the office space next to you. I'm Ken Brown, and this is a peace offering. We're going to be remodeling the office this next week. Are you here on Saturdays or Sundays?"

"Are these Casablanca lilies? They are beautiful and so fragrant. Thank you. It wasn't necessary, but they are lovely. We don't work weekends, but we'll be here on Monday."

Ella accepted the vase from Ken Brown. "I'll put the flowers on the desk."

He nodded. "All three of you will be at work on Monday?"

"Yes, we're here early," Jennifer said.

"I'm worried we may disturb you with our remodeling smells and noise; we'll be stripping the floors and painting. I hope the fumes won't bother you. They'll be pungent. We'll try to get the work done as soon as we can, but expect to be done by Wednesday or Thursday, at the latest."

"That's exciting news. What kind of business, Mr. Brown?" she asked.

"My wife and her partner are opening a beauty shop and nail salon after we get it pulled into shape."

"Are you local?" Ella asked.

"We're moving here from Charleston."

"Welcome to the community. Let us know if there's anything we can do to help you out," Jennifer said.

After Ken Brown left, Ella frowned. "We need to hang a sign or at least to have the door lettered."

"Put it on our list of things to do. We can check on that next week after we decide if we want to hang an outdoor sign on the building or have something on the door."

I collected the four sacks of clothing and peeked inside. "Jennifer, this is too much."

"No, it isn't. When was the last time you bought any clothes?"

I furrowed my brow. "I can't remember."

She snorted. "I've saved all the receipts, and no, you can't have them. Try them on, and if anything doesn't fit, I'll return it. But only if it doesn't fit."

I frowned. "Okay."

Ella laughed. "Are you busted, girlfriend?"

I glared, and Palace Guard smiled.

"Guess I better go do my laundry." I pouted. "I'm going to be up half the night."

I stomped out, and the sound of laughter followed me.

CHAPTER EIGHT

After I unloaded my packages at home and set them on the kitchen table, I pulled out each outfit and held it up. Spike put his hands on his cheeks and fluttered his eyelashes.

"Cut it out," I growled as he did his wacky dance.

I put in the first load and sent Larry a text. "Two days."

"I need to run off some energy." I changed my clothes, then Palace Guard and I ran our long, circular route past the horse farm, past my house to the goat farm, and back. When we returned, I poured a glass of tea then Lucy and I went outside. She flopped on the back porch, and I rubbed her belly then stretched out next to her and cooed.

I shifted to my rocking chair and sipped my tea. A line of dark clouds in the southwest spread across the horizon and filled the sky as it crept closer to Harperville. When the rumble of thunder announced an impending storm, Lucy padded to the door and tapped it with her nose.

"Time to go in, Lucy?"

I opened the door, and she dashed inside and leapt onto the sofa. Spike joined her, and she stuck her muzzle behind him.

My phone buzzed a text.

Larry: "What time are you leaving?"

Me: "After lunch."

Larry: "Perfect."

I stared at my phone. *Why is that perfect?*

The washer signaled the end of its cycle, and I moved the clothes to the dryer and started another load. I pulled out my overnight backpack and wrote my packing list on the back of a junk mail envelope. The crack of thunder and the flash of lightning startled me. *Hope we don't lose power until the dryer's done.* When the washer and dryer stopped, I emptied the dryer and tossed in the wet clothes to dry.

Before I carried the basket of dry clothes to my bedroom, I called Mother.

"Margaret, I was about to call you. Big D and I are taking the RV out for a few days. He called it a shakedown. Isn't that funny? Big D says we're not going far. Did you call about anything special? I need to finish packing so we can leave."

"I'm going to visit Larry for the weekend. He's been in training at the Georgia Public Safety Training Center."

"That's nice, Margaret. Are you taking Lucy? We're taking Franklin. He'll love it."

"Lucy will stay with Glenn and Jennifer."

"Lucy will have a weekend vacation too. That's wonderful."

Mother hung up.

I smiled. "Have a good time, Mother."

I clicked on the light in my bedroom then folded and hung up clothes. I held up a mossy green shirt, but it was too long. *Jennifer bought me a dress?* I slipped it on and examined myself in the mirror. *Not with running shoes.* I changed into my red boots.

I strolled into the great room and modeled. Palace Guard nodded and Spike applauded. "I'll pack it in case we go somewhere fancy for dinner Sunday night."

I hung it on my bedroom door to pack later. When I found a white shirt with small brown horses, I tried it on and checked the mirror. *This is cute.* I hung it up with the dress. The rain pounded on the roof and against my bedroom window, and I snickered. *Symphony for trying on new clothes.*

I found a flowery dress and tossed it on the bed along with a pink shirt that Mother would love. *Not my style.* My eyes widened when I pulled out a lacy bra. *What's wrong with my sports bra?* I tried it on with the horse shirt. *Not awful.* I tried on the rest of the shirts and dresses and packed two dresses, including the green one, four shirts, a second pair of jeans, and my running clothes. I added underwear, sleepwear, toiletries, and books, and my backpack still wasn't full. I hung up the dress and shirts I'd tossed to the bed.

The storm grew stronger, and the lights flickered. I hurried to the kitchen and made a grilled cheese sandwich then poured a glass of tea. When I set my food on the table, I lit a candle in case the power went off then bit into my sandwich. After I polished off my sandwich, I pulled a brownie out of the freezer and dished up a bowl of vanilla ice cream then read while Lucy and Spike napped on the other side of the sofa. When the storm moved on, Spike and I coaxed Lucy outside. I marveled at the multitude of the bright stars in the clear sky. "I love living in the country."

Spike nodded.

After we went inside, I fell into bed. *Two more days.*

Lucy's breath tickled my face, and I opened my eyes and scratched her ears. *Six o'clock.* I rolled out of bed and started a pot of coffee while Spike and Palace Guard accompanied Lucy on her early morning break.

As I poured my coffee, my phone buzzed.

Larry: "You okay with surprises?"

Me: "Good ones."

Larry: "Perfect."

Perfect again?

Palace Guard peered at my screen and raised his eyebrows.

Me: "Did you get me a new tent?"

Larry: "Made me laugh. You're close."

I frowned at my screen. "Well, that didn't help."

Palace Guard smiled.

After my yogurt and toast breakfast, Palace Guard and I ran our usual circular route to the horse farm, then the goat farm and back home. When we returned, I changed my sheets and cleaned the house while my laundry washed then dried. After I showered, dressed in a new smoky blue shirt, and packed my last-minute items, I called Jennifer.

"Is it too early to come over? I have some things to discuss with Glenn before I leave."

"We've been waiting to hear from you. See you in a few minutes."

After we loaded up, we headed to the Coyles'. Lucy placed her chin on the back of the front seat and stared out the windshield. "Are you making sure I don't miss a turn, girl?"

When I pulled into the Coyles' driveway, Lucy danced on the backseat then crowded Spike at the window and whined.

After I parked, Spike opened the door for Lucy, and she scrambled to the porch. When Jennifer opened the door, Lucy dashed past her.

"Come on in." Jennifer smiled. "Glenn's on the patio, and it sounds like Lucy's already found him. The coffee is fresh. Did all the clothes fit? I love that blue shirt on you. Did you pack any dresses in case you go somewhere nice for dinner?"

"You really went overboard, but thank you. Everything fits." We strolled together to the kitchen. "I packed two dresses just in case. I plan to wear the horse shirt tomorrow. It's my favorite."

"I thought it would be. I'll bet all the dresses are super cute with your red boots." Jennifer beamed as she poured me coffee.

Glenn smiled as I stepped out to the patio. "We hired Paul. He starts on Monday."

I sat on the patio chair next to Glenn. "Good. I've got something you can work on."

"Too much or too simple for you?" Glenn wiggled his eyebrows.

I laughed and pulled the key out of my pocket. "You decide. I found this key behind the file cabinet when we moved it. My theory is that Curtis stole Ella's key and hid this one before he bailed out the window."

I handed the key to Glenn, and he examined it. "Not a house key."

"You're right. The locksmith examined it for me, and it's a bank safe deposit key. See the number? That's the number of the box."

"So, all we need to do is figure out what bank? Something tells me there's more than that to it."

"Right, again. Only the owner, with proper identification, can use the key."

"Or a court order?" he asked.

I nodded. "I think the bank is the same one circled on the Georgia map from the courier."

"Now all we need to do is find out who the owner is then convince him or her to open the box for us. Simple, right?" He winked. "I was trying to decide what Paul could work on first. Maybe the two of us could tackle this together. I suppose it's okay if we don't solve it over the weekend? Except you know I'll get on it as soon as you're out of my hair." Glenn chuckled.

Jennifer stood in the doorway. "Why don't we invite Paul and his wife over for dinner tonight? I'd enjoy meeting her, and you and Paul can conspire."

"You're a brilliant woman," Glenn said.

"You're a smart man," she said. "I packed drinks for you and some snacks, Maggie."

"Thank you, Jennifer. I can't believe how much you've done for me."

"Kate would call it smothering," Glenn said.

"True." Jennifer laughed. "I'm glad you aren't offended, Maggie. It's nice to have somebody to spoil a bit. I have lunch ready. You choose where, Glenn. Out here or in the air conditioning?"

"It is warming up, isn't it? Let's eat inside. Maggie, I need to tell you about that cantankerous woman who masquerades as a health care aide. I'd ask you to help me get rid of her, but I'm afraid she'd put a spell on us."

"Get ready for a story, Maggie." Jennifer hurried to the kitchen. I waited for Glenn to wheel himself inside then Lucy and I followed.

While I poured drinks, and Jennifer set lunch on the table, Glenn said, "In the first place, you saw her when she came, right? Didn't she look like she left her gingerbread house to come here?" Glenn paused for a sip of tea. "A disguise. When she massaged my sore muscles, she had the hands of an angel."

Jennifer rolled her eyes, and I snickered.

"When I opened my eyes, the angel was gone, and the gingerbread woman was there. Magic."

Glenn scanned the room then whispered. "After that, I closed my eyes, and the angel washed my arms and feet with warm, magic water. I opened my eyes to watch, and the gingerbread woman rinsed my feet with icy cold water."

Jennifer and I laughed as he continued his story of the angel and the gingerbread woman.

"And then, before she left, the gingerbread woman asked me if I cared for a snack. She told me she would...ready for this? Core and slice an apple for me. I told her no, thank you, and didn't let on I knew about that poison apple trick." Glenn leaned back and his eyes crinkled.

Spike did his wacky dance. Palace Guard smiled, and I laughed even harder.

After I finished half of a ham and swiss sandwich, Jennifer said, "Saving a spot for pie and ice cream?"

"Always," I said.

"I just happen to have a cherry pie in the oven, and vanilla bean ice cream in the freezer."

When she opened the oven, the heady aroma of baked pastry and sweet cherries escaped and swirled into the dining room.

Jennifer brought in two bowls: a large serving for Glenn, and a small one for me. "Enjoy."

I spooned up hot pie and cold ice cream then blistered and froze the roof of my mouth. "So good, Jennifer."

"You need this weekend," she said. "It will give you a chance to recharge, and Larry is a wonderful man who is crazy about you, and I'm thinking the feeling is mutual."

"That's the truth," Glenn said. "I have a story, but you don't have time for it right now."

"Thank goodness," Jennifer muttered then rose. "Maggie, did you pack your computer?"

"Sure. I can look up a few things in my spare time."

"No," she said. "You need a weekend off. Leave it here."

"She's right, Maggie. You deserve a weekend off."

I glared at Glenn, and he shrugged.

I exhaled. "Not fair. Two against one."

Palace Guard held up four fingers.

"Traitor," I mumbled.

"Aha!" Jennifer said. "The men agree with me too."

"Be right back." I stomped to my car and returned to the house with my laptop.

"Thank you," Jennifer said as she carried my laptop to the den.

When Jennifer returned, she said, "I'll pack a small ice chest for you, and you can leave whenever you like. How far is it? I don't want you driving alone at night. Never mind...Palace Guard will be with you."

"It's about three hours away. I'll text you when I get there."

I hugged Glenn, and Jennifer loaded ice packs, food, and drinks into an ice chest. On our way to my car, she said, "Call or text if you have any problems or need help. Ella and I talked, and we'll be there in a flash. Literally. Have you ridden with her?"

She placed the ice chest on the backseat then hugged me. "I know you'll have a great weekend."

After I climbed in, I texted Larry.

"ETA 4:00"

Palace Guard peered at my screen and raised his eyebrows.

"Estimated Time of Arrival."

Jennifer remained in the driveway and waved as we pulled away.

After I turned onto the four-lane road at the edge of town, I accelerated to highway speed. "I'm looking forward to the weekend. I've never stayed in a bed-and-breakfast before, but it looks homey in the pictures."

As we drove along the countryside, we passed orchards with ordered rows of enormous pecan trees and fields of peanuts, cotton, and tall corn. I pointed to an abandoned shack. "Don't you know Glenn would have a story?"

Palace Guard smiled.

"Do you know about the cow game? When we pass a field of cows, if it's on your side, you get points. If it's on my side, I get points. If we pass a cemetery, the person whose side it's on loses all their points. Ready, go."

Palace Guard poked me every time we passed a field of cows on his side and slammed his hand on the dashboard when we passed a cemetery.

After almost two hours, I said, "We're about halfway there, and the interstate's coming up soon. I'll find somewhere for a stretch break."

I chuckled as I slowed to the lower speed limit of a small town. "By the way, you are a terrible loser. I can say that because I'm winning."

Palace Guard narrowed his eyes and nodded then turned his head toward his side of the road.

I pulled into the lot of an old, abandoned gas station. The pumps were gone, and the windows were covered with boards. The wind whistled through the covered canopy that once protected its customers from the sun and rain. Wildflowers and weeds poked through the cracks in the concrete drive. After we stepped out of the car, Palace Guard pointed to the ice cream shop across the road.

I stretched my back and rolled my shoulders. "It's on my side. I get ice cream points."

Palace Guard shook his head and glared, and I giggled.

We resumed our travel, and I accelerated as we entered the ramp to the interstate. After a few miles, I said, "All I can see is billboards. We'll have to suspend our game until Monday."

Palace Guard grinned and pointed out his window. *Cows.*

"Fine. You have cows. Except I got double ice cream points with sprinkles on top. I already won."

Palace Guard pointed to himself with his thumb then glared and gave me two thumbs down.

Sore loser.

Palace Guard nodded and pointed to me.

I snickered. "I argued with my imaginary man and lost. You can't tell anybody." I shook my finger at him.

Palace Guard smirked.

After we exited the interstate, I pulled over and tapped in the address of the bed-and-breakfast. "We're only five miles away."

As we rode away from the interstate, the surrounding area shifted from city outskirts to forests and farms. I slowed on the narrow country road so we could read the names of the side roads. Palace Guard pointed to an opening in the brush and trees ahead on our left.

I turned in and stopped as I scanned the dirt road with no shoulders. "We're sure, right?"

Palace Guard nodded, and I crept down the road as we drove past thickets of brush and dense forest.

"Do you feel like we're headed to Glenn's gingerbread house?"

Palace Guard pointed to a driveway that appeared on the left, and I turned in. The driveway was gravel, and the surrounding area was more groomed. A walking trail alongside the driveway turned away and disappeared into the woods. In a quarter of a mile, the driveway curved. After the curve, the driveway led to a circle in front of a two-story white house with columns and a wide porch that was dotted with rockers. A man rocked on the front porch.

I followed the small wooden signs that said *Parking*. After I parked, I sent Jennifer a text.

"Safe and sound."

Jennifer: "Thanks. Have fun."

I climbed out and stretched. I smiled at the relaxing scent of pine mixed with the light aroma of flowers then furrowed my brow as I squinted at the big white dog flopped on the porch and the man who stood next to her. "That man reminds me of Larry. I'm going to see imaginary Larry everywhere until tomorrow, won't I?"

I shrugged and opened the back door to remove my things. When the man on the porch leaped over the railing and ran toward us, I dropped my bags and raced to him.

Larry caught me up, and I wrapped my arms around his neck and breathed him in. He buried his face in my hair. "Like your hair," he mumbled.

He set me down and grinned. "Surprise."

"You win." I stood on my tiptoes and pecked the corner of his mouth with a light kiss, and he returned my kiss with one that left me breathless.

When he released me, I sighed, and he smiled then glanced at Palace Guard. "Good to see you. I wasn't worried about the trip because I knew you'd be with her."

He picked up my backpacks and the cooler. "Jennifer, right?"

"Of course. I need to hear everything." I grabbed my purse and locked the car.

"You're all checked in. I can show you to your room, ma'am." He grinned, and we strolled to the house. The white dog on the porch rose and wagged her tail.

"What about..."

"Let me give you a tour of your room and the house then we can relax on the porch and talk."

"I suppose that's logical. Will I be mad? I'm so glad to see you." I stopped on the porch step above him and hugged him, and he smiled.

The white lab nudged me, and I held my hand out for her to sniff. Her tail went into overdrive, and I scratched her ears as I cooed, "You're a pretty girl."

Larry smiled. "That's Daisy. She's the official greeter."

When Larry held the door for me, my eyes widened at the spaciousness of the foyer. I paused to glance back as Palace Guard sauntered to a rocker.

"Aren't you coming in?" I asked.

He shook his head and relaxed as he sat back in a rocker. Larry saluted him, and we continued inside. The ceiling extended to the second floor and a chandelier spread sparkles of light across the room. The stairway, however, dominated the room.

He said, "We go up the stairs, then turn right. I'll follow you."

I rubbed my hand on the smooth banister. "Feels like it's been polished by hundreds of hands."

When I reached the top of the stairs, I turned right then waited for Larry.

"Down this way to the end," he said. "Your room is the next to last on the left. There's an emergency stairway exit at the end of the hallway."

When we reached the room, he said, "Go ahead. I left it unlocked."

I opened the door, and my heart melted. The bed linens and ruffled curtains were gray, and the two overstuffed red chairs and small table in the corner near the window created a haven for conversation or relaxation.

"Wow."

Larry beamed and set down the backpacks then strode to a door and opened it. "Your closet."

He set down the cooler then pointed to the side of the closet. "There's a small refrigerator in the corner for drinks."

He strode to the door on the far side of the room and opened it. "Your bathroom."

I hurried to peek inside. "This is huge. Two sinks. Garden tub. That shower is the size of a closet. Makeup mirror." I pointed and snickered.

He smiled and opened the door at the opposite end of the bathroom.

I peeked into the room. "Shared bathroom?"

I stepped inside and scanned the room. *Gray bed linens and plain gray curtains. Black leather overstuffed chairs.* "Is this the field where you hide?"

He laughed and hugged me. "It's okay then?"

I wrapped my arms around him and returned his hug. "It's wonderful. I like my new tent too."

Larry snorted.

I grinned and turned back to my room. "I'll empty the cooler and hang up my clothes then we can go rock on the porch. Jennifer packed beer, and I'm ready to hear your details."

Larry followed me and sat on one of the red overstuffed chairs. When I hung up my last shirt, he said, "Be right back."

"This is colder." He held up two beers, and we headed downstairs.

After we sat on the porch, Larry pulled his rocker closer to mine. "I plan to smother you all weekend. Is that okay?"

I scooted closer to him. "Probably."

We clinked our beers. Palace Guard stood at the corner of the porch and scanned the property. When he strode past us to the other corner, Larry said, "Thanks, Palace Guard. It's good to know you have our backs."

Palace Guard nodded and continued his vigil.

Daisy raised her head then rose to join Palace Guard. He grinned then stroked her back, and she wagged her tail.

Larry leaned back in his rocker. "On Friday morning, we were told all of us who were left passed all tests up to that point, and the Saturday afternoon and Sunday morning makeup sessions were canceled. The rumor floated around all week, but to say we were excited is an understatement. Betsy, the bed-and-breakfast owner, changed your weekend reservation to the adjoining rooms for us."

"What about the colors? Gray and red?"

"The red was a coincidence, but they have four or five choices of sheets if people want to pick. One choice was gray. I was surprised when they said the curtains matched the sheets. I thought you'd like it here."

"It's wonderful. Can we walk around the property before it gets dark? The countryside was beautiful on the drive here, but I'm not used to sitting so long."

Larry rose. "Let's walk to the back and check out the patio."

He put his arm around my shoulder as we wandered to the side of the house. We paused to listen to the whippoorwill then resumed our stroll.

"I was gone too long." Larry brushed my hair away from my face and kissed my forehead. "At six o'clock they have light snacks and drinks in the foyer, but Betsy's partner is a retired chef and made arrangements with local chefs to deliver evening meals as takeout; the meals are delivered here at seven. I signed us up. What's different is there is no menu selection. Guests who participate list any food allergies, but it's potluck from there. Betsy said each chef tries to outdo the others. We can eat in the dining room or on the patio. What do you think?"

"Sounds interesting. Do you know what type of food?"

Larry wiggled his eyebrows and smirked. "I do. You don't."

I wrinkled my nose. "Since when are you so literal?"

When we turned the corner, I snickered at the canvas canopy with lights clipped around the perimeter. It covered four outdoor tables and chairs.

"Wouldn't this be a great tent for you for the next week?" Larry's eyes twinkled.

I giggled. "That's what I was thinking."

"Did you see the walking trail when you drove in? You can catch me up on your latest adventures."

As we strolled on the path, I told Larry about Curtis, the attack on Glenn, the key, Sierra, Paul, Jennifer, the courier, and Ella.

"All in one week." Larry shook his head as we continued along the path.

We found a bench near the end of the path. Larry put his arm around my shoulders, and I moved closer to him. We held hands as we sat in a comfortable silence and listened to the cicadas and crickets then headed back. Larry talked about his classes, his instructors, and his classmates, and I smiled. *I love seeing him so happy.*

At a few minutes before seven, a white van with *Mi Pueblito* painted in red on the side pulled into the delivery parking spot.

My eyes widened, and Larry said, "Surprise. I'm not sure if we'll have the tacos I promised you, but we'll adjust."

I nodded. "Whatever it is, we have to have beer."

"You're right. Where do you want to eat? Inside with the other people and air conditioning or outside just the two of us with the bugs?"

"Bugs over people," I said.

"Let's get two beers from their bar and carry our food out back."

Larry set the large brown paper sack on a table. I read the menu that was stapled to the side while Larry pulled out the food containers. "We have tacos three ways: flour, corn, and rolled then fried. A total of twelve tacos." My eyes widened. "No way will I be able to get up those stairs. Two sides of guacamole, two containers of salsa, and two servings of pastel de tres leches for dessert. Mmm, that sweet, moist cake is my favorite."

Larry peered into the sack. "We have plates, silverware, and napkins included." He set the remaining items on the table, and we dug in. After one taco and the guacamole, I was full.

"Do you suppose experienced guests don't bother to order but just cruise the dining room with an empty plate?" I asked.

Larry examined our untouched food. "The good news is we now have lunch for tomorrow covered. Betsy told me if I write my name on the sack, they'll refrigerate it for us then warm it up tomorrow."

"But we're eating the dessert tonight, right?"

"Of course. Let's sack this up. We can enjoy our tres leche and beer on the porch."

After we ate our dessert, Larry asked, "Ready to put your feet up?"

"I sure am. The travel wore me out."

As we climbed the stairs, Larry said, "Coffee's ready in the morning by six then breakfast is served from seven until nine-thirty."

When we reached my room, I kicked off my boots and flopped down in a red chair.

"Look underneath. There's a footstool," Larry said.

"How do you know so much?" I asked.

He chuckled. "I was here at one-thirty and explored the place for two hours until Betsy kicked me out. She said I needed to sit on the porch and watch for you."

He pulled out the other footstool and sat in the other chair.

"I didn't realize how tense I've been until I came here. I'm finally relaxed."

"So, what does Palace Guard know that you haven't told me?"

I slammed my feet to the floor and glared. "What are you talking about? Why would you ask that?"

He shrugged. "I don't know. Because I know you?"

I crossed my arms and stared while I ran through all the things Palace Guard might know that I didn't tell Larry. *I threw a fit when I couldn't open my back door? Is it okay that I cheated at the cow game? Ella thinks Palace Guard is her guardian angel? Someone shot at me?*

Larry raised his eyebrows. "Must be more than I thought. Pick the worst one."

"Someone shot at me in front of my house. I think that's the worst one."

Larry nodded. "You're probably right. When was this?"

"Tuesday morning." I raised my feet to the footstool and leaned back.

"Go through Monday night again."

"I had dinner with Sarge and Mother and met Christopher aka Curtis. Sierra was our waitress. Maurice was the host." I frowned. "I snapped a picture of Curtis, and Sierra covered me so Curtis wouldn't know, but Maurice saw me and was very unhappy. At first, I thought it was because he didn't approve of taking photos in the restaurant, but that would be odd, wouldn't it?"

"Yes. It would be odd. What do we know about Maurice?" Larry rose and paced.

"His real name is Morris, and the staff at the Vecchia Nonna call him *Morrie,* which he hates."

Larry nodded. "We'll ask Glenn and Paul to look into Maurice, and you'll stay here. Perfect plan."

"I'll see where they are with finding the safe deposit box owner, but you're right about needing to know more about Maurice." I smiled. "And wrong about me staying here. It's not going to happen."

Larry glared, and I met his glare. *Wonder how long we'll do this? Until the cows come home?* I snickered, and Larry blinked.

"I lost, didn't I?" he asked as he flopped down into his chair.

"Yes, but I have a consolation prize for you. I forgot to tell you about Moe and Ella."

I told Larry about Ella recording my conversation with Curtis before he ran to the alley, the first interview between Moe and Ella, and Moe inviting Ella to dinner that night.

"After that, it was all giggles and side glances with fluttering eyelashes. Almost as bad as Spike when he sees Heather."

Larry laughed. "Oh, man. No way can I imagine Moe as a Ladies' Man."

"I know. I almost called Kate to ask her what to do about the Moe imposter." A yawn sneaked out before I could cover my mouth.

"I'm so sorry," Larry said. "You must be exhausted. We'll talk more in the morning. You can have the bathroom first."

He moved to my chair and knelt next to me then held my face with his hands. *His blue eyes are so pretty.* He kissed me softly then I put my arms around his neck and kissed him with all the tenderness I had in my heart.

When he leaned back, he smiled. "Good night, sweetheart. See you in the morning."

He rose and placed his hand on my shoulder, and I closed my eyes as he kissed my forehead. After he went through the bathroom to his bedroom and closed the bathroom door on his side, I trudged to the bathroom and showered.

Before I dove into the soft, luxurious bed, I sighed with a longing I didn't realize I had. *I love being with Larry.*

I opened my eyes, but it was still dark outside. I snuggled into the softness of the massive bed as it enveloped me. *Kind of like Larry.* I smiled and dressed then picked up my hairbrush and slipped out. I was careful to ease the door closed without letting it click because I didn't want to wake Larry. *He deserves his rest.*

As I skipped down the stairs, the coffee aroma drew me to the coffee station. I didn't expect to see anyone, but when I made the turn at the bottom of the stairs, I froze. A tall woman who wore her brown hair piled on top of her head stood in front of the industrial-sized coffee pot and stacked clean cups on the station. She wore a white bib apron over a red and white checked shirt and jeans. She reminded me of Kate, except she was heavier and older. I tried to smooth down my unruly, unbrushed hair. She turned and grinned. "You must be Maggie. I'm Betsy. I've heard a lot about you. Welcome." She glanced at my hairbrush. "If you'd like to use the ladies' room, it's on the right near the patio doors."

When I came out of the bathroom, Betsy said, "Good timing. Coffee's ready. Your pick: front porch or the patio. I'll bring you a carafe in a few minutes."

"I have a fondness for rockers." I strolled to the front porch. Palace Guard and Daisy waited by the door.

"I appreciate that you have my back. Thank you for being here."

He smiled and nodded then strode to his corner and scanned the yard. I rubbed Daisy's face then she joined Palace Guard.

My phone buzzed.

Larry: "U awake?"

Me: "Not quite. Only on first cup."

My phone rang, and I smiled. *Larry.*

"Where are you?"

"On the front porch. Come have coffee with me."

Larry hung up then burst through the front door. "What are you doing out here by..."

He stopped and glanced at the corner. "Good morning, Palace Guard. I'm really glad to see you."

Larry went back inside then came out with a cup of coffee in one hand and a carafe in the other.

"Good morning, Maggie. How did you sleep?" He winked at Palace Guard as he sat in the rocker next to me. "More coffee?"

"Yes, please." I held out my cup. "My bed was amazing. It was like..."

Snuggling with you. "I slept really well."

CHAPTER NINE

Larry sipped his coffee. "I have another surprise. My parents planned to come to my graduation next week, but Mom decided to visit her sister in Miami before that. They're in their RV and will be here later this afternoon. Betsy said she'd schedule our dinner reservations."

Larry beamed, and I leaned over to pick up the carafe and shuddered. When I glanced at Palace Guard, he smiled and put his hand over his heart.

Larry stared at Palace Guard. "Did I do something wrong?"

I patted his arm. "Not at all. I was definitely surprised."

He relaxed. "I was afraid I was rushing something. Meeting the parents and all. Mom's excited to meet you."

I refilled our cups.

"Graduation is next Friday afternoon. I think you should stay here until then, but I've already lost that argument. Betsy put us down for Thursday through Saturday. Any way you could catch a ride here then go back with me on Saturday? I'm pretty sure Moe and maybe Heather plan to come, but they'd come on Friday."

"I'll figure something out."

"I believe you will. You always do. Let's get breakfast." Larry rose, and I joined him.

After we finished breakfast, Larry said, "There's a park not too far away with a running trail. You game?"

"I'd love it."

We raced up the stairs for a warm up. Even though Larry cleared them two at a time, I passed him two steps before the top.

"I win." When I danced my victory dance, Larry laughed.

We strolled to our rooms with our arms around each other. When I was inside my room, I sent a text to Sierra.

"Send me a sketch of Maurice?"

Sierra: "Love to. With or without the beard?"

Me: "When did he have a beard?"

Sierra: "When he first came to work here two months ago."

Me: "Both. Is that okay?"

Sierra: "Ha. Yes."

I changed to my running clothes. Larry waited for me in the hall.

"At least I change faster than you do."

I sauntered away with my nose in the air, and he snickered then caught up with me. When we got to the trail, we examined the map.

"Two-hour trail or one-hour?" Larry asked.

"In our Georgia heat, let's do the one-hour," I said.

We started with a jog to warm up then reached Larry's comfortable pace.

"I know you let me set the pace, Maggie. Thank you. I need to run with you more before I can let you set the pace."

I glanced behind us and nudged Larry. When he looked back, he said, "Glad you're here, Palace Guard."

The three of us ran the loop, and when we returned to Larry's car, I was drenched.

Larry handed me a bottle of water, and we leaned against his car and drank.

"When do you expect your parents?"

"Probably around four. We have plenty of time to go into Macon and have lunch and visit the Museum of Arts and Sciences."

"That sounds good. Indoors, right?"

"Number one criteria for an afternoon activity in Georgia."

After we showered, we headed to Macon.

I stared at the fields when we passed a sod farm. "I don't remember seeing any sod farms around home, and we have pecan orchards, not peach orchards like here."

"Cotton fields on the left, and peanuts on the right. Dairy farm coming up on the left."

Palace Guard tapped Larry on the shoulder. Larry glanced back, and Palace Guard shook his head.

Larry snickered. "I was going to ask if you wanted to play the cow game, but I have a feeling that would be a bad idea."

"You shouldn't be taking advice from a sore loser."

A car swerved around us, and Larry slammed on the brakes when it cut too close to his front bumper. "Lousy driver or a flat-out jerk. One more week, bud, and then I'll be on duty." Larry scowled. "I know about your shooting and knife skills. How are your driving skills, Maggie?"

I furrowed my brow. "I never thought about it before, but I'd label me an average civilian."

His eyes widened. "That's terrible."

Palace Guard nodded.

"Let's skip the museum and find an empty parking lot somewhere. I need to teach you a few things."

I shrugged. "Okay."

"Here we are. Plenty of practice room."

I climbed into the driver's seat, and Larry opened the trunk. "Give me a minute to set up these orange triangles," he said.

Larry walked away from the car and set the markers on the pavement in front of the car.

"We'll start with the basics: let's set the seat for you."

After two hours of driving around the markers, swerving, braking, and steering, I was exhausted.

"What do you think?" he asked. "Ready for lunch? I heard sometimes food trucks park downtown. Shall we check it out?"

"Why don't we go back and have Betsy warm up our leftovers?"

"Forgot about that. Good idea."

As he drove back to the B&B, I said, "I read everything you taught me, but it's different when it comes to performing a skill."

"It's all about muscle memory," he said.

"You're an excellent trainer. Thank you."

Larry's neck reddened, and the red crept to his cheeks. Palace Guard poked him, and he growled, "I am not blushing."

"Are too," I muttered, and Palace Guard nodded.

When we strolled into the foyer, Betsy was carrying a large pitcher of tea to the coffee station. "Ready for lunch? I'll pop it into the oven to warm. Help yourself to some sweet tea. There's a breeze on the patio. I'll bring out your lunch shortly."

"Where are we going for dinner?" I asked after we sat at a table in the shade.

"Betsy couldn't find an acceptable restaurant that was open on Sunday, so we ordered four dinners for tonight. Is that okay?"

"That's brilliant. The atmosphere here is relaxing. If they've been driving all day, they might enjoy not having to drive to dinner and then back to their RV."

"That's what I thought too."

After we ate lunch, I said, "I need a shower and some down time."

"Go ahead," Larry said. "I'll shower after you do."

After I showered, I hung up my green dress on the closet door then slipped on jeans and the blue shirt. I grabbed a book and relaxed in my chair with my feet up. When I read the same page three times, I put the book upside down on my lap. I leaned back and closed my eyes to ponder how relaxing my weekend was. *Thanks to Larry.*

"Maggie. Maggie." Larry tapped on the bathroom door.

"Come on in," I said.

"I thought you might be asleep."

So you woke me up?

"The folks will be here in thirty minutes." He whistled a long, low whistle. "Is that the dress you're wearing? Can't wait to see you in it. Come get me when you're ready to go downstairs."

He left through the bathroom.

"I guess it's just you and me, dress. You ready?" I giggled. *I'm hilarious.*

I slipped on the dress, pulled on my red cowgirl boots, and brushed my hair then made my grand entrance through the bathroom.

"What do you think?" I held out my arms and spun.

Larry's eyes widened. "You are gorgeous." He strode across the room and wrapped his arms around me, and I hugged him tightly.

"Are you nervous?" he asked.

"No."

He laughed. "Not your best lie. Let's go downstairs. Iced tea or beer?"

"Iced tea."

We carried our glasses to the front porch and pushed our rockers together. Palace Guard smiled.

An RV pulled into the driveway and stopped in the front of the bed-and-breakfast. A woman as tall as Kate stepped out, and the RV continued to the parking lot. The woman scanned the porch then her face lit up when she spotted Larry. She wore navy blue slacks and a white and medium-blue checked shirt and had pulled her sandy-brown hair back into a low ponytail. Larry strode to the walkway, and they hugged then walked arm in arm to the porch. I met her at the top of the steps, and she hugged me.

"I'm so happy to finally meet you, Maggie," she said. "Call me Lauren."

I've been broken in by Jennifer, Lauren.

"When Dad gets here, we can get some iced tea and go to the patio in the back," Larry said.

"This is a beautiful place," Lauren said. "Peaceful."

A tall man with a slight limp strode toward us. He wore jeans and a blue T-shirt. His curly gray hair, broad shoulders, lopsided grin, and the blue and white TCU ball cap in his hand left no doubt he was Larry's dad. Palace Guard saluted him.

He hugged Larry. "Where's your hat, Son?"

"Gave it to Maggie."

Mr. Ewing pulled me into their hug. "You don't have to wear that stinkin' Texas Tech cap, Maggie."

Larry grinned. "Our teams are rivals, Maggie, but we're huggers."

I smiled and leaned my head on Larry's chest. *I think I might be a hugger too.*

"Now, call him Sean, Maggie," Lauren said. "Let's grab that iced tea you offered, Kevin, and you can show us where the patio is before Dad decides to tell a story."

On our way to the patio, Lauren said, "We live in east Texas. We were sorry you and Kevin didn't have a chance to come see us when you were in Galveston. We'll have to plan a visit sometime. Georgia is beautiful. The cotton and corn in Georgia are huge and lush compared to what we're used to in Texas."

After we sat at a patio table, Sean said, "This is a beautiful place. It reminds me of the time..."

"Get ready for stories, Maggie," Lauren said. "Go ahead, honey."

I smiled and relaxed in my chair as Larry held my hand.

When Betsy announced she'd set out the snacks, Lauren said, "I'll fix a plate for us to share."

Larry scooted back her chair while she rose. "I'll grab the beers."

"I think wine for me," Lauren said as they strolled arm in arm to the foyer.

"How much of your stories are true?" I wiped away my tears of laughter.

"As much as you want to believe," Sean said. "What do your folks do?"

"My stepdad is retiring from the police department. He and Mother bought an RV and are testing it out this weekend. Mother always told her friends that raising me was a fulltime job."

Sean chuckled. "From what I hear about the adventures you and Kevin have had, I can believe it."

Lauren returned with a plate of hors d'oeuvres and a glass of wine. Larry followed with three beers and another full plate.

"Kevin tells me you have a nickname for him. Larry. It has a nice ring; how did you come up with it?" Lauren asked.

"My great-grandfather's name was Lawrence," Sean said. "Don't know how much is true, but according to the family stories, he was a character. One of my favorites..."

Sean launched into a Lawrence story that he followed up with still another. People gathered around our table and laughed along with us.

When he told his last story, Lauren said, "You never told me all that."

"That was because I didn't know you'd birthed another Larry," he said. "Larry suits you, Son. Good choice, Maggie. What does he call you?"

Crazy lady.

I glanced at Palace Guard, and he nodded.

Larry snorted. "Tell him, Maggie."

I glared at him.

"I call her sweetheart," he said.

Sean looked at me and laughed.

Betsy brought our takeout dinners and plates to our table. "Didn't want to slow down the stories. We ordered four dinners, but the chef sent three main entrées after he asked who the four people were. He said the two women will prefer to share. Maggie, I checked, and you and Mrs. Ewing will have plenty to eat. Bon Appetit, y'all."

After we ate, Lauren said, "This was lovely and so much better than going to a restaurant; you two are perfect together."

Sean nodded. "We hate to rush out, but I'd like to get situated on our campsite before it gets much later."

"We plan to be on the road early. We have reservations at a campground tomorrow near Vero Beach, Florida. It'll be a long day," Lauren said.

We hugged, and Lauren cried then they left for the parking lot.

Larry put his arm around my shoulder as we stood on the porch and waved to the back of the RV as it rumbled down the driveway.

"I love your parents," I said.

"They're pretty cool. You up for an evening walk?"

As we strolled on the walking trail, I asked, "How did you become interested in the Georgia Bureau of Investigation?"

"I told you I'd majored in math and statistics in college; I also double-majored in chemistry. I always knew I'd be a cop like Dad. Georgia Bureau of Investigation has more opportunity than a police department does to fit all my pieces. I think the experience I have at the Harperville department and my degrees in math and chemistry give me an excellent background for the G.B.I. crime scene specialist position. I'm hoping to be selected, if not this time, after a year or two in a regional office. Even if I am selected now, I'd go to a regional office for thirty to sixty days before going to the crime scene specialist training."

I stopped and peered at his face. "Next time, you have to tell me all this sooner. I think it's exciting."

He raised his eyebrows. "You do?" He held my hand, and we continued our stroll. "You are amazing. I don't know why I thought you'd be mad."

"Think about how I could pester you with questions. I've never known a crime scene specialist before. Now I have to change your entire profile in my database."

Larry chuckled. "If I didn't know you, I'd think you were joking."

When we reached the B&B, he asked, "Ready to relax with a nightcap?"

We went to my room, and while I sat in my chair, Larry opened two beers. He handed me my beer and sat on the floor next to me.

"I'll know by Thursday where my assignment is. You ready to talk?" He frowned. "That didn't come out right."

I snickered. "Cop to the core, but I'm not sure I'm ready to decide."

"I understand." He pulled out his phone. "I found these questions couples need to ask each other. Maybe this will help you." He cleared his throat. "Number one. Do you believe in Bigfoot?"

I laughed, and we spent the rest of the evening answering questions and arguing about the answers.

At ten, Larry said, "I hate it, but I need to call it a night. You have your drive in the morning, and I have to be at the training center by eight. It's going to be a long week."

When he rose, I pulled him down for a kiss that was passionate and filled with yearning for more. He pulled me to my feet, and we clung to each other. He tipped my chin and kissed me with an intensity that left me breathless. When we broke away, I sighed and hugged him, and he kissed me on my forehead. I smiled and waved my hand in front of my face.

"Good night, Crazy Lady." Larry chuckled as he closed the bathroom door behind him.

I snickered then changed for bed.

As I settled into my soft bed, I smiled at our heated discussions over the silly questions. *I can't remember why I wouldn't want to go anywhere with him.*

A tap at my bathroom door in the middle of the night woke me. "Maggie?"

"Larry? Come on in. Something wrong?"

He leaned against the door. He was sweating and short of breath. "I needed to see if you're okay. I had a terrible dream."

He strode into my bedroom and lay down on the floor next to my bed.

"I'll just sleep here."

"That doesn't sound comfortable."

"I have to keep you safe," he mumbled.

I tossed a pillow onto the floor and listened to his breathing until he fell asleep.

When I woke, I was alone in the room. I rolled over and picked up the pillow off the floor and sniffed it then inhaled Larry's man-smell. When I heard the shower running, I closed my eyes and hugged his pillow. After the shower stopped and his bathroom door closed, I lumbered to the bathroom for my shower.

After I dressed, I heard a knock and opened my door. Larry grinned as he carried in a tray.

"I brought us breakfast. I'm going to have to leave soon, but I didn't want to say goodbye downstairs."

He set the tray on our table, and we talked and ate.

"I'm all packed. I have to leave," he said. He hugged me. "I want this to be the last time we're apart for so long. I'll see you on Thursday."

He kissed me with gentleness then we shifted to a deeper, more intense kiss until he held me by the shoulders and gazed at me. "I need you to stay safe, Maggie."

He hugged me tight then left.

I dropped into my chair and cried. *We belong together.*

When my tears dried up, I washed my face and carried the tray and our dishes downstairs. Betsy smiled. "I look forward to seeing you two on Thursday, Maggie."

I packed my bags then trudged to my car. Daisy stood on the porch, and her tail drooped. *I'm sad too, girl.*

After I adjusted my seat the way Larry showed me, I headed to the interstate. Palace Guard patted my shoulder.

"Thanks, Palace Guard."

I accelerated to highway speed on the interstate. "It's hard to drive like Larry taught me: stay aware of my surroundings and look where I want the car to go."

I sighed in relief when I turned off the interstate onto the four-lane highway that led to Harperville. "I'm not a fan of interstates. Let's stop at our abandoned gas station for a stretch break."

While we were on our break, Sierra sent me texts with sketches of Maurice attached.

"He looks different with a beard." Palace Guard peered over my shoulder. "He looks rougher. Without the beard, he looks wimpy in comparison."

I forwarded the texts to Glenn then sent him an email. "Two sketches from Sierra. Beard is Maurice aka Morris three months ago. Second one is current Maurice."

After I tapped send, a black car crept past the gas station. The lone passenger pointed to my car then the car sped away.

I frowned. "Wish they were going the other way. Help me watch for them."

Palace Guard nodded, and we resumed our travel.

"We're about thirty minutes away from Harperville. Seems like a longer drive than going to see Larry." I checked my rearview mirror and frowned. "Car coming up behind us. Fast."

I tapped the cruise control button. "Larry said if the road conditions were sketchy or if the situation had the potential for instant, instinctive responses, turn off the cruise control."

The speeding car pulled up tight to my rear bumper. When I sped up slightly, it did too. When it pulled into the left lane to pass me, I said, "Let me know when it's at my rear wheel well."

Palace Guard held up his hand then brought it down and pointed, and I slammed on the brakes. The other car slammed on its brakes too, and I sped past it. The car caught up with me and rammed my back bumper on the left side, and my car swerved. I kept my eyes on the road and ignored watching where I was as the car spun. *Watch the road. Watch the road.* The car rammed me again, and my car went off the road to the shoulder then down into a ravine, and we rolled then crashed.

Palace Guard rubbed my arm, and I shook my head to clear the dazed feeling. The airbags had deployed, and I waved my hand to clear the dust. My car was on its wheels, but leaned to the right and was embedded on the passenger's side in mud and dirt. The windshield was cracked and both side front windows were gone. I couldn't move then realized my seatbelt was locked into place. Palace Guard pushed the button and freed me. I surveyed myself for injuries. My nose hurt; I had a seatbelt abrasion and cuts on my left shoulder and arm; my left foot was trapped under the brake pedal; no body parts were deformed or spurting blood.

Palace Guard patted the holster on my waistband, and I pulled out my gun. He pointed to the top of the ravine above us. A man stared down at the car and waved a gun. "I see it. She's down there," he shouted. "I got a good shot right here."

I narrowed my eyes as he shot at the car, but his wrist dropped, and he hit the dirt ten yards away from the car up the embankment.

"I hit something. I think I got her, but I'll go make sure."

I twisted to my left, and Palace Guard provided back support for me. I supported my hands on the open window and stayed with my target as he slid and fell fifteen yards then stopped and pointed his gun at the car.

"If she ain't dead, she's gonna be," he shouted.

I squeezed the trigger and hit him in the middle of his chest. At the sound of the shot, the car squealed away. Palace Guard climbed up the hill and checked the man.

When he returned, I asked, "Is he dead?"

Palace Guard nodded and reached under the seat and handed me my phone.

I called Larry, but the signal was too weak. I sent Jennifer a text.

"Need help. Don't know if text works."

"I think it went."

I tried to wiggle my foot out of my boot but couldn't free it. "Can you get my foot out?"

Palace Guard reached down to the pedal and pulled it away from my ankle and foot.

"Easy for you. Help me out of here?"

Palace Guard pried my door open then lifted me out and set me on the side of the hill.

My phone buzzed.

Jennifer: "Where are you?"

Me: "Thirty miles north of town. Car crashed near a bridge into a ravine. Need HPD and you and Ella."

Jennifer: "On it."

Palace Guard carried my backpacks and purse to a location in the shade north of the shooter and closer to the road then returned and supported me while I hobbled to my things.

"Thank you."

I sent Larry a text. "Shot bad guy. Jennifer, Ella, and HPD on the way. I'm fine thanks to your training and PG."

Larry: "Tell bad guys to cut it out."

I showed Palace Guard. "Doesn't sound mad, does he? But he is."

Palace Guard nodded.

Me: "PG and I know how mad you are."

Larry: "Darn tootin."

The faint sound of a siren came from the south. "Siren. Hear it? I expected Ella and Jennifer to be first."

Brakes screeched south of the bridge.

"Maybe they are. Help me get to where I can see."

Palace Guard helped me climb to the shoulder.

Jennifer jumped out of the car and peered into the ravine.

I waved. "Here I am. On the north side of the bridge."

Ella drove north past me then drove through the grassy median to turn south.

"You could have let me get back in the car, Ella." Jennifer was out of breath when she reached us.

Jennifer and Ella helped me into the back seat.

"Ella, my things are right down there," I said.

Ella stared at my backpacks and purse. "How did you get all that stuff from your car to there? And who is that guy lying on the side of the bank? Did my guardian angel help you?"

Palace Guard scowled, and I tightened my lips.

Jennifer examined my face. "You nose is swollen. You're going to have a black eye."

"Oh, great. Larry's graduation is on Friday."

The police car followed Ella's tracks through the median. When they reached us, Moe jumped out and peered at me. "Where's the dead guy?"

"Who said anything about a dead guy?" Ella asked.

"It's Maggie, right? As bad as she's hurt, there's a dead guy."

Ella nodded. "Down there."

Moe sent Officer Perry to check the man and my car.

An ambulance pulled in across the road.

"Go turn around at the crossover. There's a driveway on the left too if you need more turning radius."

"The guy doesn't need an ambulance," I said.

"You do," Moe growled.

Ella gathered my things and tossed them into her back seat.

"Love watching you flex those muscles," Moe whispered to Ella.

She giggled, and Palace Guard held his stomach and bent over. I coughed to hide my giggle, but I noticed Officer Perry's mouth twitch, and my cough turned into a snort.

"Are you okay?" Jennifer asked.

"I'm fine. Thank you. Don't suppose you could hide me from the ambulance? I could tell them I saw the guy breathe; although that would be right before I shot him. But that's good enough, right?"

Moe strode to me. "How many times did he shoot at you, Maggie? His gun has been discharged."

"Once then he came down the hill for a closer shot."

As I told Moe about the car and all its attempts to run me off the road, he scribbled notes then stared at me. "Good driving, Maggie. That first hit should have sent you into a spin."

The ambulance parked on the shoulder in front of us. I put my wrists together and asked Moe, "Shouldn't you put me under arrest?"

Moe glared at me. "I'll bet Kevin would pay a hefty price if I put you in jail for a few days, but I can't afford the kind of trouble you'd bring with you."

Jennifer, Ella, Officer Perry, and Moe laughed, and it was my turn to glare.

CHAPTER TEN

The ambulance crew rolled the cot out and loaded me up. "Jennifer, tell Glenn I sent him an email and two texts."

"He doesn't check his texts or emails very often. I'll call him. We'll be at the hospital in a bit," Jennifer said. "Did you contact Sarge and your mother?"

"Oh no. I forgot."

"Don't worry. I'll call. Anybody else? You let Larry know, right?"

"Oh yes. He's mad."

"Want the siren?" the paramedic asked after she closed the door and sat. "You don't remember because you were unconscious, but we transported you to the hospital when the library exploded. It's an honor to have the Gray Lady in our ambulance again, especially since your eyes are open and you're talking."

Palace Guard sat on the bench across from me. He raised his eyebrows.

I smiled. "Let's do it for old times' sake."

"You heard, right?" she asked her driver.

"Sure did," he said. "Lights and siren for the Gray Lady coming up."

"So what did you do to your hair?" she asked as she wrote her report.

I chuckled. "I thought I'd like to have my hair its natural color, and this is my mother's stylist's interpretation of what my natural color is. She included blond because that's my mother's favorite; red is my boyfriend's favorite; and all the other colors are her favorites. If you look closely, you'll see the gray woven in."

She laughed. "Your mother's hairdresser is a diplomat."

She reviewed her sheet. "Let's get a good list of your injuries. You were no help at all last time, by the way. Did you lose consciousness or feel dazed?"

"Nope."

"Right, I bet. Is anything tender on your face besides your nose?"

"No."

She completed her survey. "Don't know about that shoulder or your ankle. You'll have x-rays for sure. Your lacerations have stopped bleeding, but there may be some glass in there."

Palace Guard peered at my arm and patted my hand.

When we reached the outskirts of town, the driver changed tones, and I laughed.

"If I need to be busted out of the hospital, will you come get me if I call?"

The paramedic laughed. "In a heartbeat, Gray Lady."

The driver pulled under the emergency entrance canopy, and I had a royal ride into the emergency department then was whisked into a trauma room. I waved to my personal ambulance crew as they left.

"Don't cut anything," I said as the doctor read the report, and the nurse prepared to dress me in a hospital gown. Palace stood next to me with his arms crossed.

"I think we can work that. Wait until you see what a Houdini I am at taking off jeans. Unbutton and unzip then slip them down as far as you can without bending."

She removed my boots then tugged on the pants legs. When she was satisfied, she whipped off my jeans with one motion like a magician pulling a table cloth out from under the china. I slipped off my shirt then she put the hospital gown on me.

"Can I cut that sports bra?" she asked.

"That you can cut."

The doctor prodded and poked. "Your shoulder seems just fine, but we'll x-ray it, anyway. I'm hoping there's nothing other than bruising of your ankle, but we'll check. I can't believe your nose isn't broken. You face looks like airbag injuries. I can't promise you two black eyes, but for sure you'll have one. I was worried about glass in those lacerations, but I didn't feel any, and you didn't react when I rubbed my hand over your skin. This is all preliminary, though. We'll clean the lacerations and see what we find."

While I waited for the x-ray tech, Jennifer and Ella came into my cubicle.

"What does the doctor say?" Jennifer asked.

"X-rays."

"We'll wait here for you. I don't mind being away from the office for a while. The construction next door stirred something up. The fumes are thick," Jennifer said.

"I'm glad we knew there was a beauty shop going in next door," Ella said. "The office smells like fingernail polish remover to me."

"Really?" I sat up. "Strong?"

"Really strong," Ella said.

I frowned. "Let it air out before you spend any more time in the office."

Ella laughed. "It's just polish remover."

Jennifer stared at me. "She knows things and has good instincts. We'll let it air out."

"While we were in the waiting room, we heard a lot of sirens. Someone said there's a fire," Ella said. "Do you want to sit, Jennifer?" She pointed to the visitor's chair against the wall.

"I'm fine. Go ahead if you like." Her phone rang, and she frowned. "Glenn never calls me." As she listened, her face paled. "I'll tell Ella and Maggie."

After she hung up, she shook her head. "Our office and the new beauty shop are on fire. Someone was driving past it, and they said a fireball broke the windows. Everything is in flames. They thought I was there because my car was parked in the lot. Unfortunately, they don't know if anyone was inside the beauty shop. They can't check until they knock down the fire."

Ella dropped into the visitor's chair. "Is fingernail polish remover that flammable, Maggie?"

"It is. It's acetone. I don't understand why a beauty shop or even a nail salon would have that much though."

"I must have had construction on my mind when we were at the office because the pungent odor wasn't familiar to me at all," Jennifer said. "Now I'm trying to think what we might have lost in a fire."

"I scanned all our documents and saved them to our cloud storage except for that batch we were going to shred," Ella said. "We were lucky."

"No, we've got Maggie." Jennifer shook her head.

The x-ray tech pulled back the curtain. "Maggie Sloan?"

Jennifer said, "You're going to be busy for a while. Got your phone?"

I held it up, and she nodded. "Call us when your tests are done. I don't think we'll be able to pick up my car right now, so we'll go to the house."

"Car," I said. "I need a new car."

Palace Guard nodded and stayed by my side as the tech rolled me down the hallway.

At eleven, my doctor pulled away my curtain. She smiled and her eyes twinkled. "Nothing's broken, which actually surprised me. Your ankle is bruised, and the ligaments are torn. We'll wrap it, and you'll need to elevate and stay off it for at least two weeks. Ice it and your shoulder. You want to go home after lunch or now? If you promise you won't write us up for depriving you of a nutritious hospital meal, I'll sign the release papers."

I rolled my eyes. "I promise. Sign the papers."

She nodded to the nurse who came into my cubicle.

"See you, Maggie Sloan. But not soon, okay?" The doctor waved and left.

"Doc's a comedian," the nurse said. "I have your signed release papers and will help you dress."

I texted Jennifer: "Being released."

Jennifer: "Be right there."

The nurse closed the curtain then went over my release papers. After I was dressed, she said, "Might want to relax for a day or two." She peered at me. "We both know that won't happen, but I feel better saying it."

An aide showed up with a wheelchair. "You ready, Miss?"

"Let's get your right boot on," the nurse said. "I don't think I can force the left one on without causing a lot of pain. I'll drop it in a sack. By the way, my personal opinion is that your boot protected your ankle. Only an observation."

The aide helped me into the wheelchair, and the nurse handed me my papers and the sack.

"Will Maggie be staying with you?" the nurse asked Jennifer.

"Yes, we've got her all set up at my house."

"Good. Check her foot later. The compression bandage is tight. You may need to re-wrap it. Be careful, Maggie.".

When the aide rolled me outside, Ella's car blocked the entrance, and Jennifer smiled and opened the back door. The aide and Jennifer helped me into the backseat, and Jennifer slammed the door. "Drive slow and easy, Ella."

"Always do," she said.

I snickered as she accelerated out of the parking lot and zoomed toward Jennifer's house.

I sent Larry a text: "Cleared hospital. Nothing broken. On way to J's."

"Did you have lunch?" Jennifer asked.

"I declined."

"Good. I have lunch fixings at my house, and Glenn and Paul can't wait to hear details and have news for you."

When we reached the house, Jennifer opened my car door, and Ella helped me hobble up the steps as Palace Guard hovered. Jennifer opened the front door, and we all went inside.

Lucy bounded to me and pranced as fancy a dance as her old arthritic legs allowed. Spike beamed.

"Did you teach her to dance?"

Spike broke into his wacky dance, and Lucy danced with him.

Jennifer stared at Lucy. "No, I didn't even know she could dance."

Palace Guard rolled his eyes.

I did ask, didn't I?

I knelt down and cuddled Lucy. "Good girl."

Lucy led the way to the den. Glenn and Paul came in from the patio.

Glenn smiled. "Glad you're okay. Jennifer said we can eat and talk."

"Sit at the table, Maggie. I'll bring you some iced tea," Jennifer said.

After Ella helped me sit, she went to her car and gathered up my things.

"Where do I put these, Jennifer?" Ella held the bags up as she walked in.

"In that first bedroom, for now."

Jennifer set out lunch fixings and pointed as everyone came to the table. "This is make-your-own sandwich day. Meat choices are chicken salad, ham, or roast beef, and your pick of bread and cheese. Mayonnaise, mustard, horseradish, pickles, and chips are in the middle."

I dished up a small serving of chicken salad and added pickles on the side; everyone else made a sandwich.

While we were eating, Glenn said, "We went to the office, Jennifer. Before you say anything, Paul pushed my wheelchair, but the closest we could get was a block away. The building is gone, and a tow truck driver said the fire destroyed all the cars parked in the rear lot and at the curb. I'm sorry about your car."

Jennifer sighed. "I've had that car for seven years. I just got it broken in. I'll do some research then we'll go car shopping, Ella."

"I could ask Mother, except I forgot to tell her I'm out of the hospital."

"Already done," Jennifer said. "She and Sarge were ready to leave their campground for the hospital, but I told them you'd be here, and there was no hurry. She'll call you later, but you might want to call her after lunch."

She peered at my face. "Your eyes are showing bruising. You're going to have two black eyes. Let me grab some ice for you."

She handed me a small icepack, and I held it on one eye then the other. "Can you put some makeup on me?"

"I can try, but I don't have much confidence in being able to cover both of them. If it was just one, we could use an eye patch."

Glenn finished his sandwich and gulped down his tea. "Maggie, Paul had a phenomenal breakthrough. You tell her."

"I was able to get the name of the safe deposit box owner. It's Clara Hayden, widow of Bruce Hayden, and she lives in Athens. He was a lawyer. She's ninety-two and sounds frail, but her mind is sharp. She discovered her safe deposit box key had disappeared at least a month ago when she decided to turn it in for her five-dollar key deposit, but she had emptied the box ten years ago because she didn't trust banks."

"I don't blame her for that. She's lived through every economic crisis imaginable. Wonder if she has any money in banks? Now I want to empty our bank accounts and buy gold," Jennifer said.

Paul nodded." She gave all of the box contents to her lawyer except for one letter from her deceased husband. The letter talks about three pieces of art at another friend's house. She said she couldn't send it to us, but she'd let us read it if we came to her house and ignored the mushy stuff. Her words. She didn't open up or even offer for us to see the letter until I told her about Maggie who was trying to locate her grandmother's art. Maggie, you and

I will have to go. Sorry. Sometimes my efforts to think fast aren't that well thought out."

"I don't mind at all, but Athens is a five hour drive from here," I said. "It would be hard to get there before the end of the day."

"It will be hard for you to manage a five-hour, one-way trip at all," Jennifer said.

"Thought about that," Paul said. "I have a friend with a small plane who owes me. He'll fly us this afternoon. Mrs. Hayden expects us at four."

"Perfect. What do I wear, Jennifer?"

"Wear a dress. I'll re-wrap your foot if it's too tight, and we'll get you some crutches that are your size so you can get around. Ella, how are you at sizing crutches?"

"I'm an expert. Just need a measuring tape."

"It's about an hour's flight, and I already have arrangements for a car when we get there," Paul said.

Jennifer handed Ella a measuring tape.

"Stand up, Maggie." Ella measured from my armpit down to the floor in two places and left.

Jennifer frowned. "What about a dress, Maggie? Do you have any packed?"

"I wore the green one, but the blue and white one is in my bag."

"I'll grab it and toss it into the dryer for a few minutes. How are we doing on time, Paul?"

"We're good. It's twelve-thirty. We'll need to be at the airport before two. Plenty of time with everything we have in motion."

"If that's it, I need to call Mother," I said.

"Where do you want to go?" Paul asked and offered his arm. "Patio's fine."

Paul helped me up, and I leaned on his arm as he walked with me to the patio. I sat on the cushioned chair and called Mother.

"Margaret, are you okay? Jennifer said your foot was injured, and not broken like they thought. That was wonderful to hear. We were going to pick up sticks, which is what Big D said. Or maybe it was pull up stakes, I'm not sure. Isn't that funny? We planned to visit you in the hospital, but Jennifer called and said you'd been released and were fine. I'll bet you'll be sore tomorrow. Isn't that what they say? If you don't need us there right away, then we'll stay here until tomorrow."

"Mother, Larry graduates on Friday. I thought you and Sarge would like to go. His parents drive an RV too and will be there. I can tell you which campground they use."

"What a wonderful idea, Margaret. I'll talk to Big D and let you know. Things are getting pretty serious between you and Larry? Big D likes him and says he's a fine young man. I'm glad you're having fun."

"Thank you, Mother. If you and Sarge decide to go, could I ride with you on Thursday? Larry made a reservation for me at a bed-and-breakfast and wants me to ride back with him."

"That sounds like a great idea. You'll get to ride in the RV with us and be comfortable. I love it. I'm sure Sarge will agree."

Mother hung up, and I smiled. *Goodbye, Mother.*

Glenn rolled to the patio door. "Everything okay?"

"Yes. Mother and Sarge are happy together and enjoying life. I think it's great."

"Your nurse said we need to check the wrap." Jennifer touched my toes and frowned. "They're cold. I need to re-wrap. Let's go."

Jennifer helped me into the bedroom, and I sat on the bed. "Let's get your dress on then I'll re-wrap your foot."

Jennifer removed the compression bandage then re-wrapped it.

"How is it? Too tight? It's supposed to be tight enough to compress but loose enough for your toes to get good circulation." Jennifer furrowed her brow.

"It doesn't feel so tight," I said.

"Good. I know you wanted to try makeup, but I can tell your bruises are too dark to cover up. You'll need to come up with a good story, but I think faulty airbags would work."

"Dang. I think a cover story's a good idea. Thanks."

"When Ella gets here, you'll be ready to go. Do you want to carry your purse or backpack?"

"Backpack."

"You sit right there and tell me what to move from your purse."

After my backpack was ready for the flight, my phone rang as Jennifer helped me to the den.

"Larry." I heard the squeal in my voice, and Jennifer smiled.

"Sit here." She helped me to a soft chair in the living room as I answered.

"I don't have long, but I needed to talk to you. Catch me up."

I told him about the fire, the safe deposit document, and the plan to fly to Athens.

"My nightmare was about a fire at your house, and you were trapped. Would you mind asking Jennifer if you could stay at their house until Thursday? I'm sorry, but it was too real, and I can't shake it. I gotta go."

Jennifer stood in the doorway. "Everything okay?"

"Larry had a nightmare last night. It was about me, and I was trapped in a fire at my house. The nightmare has him nervous; he'd like for me to stay with you."

"That's easy. Can Ella and I run pick up more clothes for you while you're gone this afternoon?"

"That would be great. I only packed for the weekend."

I sent Larry a text: "J & E will pick up clothes this PM."

Larry: "Thanks."

Ella rushed into the house. "Sorry I was so long. Evidently, only tall people are allowed to have crutches around here. What do you think?"

The polished wood crutches were stained a deep red reminiscent of a dark wine.

"They're beautiful," Jennifer said. "Try them out."

I headed to the patio.

"Stop," Ella said. "Let me give you a quick lesson."

After she showed me, I walked to the kitchen. "That's much easier. I was fighting the crutches instead of letting them help me. How do you know so much?"

"I have a friend who's a librarian, and I read." Ella cackled, and Jennifer laughed.

"Are you ready?" Paul asked. "It wouldn't hurt to get there a little early. Glenn's still researching Maurice. Don't suppose you have a last name?"

"Don't know why I didn't think of that."

I texted Sierra. "What is Maurice/Morrie's last name?"

Sierra: "Rhodes."

"Hey, Glenn. Maurice's last name is Rhodes," Paul said.

"My first guess." Glenn laughed.

On our way to the airport, Paul asked, "Have you ever flown in a small plane?"

"No."

"They're nosier inside than commercial planes, but the view is like no other. And there's no wait. Walk up to your plane and go. Remember, if you get anxious or nervous, just breathe."

After we parked, Paul said, "Let's go inside. I'll see if our pilot is in the building before we walk out to the plane. You might enjoy seeing a bit of the operation."

I slipped on my backpack, and we went inside. A young woman with black hair and a double heart tattoo on her wrist smiled when we walked in. "Hey, Pablo. Rich is waiting for you at the plane."

On our way to the plane, Paul said, "Family still calls me Pablo even though my birth name is Paul. It's like a family joke." He glanced at me. "Yeah, I don't get it either."

"This one." He pointed to a nearby plane.

Can this even hold three people?

Palace Guard patted my back, and I relaxed.

"Hey, Paul. Ready to go? Is this Maggie?"

"Maggie, Rich."

"Let's load up," Rich said. "What happened to you?"

"I got the last beer."

Paul and Rich guffawed then Paul helped me inside the plane. "Put your headset on."

Rich hopped in and started the engines. "Let's go."

I breathed.

After we were airborne, I smiled at the ground below. *Paul was right. The view is phenomenal.*

Palace Guard sat in the co-pilot's seat. He nodded.

I was so mesmerized by the flight that I was surprised when Rich started our descent.

"Are you hooked, Maggie?" Paul smiled.

I nodded. "Yes."

"Anytime you want to become a pilot, let me know," Rich said.

After we landed, Rich parked then came around to help me out of the plane. Paul jumped out and handed me my crutches and my backpack. Rich saluted me, and I nodded then followed Paul to the small building.

He picked up the keys for our car. "Wait here." Paul headed to the parking lot then returned with a car and helped me into my seat.

"What else did you say to Mrs. Hayden about my grandmother?" I asked.

"Nothing else. I was counting on you to wing it."

"I can do that," I said.

"We're here. Ready, Undercover Maggie?"

"Sure am."

We were in a historic section of town. Mrs. Hayden's house was surrounded by similar grand homes. When Paul knocked on the door, an elderly woman that barely came to my shoulder opened the door. Her sparse gray hair created a halo around her head, and she wore a navy-blue dress with a white lace collar, white pearls, and high-top tennis shoes. The edge of her hem brushed the tops of her shoes.

"Come in, Mr. Vargas. You must be Maggie. You have two black eyes, and what happened to your foot?"

"Hello, Mrs. Hayden. It was only a fender bender, but my airbag deployed. I was so startled that I jumped out of my car and sprained my ankle. Not very exciting; I wish it was something more interesting." I smiled.

Mrs. Hayden nodded. "I understand. We need to come up with a more dramatic story for you. Maybe a kickboxer championship, and you won?"

We chuckled, and Paul snorted. When we followed her into the house, I was awestruck by the two-story tall ceiling in the entryway and the impressive, carved crown molding scroll work. The walls were covered with paintings: Renaissance,

Impressionism, and other styles that were beyond my art history knowledge. The art, frayed furniture, and faded wallpaper added to the ambiance of a preserved museum and a time long ago.

"I have a nice footstool you can use to elevate your foot in the parlor," Mrs. Hayden said.

When we reached the parlor, Mrs. Hayden pointed to the tray on a round coffee table with three glasses of lemonade, cloth napkins, a plate of cookies, and three small plates. I was afraid to pick up one of the delicate plates. "Please. Help yourself."

What if I crush the plate between my fingers when I pick it up?

Palace Guard nodded. I selected a glass of lemonade and picked up a cloth napkin.

"Don't you care for any cookies, Maggie?" she asked.

An old gray cat flicked its tail and stared at me from under the table then raced away when I sneezed. I smiled. *Mother told me her grandmother always said, Scat cat, when Mother sneezed.*

"They look delicious, but I'm a novice flyer."

"I can just imagine how frightening that would be. You're here about art, right? My husband wrote me a letter about some art, and it may be interesting to you." She opened a drawer on the lamp table next to her and pulled out a triple-folded sheet of yellow legal-sized paper.

"Tell me about your grandmother. What kind of art did she collect?" she asked.

I smiled. "She was my great-grandmother. I don't know much about her, but Mother said her grandmother loved art and gave her best pieces to a lawyer for safekeeping."

"What was your great-grandmother's maiden name?"

I cocked my head and frowned. "I'm not sure, but Mother said her grandmother was Irish."

"I knew it. With your green eyes and red hair." She waved away anything I might say. "I know you have your hair colored or streaked, or whatever you girls call it nowadays, but I see your natural red. You're a Flanagan, Maggie, just like Margarite. I'm sure of it. Are you allergic to cats too?" She tittered, and Paul smiled.

Palace Guard rolled his eyes.

"Here, Maggie Flanagan. Read this," she said.

I read and felt my cheeks grow warm midway through the first page. Mrs. Hayden tittered again. "He was a romantic."

I nodded. Paul eased closer to read.

When I turned the page, I found the mention of three pieces of art that Hayden's woman friend wanted him to keep, but he disguised the art to keep the government from taking the pieces. Then later in the letter, a ramble about black velvet and art mixed in with an in-depth description of a woman's breasts.

Mrs. Hayden peered at me. "You know who he's talking about there at the end. His Irish beauty."

I smiled. "My mother would get a kick out of this letter. She always said her grandmother had a wild side. This letter reminds me of some of the stories Mother told me."

"I've read that letter so many times, I've got it memorized. There's nobody I'd rather see have possession of it after I'm gone than Maggie Flanagan's mother. Please, deliver it to your mother."

"You know, I could just snap a picture."

"No, no. Your mother needs to hold the paper when she reads it."

"This is wonderful. Thank you. I am so sorry, but we're going to have to leave. I don't want to fly back in the dark, and we don't want to wear you out."

Paul set my lemonade on the table next to his then helped me up.

"You were a delight, Maggie Flanagan. I loved your story. Well done." She smiled, and I returned her smile.

She walked us to the door, and Paul helped me down the steps.

On our way to the airport, Paul said, "That was amazing. What a coincidence."

"What? That an old liar like Mrs. Hayden had an entertaining afternoon? She knew I'd memorized the letter the second I saw it. She just wanted to see if she could trap me. Part of me wonders if she wrote it after you said we were coming to see her to test us and to give us a puzzle to solve. Remember when she said well done?"

"I just watched a young liar entertain an old liar?"

I cocked my head and peered at him. "No, she filled in all the holes herself."

"Why didn't you drink your lemonade? I noticed you didn't after your cookie comment, so I didn't either."

I chuckled. "I was glad you didn't. Saved me from spilling yours. I'm a librarian. I read books, and we were in the perfect setting for a murder mystery. The witless visitors are always poisoned in the parlor."

Paul snorted. "I knew there was a logical reason. Was this a wasted trip?"

"If her husband wrote the letter, it wasn't to her, and she was happy to get rid of it. I suspect it's been a long time since anyone gave her the opportunity to show off her keen mind. What's true is we have the letter; not a wasted trip."

Paul shook his head. "She handed off a letter she didn't want to a worthy sparring partner."

Palace Guard grinned and nodded.

When we reached the airport, Rich was waiting. Paul turned in the car and keys, and we boarded the plane for our trip back.

When the plane bumped and rolled during our flight, I checked Rich's hands and posture.

He's relaxed.

I leaned back and enjoyed the ride.

After we landed, Rich said, "Sorry about that turbulence. It's fairly common in the late afternoon. Would you fly again, Maggie?"

I grinned. "In a heartbeat."

On the way back to Glenn's house, Paul asked, "What's our next step? Do we go to the address in Columbus that the letter mentioned to see if we can find the art?"

"First, I want to do some research, and we need an art expert." I sent a text to Sierra. "I have ?? about art. Call when you have time."

Paul said, "All I know about Columbus, Georgia, is that it's on the Chattahoochee River and is directly across from Alabama."

"Mother called it an artsy river town. We'd visit in the fall while everyone else dashed to the north Georgia mountains."

After Paul parked in the Coyles' driveway, he asked, "Are you worn out, Maggie?"

"More exhausted and sore than I expected to be."

Paul nodded as he helped me out of his car. "I suspect Jennifer is ready to hover."

When Jennifer opened the front door, Lucy scrambled through the house and barreled at me. Before she could jump, Spike caught her, and I reached for her and cooed. Palace Guard helped me bend over so I could scratch her ears and hug her neck.

Paul's eyes were wide as Palace Guard helped me rise.

"You're a gymnast, Maggie Flanagan." Paul guffawed.

Jennifer narrowed her eyes then laughed.

CHAPTER ELEVEN

After Paul left, and I was situated with my feet up, Jennifer said, "The hospital sent you home with pain meds. Do you want one?"

"No. I need a beer and my laptop."

"I'm ready to hear what happened," Glenn said.

Jennifer brought me a beer then sat in her soft chair while Palace Guard joined me on the sofa.

"Laptop later. Talk," Jennifer said.

Glenn snorted. "It's her interrogation technique. Very effective. Probably illegal."

I told them about the flight, the remarkable Mrs. Hayden, and Maggie Flanagan then handed the letter to Glenn. After he read it, he handed it to Jennifer.

"What's next, Maggie?" he asked.

"Research. Speaking of which, have you learned anything about Maurice?"

"Not much other than his name isn't Morris Rhodes. Dead end there which actually is even more suspicious, don't you think? Paul and I are going over my notes tomorrow. Maybe he'll have some ideas."

Jennifer handed the letter to me. "If we didn't know the significance of this letter, we'd think it was too personal to be read by anyone else except the recipient. If I were Mrs. Hayden and found it, I would have burned it on his grave." She rose. "I'll get supper on the table."

After we were seated at the table, Lucy plopped down on the floor next to me.

While we ate, Jennifer said, "Ella is amazing. We picked up a few boxes on the way to your house, and she explained her plan of attack like we were packing a large order in a distribution warehouse. The two of us packed the entire house in less than thirty minutes including stripping the beds. We'll go back tomorrow and wipe down the walls and cabinets and mop the floor. Whether you go back home or move with Larry, your house is set."

"When they unloaded Ella's car, each box was numbered and labeled," Glenn said. "Jennifer unpacked the box with your clothes and a small box with your bedsheets and laundry. The rest are in the garage. Never saw anything like it.".

"I hung up your clothes in your closet, and your guns are in Glenn's gun safe," Jennifer added.

I stared at her. "I thought you might throw a few things into a suitcase. That's wonderful. Thank you."

"It's Ella. She's amazing."

Glenn nodded. "I would have spent thirty minutes in the great room while I decided where to start."

"Ella would have fired you. Ready for dessert?" Jennifer asked.

Jennifer poured half of a small carton of heavy cream into a bowl then added a dollop of honey and a splash of vanilla. She used her hand mixer, and when it was fluffy and peaked, she opened the refrigerator door and pulled out dessert.

"Your grandma's ice box lemon pie." Glenn wiped his mouth with his napkin. "I think I drooled."

"I was inspired by the heat and Maggie's trip to see a little old lady in Athens." Jennifer placed generous slices of pie covered with impressive servings of whipped cream in front of us, and we dug in.

I stared at my empty plate. "That was so good, Jennifer. I've never eaten icebox pie before."

She smiled. "I'll be sure you have the recipe before you leave."

"I'd love it. When you have time, would you unwrap my foot and pull off my boot? I need a shower."

Glenn and I relaxed on the patio while Jennifer cleared the table and started the dishwasher.

"I'm glad you've decided to go with Larry," he said. "You'd be miserable here by yourself. In fact, I suspect Ella and Jennifer would have loaded you up and dumped you on his doorstep." Glenn chuckled.

I stared at him. "I'm not sure..."

"Really?" Jennifer laughed from the kitchen.

"She hears everything," Glenn whispered.

"Do not." Jennifer came out to the patio. "I'll unwrap your foot, then pull off your boot. Ready?"

When my foot was free, I wiggled my toes while Jennifer pulled off my boot. "It worked well to have it wrapped. I remembered to stay off it."

Jennifer smiled. "Let me know if you can't find anything."

When I reached the bathroom, Lucy pushed past me and flopped down on the cool tile. "You supervising?" I closed the door, and Lucy grinned.

After my shower, I towel-dried my hair. Jennifer tapped on the door then opened it a crack. "Here's your robe."

"Thanks." *Guess I'm more tired than I thought.*

Lucy and I went into my bedroom, and I put on my pajamas then opened the door for her.

Jennifer came into my room. "Here's your phone. Just whisper if you need anything else."

I grinned, and she chuckled as she left. I climbed into bed and texted Larry. "Call?"

I fluffed up my pillows, but before I could lean back, my phone rang.

"You okay?"

Maybe someday he'll say hello.

"I'm fine. How did today go?"

"Horrible. You were there, and I was here. Other than that, good. We have one final tomorrow. It's written, and I'm prepared, so that's not a worry. How was your flight? How was Athens?"

I told him about the flight, Mrs. Hayden, the letter, and Ella's warehouse skills.

"I feel much better with you at the Coyles'."

"I am glad I'm here. I'm not sure I would have had the energy to cook this evening. Jennifer's been hovering and pampering me. Lucy loves Glenn, but she's been glued to my side since I got out of the hospital."

"I've already cleared it with Betsy to have Lucy with us at the B&B. Will Sarge and your mother be okay with Lucy coming in the RV, or will we pick her up when we return to Harperville for my things? You are coming with me and Lucy, aren't you?"

Tears slipped down my face. *He thought about Lucy.*

"Maggie? Are you there? You must be exhausted."

"I am surprised at how tired I am."

"Let me know what your plan is for tomorrow. I worry about everything when you don't give me specific details of what to worry about." He chuckled.

"Glenn said I'd be miserable if I didn't go with you. He said Jennifer and Ella would dump me on your doorstep."

Larry laughed. "Whatever works. Does that mean you're going with me?"

"If it were my choice..."

"You'd be here right now. Did I get it right?"

I laughed. "Dang it. I paused for dramatic effect. Yes, you got it right."

"Knew it. Sleep well. Can't wait to hold you."

"You too. Good night."

I smiled then did a quick search on my phone.

"Ah ha. An art sale. This is perfect timing."

I submitted an application then turned off the light and flopped back on my pillows.

Lucy click-clicked out of the room, and I opened my eyes. It was still dark, but the heady aroma of coffee enticed me to sit up and reach for my crutches. I grabbed them and swung out of bed then headed to the kitchen with my expert stabilize and swing rhythm.

Jennifer smiled. "I didn't expect you up so early; it's not even six yet. Coffee?"

"Yes, please. I think I'll go to the patio and listen to the birds while I check some things on my laptop." Lucy and Spike followed me to the patio.

I texted Larry. "Good morning. Two days."

Larry: "Hurry up, two days."

I turned on my laptop and searched the internet then read reviews.

"Maggie?" Glenn was in the patio doorway. "You were deep in concentration."

"Playing with some facial recognition software. I've been tweaking it."

"Jennifer said you've been out here for over an hour. Come inside and have breakfast with me."

I rose but kept peering at my screen then picked up my crutches and turned to Glenn. "Doesn't seem like that long." I followed him to the table.

"Eggs, bacon, and cinnamon rolls today." Jennifer set our plates in front of us.

After we ate, Glenn asked. "What were you doing with the facial recognition?"

"I tried to run both sketches together but overloaded my bandwidth and couldn't get it to work. I'm doing two searches now: one for each sketch then I hope I can narrow them down to a manageable list."

"Before that, I searched the Columbus, Georgia, address. It's an old house, but there is a private estate sale today. It's by invitation only then the sale opens to the public this weekend. I applied for an invitation and was accepted. I thought being my mother's daughter would help, and I was right. Next weekend is the public auction for any items not sold today."

On my way to the patio, my phone rang. Sierra.

"Hi, Maggie. Got your text. I'm off for the next two days. Whatcha got for us to do?"

"I think there's some artwork in Columbus, Georgia, but I need an experienced artist to advise me."

"What kind of art?"

"I suspect there might be three pieces by Rembrandt Van Rijn hidden behind some other art."

"Whoa. Are we talking about works that were stolen? My art history teacher in college was fanatical about how wrong that theft was."

"May be. Also, I have no idea what I'm talking about, but what do you know about black velvet and art?"

She laughed. "My art history teacher said at one time you could buy pictures painted on black velvet along the side of any highway. Now, they've become a collector's item. You could have paid up to five dollars back then. They sell online for three to six hundred dollars easy. The price depends more on the size, I think, rather than the quality of the work. If we ever build a time machine, you and I would be filthy rich." Sierra giggled.

"The auction starts at one and includes light snacks according to the information on the submission form. I can invite two guests, and I have a driver. He may or may not go inside the sale with us. Can you be here by nine?"

"Sure can. I'm the art expert, right? So I can dress artsy. I've always wanted to do that."

I laughed. "Sounds like a good idea." I gave her Jennifer's address before we hung up.

I didn't even think about what I should wear.

I trudged as well as anyone could trudge with crutches into the kitchen.

"I'm going to a by-invitation-only private art sale in Columbus, Georgia. I'm hoping Paul will drive. Sierra's going with me. She's an artist and will dress artsy. I invoked Mother's name to get an invitation. What do I wear?"

Jennifer smiled.

Now I know where Kate got her wicked smile.

"You have two choices. The obvious one is to dress flamboyantly like your mother; or you can dress like Olivia left you money, which she did."

I sighed. "You're saying dress, but I can still wear my boots, right?"

"The boots are your signature, and thanks to Ella, they match your crutches."

"Flower dress, I suppose."

"Yes, and I'll wrap your foot."

I held my breath then slipped on the dress. Jennifer came into the room. "You are so pretty. Your hair's long enough for a single braid in the back."

"As long as I don't have to wear a floppy hat," I grumbled.

"What a good idea." Jennifer chuckled. "I was kidding. Besides, you can't wear a hat with a braid."

"Somebody's at the door. I'll be right back. Don't move."

Jennifer returned. "It was Paul. He'll drive you."

Jennifer finished my foot wrap then braided my hair.

"That was fast. I've never had my hair braided before."

"It suits you. You need to wear sunglasses too. I've got a pair that will hide your black eyes. You're rich. You can be eccentric and wear them indoors."

"That's brilliant. Why didn't I wear sunglasses yesterday?"

"Glenn's idea. He suggested it this morning."

"I need to check my computer. Am I released?"

"One more thing. You need a small purse that's large enough for your wallet and your gun. I've got the perfect one. It's forest green, which goes with your dress and your boots, and it has a long, skinny strap you can wear across your chest. Be right back."

She returned with the purse. "Here, try it on. It won't hinder you with the crutches, and you'll have your gun. Your knife might fit in too."

I placed my wallet and gun into the purse and slung it over my shoulder.

"Good. Your gun doesn't show its outline. Try it out. Keep it if you like it. I bought it in case you needed something to go with your dress."

"Thank you. Now can I go?"

"Go, go." Jennifer waved me away.

I hurried to the patio and checked my laptop. "Both searches are done."

Glenn rolled closer to look at my screen. "Facial recognition software, Paul. She searched the two sketches of Maurice."

"Bearded Maurice has seventy-two total near-matches. Near-matches are what I expected. Shaven Maurice has thirty-eight near-matches."

"I've got my day planned for me," Glenn said.

"My turn," Jennifer said. "As soon as Ella gets here, we'll talk through what we want for a new office. We might as well get what works for us instead of trying to scrape by. We may wait until tomorrow before we finish cleaning your little house, Maggie. Harriet will be here at eleven. Your mother said she's the best agent in town. You worked with her, Maggie. What did you think?"

"She knows her real estate business. She's my landlord, but she waited for me to decide before she told me she owned the little house."

Ella tapped at the door and came to the patio. Her eyes widened, and Jennifer shook her head. "I cruised past your house, Maggie. I was relieved to see it was still standing."

"Our new real estate agent, Harriet, will be here later this morning, Ella. Let's work at the dining table. First, we'll brainstorm, and I'll jot down notes."

Jennifer answered the knock at the door. "You must be Sierra. I'm Jennifer. Come on in."

Sierra wore a bright turquoise peasant blouse with an asymmetrical, midi-length, multicolor skirt and hot pink, fringed boots. The purple streaks in her dark-brown hair and her lip ring matched her style to perfection.

"Outstanding, Sierra. You look artsy."

Jennifer handed me her sunglasses, and I put them on. When I peered over the top of the glasses, Sierra laughed. "You look ritzy."

"I feel underdressed. I need a bow tie or something," Paul said.

I gave Paul the address then I hugged Lucy, and Spike waved goodbye.

On the way to his car, Paul said, "Maggie, you might be more comfortable in the back seat. You can prop up your leg."

After we cleared town and were on the open road, I leaned against the door so I could put my leg on the seat. Palace Guard scooted closer to his door to allow more room for my leg. *Good thing I'm short.* Palace Guard grinned.

"Sierra, I have the dimensions of the three stolen paintings. I thought it might be helpful." I handed her my notes, and she read it.

"This will steer us away from anything too small." She stuck the paper into her pocket then turned to talk. "I went by Vecchia Nonna after I got off work yesterday to pick up my last paycheck. When I was on my way out, Maurice asked if I'd talked to you. He said you'd been in a major crash and wanted to know if you were okay. When I told him I had no idea what he was talking about, he tried to pass it off and said it must have been somebody else. He seems obsessed with you. Creepy."

"I'm having a hard time finding any prior history for him," I said. "Turns out his last name isn't Rhodes. Did he ever say anything that hinted where he lived before he came here?"

"Not really, but I've noticed his southern accent has deepened since he's been here. When he first came, it was more like French or something. I'll let you know if I remember anything more specific."

I nodded. "I've been thinking about our approach when we get to the sale. The website lists a partial catalog of the items. I assume they'll have a full catalog when we get there. Would it be helpful if we examine all the black velvet paintings first?"

"It will save us a lot of time. I suspect their catalog is organized by room, so it is easier for their patrons to find a particular piece. I don't expect to see people milling around like an art show. The people in attendance are there to buy and art dealers know that. Expect fancy finger foods and champagne. It's perfectly acceptable to decline. Maybe we can grab a burger on our way out of town to get rid of the hoity-toity taste."

I snickered, and Paul snorted.

"Sounds so appealing, Sierra," Paul said, "but I think I'll get the oil changed in my car. You can text me when you're ready to leave or if you run into any problems. I'll give you my cell number when we get there."

Paul pulled into the long driveway that was lined with majestic, old pecan trees. The long-term neglect and deferred maintenance became apparent as we approached the once grand home. The bases of the columns showed signs of dry rot, gutters sagged, and algae and flaking paint marred the once white mansion. A crowd of people with drinks in their hands chatted on the wide veranda and blocked the entry to the house. My eyes widened. I felt my heart race, and my breathing became rapid and shallow.

"Maggie, breathe." Paul opened my door. "They're all assassins. You got this."

I laughed. "You're right. I can handle a crowd of killers."

"I've got your back, Maggie," Sierra said as she climbed out of the car.

I slung Jennifer's purse across my chest and handed my crutches to Paul, who helped me out of the car.

Paul told us his cell number and noted ours then Sierra helped me to the front porch. I scanned the crowd for anyone whose behavior was not typical or who seemed particularly nervous. I picked out four people who didn't belong: three women and a man.

People cleared a path to the front door for me and my crutches. *Didn't think about that.* The front door was open, and when we stepped inside, an overweight man in a suit hurried to greet me. His sparse hair stuck to his damp forehead.

"Ms. Sloan, so nice to finally meet you. I'm Darren Martin. Welcome to my mother's family home. I've been watching for you. Your mother is well known in our small circle, and your benefactor was a major supporter of the arts. She is greatly missed. Here is our full catalog and my card. I'll be happy to answer any questions you may have. We have guides if you care for one, but I see you've brought..."

"Sierra," she said.

"Yes, that's right. Sierra." He gave Sierra a booklet. "Our catalog. There's an order form enclosed."

Mr. Martin pulled a silver pen out of his pocket and handed it to Sierra. I sat on a bench, and Sierra joined me. Palace Guard stood next to me. While she read through the catalog and circled items, I copied Darren Martin's contact information into my phone then examined the other occupants of the room. *All assassins. Nothing else.*

A man in a tuxedo approached us and offered the tray of drinks he carried. Sierra waved him away.

"I think I've found ten possibilities," Sierra said. "Let's start with the room to the right."

We were alone in the room. "There are three in here." She pointed. "That one is too small. That leaves us two."

The two black velvet paintings sat next to each other. "Ugly, aren't they?" Sierra whispered.

"Remarkably. Mark them on our order sheet. Cross the other one off so we don't think we missed one."

"Good idea. We'll work our way back to the front door and go counterclockwise."

"Lead on."

"Let me know when you need a break. We can sit, and I'll bet we could get decent lemonade here."

When we got to the next room, Sierra said, "Should be two in here."

After we examined the paintings, she said, "Both of them are too small."

I nodded, and we moved on. The next room was a banquet-sized dining room.

"Four in here." The last one was too small. Sierra marked the other three.

When we came to the last open room, I said, "The last one of our ten should be here."

"Too small," Sierra said.

There was one more room, but a handmade sign was taped to the door: *Invitation Only.*

Mr. Martin rushed to us. "The items in this room are not in the catalog. I found them in the attic. You're welcome to go in." He unlocked the door and opened it for us then hovered in the doorway.

"Jackpot," Sierra whispered.

She turned to him. "Are the items in this room priced?"

"Yes, sorry. Here is the price sheet." He handed her a printout.

I sat on a Queen Anne chair while Sierra viewed each painting in the room with care. She showed me the sheet and pointed to the three paintings she marked. I nodded and texted Paul then rose. "We have our selections. Our car will be here in a few minutes. Could someone help us load the paintings?"

"You're taking them with you? Of course, you are. No reason for you to come back; although, we'd be happy to see you again, Ms. Sloan. Or we could deliver them, if that's easier for you."

"We'll need someone to help load them into our car," Sierra said. "Is there any lemonade?"

"Certainly. I'll send some right in unless you prefer to wait on the porch. Does this come out of your reserve, Ms. Sloan?"

Sierra recorded the prices and showed me the total on her phone.

"Yes, that's perfect." I rose. "Lemonade on the porch sounds refreshing. Your mother's home is grand, and her art is impressive. Thank you for including me in the sale."

Darren Martin's face reddened. "You're welcome. The house was grand at one time but came to be more than Mother and I could manage. Mother always hoped someone with a large family would buy the house. She said the house needed children again." He smiled. "Mother always encouraged my friends to visit. It was my pleasure to meet you."

Sierra and I claimed the empty porch swing, and a young woman brought out two tall glasses of lemonade. I sipped my lemonade and observed the people on the porch without being too obvious. Palace Guard pointed to one of the women I'd noticed. A large man with a gun bulge on his hip was escorting her to his car. *Cop.*

"What do you think?" Sierra glanced toward the woman and the man.

"My money would be on a pickpocket. This crowd is ripe."

Paul parked in front of the house, and when he climbed out of the car, Sierra snorted at his bow tie. "Where do you suppose he got that?" she asked.

Mr. Martin directed the four young men who carried our art wrapped in brown paper to Paul's car. Paul popped open the trunk.

Mr. Martin waited for me on the steps and helped me navigate them. "Thank you again, Ms. Sloan. It was a pleasure doing business with you, and I hope we'll see you again soon."

Paul closed the trunk and opened the back door for me. Palace Guard jumped in, and I slid into my seat.

As we drove away, I leaned back in the seat. "I'm exhausted."

"Successful trip?" Paul asked.

"We think so," Sierra answered.

"How were the assassins?"

"That was brilliant, Paul. It helped. One of the four pickpockets I saw was arrested."

"It was slick," Sierra said. "I'm not sure I would have noticed if I hadn't been sitting next to Maggie. Where'd you get the bow tie, and are we going to stop for lunch?"

He chuckled. "My secret, and there's a great diner about thirty miles from here if you can hold off."

When we were out of town and on the four-lane highway, Paul glanced in his rearview mirror. "We have a fast-moving car coming up behind us. I don't like the looks of this. Hang on. I might be doing some fancy maneuvering."

I swung my leg to the floor and jerked on my seatbelt to lock me in place, and Sierra locked her seatbelt too. Paul moved to the left lane, and the car moved to the right lane.

Paul narrowed his eyes and sped up. "We're in for a bumpy ride."

When the car sped up to our bumper, Paul slammed on the brakes and skidded across the median on the left. He whipped into another hard-left turn onto the northbound highway and sped away. I peered at the speedometer and gulped. *110 miles per hour.*

"In two miles, a county road intersects with a two-lane road that goes south. We'll be making another stock car race turn." Paul grinned.

He's having fun.

Paul slowed to fifty miles an hour as he exited on the ramp. "Good thing the road engineers know how to bank a curve," he said.

Palace Guard grinned and winked.

You're just as bad as he is.

Paul turned left and sped away from the four-lane road.

"They may figure out how we lost them, but they'll have a hard time catching up. Even if they had a second car, the odds are slim that it's south of us on this road. I don't think they'd abandon the four-lane. But we'll see, won't we?"

"There's a drive-in lunch spot maybe twenty miles ahead," Sierra said.

"How do you know that?" Paul asked.

"I had a boyfriend with a motorcycle. We stuck to the back roads."

"We are a most interesting trio." Paul chuckled.

In twenty miles, the speed limit dropped ten miles per hour every few hundred yards until it was thirty-five. "Not much farther," Sierra said. "There it is, on the left. It's late in the day for lunch. I'm not sure they're still open, but there's nothing else between here and Harperville."

Palace Guard pointed to the back of the diner. I squinted at the trunk of a black car.

"Paul, there's a black car behind the diner."

"Is that where the cook parks, Sierra?"

"Never did when I was here. He's the owner and always parked in the prime spot in front of the diner. He drove an old jeep."

Paul maintained his slow speed and kept going. After we cleared the town limits, he sped up to ten miles an hour over the speed limit. "Maybe we're all just paranoid, but I think they expected us to blow through town."

CHAPTER TWELVE

After forty-five minutes, we reached the Harperville city limits. When we pulled in front of the Coyles', both Sierra and I exhaled long, slow breaths.

"I agree," Paul said. "Let's get those paintings inside."

"Is it okay if I stick around?" Sierra asked. "I want to see if we found the stolen paintings. I'm curious about those three from the private room."

Paul popped the trunk, and I headed to the house while Paul and Sierra lifted paintings out of his car. I opened the door, and Lucy wagged her tail while Spike held her. I cuddled her, and when she whined, Spike released her and scratched her ears. Paul and Sierra set the wrapped paintings in the den then returned for more.

"Are these the stolen works of art?"

"We don't know. I need to check first." I cut the string around one of the paintings then removed the wrapping. The back of the painting was protected with art paper, and I slit a small T in it then peered at the back of the painting.

"I need Sierra to confirm, but this looks more like the nineteen seventies than sixteen hundred to me."

Jennifer moved the painting to the dining room. "I never understood the fascination with the black velvet paintings. This is ugly."

Paul and Sierra brought in the rest of the paintings while I unwrapped the next painting.

"Sierra, check the back of this painting," Jennifer said. "Did you have lunch?"

"No," Sierra said. "They starved me."

Jennifer glared at Paul then hurried into the kitchen.

"This is black velvet." Sierra examined the back. "It's sturdy, but cheap. No masterpiece hidden here."

I cut the small slits in the back of the second painting.

"Give me a minute," Jennifer called from the kitchen. "I want to check the next one."

Sierra hurried to the kitchen to help Jennifer. They returned with ham sandwiches, chips, tea, and a plate of brownies.

"Break," Sierra said.

While we ate, Glenn asked, "Anything interesting happen on your trip?"

Sierra and I laughed.

Paul snorted. "Here's my summary: I'll never travel with those two again. I'll fill you in later. Let's go to your outside office to work."

After Glenn and Paul left for the patio, Jennifer rose from the table and examined the back of the first painting through the paper. "I see what you're talking about, Sierra. This is velvet."

Jennifer removed the wrapping paper from the paintings, I slit the protective backings, and Sierra declared each one, "Velvet."

After our assembly line unwrapped, sliced, and inspected the ten paintings, we lined them up for an art review.

"You can't leave them here, Maggie, unless we re-wrap them and put them in the attic," Jennifer said.

"We can sell them for at least twice more than Maggie paid for them," Sierra said.

I cocked my head and stared at her. "Could you sell them, Sierra? Unless that was a joke. I'm not good at understanding jokes."

Sierra snickered. "Not a joke. I could sell them in less than a week."

"Go ahead then. Use the proceeds for Toby's schooling or whatever he needs."

"Really?" Tears slipped down Sierra's face.

Jennifer raised her eyebrows and peered at me.

"Toby is Sierra's brother," I said. "He has a job waiting for him after he is a certified mechanic."

Sierra hugged me then Jennifer hugged both of us. Spike elbowed Palace Guard.

"Thank you, Maggie," Sierra said.

"You can leave them here, if you like, Sierra, if it's easier for you." Jennifer shook her head as she stared at the paintings. "No accounting for taste."

"I'm off today and tomorrow. Unless you need me for anything else, Maggie, I'm going home to get to work."

Paul stood in the patio doorway. "Maggie, Glenn went through all the potential Maurices. Come out here when you have time."

Jennifer walked with Sierra to the door, and I clipped along to the patio on my crutches then sat at the table next to Glenn.

"You left me with a total of one hundred and ten photos to go through, Maggie," Glenn said.

Paul snorted. "You had the easy job."

Glenn grinned. "I agree. I started with the names, but there was zero duplication of names between the two sets. That would have been too easy, right? After that, I spent the day trying to cross-match bearded versus unbearded. Not very scientific, but I eyeballed them and narrowed it down to seventeen matches. I'll show you what I have; I'm sure you have some thoughts about where to go from here."

Glenn showed me his list on his computer then I created a folder with the thirty-four photos and matched up the bearded and unbearded pairs.

Paul peered over my shoulder. "Glenn, we would have needed a month to do what Maggie did in just a few minutes." He tilted his head and grinned. "My wife deserves a night off. We'll go out to dinner."

Glenn chuckled. "Italian?"

Paul rubbed his chin. "What a good idea, Glenn. I'll give Julie a call."

Jennifer stood in the doorway. "You two are comedians."

"You deserve a night off too," Glenn said. "It wouldn't hurt for the two of us to get out."

Jennifer smiled. "Can we plan on six-thirty? I'll call for reservations at Vecchia Nonna."

"I'll call Julie." Paul grabbed his phone and stepped outside.

"I'll see if I can prioritize these photos for you," I said.

"Want me to call Ella and Lester to keep you company this evening, Maggie?"

"What? No!"

Glenn chuckled, and Jennifer swatted him.

"Did I miss something?" Paul asked as he came inside.

"No," I growled.

"Julie said six-thirty is fine. Shall we meet you there?"

"Yes, and we need to leave Maggie alone so she can work; otherwise, no dinner for anyone," Jennifer said.

"I'll go. See you at six-thirty," Paul said. "Maggie, can you email me your most-likely pairs?"

"Will do."

I reviewed the seventeen unbearded first then examined the bearded photos as I imagined Maurice with a beard.

I leaned back into my chair then Jennifer joined me.

"Need a break?" she asked. "I talked Glenn into lying down for a nap, and he's out. Shall I unwrap your foot?"

"I'd love that. Would I disturb Glenn if I go into my room so I can change?"

"Not at all. Your dinner is in the refrigerator. You can pop it into the oven when you're ready. I'll unwrap first."

I held out my foot, and after Jennifer removed the wrap, I sighed. "That feels so good."

"If you'd like to shower before we leave, you won't bother Glenn." Jennifer smiled.

"I think I will." I used my crutches to rise and headed to my bedroom. Lucy followed me, and I closed the door.

While I gathered clean clothes to change into after my shower, my phone buzzed a text.

Larry: "Call?"

I relaxed on the soft chair next to my bed and called.

"Are you okay?" he asked.

"What kind of hello was that?"

I felt his smile broadcast through the phone. "Hello, sweetheart. How was your day?"

I snickered. "Thanks for asking. Now, let me talk to my Larry."

He burst out laughing, and Lucy ambled over to sniff my phone. I told him about Columbus, the art show, and how Paul Vargas outmaneuvered a car.

"Paul Vargas used to be with the police department, right?" he asked.

"Yes."

"My dad told me about him. Dad thought Paul got a raw deal."

"He's working with Glenn now. I'd like to go back to Columbus. Is that something we could do on Saturday?"

"Whatever you want to do as long as we're together."

His words warmed my heart. *As long as we're together.*

"Maggie? Are you there?"

"That's absolutely the nicest thing you could have said. I do have one more thing. I have black eyes, and I wore Jennifer's sunglasses today. I may have to borrow them for the weekend."

"What's your cover story?" he asked.

I smiled. *You know me too well.* "I have two. The first one is I got the last beer; the second, I won the kickboxing championship."

Larry's laughter was out of control. I moved the phone away from my ear and stared at it. *I didn't know it was that funny.*

When he settled down, I asked, "How was your day?"

"I've survived another day of being away from you. The final test was easy, but I'm glad I studied. I'm sure we'll hear tomorrow where we're going. Are you going with me?"

"Of course. Didn't we already decide?"

"You are? I needed to hear you say it. You're going. We'll be together. That's perfect. As soon as we know where, we'll find a house that works for us and Lucy. No steps or at least only a few, and Lucy needs a fenced yard too. I know Spike keeps an eye on her, but she's safer with the fence. We'll need to think about a car for you, but we can get that after we move. How quick can you pack? We have a week to move then I start my new job."

I listened to his voice and tingled with growing excitement.

"Maggie? Are you there?"

"I'm excited too."

"We'll be together. I have to go. Love you."

He hung up, and I stared at the phone.

"Did you hear what he said, Lucy? What do we think about that?"

Lucy put her head on my lap, and I cuddled her. "Good answer, girl. I need to shower, so Jennifer and Glenn won't be late for their dinner date."

Lucy followed me into the bathroom. She flopped down on the floor, and I turned on the shower to warm up while I stripped. After I shampooed my hair and washed, I turned off the water and grabbed my towel. I dried and dressed then combed my hair to get out the tangles. Lucy and I went to the bedroom for my crutches.

Jennifer stopped by my door. "Glenn will be ready to go in ten minutes. I put your dinner in the oven for you. It should be ready to eat in thirty minutes. I feel like I've been on the go since early this morning. Come to the patio with me while I wait for Glenn."

Jennifer stopped by the kitchen and poured two glasses of tea then we went out to the patio. Palace Guard, Spike, and Lucy joined us. Lucy circled her soft pad twice then returned to the air conditioning in the den. Spike glanced at the patio thermometer then followed her.

"What did Larry say?" Jennifer asked.

"Excellent deduction, Watson. Who else would I be on the phone with for so long? He aced his last test today and will find out where we're going tomorrow. He said love you right before he hung up."

Palace Guard grinned, and Jennifer laughed. "Slick. Him and you. He didn't give you a chance to say anything, did he? I'll bet you a brownie that he's dying inside. Call him after you eat your dinner. When did you first meet Larry?"

I thought back to the first time we met and smiled. "We met at the library after the murder and before the explosion. I thought he was tall."

Jennifer nodded. "Larry is tall, especially to you and me. What's the first thing he said to you?"

"We were assigned to return the patrons' cell phones after the detectives released them. When the reporter snagged specific people to interview as they left, he asked me how the reporter selected them, and I answered him. Simple, right?" I shook my head. "That's when he told me *you are the funniest librarian I've ever met.*"

Jennifer snorted. "I'm curious. What was your answer to his question about the reporter?"

"I told him she listened for our most imaginative patrons, and I couldn't wait to get home to hear what really happened according to our in-house eyewitness experts."

Jennifer laughed. "And that's why he said you were the funniest librarian? He got that right. When did you name him Larry?"

"It was the day after Sarge announced his and Mother's engagement. Kate told me police officers were in my apartment, but I was not to talk to them in case bad guys were listening because I was supposed to be alone. Two men were in my apartment: one had curly hair and smiled; the other, black hair with bangs cut straight across his forehead. He scowled. Larry and Moe, right?"

Jennifer laughed until tears ran down her face. "What did Larry say when he found out he was Larry?"

I thought about his red, angry face. "He was mad. He asked me if a third officer who was bald was there, would he be Curly? I said no, and he got madder and said *not convinced*. I think that was the first time he accused me of lying."

Jennifer threw her head back and laughed even harder. After she caught her breath, she said, "No wonder you two get along so well with a start like that. Nowhere to go but up."

Glenn rolled to the patio door. "You two are having too much fun. I'm ready, Jennifer."

Jennifer hugged me. "I loved our chat. We won't be late."

"You don't know," Glenn said as he wheeled to the front door. "We might go dancing."

"Right," Jennifer said.

I sat at the computer and scrolled through the photos, but not one struck me as even close to Maurice. I pulled up the original one hundred plus and scrolled through them to select my own possibilities then checked my six choices against Glenn's seventeen pairs.

"I have zero matches."

Palace Guard frowned at the screen.

"My original database has insufficient data. I'll start another scan on a broader database."

I kicked off a search on a database with more records. "Nothing to do now, but let it run."

A buzzer sounded in the kitchen. "Jennifer set a timer. My dinner's ready."

I used one crutch as I carried my glass of tea to the kitchen. After I refilled it and added more ice, I pulled my dinner out of the oven. Palace Guard sat with me at the table then Spike and Lucy joined us.

"Thanks. I don't mind eating alone, but it's nice to have company. Can I talk to you about Larry while I eat?"

Palace Guard smiled, and Spike covered his ears and grinned.

"Then don't listen, Spike." I cut the oven-fried chicken into bite-sized pieces. "The only logical explanation I have for my hesitation to go with him in the first place is a fear of the unknown. What do you think?"

Palace Guard frowned, and Spike shook his head. I scooped up mashed potatoes and speared a bite of chicken then chewed my food.

"Doesn't sound logical to me either, now that I say it. Larry isn't the unknown, so there isn't a reasonable explanation other than I thrive on data and this relationship stuff doesn't yield data I can analyze."

Palace Guard rolled his eyes, and Spike lolled his head backward and hung out his tongue. I used my scoop of mashed potatoes to pick up some peas then stabbed a piece of chicken. Spike crossed his eyes and held his nose. I glared and ate my multilevel bite of supper.

"It used to drive Mother crazy when I stacked food on my fork so I could have one bite of everything all at one time. It was efficient. I never thought she was logical. Why would she care? I was the one eating it. I think I did it to annoy her. Maybe that wasn't logical."

Spike nodded.

I waved my fork and its piece of chicken. "About Larry: I do have some data. It's a fact that I can't stand to be away from Larry, and he feels the same about me. He's just better at expressing his feelings than I am."

Palace Guard and Spike high-fived.

"That's it. It wouldn't hurt me to learn a new skill, would it?"

Palace Guard smiled, Spike nodded, and I laughed.

I rose and carried my dishes to the kitchen. I hobbled to the patio, but the system was still searching.

I sent a text to Larry. "Call? No hurry."

My phone rang. When I answered, Larry asked, "What's wrong? What do you mean no hurry?"

"Larry, stop. Breathe. Nothing's wrong, and what I meant was to call me at your convenience. No hurry was easier to text."

Larry inhaled then exhaled a long breath. "There. Hello, sweetheart. How's your day? You can answer at your convenience."

I chuckled. "I figured something out. You know how I love to analyze data, and I'm good at it. Here's some data. It is a fact that I can't bear to be away from you. Another fact is that I know you can't stand being away from me, either."

I listened. "Are you still there?"

"Yes. I just know you, and there's more. I'm listening."

I sat on the patio chair. "There is more data. You know how to express your feelings. I don't; however, I'm smart and can learn. Here's another fact. You are an excellent teacher. I can't think of anyone I'd rather learn from than you."

"I was running a trail in the woods. I'm sitting on a bench. Where are you?"

"I'm sitting on the patio. It's comforting to know you are outside too, but I don't have the gnats."

Larry chuckled. "You're right about the gnats. I love listening to your voice. You have a lilt when you speak. I'm still listening because you have more."

"You make me laugh. That isn't easy because I don't understand jokes."

"You sure don't, and that's no joke."

I smiled. "When we talked earlier, you ended the conversation by saying love you."

I waited.

"You're waiting to build suspense," he said. "I'll wait with you."

"See? That's why I love you too."

I waited. "Are you building suspense now?" I asked.

"No. I'm at a loss for words. You don't know how long I've waited for you to say that, but I was afraid at the same time that you never would because that wasn't how you felt, and I know you. You wouldn't say it if you didn't mean it. Say it again. I have to hear it."

"I love you, Larry Kevin Ewing."

"Now I need to see your face while you say it. I want to watch your mouth move and your green eyes light up. Can you be here tomorrow? I'll call Betsy just in case. I have to get back for a meeting. Text me no hurry anytime, and I love you, Maggie Gray Lady Sloan."

"Bye, love you," I said as we hung up.

Palace Guard smiled, and Spike fluttered his eyelashes.

"It was that bad, Spike? You didn't have to stay and listen, you know."

Spike did his wacky dance, and I did a modified one-foot dance. Palace Guard stood next to me in case I fell.

I stretched. "I'm tired, but I want to hear about Jennifer and Glenn's evening."

I peered at the computer screen. "The system completed its search."

I began the analysis of my data. Two hours later, Jennifer and Glenn came home. Lucy woke and trotted to the front door when they parked in the driveway.

When Glenn rolled into the house, he asked, "What have you got?"

"I ran a new search on a larger, more extensive database. I have a larger batch of photos for you to review."

He eased himself onto his recliner and raised his feet.

Jennifer joined us. "We had an enjoyable evening with Julie and Paul. It was nice to get out even if we were working. That Maurice is charming."

Glenn said, "By charming, she means slick."

Jennifer nodded. "It was hard to get past that, but once I did, I saw how smart he is. Cunning. He studies people and is skilled at characterizing them. That's how he decides his best approach."

"To answer your question, Maggie," Glenn said, "it was smart to see him in action, but it didn't help as far as narrowing down his photos to a name. What's up with you?"

"Did you talk to Larry?" Jennifer asked.

"Yes, I did. He hears tomorrow where we're going. I'm catching his excitement and am looking forward to his graduation on Friday. Do you think I'll be off crutches by then? Can I borrow your sunglasses over the weekend?"

Jennifer raised her eyebrows. "You're welcome to wear the sunglasses as long as you like, but weren't you supposed to stay off your ankle for a week or two?"

"Yes, but that's annoying." I pouted, and Jennifer laughed.

"I'm beat," Glenn said. "I'll examine photos in the morning."

I yawned. "I guess I am too. Goodnight all."

Lucy beat me to the bedroom. "You're tired too, girl?"

She flopped onto her pad while I changed for bed then opened the door so she could wander.

After I was in bed, I thought about Larry. *How can I leave tomorrow?*

The sound of sirens woke me in the middle of the night. *It's a dream.* I rolled over and snuggled my pillow.

When I woke, it was still dark. I rolled over to sleep a little longer, but my foot throbbed. When I sat up, I realized Lucy had left the bedroom. As I grabbed my crutches, the enticing aroma of coffee lured me to the kitchen.

"There you are, sleepy head." Jennifer smiled as she turned on the oven then poured a cup of coffee for me.

I peered at the clock. *It's only six.* I rolled my eyes. "Thank you for the coffee. I might need to ice my foot."

"Lucy and I guess Spike went out back; or maybe Lucy has learned how to unlock and open the door now."

I smiled. "Now that's funny."

Jennifer curtsied. "Pants don't work all that well for a grand curtsy, do they? Go sit where you're comfortable, and I'll bring you an icepack for your foot."

CHAPTER THIRTEEN

When I opened the patio door, the early birds serenaded me. I propped up my foot, turned on the computer, and set up the new batch of photos for Glenn then picked up my phone.

"Do you think it's too early to call Mother? She was always an early riser," I asked as Jennifer came into the room with an ice pack.

"You can leave a message. What's up?"

"Larry wants me to come to Macon today. I can't think of any reason why not, other than I don't know how much of an imposition it is to ask Mother if she and Sarge can leave today instead of tomorrow."

"It doesn't hurt to ask, but if it doesn't work out for them, Ella and I could have you there in no time. I wouldn't mind getting away for a day, and it's been ages since I've been outside of town."

"Really? That's really generous of you."

Jennifer rose. "Call your mother. I'll bring you more coffee."

I called Mother.

"Margaret, how nice to hear from you. We got back early on Tuesday. It was a great shakedown trip, and Franklin loved it. Big D is ready to leave again. He filled the RV with fuel yesterday, and I cleaned the RV and changed our sheets. I have a short grocery list, and Big D has gone to the store. We may be circling the Coyles' house in the RV until tomorrow." Mother laughed.

"If you wanted to leave today, Larry would love it. He asked me last night if there was a possibility. He's completed all his classes earlier than he thought and is packing up today."

"Big D asked me what the possibilities were of leaving today, and I told him I didn't want to put any pressure on you. Isn't that funny? I'll talk to him when he gets back and call you. I'm excited you're going to ride with us in the new RV."

Mother hung up. I set down my phone. "Bye, Mother."

Jennifer raised her eyebrows as she brought the coffee pot and her cup to the patio.

I snickered. "Mother is checking with Sarge, but she said Sarge was ready to leave this morning. She has never said goodbye to me. She just hangs up. I always tell her bye. It's my version of a joke, but one of these days, I'll be faster than she is."

Jennifer chuckled. "It's actually a good one, especially coming from you. What are your plans?"

"Only high level. Larry hears today where his assignment is. We'll be back here on Saturday and load our things then hopefully find a place next week and move."

"When I hear Glenn stirring, I'll put the cinnamon rolls in the oven. Let's check your foot."

Jennifer unwrapped my foot and examined it. "Your toes are warm. I'll re-wrap it."

Palace Guard frowned and pointed to the front door, and Spike and Lucy came inside.

I peered at Palace Guard. "Somebody's here? This early?"

He nodded.

Jennifer asked, "What do you mean somebody's here? Did your men hear something?"

I nodded, and she hurried to the front of the house.

"Hello, Detective," she said.

"Sorry to disturb you so early in the morning," Moe said. "We need to talk to Maggie. She's here, isn't she? Is she awake?"

"Yes, come on in. Care for coffee?"

"We won't be here long," Moe said.

"Good morning, Mrs. Coyle," a male voice said. "Sorry for calling on you unannounced at such an early hour."

I frowned. *Not a voice I know.*

Jennifer, Moe, and the fire chief, who wore his jacket, joined us on the patio. *Official visit.*

"Maggie, we need to talk." Moe had a softness in his face that scared me.

Jennifer grabbed his arm. "Is Kevin Ewing okay?"

"What? Yes, as far as I know," he said. "Maggie, your house caught fire sometime in the middle of the night. It was gone by the time the neighbors realized there was a fire and called it in."

Palace Guard's eyes widened then he put his hand on my shoulder, and Spike sat on the floor with Lucy.

I'm glad we were all here. My men nodded.

The fire chief cleared his throat. "Ms. Sloan, we have strong evidence that points to arson. The neighbors were frantic because no one knew where you were. The onsite police officers called Detective Ross. I'm sorry, but all the contents were lost; however, the entire fire department is relieved that you are safe."

"Thank you. Does Harriet know? She owns the house," I said.

"We're going to see her next," Moe said. "She'll ask about you, and I wanted to see you for myself first." Moe reached toward me with one arm and laid it on my shoulder then patted my back. Jennifer walked with them to the door.

After they left, she returned to the patio with the coffee pot. "That was the most awkward hug I've seen in my entire life. Excellent example of a Moe version of a tender moment, though." She peered at my face. "You must be in shock about that beautiful little house. I know I am. More coffee?" She refilled our cups.

My tears overflowed and streamed down my cheeks. "I am. I loved that house, and I feel terrible for Harriet."

Jennifer nodded then we sipped our coffee in silence.

My eyes widened. "Larry. I need to call him."

The phone rang over to voice mail, so I hung up and tapped in a text. "I'm at the Coyles' and fine. Call. No hurry." I showed my text to Jennifer, and she nodded. I tapped send.

"I'll re-wrap your foot then put the cinnamon rolls in the oven. That will get Glenn up for sure. I'll help you pack after breakfast." After she tended to my foot, she hurried to the kitchen.

"I'm going to miss that house: our first house, really." I sighed, and Palace Guard patted my shoulder.

My phone rang, and I smiled. *Mother.*

"Margaret, we just heard about your little house. We feel terrible. Do you need me to buy you something to wear? Big D said everything was gone. Are you doing okay? I know Harriet is devastated, but she'll rebuild. She's a survivor like we are. Are we still going to Macon? We're ready when you are. Big D wants to leave now."

"I'll be ready in an hour."

"Good." Mother hung up.

"Bye, Mother."

Jennifer stood at the patio door. "Glenn's up and moving around. Let's get you packed. You point; I'll pack." As we headed to my bedroom, she asked, "An hour?"

I chuckled. "Mother said Sarge was ready to leave now. I'm not leaving until I have a cinnamon roll, though."

Jennifer opened the closet door, and I sat in the soft chair. "You're planning to be back on Saturday, right? Let's plan clothes through Monday."

I smiled. "I think that's brilliant. I'll need a dress for the graduation and one more dress in case there's a party or something. Jeans and shirts. I don't need my running clothes, darn it."

"You can add your toiletries after I pack. Would you check the cinnamon rolls? They'll be ready to come out of the oven in five minutes, and I'll finish up here."

I pulled out the cinnamon rolls, started a fresh pot of coffee, and set the table. Glenn rolled into the dining room, and Jennifer rushed to the kitchen.

"Jennifer told me about your house. I'm so sorry. That was a special place, wasn't it?"

"I loved being in the country, and Palace Guard and I ran almost every day with the horses and goats. It was a wonderful house."

"I agree," he said.

"That's two fires too many." Jennifer poured a cup of coffee for Glenn.

I stared at her. "What?"

"Two fires. Too many." She hurried back to the kitchen.

"Three fires," I mumbled.

"What are you talking about?" Glenn peered at me over his cup.

"The warehouse fire the night before Ella was furloughed. I have no idea if it's related or how it could be, but I didn't think of it until Jennifer said two fires."

"Breakfast." Jennifer glided into the dining room carrying three plates with the ease and grace of an Olympic ice-skating champion. I smiled. *Reminds me of the first time I met Kate.*

After breakfast, I packed my hairbrush, toothbrush, and the rest of my small items that must have fallen into the toiletries' category.

"Ready?" Jennifer asked when my crutches and I swung into the den.

I tapped the bill of my Texas Tech ball cap. "Yes, ma'am."

"Here are my sunglasses. Your eyes are still black. Doc said your nose wasn't broken, didn't she? It's hard to see how that's possible, but at least the swelling's gone down."

"Are you hovering, Jennifer?" Glenn chuckled.

"Only a little."

The drone of a diesel engine in front of the house announced Mother and Sarge's arrival. Jennifer stacked my bags next to the front door. "You have your packed duffle bag, go-bag, backpack, and computer. I put your small purse in the duffle bag in case you go somewhere besides the patio or for a short stroll."

"Paul and I plan to find out what Maurice's real name is, and I'm interested in who owns that warehouse," Glenn said. "Let me know if there's anything else we can research. I'll beat Jennifer to the punch. Be safe."

Palace Guard joined me at the door then Lucy and Spike came in from the back yard. Lucy claimed her position between me and the front door.

"Not this time, girl. Soon." I snuggled her then waved to Glenn and Spike as I opened the door.

Sarge stepped onto the porch. "Good morning, Maggie. We aren't rushing you, are we? I'll carry your things to the RV. Your mother is waiting at the door."

He picked up all my bags, and Jennifer hugged me. "Be safe." She accompanied me to the RV.

"Remember, Ella and I can come anytime. Just text, call, or holler." She grinned.

"Wow," I said when I went inside the RV. "This is nice." I'd seen pictures of RVs, but I wasn't prepared for how much room there was. When I peered at the back, I saw a Sarge-sized bed and a door that must be a bathroom. The bright pink, purple, and turquoise throw and deep orange and red fluffy pillows gave Mother's unique signature of colors to the light tan leather sofa.

"It is, isn't it?" Mother beamed. "Here, sit on the sofa next to the window and prop up your leg. The sofa becomes a bed and so do the dining benches."

When Palace Guard climbed in, his eyes widened, and I nodded.

I waved to Jennifer who was in the front yard, Glenn, who was at the front window, and Spike who stood behind Glenn. After I settled down on the sofa, I said, "I feel like we're going on a voyage. No wonder you enjoy traveling in your RV."

Sarge climbed into the driver's seat. "Everyone ready? Let's hit the road."

I texted Larry. "On the road."

"We're going the scenic route, if that's okay with you," Sarge said. "Old friends of mine have a farm along the way, and I'd like to stop to see them. It will be a brief stop. I'd like to introduce them to Izzy. They have alpaca."

"That's fine with me. I'm not sure I've ever seen alpaca on a farm."

"Mother, do you know Darren Martin in Columbus?"

Mother moved from the front passenger's seat to the upholstered chair. "I knew his mother. She was quite a bit older than I am, but she was an artist and knew art. Darren doesn't have her art talent or knowledge, but I understand he's a talented art salesman."

Mother told me more about her mother's interest in art and growing up in the artsy crowd until my phone buzzed. She smiled. "Check your phone, Margaret."

I picked up my phone and read the text.

Larry: "Was in a meeting. Excited to see you. What time?"

Me: "After lunch."

Larry: "Lunch at 10? A joke."

Me: "Ha."

"Was that Larry?" she asked. "Has he heard where he's going to be assigned?"

"It was, but he hasn't heard yet."

Mother's phone rang, and she chatted with her friend who called. I gazed at the countryside then I saw them.

"Cows," I said.

Palace Guard smiled and turned toward the window on his side.

Game on.

"Dang. Cemetery. I have to start over."

Palace Guard grinned, and I wrinkled my nose and turned back to my window. *Come on, cows.*

After thirty minutes, I was ahead, and then Palace Guard poked me from across the aisle and raised his hand. I stared out his window. Sarge slowed the RV to creep through a small town, and there it was on Palace Guard's side. *Ice cream shop.*

I sighed and smacked a high-five. "Fine. You win."

Mother raised her eyebrows, and Palace Guard shook his shoulders in a silent chuckle.

Mother hung up. "Now, where was I?"

"Mother, tell me more about your grandmother. Did she ever live around Athens? What was her maiden name?"

"My grandmother and mother moved from Columbus to Athens sometime after my grandfather died, but I never got the dates quite straight in my head. Mother's name was Devlin Grace. She was named after Anne Devlin, a key leader of the 1798 Irish Rebellion, and Grace O'Malley, the Pirate Queen in the late 1500s. Mother always said that she regretted she couldn't remember her father. She was an outstanding storyteller, which she inherited from her father, according to Grandmother. Grandmother's maiden name was Flanagan, and she had red hair and green eyes. Mother told the funniest stories about her wild mother and her artsy friends. According to my mother, her mother had ninety percent of the men in Athens wrapped around her finger; the other ten percent were blind." Mother laughed, and I smiled.

"Mother said a group of women, led by a woman named Clara Hayden, tried to ostracize Margarite. Rumors were that Mr. Hayden was her number one admirer. Did I ever tell you that you were named after her? Anyway, Margarite's friends rallied around her. They were the wild, artsy crowd. Margarite collected and sold art at a hefty profit and left a sizeable inheritance for Mother and me. My father died in the war before I was born. I told you that, didn't I? Mother named me after the Irish princess, Isolde, who, according to the legend, was married to King Mark of Cornwell and was loved by Tristan. Mother always told me I inherited the Flanagan flair for color and style. Mother and I lived with Grandmother Margarite then it was just the two of us after Mother left town for a new job. Grandmother told me stories about fairies. I used to tell you stories when you were little."

I don't remember Mother telling any stories. "Tell me again, Mother."

I leaned back and listened to the stories of fairies and the wild, artsy crowds in the small towns of Columbus and Athens, Georgia, in the late 1920s.

Sarge slowed then turned the RV at a gravel driveway. As the RV crunched gravel and rumbled down the driveway, my eyes widened at the alpaca in the field. "They're beautiful."

Sarge chuckled. "Pete said he had a few alpacas. There appear to be more than a few."

As we approached the farmhouse, Mother pointed to a small building. "They have a country store. I'll have to see what they have. Are you getting out of the RV, Margaret?"

"I wouldn't miss it."

When we stopped, Sarge blew his air horn then came around to the passenger's door. He helped me down the steps then handed me my crutches. Mother beelined to the open store, and Sarge helped me as we headed to the farmhouse. A large German shepherd rose from the porch and ambled our way. We stopped, and she nuzzled Sarge's hand. He laughed and offered her his fingers to smell. She nudged his hand again, and he spoke to her in a soft voice. She grinned and trotted back to her shady spot on the porch. A man who was Sarge's age drove a tractor from a back field and met us at the door. The two men shook hands and pounded each other on the back.

Sarge said, "Pete, this is my new daughter, Maggie."

Pete sported a gray handlebar moustache and wore overalls. "You got yourself a winner there, Sarge. Hello, Maggie. You met

Bailey. She's our official greeter for the store. Kid magnet. Where's your bride?"

He chuckled at the squeals from the country store. "Never mind. She and my wife are already fast friends. Need a cold drink, or are you two ready to see the alpacas? I have to see inside that yacht you sailed into here before you leave. Do we call you Captain now?" Pete's booming laugh was contagious, and even Palace Guard smiled.

When we reached the fence, two of the alpacas loped from the middle of the field to the fence. "These two are the oldest; they're looking for a treat. My wife brings them treats of carrots, apples, turnips, or whatever we have in the afternoons. It's too early, girls."

The alpaca spit then wandered off.

"Some people say alpaca don't understand us. What do you think?"

Sarge and I laughed.

"I got a new tractor, Sarge. Come to the barn."

"I'll check out the store," I said.

When I reached the store doorway, Mother said, "Come on in, Margaret. This is Martha. There's a chair here where you can sit, or you can browse."

I picked up a knitted winter cap. "Ms. Martha, this is so soft."

"Isn't it?" Mother said. "Pick out one. I couldn't decide which one you'd like, so I waited for you."

I spotted a sage-green cap and showed it to Mother. "This is beautiful."

"Try it on," Martha said.

I put it on. "Soft. I'll bet it will be warm in cold weather."

"Like no other." Martha smiled. "Here's the scarf that goes with it."

"Ring up those two and two sets of the dryer balls then I have to leave the store."

Martha placed the items into two brown craft sacks with ribbons tied onto their handles.

"Thank you. I love your store," Mother said.

When we strolled to the RV, Sarge and Pete stood next to the engine compartment at the back.

"This is some ride you got, missus," Pete said. He and Sarge shook hands. "Come back again when you can stay for lunch or even supper. I've got that hookup near the store."

Sarge helped me inside, and Mother hopped in behind me.

"I'll send you your cap and scarf when the weather gets colder," Mother said. "No reason for you to carry them around just to pack them for your move."

Sarge climbed in, started the engine then drove around the circle driveway back to the road. "Lunch in about an hour?" he asked. "There's a roadside park with shade up ahead."

"That works, Big D," Mother said.

When we were back on the road, I asked, "Did Mrs. Hayden buy and sell art too? Could that have added to her trying to ostracize Margarite?"

"According to Mother, Clara Hayden was a larcenous conniver who didn't have a smidgeon of art sense in her. Mother said she'd gyp people out of their art. Did you ever hear of the art theft from the Gardner Museum in Boston? Everyone knew Clara Hayden purchased at least three if not more of the stolen paintings with the plan to lie low and sell them after the museum forgot about them, but the museum kept increasing the reward for them and scared Clara. Mother said Clara's grandson inherited her meanspirited streak of larceny. Mother knew him and didn't like him at all. His family moved up north somewhere when he was in his early twenties, but I can't remember where. I never knew him. But I'm rambling. You aren't interested in all this ancient history."

Sarge chuckled. "Think about who you're talking to, Izzy. Our Maggie thrives on crime and larceny."

"Is that right, Margaret?"

I nodded. "Do you remember the grandson's name?"

"I'm not sure Mother ever said his name. She always called him Clara's thieving progeny."

I snickered. "I love Grandmother's way with words."

"She might not have considered herself an artist, but she sure could paint a story with her words."

I covered my mouth and yawned, but Mother said, "I'll go sit up front. You need to rest before your exciting weekend starts."

I smiled and leaned back, and Mother handed me a bright yellow pillow before she moved up to the passenger's seat.

When I opened my eyes, we were parked in the shade, and Sarge was not in the driver's seat. I heard a scrape behind me and turned. Mother stood at the dining table as she made sandwiches.

"We were going to let you sleep, but Big D reminded me you should eat before we get there. He went for a walk while I pull lunch together. He said I couldn't talk to him if he wasn't here. Would you like some tea?" Mother handed me a bottle of peach tea.

"Thanks, Mother. This is my favorite."

She smiled. "I know."

Sarge came inside. "Hello, Maggie. Glad you could catch a nap. We're about thirty minutes away from the B&B."

Mother set a placemat and a plate on a lap tray then brought it to me. She cut my half sandwich into a triangle and added a few chips.

"This is perfect, Mother, thank you."

She and Sarge sat at the dining table. After Sarge finished two sandwiches, he asked, "Ready for me to head out?"

I nodded, and Mother removed my empty plate and tray. I leaned back and gazed at the passing landscape and farm animals.

"If you need anything this weekend, let us know," Mother said. "Sarge has another friend who lives about an hour west of here, but we'll be at the campground tomorrow. I'll let you know when we're there."

When we reached the entrance of the B&B, I smiled at Palace Guard, and he held up a thumb.

I sent Larry a text: "I'm HERE!"

Larry: "Where?"

I leaned across the aisle and showed my phone to Palace Guard, and he grinned.

When Sarge pulled in front of the B&B, Larry stood at the curb. His big smile gave me goosebumps. After Sarge stopped, I said, "Thank you so much for bringing me. I love the RV. It was a wonderful trip. Bye, Mother."

She smiled as I made my way to the passenger's door. Sarge pushed a button, and the door opened.

"Hello, Mrs. Arrington. Sarge." Larry smiled and waved to Mother then snatched me off the step into a big hug.

I snuggled his neck. "I missed you."

He set me on the ground and gazed at me. "Missed you more."

I narrowed my eyes. "Did not."

"Did too."

Mother laughed, and Sarge handed Larry my crutches.

"Finish your fight somewhere else. I can't unload Maggie's things with you in my way," Sarge said in his gruff voice then smiled.

As I headed to the porch, Daisy wagged, and Larry hovered. "Are you okay? Should I help you up the stairs? Betsy gave us rooms on the first floor."

"I can go up the steps. I need help to go down. Are you going to hover all weekend?"

"Hadn't thought of that." He laughed and Sarge joined in.

"Comedian." I rolled my eyes.

Sarge set my things on the porch, and Larry said, "I'll carry them inside."

Sarge nodded. "Thanks for riding along, Maggie. See you on Friday. Congratulations, Kevin."

As the RV rumbled away. Larry asked, "What do you want to do, Maggie?"

"See my room then sit on the patio with a glass of tea and my sweetie."

Larry grinned and picked up my bags. "I'll hold the door; turn right."

When I stepped inside, I inhaled the homey essence of the B&B then made my way to the hallway on the right.

"Second door on the left." Larry rushed past me and opened the door.

I stepped inside the room. "This is pretty." The walls were soft green, the curtains were a deeper sage green, and the bed linens were white with tiny red roses.

"Good. Betsy said she didn't like the other room for you after she met you. She said this is your room. I wouldn't have picked it. Is this your room?"

"I wouldn't have picked it either, but she's right. I love it."

"Oh good. I hoped I wasn't going to have to change rooms with you."

I smirked, and he laughed. "Too late. You already said you like it."

I swung on my crutches then went into the bathroom. "This is a little larger than the other one."

"Shall I put your clothes away for you?"

"I can do it, but I wouldn't mind some help. If I stand in the closet, would you bring me my hang-up items?"

Larry opened my duffle bag, and I balanced against the wall. I hung up the dresses, shirts, and pants then moved to the dresser and opened a drawer. "Just dump everything in here for now. I'll organize my things later."

Larry put two handfuls of underthings, socks, and sleepwear in the drawer then closed it. When I headed to the door, he stopped me then pulled me into his arms and kissed me with a passion that sent electricity to my core. I matched his passion, and he moaned as he eased into a soft, tender kiss and nibbled on my lip. When he gazed at me, I met his gaze. "I love you, Larry Kevin Ewing."

"I know. I love you too, Maggie Crazy Lady Sloan." He smiled, and I leaned against him. We held each other, and I sighed. *I belong with Larry.*

"Ready for tea on the patio?" he asked.

I headed to the door then glanced back with my best flirtatious look. "You going too?"

He laughed. "Are you getting even?"

"Every chance I get." I tossed my hair then opened the door.

"I'll bring the tea. You go ahead and sit," he said.

On my way to the patio, Betsy bustled into the foyer. "Maggie, I heard you were hurt. I should have known you'd have the perfect Maggie crutches. Let me grab that door for you."

She smiled as she opened the door. "Good to see you. I'll bring y'all a little snack in a few minutes."

Chapter Fourteen

Larry came out to the patio with our tea. "We've got a lot to talk about."

"You first."

He glared. "That's not good. That means you have something to tell me that no one else already has, right? You first."

"We can do this all night," I said.

Larry held his glare as he sipped his tea.

"Fine. I'll jump to the punchline then fill you in later. How's that? Instead of going to Columbus on Saturday, can we go to Athens?"

His eyes widened. "You're right. That is a good punchline, and I was right because nobody told me about that. It's only about two hours away, same as Columbus. I have to go to the training center tomorrow morning, and I expect to be back before lunch. If I am, we could go to Athens tomorrow then we'll have Saturday for any follow up. Maybe we should plan to stay here Saturday night too. What do you think?"

"Good idea. We may have follow-up because I'm not positive what I'll be able to learn in Athens. Details later. Your turn."

Larry drained his glass. "I'll talk to Betsy first. Be right back."

I glanced at Palace Guard. "Was that cheating?"

Palace Guard grinned and nodded.

"I thought so too."

Larry rushed back. "Betsy was fine with us leaving on Sunday. My turn, right?" He sat in his rocker then leaned forward and scanned the area.

This is top secret?

"I know where we're going. You ready?"

My eyes widened, and my heart rate increased in anticipation. "You know? That's exciting. Where?"

He sat back. "The regional office in Midland."

I frowned. "In Georgia, right? Where is it?" I wiped the dripping condensation off my tea glass with my paper napkin then folded my napkin and placed it under my glass of tea.

"On the outskirts of Columbus."

"That's great! Can we stalk the office tomorrow or Saturday?"

"It would be better on Saturday. It would be embarrassing to get caught." He peered at the bottom of his glass. "I need more tea. Your glass is still full. Need it refreshed? More ice?"

"No." *Something's up.*

When he returned, he leaned back and drank his tea.

"What else?" I asked.

"What do you mean, what else?"

I raised my eyebrows, and so did Palace Guard.

"Okay." He sighed. "I've been selected for Crime Scene Specialist."

I jumped up but almost fell because I forgot about my foot. I grabbed my crutches and waved him off. "Didn't expect the pain. That is amazing news. Why did you wait so long to tell me? Aren't you excited? I'm excited. Were you building up the suspense?" I stared at his face. "What's wrong?"

"It means ten weeks of training in Tennessee and maybe additional time for practicals."

"What's bad about that? Do you have to stay at their training facility? I'll camp. That will be fun because I've never camped in Tennessee. I'm not afraid of a little adventure."

He stared at me. "You'd go with me to Tennessee?"

I narrowed my eyes. "Do you have a reason I shouldn't? Do I need to get shots or something?"

Larry stared at me then burst out laughing.

"What's so funny?" I asked. "You thought I'd go to Midland that is almost Columbus but not Tennessee? Why?"

"Because I'm an idiot."

"Oh, okay. As long as you have a good reason." I swatted him and laughed. "You are goofy sometimes."

Betsy carried a plate of crackers and cheese out to the patio. "The crackers are homemade, and I bought the cheese at the shop down the road. Their grand opening was last week. Will your folks be here this evening for supper, Maggie? I was going to call in our order, but thought I'd better check with you first."

"No, just the two of us tonight," I said.

Betsy nodded. "Seems like you could use some relaxation time, and that's our specialty."

After Betsy left, we munched on crackers and cheese.

"Do we go back to Midland after your training in Tennessee?" I asked.

"I'm not sure, but it's a question I can ask tomorrow. If I do, would you want to stay in Midland while I go to Tennessee?"

"For ten or twelve or whatever weeks? No."

I drank the rest of my tea and held an ice cube in my mouth to melt. "I need a car."

"We need a truck to haul a few things to Tennessee and back. I'll give you my car. We can rent furniture or find a furnished place, right?"

"All except beds," I said. "Mother has contacts in Columbus. Maybe she could find a real estate agent to show us around on Saturday."

"That sounds smart. My first day is a week from this Monday. At first, I was glad to have a week, but now I realize we have only a few days to find something so we can move and get settled in a week."

"If we can find something on Saturday, that will ease some of the pressure," I said.

A light breeze rustled in the trees and across the patio. Larry lightly touched my forehead with his fingertips then he brushed the hair away from my face. "You distracted me. I want to hear more about Athens and what all led up to the punchline."

Larry reached for crackers and cheese and left one of each on the plate.

"No reason to leave any for me. I'm saving room for our fancy outdoor dinner."

"Athens." He made a cracker and cheese sandwich then popped it into his mouth.

I told him about Margarite Flanagan, Darren Martin, Clara Hayden, Clara's grandson, and my mother's impressions of the Hayden family and the possible tie in with the Gardner theft.

"I just thought of something else. Glenn and Paul. I can ask them to see if they can come up with Clara Hayden's grandson's name and any details about him."

Larry's eyes twinkled. "I was going to say that."

I grinned and sent the text to Glenn.

"I wouldn't have thought of it if we hadn't gone over it together." I shifted my leg and winced.

Larry frowned. "You need to elevate your foot and ice it. Let's get you to your room, and you can rest before dinner. I'll get ice from Betsy."

I was too tired to argue. He helped me up, and I made my way to my room while he hurried to find Betsy. I eased down onto the soft chair and elevated my foot on the footstool. Larry brought the icepack to my room. After he unwrapped my bandage, he placed the icepack around my ankle.

"Do you have any pain med with you?"

"This is fine. You're right. I just need to rest."

"I'm right." He chuckled as he turned on the ceiling fan then left.

I leaned back in my chair and relaxed to the faint whir and soft breeze of the fan.

I woke to a tap on my door then Larry opened the door.

"Ready for dinner? It will be here in a few minutes. Where do you want to eat? Here? Dining room? Patio?"

"Patio. Always." I scooted up in the chair.

He held up a fresh bandage. "I'll wrap your ankle. Jennifer sent two extra wraps. Betsy washed the one we used earlier, and it's drying."

After he wrapped my foot, he helped me up and held me as he kissed me lightly. "I love you."

"I know. I love you too."

"I know. Let's head to the patio. I'm starved and ready for a beer. Want one?"

"Absolutely."

When I stepped onto the patio, a cold wind chilled me. The tops of the trees swayed in the strong northwest wind, and a low rumble of thunder rolled in. Palace Guard frowned and pointed to the doorway as Larry hurried out. "Betsy said there's a severe storm headed our way. She has our dinner in the dining room, unless you'd rather eat in your room."

"I'd be more comfortable eating at the table, and I don't have any B&B customers in my database."

Larry shook his head and held the door open for me. When we entered the dining room, Betsy was bringing in sacks on a rolling utility cart. "Pick out a table. I'll bring you your dinner."

"Here?" I pointed to the table nearest to the door and next to the wall.

"Perfect. Did you know you think like a cop?" He held my chair for me then set my crutches against the spare chair next to me before he sat. He handed me my beer, and we clinked bottles.

"Ready to Thai one on?" Betsy chuckled as brought our food to the table. "Chicken or tofu?"

"Tofu," I said.

"Then chicken for you, Larry." Betsy set our dinners in front of us. When I opened my sack, I inhaled the mingled aromas of Thai sauce, cilantro, and spicy red peppers.

"And here's your Tom Yum soup." Betsy set two smaller sacks on our table. "Enjoy."

We dug in as three more couples came into the dining room at the same time and hurried to the tables across the room. The first two couples sat at the two tables next to the windows, and the third couple hesitated then sat at the last table left on the perimeter. Another couple opened the door and scanned the room. They held an animated, whispered conversation, then left.

"No one wants to sit in the middle of the room. Is that common behavior in a restaurant?" Larry asked.

"I don't know. Maybe that's why diners have booths, and restaurants have a host. Maybe Betsy needs a counter or a bar and stools."

While we ate, wind whistled through the drafty old home and sheets of rain pounded the windows. One of the couples next to a window moved to the center of the room. The other couple left the dining room with their food in-hand.

"You okay?" Larry peered at me.

"Wonder what's for dessert?"

Betsy set a covered tray on the table near the iced tea then came to our table. "I'll bring dessert after both of you have finished. No rush. I see you've eaten your usual, Maggie. I won't save it for you this time, though. It's not the same heated."

She spoke to her other guests then left the dining room.

"What time do you leave in the morning?" I asked.

"I'm supposed to be there at eight. I plan to be there by seven-thirty. What do you have planned to do in the morning?"

"I'll call Glenn and pester him then I'll call Mother and ask about a real estate agent in Columbus. Can you think of anything else?"

"I need a truck, but I'm not exactly sure what I want. Let's research it this evening. Here comes dessert."

Betsy set our desserts on the table. "Key lime pie. It will cool your mouths after the hot peppers. Let me know what you think. It's a new recipe."

I closed my eyes and enjoyed the creaminess of the tangy pie in my mouth. "Mmm. If you love this, Larry, I'll pester Betsy for the recipe."

"You could bake this?" He pointed with his fork before he ate his next bite.

"Of course. I'm a cook and a librarian. I can whip up any recipe I can read."

He chuckled. "And I'm a cop and a scientist, and I'll eat whatever you put on the table. You're an exceptional cook."

After we finished eating, Larry squinted at the windows. "Rain's slowing down. Ready to research trucks?"

When we got to my room, I propped up my foot while Larry handed me my computer. "Do you think it would be okay if we unwrap my foot for the evening?"

"Sure." Larry removed the bandage and inspected my ankle. "Swelling's gone. We can leave it off and see how it is in the morning."

Larry sat on the arm of my chair and commented on the trucks we found online. After an hour, he rose and stretched. "Thanks, Maggie. I've got a better idea of what I want. Last year's model would be ideal."

He knelt next to me and pointed at my computer screen. "All the trucks have a five-year warranty."

"That's pretty much the minimum now, isn't it? At least for trucks."

He gazed at me. "They all offer an extended warranty too."

I scrolled and nodded then stopped scrolling and met his gaze. "Is that important?"

"I've had my car for seven years," he said.

I cocked my head and smiled. "A lot of people never keep a truck or car over two years."

He shook his head. "Isn't that the truth. Not my style."

I think I'm lost. What are we talking about exactly?

He hugged me. "Good talk."

When he shifted to rise, I wrapped my arms around him. "So, did you decide what you want?"

He gave me an extra squeeze then nuzzled my hair. "Sure did."

"Are you going to tell me, or is it a secret?"

"Not much of a secret. Where do you see yourself in five years?"

"With you." My eyes widened. "Never thought about that before."

"I think about it all the time. That's where I want to be. With you."

"A warranty?"

"We'll want the extended warranty." He brushed back my hair and caressed my cheek then gave me a light kiss.

Still lost. I waited.

He sat back on his heels and grinned. "I love how literal you are."

I furrowed my brow and went back over the conversation. "Extended warranty."

"Maggie Crazy Lady Sloan, our extended warranty is to be married."

I gazed at his intense blue eyes. *Cute and sensible.* "You're right. We belong together."

Larry lifted me off the chair in a hug. I wrapped my arms around his neck; when he gazed at me, I smiled then kissed him with my full heart. When I snuggled his neck, he chuckled. "Excellent cook, outstanding shot, remarkable knife skills, brilliant, beautiful, and a good kisser. We were made for each other."

He set me back down on my chair and sat on the footstool as we held hands. "Georgia has no waiting period for a marriage license or to be married, but it's better to have an appointment for the marriage license. Monday would be good. You don't see any reason to wait, do you?"

"Does having a sudden case of the nerves count? Because that's what I think I have."

He kissed my fingers. "So do I, so that's okay."

"You do? Good. I'll call for an appointment on Monday."

"Let me know when you get cold feet. I'll let you be first then I'll have my turn." He smiled, and I giggled as we snuggled.

"I don't have an engagement ring." His voice was muffled by my hair.

"I don't want one. Do you?"

He laughed. "No, but we can shop for wedding rings next week."

I yawned. "We have a million things to do before we leave for Midland."

"Yes, we do, sweetheart, but you need your rest, and I'll pretend to sleep too."

He went into the bathroom and closed the door. I listened to the shower and dozed. When he turned off the water, I waited a few minutes then showered. I closed my bathroom door and climbed into bed.

The bathroom door opened, and Larry came into my room with his pillow under his arm and a blanket over his shoulder. "Thought I'd save time. I need to be close. Good night." He leaned over and pecked my cheek then lay down on the floor.

I feel safe.

A little after six, I opened my eyes, but Larry was gone. I grabbed his pillow off the floor and inhaled to soak up his man-smell. Larry whistled in the bathroom.

I feel like whistling too. I reached for my crutches and went to my closet to pick out my clothes to wear for the day. After I dressed, I called Mother.

"Margaret, I've been waiting to hear from you. I almost called you earlier. How are you? How is Larry? I can't wait to see you tomorrow. Anything new?"

"Mother, Larry and I are going to be married."

"You are? We, I mean, I think that's wonderful. What can I do for you? How can I help?"

"Do you know any real estate or property agents in Columbus that could help us find something on a month-to-month basis? We'll have Lucy. We're going to Columbus on Saturday, so it would be nice if we could meet with someone and at least talk about our options."

"I sure do. Let me check to be sure she'll be available on Saturday; otherwise, I can think of one other person. What else?"

"We need to get Larry a pickup truck. We'll be moving several times until we're settled, so it would be convenient if we have a truck to pull a small trailer. I'll have his car."

"Maybe look for one here on Monday or Tuesday? I can line that up. When are you planning to be married? Will you be married here?"

"We hope to pick up the marriage license on Monday. I'll schedule an appointment. After that, we'd like to be married before we go to Columbus."

"Call Jennifer. That's more in her department, but tell her I'll arrange whatever she likes. She can just call me. What else?"

"We'll need wedding rings. I thought you might have a recommendation."

"Let me know what time your license appointment is on Monday, and I'll schedule you with a meeting with your lawyer.

Her admin, Shantelle, is a jewelry expert, and if there are any legal things, Ms. Rodriquez can answer your questions and advise you. I'm so excited. I have to tell Big D."

Mother hung up.

"Bye, Mother." I rolled my eyes. *She already knew. Mr. Larry Kevin Ewing's in for it now.*

Larry tapped on the bathroom door then smiled as he strode to me. He helped me up from my chair and hugged me. "Good morning, sweetheart." He nuzzled my hair with his face then kissed my neck.

"I talked to Mother."

He stiffened. "Everything okay?"

"She was excited. She'll find a real estate agent who can meet with us on Saturday, and she'll arrange for us to look at trucks. Oh, and she'll schedule a meeting with my lawyer." I reached for my crutches.

Larry frowned as he handed me the crutches. "Why do we need to meet with a lawyer? Is it for a prenup? Why do you want a prenup? Do you think a prenup is necessary?"

I shrugged and headed to the door. "Let's get coffee. I've got brain fog."

Larry walked along with me. "You must have brain fog if you think we need a prenup. Do I need to get a lawyer too? What even made you think we'd need a prenup?"

I shrugged and poured two cups of coffee for him to carry to the patio then swung on my crutches to the door. Larry caught up with me. "Is carrying your coffee part of the prenup? I haven't wrapped your foot because you left too quickly. Will that go into the prenup too?"

Palace Guard was on the patio. His eyes widened then I winked at him. He turned his back on us. *On duty now?*

He nodded, and Larry continued his rant about the lawyer and a prenup while I sipped my coffee.

"Larry, honey." I interrupted him. "I have a question."

He stopped mid-sentence. "What?"

"Who said anything about a prenup?"

Palace Guard's shoulders shook.

"Well, you did."

I raised one eyebrow and peered at him. "No, I said Mother was going to schedule an appointment at my lawyer's office."

I sipped my coffee while Larry glared.

"You let me go on," he growled.

"You were on a roll. I'm too polite to interrupt you." I tossed my hair.

Larry stormed into the B&B. Palace Guard raised his eyebrows.

"Larry asked me to marry him last night, and I said yes. I called Mother this morning, but I'm sure she already knew. The lawyer's admin is a jewelry expert. She'll help us find wedding rings. I may have let him jump to his own conclusion. Was that mean?"

Palace Guard rolled his eyes then nodded his head.

"Good."

I stared at the bottom of my empty coffee cup. "I may have made a tactical error because now I don't have any coffee."

Betsy came outside and picked up my cup. "I don't ordinarily get in the middle of a family fight, but this one's too delicious to miss. I have a message from Larry. He said to tell *her* that breakfast was ready. I assume you are the dreaded *her* to whom I am to deliver this scathing remark." She laughed. "Come on, Maggie. I'll carry your cup. All I ask is don't break any of my dishes."

I hung my head as we went inside.

"You going for pitiful?" Betsy whispered.

"I was trying for contrite," I said in a quiet voice.

Betsy snorted. "I'll bring you your breakfast. Patio or dining room? Silly question. Patio."

I glanced at Larry and sighed, and he rolled his eyes. I stood by the door, and he picked up his cup and plate then pushed the door open and held it for me. Betsy brought my plate, cup, and a carafe and snickered as she left.

I sipped my coffee and cut my fried egg into small pieces with my fork. "How did Mother know?"

"Dang. So that's it. Did she tell you I called Sarge yesterday and talked to him?"

"You talked to Sarge about us getting married before you asked me?"

He set down his cup and glared. "Your interrogation techniques are on the level of cruel. You flash those beautiful green eyes and speak with your soft lilt, and I confess everything. What's next? A sweet smile and a peek at your ankle?"

I pushed the neck of my shirt toward my shoulder in a seductive reveal of skin and side-glanced at him with my best come-hither flutter of eyelashes. He laughed then I laughed until tears ran down my face. Palace Guard smacked his forehead, made a Spike gagging face, and turned away. We laughed harder.

After we settled down, Larry said, "I called my dad and talked to him because I wasn't sure what you'd say. I called for moral support. He listened then told me if I didn't know how you felt then I was blind. So then I called Sarge, and he laughed at me but didn't say a word. When I called Glenn, he told to be brave. He said he was afraid of you too, then he laughed and hung up."

I shook my head. "Good advice and sympathy are hard to find sometimes, aren't they? That whole truck warranty thing was brilliant. I didn't know what on earth you were talking about. I loved it."

"Really? Then it was all worth it. Except for the part that my mom, your mother, and Jennifer have already planned the wedding."

"That's not all bad. If they go overboard, I'll have the lawyer write them out of the will. Easy."

"Why are we seeing your lawyer?"

"Eat your breakfast. You'll want to leave soon. We're actually seeing the lawyer's assistant because she's a jewelry expert and can help us find rings. I'd forgotten I'd turned over all of Olivia's jewelry to her, and she sold most of it and kept a few of the better pieces."

Larry refilled his coffee, topped off mine, and finished his breakfast in four bites then kissed me on the cheek. "Bye, sweetie."

I sipped my coffee and called Jennifer.

"Hello, Maggie. Before you say anything, Glenn told me about Larry's call, and I'm absolutely thrilled for you. Larry is a wonderful man, and he's crazy about you."

"Thank you. He told me about his calls this morning under coercion, according to him. We're going to Athens this afternoon. I'll call Glenn and fill him in. Larry graduates tomorrow, and his folks, Sarge, and Mother will be here for graduation."

"I'll sit so I can record notes," Jennifer said. "It's okay if I fill in Ella, right?"

"Sure is."

I told Jennifer about Tennessee, our plans to go to Columbus on Saturday, pick up our marriage license on Monday, and get Larry a truck and our wedding rings on Monday or Tuesday.

"It's a tight schedule because Larry reports for his first day of work a week from this coming Monday."

"Aha. I know what I need to do. Arrange a small wedding and find a wedding dress that you'll wear. Wednesday would be ideal for the ceremony because you could pack on Thursday and leave for Columbus on Friday. That gives you the weekend to unpack at least the essentials, except you'll have everything unpacked, washed, and put away before Sunday." Jennifer chuckled.

"I think you're right about Wednesday. I hadn't put the pieces together. Mother said to tell you to call her with her assignments."

"I'll do that as soon as we hang up. I have some questions for you. First, do you want to have any input on the details? If you don't, no worries. We'll plan a lovely wedding. Second, I'm thinking we'll have a simple, small wedding. Parents, of course. I assume it's okay if we invite Ella and Moe. It would be nice if Kate could be here, but no guarantees. Is there anyone else you want us to invite? Can all the details: time, place, guests, and everything else I haven't thought of yet be ours to decide and handle?"

"That actually would be great. You have carte blanche. The only thing is not a big frilly dress."

"Never. You'd sneak and change into jeans and Larry's Texas Tech ball cap. Another thing for you to think about: when you do your paperwork for the license, you'll declare your married name. You and Larry might want to talk about that."

"Thanks, I didn't think about that. Anything else?"

"When you're in town next week, you're more than welcome to stay here with Lucy. And Larry too if he's already released his apartment."

"I don't know about Larry's apartment. I'll ask him and get back to you, and I would love to stay with you. I am so relieved to hand off the wedding plans. I wouldn't have known where to start. Thank you."

"We'll do our best. If you hate anything, tell us, and we'll call you Bridezilla." She laughed, and I joined her.

Chapter Fifteen

After we hung up, I called the county. Of course, I called the wrong office, but the assessor's clerk was nice and gave me the correct number to call with instructions to call her back if I had any problems. *I love the people at the county offices.* I called the number she gave me and reached the right person. We scheduled the appointment for Monday at ten, and she reminded me of the papers to bring and congratulated me on my upcoming wedding.

My wedding? I shook off the dread and texted Mother and Jennifer the appointment time then called Glenn.

"We're going to Athens today because I want to talk to Mrs. Hayden again. I think she was involved with the Gardner theft somehow, but I don't think she's responsible for the fires. It's hard to tell because she weaves her truth and lies together with the skill of an experienced artisan. Do you know the name of her grandson?"

"We have a tentative name. It was harder than it should have been. Somebody's worked to erase the ties. We think his name is Ross Walker. Paul hopes to have it confirmed later today. The owner of the warehouse is Arlo Siddall. Interestingly enough, there are rumors of a string of warehouse fires in his past. He's never been charged or investigated, but there's that lingering cloud of doubt. Paul's digging and talking to people. That's all we've got so far."

"It's a lot. I'll ask Mrs. Hayden what her grandson's name is. I can't remember if I asked you to see what you could find on Darren Martin. He's the art dealer in Columbus. I don't think he fits in anywhere, but there was just something...I don't know."

"Will do. Maggie, I wanted you to know how happy I am that you and Larry will be spending your lives together. You're a perfect match. We love you, Maggie, and always want the best for you. Larry is the best."

Tears rolled down my face as Glenn spoke. I cleared my throat. "It means a lot to me to hear that from you. Thank you, Glenn. I had thought you'd be my father-in-law, but instead, you're my real dad."

"Gotta go."

Glenn hung up, and I smiled. *He's a softie too.*

I texted Larry. "Marriage license 10 am Monday. The machine is in gear."

I sat back in my chair and sipped my cold coffee. "Jennifer and Mother are in charge of next week's details. I am so relieved. Now all we have to do is find a thief, an arsonist, and a killer."

Palace Guard smiled and held his hand low and close to me. I smacked it.

I closed my eyes and listened to the birds sing. "I have so many things to do that I can't pick out anything to focus on. Any suggestions?"

I squinted at Palace Guard as he smiled and rocked forward then back.

"Perfect. I think rocking on the front porch is what I need to unwind. Thanks."

As we headed to the front lobby, my phone buzzed a text.

Larry: "Two more hours. I may survive."

I showed my phone to Palace Guard, and he rolled his eyes. The front porch was shaded from the sun by the towering trees. While I rocked and Palace Guard and Daisy were sentries, Betsy joined me on the porch.

"I thought I'd follow your lead and relax myself. It's none of my business but catch me up, anyway."

I told her about the wedding and all the plans, and she smiled as she listened.

"I've heard a lot of angry stories. We're a bed-and-breakfast. It's supposed to be a nice place and a place to be nice. I have loved hosting you and Larry. You doused all those hateful words that lingered on this porch. Thank you. I think I'll have a sign made. No, my business would tank if I put up a sign that said, *Be nice or leave.*" She rose and chuckled as she went inside.

The sun had cleared the trees, and the hot rays chased me inside. I changed to a dress to wear to Athens. I strapped on my knife holster then pulled on my boot. I examined myself in the full-length mirror as I checked for any telltale signs of my knife.

I frowned. "If I wear a dress very often, I'll want a bra with a holster. I'm not crazy about not having my gun." I stuck my gun into my bra, but the imprint was too obvious.

I texted Jennifer. "Is a bra with a holster a thing?"

Jennifer: "I'm sure it is. I'll put Ella on it."

I rolled my eyes. *I need to be more careful about the questions I ask Jennifer for the next week. She's in action mode.*

I created a timeline checklist for the next ten days on my phone then stared at my list and sent a text to Mother. "I have a list of documents I need for Monday. Might need help."

Mother: "Larry needs them too? Send me the list. Will share with Lauren."

Why didn't I let Mother help me when I was growing up? She's a force.

I shook my head and sent the county list to Mother then turned my attention back to my checklist and realized I'd missed an important detail.

We can talk about my name today on the road to Athens. As I added *name change* to my checklist, Larry burst through the door.

"Hi, honey. I'm home." He chuckled as he rushed in. "You don't know how long I've been waiting to say that. All done until tomorrow's graduation. I need to wrap your foot. Anything else? I know a good place to pick up sandwiches on our way to Athens, and I've ordered dinner for the six of us..."

I rose and interrupted him with a big, sloppy kiss. "Wrap my foot, please. I'm excited too."

After Larry wrapped my ankle, I pulled myself up with my crutches. "Perfect. Thank you." I put my holstered pistol inside the sling purse. *I need that holster-bra too.*

When we reached the front porch, Larry said, "Wait here, honey. I'll drive around to pick you up."

After he parked in front of the B&B, he hurried to help me into the car. I glanced at the back seat, and Palace Guard smiled. "I'd glad you're going, Palace Guard because I'll need your insight into what Clara Hayden says and what she means."

A half hour down the road, I said, "I have something we need to talk over. Jennifer told me that part of the marriage license paperwork includes my legal name after we are married. I hadn't thought about that."

"It can be whatever you want, right? What do you want to do?"

"Talk it over with you."

Larry laughed. "You'll always be Maggie, my Crazy Lady to me, but let's not write that on the document for your legal name."

I snickered. "That's one down. It would be logical for me to be Maggie Ewing."

"I want you to be a Ewing," Larry said, "but you're Maggie Sloan."

"Maggie Sloan Ewing?"

"A lot of people hyphenate. What do you think about that?"

I glanced back at Palace Guard, and Larry peered at the rearview mirror. Palace Guard held his nose.

"I agree. Too pretentious or something."

"Maggie Sloan Ewing. You'll have options then. Maggie Sloan when you shoot somebody, and Maggie Ewing when you aren't busy shooting someone. How does that sound?"

"I kind of like it. Very convenient."

Palace Guard nodded.

"It's unanimous. That was easy."

I frowned. "Do you think Mother will be hurt if I'm legally Maggie, not Margaret?"

"I suspect she'll still call you Margaret no matter what you put on the paper."

"That's true." I leaned back and watched for cows. Palace Guard tapped me on the shoulder and pointed to his side of the road. *Cows.*

I narrowed my eyes and scanned the fields.

"Now I have a question for you," Larry said. "Are you okay with being married to Kevin Ewing?"

I thought about Kevin Ewing and Larry.

"I love you, Kevin Ewing."

He frowned. "What about Larry?"

"That's your maiden name. I love you, Kevin Larry Ewing."

Larry guffawed. "Dang, Maggie Sloan. You are brilliant."

"Do you remember what you said the first time we met?"

"Of course, I do. I said you were the funniest librarian I'd ever met."

"That's right. How did you remember that?"

"I cheated. Learned it from you." He wiggled his eyebrows.

I narrowed my eyes. "Jennifer told you."

"Nope. She told your mother, and your mother told Mom who told Dad, and he told me."

"It will always be like that, won't it?"

"Sure will. So, do you remember the first thing you said to me?"

I furrowed my brow in deep thought. "We could sit in the children's story room?"

"Nope. You said, *Officer Ewing, you are the cutest cop I've ever met. I'm going to marry you someday.*"

I raised my eyebrows. "What? I don't remember saying anything like that."

Larry shook his head. "Faulty memory. How are your teeth? They're the next to go."

I fumed. "You are absolutely..."

I glared, and Larry guffawed and held up his hand. When Palace Guard smacked a high-five, I scowled at Palace Guard and crossed my arms then turned to the window so they couldn't see my growing smile. *Game on, Larry.*

Larry whistled as he drove, and I pursed my lips tight to keep my rising laugh from escaping.

"You okay, Maggie?" There was no inkling of concern in his voice.

Stinker. Do I laugh or explode?

I couldn't hold it in any longer; I laughed, and so did Larry.

"I got you." He preened and puffed out his chest, and I rolled my eyes.

He slowed then pulled into a gas station that I assumed had closed years ago. There was no paint left on the side of the building, and the bare wood showed signs of termites and dry rot. The faded blue tarp on the roof was torn and flapped in the wind. The front windows had lost their seal and were cloudy. "Here's our sandwich shop. Turkey sandwich? They roast a turkey here every morning. They run out early, but we're here ahead of the lunch crowd."

My eyes widened. *Larry doesn't joke about good food.* "Sounds good."

It wasn't long before he came out of the no-name gas station with a sack and a drink holder with two large cups. He handed me the cups then climbed into the car. "There's a park a few miles down the road, or we can eat here."

"Let's go to the park. I wouldn't mind getting out of the car to stretch."

We pulled off the road to a wide spot that was within three feet of the shoulder. Two pecan trees shaded the lone wooden picnic table that was perpendicular to the road. The planks on the top of the table were warped, and the wood on the benches was split. The fence to the adjoining field was four feet away from the table, and cows ambled our way to be nosy, to share in our lunch, or both.

"Don't sit down yet," Larry said. "I have a blanket I can throw over the seat."

He threw the blanket onto the bench that faced away from the direction of our travel. Palace Guard sat across from us.

While Larry unpacked our lunch, I contemplated the cows. "If we find a place next to a cattle farm, the cows wouldn't run with us, but the calves might."

"Wouldn't that be ideal? Would you be tempted to wager that we'd go back to Columbus and sign a longer lease than a month to month?"

I sipped my tea. "That's a hard question. It would be tempting."

A fast-moving car appeared over the rise behind us, and Larry rose and stood next to Palace Guard. As the car zoomed past us, a young boy in the back seat pointed to the cows then the car was gone.

"You've eaten only half your sandwich," Larry said.

"You can have the other half or toss it. I'm full, and there are cookies in the sack that look homemade."

"What kind?" he asked after he finished off the half sandwich.

"Chocolate chip."

"Let's eat them on the road." Larry picked up our trash sack and carried our tea to the car then came back for the cookies and me.

After he pulled onto the road, I gave him a cookie and bit into mine.

"Mmm. Good. When will we be there?"

"Thirty to forty-five minutes: it depends on how heavy the traffic is when we get closer to town."

When we neared Clara Hayden's neighborhood, Larry asked, "Do I go in with you?"

"Yes. I don't trust her. With my cousin Larry and Palace Guard with me, I'll feel safe."

Larry laughed. "Did you know cousins can marry in Georgia?"

"Really? Did you make that up?"

He raised one eyebrow. "I don't make up things. That's your department."

I cocked my head. "When did you research that?"

"Oh, you know..." He pointed to the field ahead. "There's another field of cows with calves."

I let myself be distracted. *I'll get the details out of you later, cuz.*

Larry parked in front of the old house and helped me out of the car. I dawdled on my way to the porch while he scanned the area. Palace Guard strode around the house. When we reached the front door, I knocked, and the door swung open. Larry pointed to the door jamb and the signs of a forced entry. Larry pulled out his gun and entered. The foyer was in shambles. Chairs were broken, and all the art was gone. Larry entered first, and I followed.

We scanned the foyer then Palace Guard joined us. We stayed in the foyer while Palace Guard checked the parlor then he waved for us to come in. Larry followed me to the parlor.

"There you are, Maggie Flanagan. I've been waiting for you." Clara Hayden was perched at the edge of her settee with her hands palms up in her lap. She wore her navy-blue dress with the white lace collar, white pearls, and her high-top tennis shoes. Dust and damp dirt clung to her dress. Her palms were scraped, her left cheek was lacerated and oozing blood, and her left eye was swollen.

"Is this your young man? He can put his gun away. They're gone and so is all my art except the paintings that have value. They're in my basement."

"Larry is my cousin, Mrs. Hayden. Have you called for an ambulance? What happened?" I sat next to her, and Larry headed to the kitchen. Palace Guard stood where he could see the foyer, and I could see him.

"Some thugs broke in, and I decided to hide in my basement with my cat when I heard the front door crash in. I hurried down the steps but didn't want to turn on a light. I tripped over something about halfway down then stayed still on the basement floor. I was afraid they heard me fall, but they must have been too busy wrecking my house. They stole all my wall art. The only paintings I have of value, though, are in the basement because an elderly woman is a target for thefts."

Larry stood in the kitchen doorway and nodded his head toward the kitchen.

"When did this happen? Is it okay if my cousin checks the basement?"

"Of course. Tell him the light switch is on the left."

"Larry," I called out. "Would you check the basement? Light switch is on the left."

"Sure will," he called from the kitchen.

"They broke in around nine this morning. Don't robbers usually break in at night? I know who hired them. It was that Darren Martin. His mother wanted my art, and now he does. He even sent a document to the FBI and told them in some kind of code that there were stolen paintings at my house. He's the thief, not me."

I cocked my head. "How do you know that?"

"Somebody told me. Do you suppose you could get me a drink of water, Maggie Flanagan?"

"I'll be right back."

When I returned to the parlor, Palace Guard pointed to the small table drawer. I gave Mrs. Hayden the glass of cool water.

She sipped then set her glass on a coaster on the table. "The Irish Beauty and I could have been friends except for that Rebecca Herkes. I think she married that Martin boy because she hated her name, but we all still called her Rebecca Herkes. Rebecca Herkes said Margarite Flanagan's fairies told lies about me. I'm sure it was true. I never trusted the Irish, and we all knew Margarite told her fairies to spy on us, but I got a cat to keep the fairies away. Cat Two is my second cat. A friend of mine will come to get him later today. I'm afraid the robbers will come back and hurt him."

Her face tightened, and her eyes narrowed. "Do you have fairies too, Maggie Flanagan? I think your green eyes see more than you will say."

Palace Guard rolled his eyes.

Mrs. Hayden continued, "Margarite Flanagan stole paintings from me and said I stole them. I went to the sheriff, but he was under her spell. I got even with her, though. When she bought paintings, I contacted the seller and tripled the price. The sellers folded and told Flanagan that they'd been sold in a prior sale and refunded her money. I sold the paintings for twice what I'd paid. She thought she was so shrewd, but not as shrewd as I was, but then she had her fairies put a hex on me. My grandson cannot be trusted. It's all her fault. That's when I got Cat One."

"What's your grandson's name?" I asked.

"Thought I told you: Henry Crawford."

She crossed her arms. "I organized a group to finance a scheme for rare art. Rebecca Herkes, Vera Willis, and me. I didn't include Margarite Flanagan because I had shunned her for hexing me. I planned everything, and Vera hired the talent. Rebecca Herkes was worthless. Just like her son. After she arranged all the sales and collected the money, she tried to short me. Claimed she deserved an equal share."

She snapped her fingers. "Phfft."

"That Vera." Clara shook her head and gazed at the fireplace. "She was a firebug when she was a kid and never outgrew it. She'd set fires then she'd come get me to watch the burn with her and her boy, Arlo. Nobody enjoyed a good conflagration like those two."

Clara cleared her throat. "Of course, I never went. After she left town, the years of unexplained fires suddenly stopped." She chuckled. "Imagine that."

Larry appeared in the doorway. "Mrs. Hayden, there was a shovel on the fourth step down. There are five paintings in the basement."

"Oh, the shovel. I planted some summer bulbs in my backyard and thought I carried the shovel to the basement. I must have been distracted."

Palace Guard shook his head then pointed to the table drawer.

Larry strode into the parlor. "Mrs. Hayden, shall I bring the paintings up? The damp basement might not be the right place for them."

Clara rose from the settee. "I hadn't thought of that. Help me to the kitchen, then bring them up. I need to examine them."

Larry offered her his arm, and she clung to him as he helped her walk to the kitchen. She turned and winked at me when she reached the doorway.

That old stinker.

I listened to Larry's footsteps as he went down into the basement. After he came back up, he said, "Here's two. They're both about two feet square. One of them feels like a piece of wood, but I couldn't tell because they're all wrapped in what looks like bedsheets. Is this what I'm supposed to get?"

"Oh my," Mrs. Hayden said. "They feel damp. That's not good. I don't have anywhere else to store them. Bring the rest up, dear. One is a little smaller than these, and there are two that are wrapped in the sheets like blueprints."

I opened the table drawer and furrowed my brow at the small fabric-covered ring box. The roses on the dirty, frayed fabric had faded. When I opened the box, a tiny piece of paper fluttered to the floor, and my eyes widened as I stared at the ring. The heirloom emerald set in the gold Celtic knot sparkled in the light of the sunrays from the window. I slipped on the ring and the soft round edges hugged my finger. I removed the ring and looked inside the band. It was stamped with 14K and had a tiny inscription, *BH & MF.*

Wow.

Palace Guard nodded.

I placed the ring and the note back into the box, returned the box to the drawer, and eased the drawer closed then strode into the kitchen. "I suppose the soft cotton protects the surfaces. Do you have somewhere safe you can keep them besides in the basement?"

She frowned. "No, I don't. If you have them for safekeeping, I can arrange for proper storage with the appropriate environmental conditions. I'm sure it won't be more than a week or so. Will you do this for me, Maggie Flanagan?"

"I don't know. I'm worried because you said they were valuable."

"I've never relied on anyone; I trust you." Her gaze was direct then she glanced to the left. "They are valuable reproductions. I want them safe from Darren Martin."

First time she's said anything that I believe then she lies.

Palace Guard nodded.

I met her gaze. "I can do that for you, Mrs. Hayden. Do you have anywhere that you can go where you'll feel safe?"

She snorted. "I'm safe here. There's nothing left to steal. I have my handyman coming to fix the door this afternoon, and my lawyer will be here to review my will. Now that your cousin has moved my shovel, I always have my basement." She cocked her head. "Is Larry your cousin on your mother's side?"

I smiled. "No, he isn't."

She nodded. "That's good; I didn't think so. You're an only child, right?"

"Yes. Mother told her friends I was enough of a handful."

Where is she going with this?

"I think I would like your mother." She held out her hand. "Help me up, Maggie Flanagan. Let's wait in the parlor while your Larry carries the rest of the art upstairs and to your car."

After I helped her up, I left my right crutch against the table and offered my arm. Her light touch was a bird that was ready for flight, and I smiled. *She's fine to walk without any support. Once a faker...*

I helped her to the settee then returned to the kitchen for my crutch. On my way back to the parlor, I heard the table drawer close.

Checking on me, Mrs. Hayden? Thought you trusted me.

"Is my table drawer too small for a gun?" she asked.

"I'm not too familiar with guns. We can ask my cousin because he hunts turkeys in the fall, but I suspect he wouldn't approve of having a gun without knowing how to use it."

"You're probably right. The noise alone would give me a heart attack. My old ticker hiccups enough without any extra help." She cackled, and I smiled.

Larry returned to the parlor. "All loaded up."

"Are you sure you're going to be okay by yourself?" I asked. "Maybe your lawyer will have a suggestion of the best place for you."

"Thank you, Maggie Flanagan. If I need you again, I'll send your fairies with a message." She tittered then pretended to struggle to rise.

"You just relax, Clara Hayden. We'll see ourselves out. Let me know when you're ready to put your art in proper storage."

After we were in the car, Larry said, "She's a trip. I would have called her basement a root cellar. Even the door was narrow and only five feet high. Did you notice? It was tight getting up and down the stairs. I can see why she'd fall if she didn't have the lights on. Everything in that house sent my detective radar off the charts, but at least you got her grandson's name."

I snorted. "You heard that? I don't know why, but she lied about his name. Do you know who Henry Crawford is? He's the villain in *Mansfield Park* by Jane Austin."

Larry stopped the car at the intersection and turned to stare at me. "You have got to be kidding. Except I know you aren't."

After his right turn, he smirked. "You need to wear a warning sign. *Caution. Librarian on Duty.*"

"Why do you suppose she sent me out the door with her art? Will she call the sheriff and have me arrested?"

"Didn't think of that. Are you worried?"

"About going to jail? Yes. I have plans next Wednesday that don't include being incarcerated."

"Yes, you do. Six days," Larry said. "And just when I thought I was over counting the days."

"We could have done something dumb like planning the wedding to be after you finished your training in Tennessee, except neither one of us would last if we had a marriage license in hand."

Larry grinned. "Now that you mention it, what are you doing Tuesday?"

"I have no plans, except Jennifer, my mother, your mother, and Ella would have broken hearts if we skipped the simple ceremony they planned. Can you imagine what the wedding would be like if we gave them even an extra week?"

Larry laughed. "No messing with the Mom Force."

I smiled. "It's so nice to hear a true statement to clear out the pit of lies from Clara Hayden."

"Do you think she'll stay in her house alone?"

"She may already have had plans to go somewhere else. No telling."

"What do we do about the paintings?"

"I'd like to carry them to my room and unwrap them. I have no art training at all, but I'd feel better if we at least look at them."

"I agree. I'm not comfortable about the idea of potentially hauling around stolen goods."

"I need to send Glenn more names to research." I picked up my phone and texted.

"Rebecca Herkes, Darren Martin's mother; Vera Willis, probably arsonist. Both at one time residents of Athens."

Glenn: "On it."

Larry checked the time. "The parents will be at the B&B later this afternoon. We have time to look at the paintings and relax before we're inundated with smiling faces."

"I have a smiling face, and so do you." I leaned back and closed my eyes.

The tires crunched on the gravel driveway as Larry turned at the B&B, and I opened my eyes then yawned.

"Your face is so peaceful when you sleep. I almost believed that you really aren't hatching your next plan." Larry rubbed my shoulder.

I snickered. "There you go. Sweet-talking again."

Larry chuckled. "Whatever works."

I glanced at Palace Guard, who rolled his eyes.

When Larry stopped at the B&B entrance to let me out, I exhaled. "Good. They aren't here yet. After we look at the paintings, I need time to get out of these sissy clothes and relax on the porch or the patio with you."

After Larry helped me out and closed my door, I added, "And maybe read a book and have a beer."

Larry snorted. "I'll grab the luggage cart."

When he rolled the cart to the door he asked, "If I load the paintings, can you push it to your room?"

"Easy. Good idea."

He loaded the cart then left to park, and I placed my crutches on the cart next to the paintings and pushed.

CHAPTER SIXTEEN

I rolled the cart into my room and unloaded the paintings onto my bed. After I moved the cart to the hallway, I sliced the tape on the smallest painting and unwrapped the sheet then stared at the man dressed in black. He wore a tall, black hat and sat at a table as he glared at the artist who had interrupted him while he was writing an important letter. *Manet.* I pulled up the photos of the paintings stolen from the Isabella Stewart Gardner Museum in 1990. *Chez Tortoni by Manet.*

My hand shook as I sliced the tape on the bedsheet that wrapped the piece of wood. I inhaled then exhaled slowly to calm myself and unfolded the sheet. I gazed at the obelisk and dropped onto the bed as Larry came into my room.

"Maggie, are you okay?" He rushed to my side.

"No. I'm not." I picked up my phone and scrolled to the *Landscape with Obelisk* and handed my phone to Larry. He frowned at the screen then stared at the paintings. He scrolled to *Chez Tortoni.* "Reproductions or originals?"

"I don't know. Let's unwrap the rest then I'll text Kate. I'm afraid I know which one this next one is." I sliced the tape then Larry unwrapped it.

"Is it *The Concert*?" I asked while I scrolled my phone.

I gaped at the painting as I handed my phone to Larry, and his eyes widened as he stared at the screen.

"I'm texting Kate right now. The rolled paintings must be the two Rembrandts that were cut out of their frames. They're huge."

I hobbled to my chair and sent Kate a text. "Call. Urgent."

My phone rang.

"Go," Kate said.

"I have either reproductions or the originals of five of the paintings that were stolen from the Gardner Museum in 1990."

"You've got my attention. Tell."

"Clara Hayden, a woman in Athens, gave me five pieces of art wrapped in sheets. She had hidden them in her basement. After her home was broken into this morning, she asked me to keep them for her because they were damp from being stored in her basement. We're at the Bed and Breakfast outside of Macon. We just unwrapped them. They are either excellent reproductions or the originals. We've looked at three: *Chez Tortoni*, *Landscape with Obelisk*, and *The Concert*. The other two are not framed but are rolled in bedsheets like banners would be."

"Unroll them. *The Concert*? You know what the original is worth?" Kate asked.

"Yes. Two hundred million dollars if the internet is accurate. Give me a minute."

Larry whistled a long, low whistle, and we unrolled with care. When we had unfurled the half of one, I gasped. "Kate, we partially unwrapped the smaller of the two. *It's A Lady and a Gentleman in Black*."

Kate exhaled. "Rembrandt. Be careful as you roll it back up. Unroll the other one. Real easy."

I know what's there. We unrolled with care.

"Kate, it's *Christ in the Storm on the Sea of Galilee*." My voice cracked. "Kate?"

"You're at the Bed and Breakfast outside of Macon? Put me on speakerphone. I want Larry to hear too."

I put the phone on speakerphone even though Larry's face was pressed against mine. "Okay," I said, "speakerphone."

"Good. An agent will be there first thing in the morning to pick them up unless I can find someone available this evening. I'll text you his photo and contact the training center to have someone that Larry knows be there to verify the identity of the agent. Don't release the art to anyone without someone there that Larry knows. Lord, girl. I need a couple of days off for you and Larry to tell me the full story. If I try to commandeer you at the wedding, Mom will ban me from the house."

After we hung up, I asked, "What do we do now? We have the folks coming."

"I'll ask Palace Guard to stay with the paintings while we're hosting the parents."

I exhaled. "That will work. Let's put the paintings in your room and close the bathroom doors. It's not perfect, but while the thugs tear my room apart, Palace Guard will have time to let us know before they snatch the art."

"I'll move the art first, then while you change, I'll talk to Palace Guard. He can stay in my room, and we'll have yours. I'm in here all the time, anyway." He grinned then carried the art to his room and closed the bathroom door.

I stared at the shirts in the closet. *Why did Jennifer buy me this orange shirt?* I put on the shirt then swung on my crutches into my room near the window, and my eyes widened. *It's fiery orange. I'll see what Larry says.* I tucked in my shirt and tapped on the bathroom door. When it flew open, I almost fell.

Larry's face reddened. "I wanted to be sure I heard you."

"I'm ready to relax on the porch." When I headed to my door, he rushed past me and blocked my way. I dropped my crutches, wrapped my arms around his neck, and pulled him close then kissed him lightly. He squeezed me and returned my kiss with a passion that promised a lifetime of being together.

When he broke away, he smiled as he picked up my crutches then caressed my neck and face.

I'm going to melt.

"Is that a new shirt?" He massaged my upper back. "Did you know your shirt shoots sparks of fire in the sunlight? It reminds me of your fiery spirit and is a perfect match for the red streaks in your hair."

He nuzzled my neck. "Mmm. Soft." His eyes twinkled. "And so is the shirt."

A win for Jennifer.

He handed me my crutches, and I frowned as I tucked them under my arms. "Even if I'm still on crutches on Wednesday, I want to marry you on my own two feet."

"More terms for the prenup?" He kissed my open mouth then reached for the door before I could retaliate. "I'll see you in a few minutes."

After I sat in my rocker, Daisy flopped next to me for a face rub then Betsy came out with a glass of tea. "I was watching for you. I almost feel like I'm part of the wedding planners. Can I pretend this is your rehearsal dinner or would that scare you? Do we want to set up outside on the patio or inside the dining room for the dinner this evening? I suggest outside. There's no rain in the forecast, and our light breeze will keep the bugs away."

"Rehearsal dinner would scare me. Is there such a thing as a pre-graduation dinner? That was the original plan. If we're outside, our two sets of RV campers will think we're roughing it."

Betsy chuckled. "Good point on both counts. I'll set up the round table."

I rocked as I waited and drank half my tea before Larry came to the door. "Let's move to the patio," I said. "All the shade's gone, and it's hot in the sun."

Larry carried my glass as we headed to the patio. We discovered Betsy had set up an oversized round table with six chairs.

Larry asked, "Do you want your tea refreshed? All your ice has melted."

"They're on the patio," Betsy said, and my heart rate jumped. *What am I so nervous about?*

"No, I think beer will be in order before long."

Mother and Sarge burst through the door from the foyer. Mother carried Franklin in his carrier.

Sarge scanned the patio. "Sure am glad you're out here. It's nice to be outdoors after all our time on the road. We drove around an extra half-hour, so we wouldn't get here too early. Izzy wanted to cruise the parking lot." Sarge bellowed his hearty laugh, and we laughed with him.

Mother swatted at him. "I did not. You said we could cruise the parking lot. I forgot how small it was."

Sarge grabbed me into a hug, and Larry hugged Mother. Sarge and Larry did the man-hug thing, and Mother patted my shoulder. *What the heck. I'm a hugger.* After I hugged her, she burst into tears. I stared at her then stepped back.

Sarge asked, "Are you okay, Izzy?"

She sniffled. "Margaret never wanted to be hugged when she was little. I thought her skin was sensitive or something. She's all better. It's wonderful to see her healed."

Larry and Palace Guard raised their eyebrows then Larry hugged me and whispered, "I'm a hugger healer."

I rolled my eyes.

"This is beautiful back here, isn't it? Just like being in the woods." Mother sat next to me. "Margaret, I love your blouse. It's a beautiful fiery color that reminds me of a sunset on the beach. Before I forget, your appointment with Shantelle at the lawyer's office is at one o'clock on Monday."

Sarge scooted his chair close to hers and draped his arm around her shoulder.

I smiled. "Thank you, Mother. I'm glad you're here. How was your visit?"

Mother told us about the friend's farm and the chickens and pigs. "Baby pigs are cute. I never knew that. Big D and I might think about a small farm if we get tired of traveling."

"That's right," Sarge said. "One thing we learned is that we have to do all our traveling before we have animals."

Mother peeked into Franklin's carrier. "Still sleeping. Nothing disturbs him. I left all of your paperwork with Jennifer, Margaret. Thank you for letting me help."

Sean and Lauren came through the door, and Betsy followed them. After a round of hugs, Betsy said, "The bar is open in the dining room, and we have hors d'oeuvres next to the drink table."

"Beer?" Larry asked as he rose.

"I want wine, but I'll pick my own," Lauren said.

"So will I." Lauren and Mother strolled to the door arm in arm. Larry and Sarge went in together.

"Maggie, Lauren and I have always been proud of Kevin, your Larry, but I am surprised he had sense enough to find a brilliant, beautiful woman to marry."

I snickered, and Sean laughed. "Just wanted you to know that's the end of my flowery speech."

Larry returned with three beers and narrowed his eyes. "What stories did you tell, Dad?"

"No stories yet. Thanks for the beer, son. Cheers."

We clinked bottles.

I sipped my beer. "My favorite."

"Mine too." Larry winked.

Sarge, Mother, and Lauren returned with enormous platters of hors d'oeuvres and six small plates, and Sean began his first story.

Betsy interrupted in the middle of the third story. "Your food is here. Special treat, Larry and Maggie. Tacos."

She set a large bowl of tortilla chips in the middle of the table then Lauren helped her open the sacks and serve the plates.

Sean told stories about Kevin, and Mother told Margaret stories about being startled every time I'd appear from behind furniture or in a cabinet.

"You can't imagine what it's like to open a cabinet where the pots are and find a tiny girl inside the cabinet. I became cautious and peered around corners and opened cabinets with care because I had a child that popped up out of nowhere."

We had more rounds of embarrassing Kevin stories interspersed with equally embarrassing Margaret stories during dinner. Finally, Sarge said, "We need to set up at the campground before it's much later. Great evening."

Mother picked up Franklin who was still sleeping. "See you tomorrow."

Sarge whisked Mother away before she lingered with more stories.

"Let's go, Sean. I'm tired too." Lauren hugged Larry and me. "We'll see you at graduation. Have a good evening."

After they left, the patio was quiet.

"Happy?" Larry asked.

I exhaled. "Yes."

"Good. Mom gave me all my paperwork I'd need for the marriage license, and I put it in my backpack. So, let's talk about Clara Hayden. I need to know what she said while I was getting the paintings in that creepy basement."

"The truth is quicker to tell. Thugs did break in, and she fell on her way to hide in the basement. Sifting through the lies, Darren Martin may have sent the brochure and map through the real courier that mailed it to Kate at the Coyles' office, but Clara said Darren Martin sent a document to the FBI by a courier, which points to Christopher Arrington. Clara must have had a hand in that too. She's seeing her lawyer today. That is probably true. All the rest I gleaned from parts of conversations. You ready to hear more?"

"I'm game."

"I'm sure she either lied about the art being reproductions or lied about it being valuable. I still don't know. I understand reproductions are hard to identify. While the two of you were in the kitchen, Palace Guard told me to check the table drawer. I know what she dug up. It was a ring box with a ring inside: a beautiful emerald stone set on a Celtic knot. The inscription inside the ring was BH plus MF. I put the box back after I looked at it, and she double-checked the drawer after she returned. So much for I'm the only one she trusts."

"Wow. That's a shocker. You think she had it buried all these years? Wonder why she dug it up?"

"I have no idea, but it was not on a whim. She's too conniving. I believe she was the brains behind the Gardner theft, but of course, I have no proof. Sifting through her lies, I think Vera Willis hired the thieves. Vera was a firebug and shared her fascination with her son. Rebecca Herkes sold the art and either tried to gyp Clara or wanted her fair share. I don't know if the paintings she had in the basement are copies or originals, but if they are originals, we have proof, but I don't know of what."

"Are you going to be able to sleep tonight with all that whirling around your head?"

I snorted. "I have much more important things to keep me awake, like a wedding."

Larry lifted my chin and kissed me. "After hearing all those stories tonight, I sure am glad we're not like that Kevin kid or that Margaret girl." He smirked, and I snickered.

"No kidding." I stifled a yawn, but Larry caught me and smiled.

"Let's go to our rooms, Maggie Flanagan Sloan almost Ewing."

I moaned as I rose. "It was a long day. Tomorrow's your graduation day. I'm excited about that too."

"And one day closer to our wedding day."

When we went into my room, I flopped down on my chair. "I thought of one more thing I forgot to tell you. Margarite Flanagan had fairies, according to Clara. The fairies saw what other people did, and no one else saw them except Margarite. Clara was convinced that Margarite told her fairies to hex Clara, and it worked because her grandson cannot be trusted, but it isn't his fault. It's Margarite's. Mother told me stories about Margarite's fairies too."

"Wow. What did Palace Guard think?"

"He rolled his eyes."

Larry knelt at my feet. "I'll remove your bandage then you can go to sleep with dreams of fairies."

After he unwrapped my foot, he said, "You can shower first. I need to organize my clothes for tomorrow. I'll be in later with my pillow and my blanket."

He hugged me then left for his room. I gathered my sleeping stuff and showered then hobbled to my bed and fell in. When he came into my room with his pillow and blanket, he kissed my forehead.

At one in the morning, I heard the buzz of a text, and Larry fumbled for his phone that was next to him on the floor.

He peered at his phone then me. "You're awake. Good. My chief trainer will be here in thirty minutes, and the FBI will be here by two. You want to get up?"

"Yes." I slipped out of bed and hobbled to the bathroom. "My hair is scary before I brush it."

Larry came into the bathroom while I brushed my hair. "I'm going to throw on some jeans." He closed the door behind him as he went into the other bedroom. I hurried to dress too.

When he returned, he said, "I told Palace Guard what was going on. I'm going to the dining room for coffee. Want to go along?" He handed me my crutches.

"Subtle." I sniffed, and he wiggled his eyebrows.

Betsy sat at a table in the dining room, and Daisy was under the table asleep. Betsy placed her book facedown to keep her place. "Everything okay?"

"One of my trainers and another man will be here in about a half hour or so to pick up some items from us. I'm sorry for the inconvenience. We didn't have any control over their timing."

Betsy waved her hand. "Don't worry about it. As long as they aren't here about my still, I'm fine."

She laughed. "My partner says one of these days I'm going to joke about a still, and they'll find hers."

She snort-laughed. I giggled, and Larry smiled.

"Coffee's fresh," Betsy said.

"I got it," Larry said. "What about you, Betsy? Need a refill?"

"I just poured my second cup. I had fallen asleep, but I dreamed about this book I'm reading and had to get up to see what really happened in the book. You know how convoluted dreams can get."

"Is it okay if we wait in the foyer?" Larry asked.

"That's fine." Betsy opened her book and disappeared into the story.

After twenty minutes, Betsy padded to the foyer, and Daisy trailed after her. "You're in charge. I got past the part in the book that worried me. See you in the morning."

We finished our coffee, and Larry returned our cups to the dining room then rolled the luggage cart to his room. Five minutes after he joined me in the foyer, a car pulled up in front of the B&B.

"It's Lieutenant Baker. I wasn't expecting him." Larry stood at the door and waited until the Lieutenant approached the door.

My phone buzzed a text.

Kate: "Sorry to be slow. Several changes. Here's the photo. Lt. Baker knows her." I smiled. The photo was of a woman with a thin face, oversized glasses, and a large Western hat. Her gray hair was pulled back and her porcelain skin was wrinkled, but her severe look was softened by the dimples in her cheeks.

I showed the photo to Larry and handed him my phone, and he opened the door. The two men shook hands.

"This is Maggie Sloan. Our wedding is on Wednesday." Larry beamed, and I felt my face warm.

"Nice to meet you, Ms. Sloan, soon to be Mrs. Ewing. My best wishes to you both."

"This is the photo Maggie received from Kate Coyle."

Lieutenant Baker nodded. "I'd heard there was a last-minute change because Della was closer."

A ten-year-old white truck with a topper on the pickup bed pulled up and parked with the driver's side at the curb. A tall, thin woman opened the driver's door and scanned the area then stepped out. She wore brown leather work boots and jeans and the same Western hat as her photo.

Lieutenant Baker grinned and hurried to the door. "About time you got here, Della."

"Hush yourself. Where's my treasures? Who are these lovely people?" She narrowed her eyes. "They look too wholesome to me. Must be the dastardly thieves." She cackled and strode to us with her hand outstretched. "I'm Della."

Larry held out his hand. "I'm Kevin, and this is Maggie."

Della shook his hand and turned to me. I held out my hand, and she grabbed it. "Maggie? No, this is the Gray Lady. Didn't recognize you right off, but that's how you operate, isn't it? It's an honor to shake your hand. Everyone knows you are brilliant, but nobody mentioned how gorgeous you are, Maggie Sloan."

My eyes widened, and my face warmed.

Della smiled. "Sorry. You must get that all the time, but I'm one of your biggest fans. You're a legend, so where's this alleged purloined loot?"

Lieutenant Baker stared at me, and Larry rubbed his face to hide his smirk.

"It's in my room." Larry strode to his room then rolled out the luggage cart.

Larry and the lieutenant loaded the art into the back of the truck under Della's close supervision. When she was satisfied, she closed the topper and hurried to the porch where I waited. She hugged me and gave me a card. "This is my cell. Put me under Grandma D. in your contacts. Burn the card. You can call or text me anytime. I love a good fight."

When she drove away, Lieutenant Baker cleared his throat. "I'll see you at graduation." He stared at me. "The actual Gray Lady." He shook his head and hurried to his car.

"Think you can sleep tonight, Gray Lady?" Larry asked as we went inside the B&B. After we were in my room, he said, "I'll give you a chance to change. I'll be back in a few minutes, sweetie."

After the bathroom door closed, I changed and hopped into bed.

Larry returned and lay down on the floor next to me. He whispered, "Are you glad the art is gone?"

"Yes." I relaxed.

I woke before daylight and listened to Larry breathe. I rolled over so I would be closer to him. *Five more days.*

I closed my eyes and listened to his even, relaxed breaths then timed my breaths to his.

"Maggie?"

I opened my eyes, and the daylight surprised me, but Larry's face two inches from mine surprised me more.

I blinked. "Hi. How long have you been there?"

"Not long. I enjoy looking at you." He kissed my nose. "Cute nose. Five days. I already showered. I'll go for coffee."

"What time is it?"

"You don't want to know." He chuckled as he left.

I glanced at the clock. *Six.* After I showered and dressed, I was drying my hair when Larry came into my room from the hallway.

"I knocked on the door. I thought you might still be in the shower when you didn't answer. Here's your coffee."

"Hair dryer's noisy. I usually just run out the door and run to let it dry."

"I know." He grinned. "Have some coffee. Graduation is at one, and I need to be there about noon. I don't expect it to last more than an hour. Mom sent me a text while I was getting the coffee. They would like to invite your folks and us to lunch after graduation. Ready for more stories?"

I leaned on my crutches at the window and sipped my coffee as I peered at the gathering clouds in the sky. "We may get rain this afternoon."

"The ceremony is indoors, so we'll be okay for the graduation." Larry yawned. "I'll be ready for a nap this afternoon. I'll wrap your foot before we leave. Ready for breakfast?"

He handed me my crutches, and we headed to the dining room to find more coffee.

Betsy came inside from the patio. "My partner set up a new birdfeeder on the patio. The birds haven't found it yet. Maybe they're waiting for me to quit hovering. You'll want to have breakfast on the patio, right? I'll bring it out if you want to grab the coffee, Larry."

When I stepped outside, I breathed in the cool air then sat at the farthest patio table from the trees that dripped their overnight moisture. A bright-red cardinal perched on the top of the birdfeeder while his less colorful mate picked through the seeds. My phone rang as Larry carried out our coffee. I raised my eyebrows. "It's Glenn."

When I answered, Glenn said, "Hope it's not too early for you. Larry there? You might want to put me on speakerphone."

"Done. It's not too early. We're outside with our coffee."

"Good. I wanted to call you last night, but Jennifer said it was too late. The state fire marshal visited me. He's an old friend, so we spent a while catching up after we talked about fire business. I think we'd still be talking about old times if Jennifer hadn't thrown him out." Glenn chuckled. "Might be an exaggeration. Don't tell her I said that."

Glenn cleared his throat. "Back to the fire marshal's visit; his results aren't final, but he said the fires at the warehouse, my office, and your house were arson and not accidental or caused by electrical or other failures. However, the warehouse fire signature differs from the office and your house. He said arson fires are often set to hide criminal activities, typically insurance fraud, burglary, murder, or to destroy evidence, but it's not common to have two arsonists at work in a small town like ours. He thanked me for giving him the name of the warehouse owner. Arlo Siddall bought the building in Harperville under an alias. He has a history of unexplained warehouse fires. The fire marshal will get back to me with more about the office and house fires later. That's about it. Do you have any questions?"

Larry shook his head.

"No, we'll let you know if we think of anything," I said.

"Larry, Jennifer and I wanted to congratulate you on your graduation today. That's not an easy course to get into or to complete. We're proud of you."

Larry blushed. "Thank you, Glenn."

After we hung up, Larry asked, "Are you surprised about two arsonists?"

"Not really. It would have been easier if there were only one arsonist, but I couldn't fit the motives together. I'd be interested in hearing about the fire signatures for the office and my house."

Betsy carried out our breakfasts. "Chef made you a treat for your graduation day, Larry." She lifted off the cover and smiled. "Breakfast tacos. Enjoy."

"Thank you." Larry grinned. "This is great. I can't think of a better graduation present."

After Betsy left, we dug in. Larry finished his taco as Betsy set the carafe on our table.

She pointed to my plate then chuckled. "You waiting patiently for the half that Maggie is saving for you, Larry?"

"It's my best skill," he said.

I snickered. "Help yourself."

Larry slid the half onto his plate, and I refilled our coffee.

"Can we talk about motives?" I asked. "The motive for the office fire might have been to destroy the copy of the document, but Ken Brown, the guy who was supposed to be from the beauty shop, asked straight out if all three of us would be there. It's hard to say about the house fire unless whoever ordered the fire thought I had the evidence they needed to destroy or knew my car was wrecked and planned for me to be at home asleep."

"Call Glenn," Larry said. "The fire marshal needs to hear this. Glenn will explain the evidence is skimpy, but it still may help."

I called Glenn and told him my theories about motives.

"I'll call the fire marshal," Glenn said. "I'm glad Palace Guard and Larry are with you."

I heard the concern in his voice. "So am I."

After I hung up, I rose and held onto the chair. "I'm tired of sitting and tired of my crutches." I smiled as another pair of cardinals flew to the feeder. "We need a birdfeeder wherever we are."

Larry rose and stood behind me, and I leaned against him. He wrapped his arms around my ribcage.

"Where's your sports bra?" he asked.

I pushed away and glared as I faced him. "What? How do you know about my sports bra?"

He shrugged. "You know. That's what you always wear. I told you I like to look at you. I mean..."

He rubbed the top of my bra. "See? It's like lacy or something. Your sports bra isn't lacy, and it isn't just because I leer at you; I've done your laundry." He wiggled his eyebrows.

I giggled. "I'd forgotten about the laundry. Do you really leer?"

"Of course. You're nice to leer at." He massaged the top of my bra and grinned. "I like lace." When he leaned down and kissed me with tenderness, I pressed my body against him and nibbled on his lip.

He sighed and released me, and I met his gaze. He squeezed me close to him and I clung to him with my arms around his waist.

"What are you and your lacy bra doing on Monday afternoon?" he asked.

"Should I call Jennifer?"

"Yes," he murmured then said, "Wait. What are you going to tell her, so it's my fault, not yours?"

I snorted. "I don't know, but it will be good."

"No doubt. Let's go for a walk." Larry handed me my crutches. "I don't want to wear you out, so let's walk around the parking lot. If we have time, we can relax on the front porch."

When we were halfway around the parking lot, my phone rang.

"It's Mother. I hope everything's okay."

CHAPTER SEVENTEEN

After I turned down the phone volume, Larry pressed his face close to mine and listened as Mother spoke in her loud voice. "Margaret, Harriet called me. Did you know your lawyer hired her to manage Olivia's apartment? Something about the lease being automatically renewed or something. You can ask the lawyer about the details. Harriet said she's been renting it out for you, but it's vacant now. I talked to Jennifer, and we think that's the perfect place for you and Larry to stay before you leave for Columbus. What do you think?"

"I didn't even think of Olivia's apartment. That's a great idea. I'll talk to Larry and call you back."

Mother hung up.

"Bye, Mother."

"Did you hear? What do you think?" I asked.

"Olivia's apartment is still yours? We could drink beer on the balcony, write notes, and get a Maggie pizza just like old times. I was thinking maybe you and Lucy could stay at my place, but it's pretty sparse and doesn't have any yard for Lucy. This is perfect," he chuckled. "The Mom Force strikes again."

I called Mother back. "That is great, Mother. Thanks to you and Harriet for thinking of it."

"I'll call Harriet and Jennifer. Harriet will have someone clean it tomorrow. Big D said we're going straight to the training center for Larry's graduation, so we'll see you there."

She hung up.

"Bye, Mother," Larry said.

I grinned. "Were you trying to beat her or me?"

"I'll write you a note later. Let's go change. It's almost time to leave."

After I dressed, I peered at my face in the mirror. "My eyes are still discolored. Should I wear my sunglasses?"

Larry came into the bathroom and squeezed in between me and the mirror then lifted my face and kissed my eyes. "No. All better."

When we approached the front porch, Daisy rose from her spot and ambled to the top of the steps.

"Does she look irritated to you?" Larry asked.

"We haven't talked to her all morning. Could we spend a little time with her on the porch?"

Larry stooped next to her, and she rolled for her belly rub. After I sat on my rocker, she padded to me, and I scratched her ears and hugged her. When I rose, she ambled to the corner of the porch where Palace Guard stood.

"Thanks," Larry said, and Palace Guard saluted.

Larry hurried to his room, and I pulled on my teal dress Jennifer said was a wrap dress. I wrapped the fabric around me then tied it at my waist with a square knot. I glanced at the mirror. *Jennifer got me a dress that flashes cleavage? I need to change.*

Before I returned to the closet to find something else to wear, Larry opened the bathroom door. My eyes widened at his dark charcoal suit, crisp white shirt, and teal tie. *You are one sexy man, Kevin Larry Ewing.*

"You look gorgeous, Larry," I said.

He stared at me.

I waved my hand. "Don't worry; I know I need to change."

"Why?" he asked. "I have loved you since forever, and every day you remind me why we belong together."

He strode across the room and put his hands on my shoulders and gazed at me. "Five days." He kissed me then smiled. "I'll wrap your foot then we can go."

I sat on my soft chair while Larry wrapped my foot.

"Are you and your lacy bra ready to leave?"

I giggled then fluttered my eyelashes. "Love your teal tie. I can't wait to get it off you."

"How do you do that?" he asked as he opened the door. "You always win."

After he locked the door, he whispered, "You are so sexy in your dress, red boots, red crutches, and your gun inside your girly purse."

We laughed together as we headed to the foyer.

When we stepped onto the porch, Daisy raised her head, and Betsy stared. "You just raised this establishment to a new level. We've never hosted royalty before. You two are absolutely stunning."

My face warmed, and Larry said, "Thanks."

Larry returned with the car to pick me up. When Larry opened the passenger door for me, Palace Guard saluted Larry from the backseat then smiled.

On our way to the training center, I gazed at the sky. "The clouds have cleared up. Did your mother say where we're going for lunch? Not that it matters."

"Besides the fact that you are the sexiest woman I know, I love you aren't picky about food. You might not eat a lot, but you'll eat half of anything that's on your plate."

"I love that you're willing to eat the other half of whatever's on my plate," I snickered and glanced at Larry.

"Don't flash your eyes at me while I'm driving, honey. Distracted driving is against the law. After I graduate, I'd have to arrest myself and you as an accomplice."

I stared. "Accomplice. I've been so focused on one person, Clara, being the mastermind of all the events. What if there are actually two?"

Larry frowned. "Could that be why it's hard to pinpoint one person? What if the second person isn't an accomplice, but has his own agenda?"

"Two conflicting agendas?" I narrowed my eyes. "As if Clara wasn't complicated enough; I wonder if Vera or Rebecca still work with her."

I sent Glenn a text. "Vera Willis. Rebecca Herkes. Still around?"

"Clara didn't seem to think much of either one," Larry said.

"True, but she didn't think much of anyone. I think she'd stick to known factors."

Known factors. I glanced at Palace Guard, and he nodded.

I rubbed my forehead. "Mother said she knew Darren Martin's mother, and Clara said Rebecca Herkes married a Martin."

I sent Mother a text. "What is Darren Martin's mother's name?"

Mother: "Rebecca Herkes Martin. Always went by Rebecca. Got huffy if anyone called her Becky."

Me: "Is she still in Columbus?"

Mother: "As far as I know. Hadn't heard that she left."

I read the texts to Larry. "I need to tell Glenn."

After I sent the text to Glenn, Larry reached over and rubbed the back of my neck. "You okay?"

"Frustrated that I'm so slow putting these pieces together, and I've got another one. Clara told me Vera Willis's son's name was Arlo, and the two of them were firebugs. Not a very common name, is it? And Glenn said he and Paul discovered that the owner of the warehouse is Arlo Siddall."

"You're definitely keeping Glenn from being bored in his recuperation," Larry chuckled.

"There is that."

I texted Glenn. "Vera Willis had a son named Arlo. Clara said Vera and her son were firebugs. String of arson stopped after Vera left town."

My phone buzzed a text.

Glenn: "Paul is scrambling. Keep 'em coming."

I read the text to Larry, and he chuckled. "That's terrific, and I'm proud of you for letting them work it. Both of them needed a challenge, and you've handed them a doozy."

A tear escaped down my cheek. "Thank you. I felt like I was dumping it on them."

"I know. That's how you are, sweetie."

I leaned back. *Nobody knows me as well as Larry does.*

Palace Guard patted me on my shoulder and nodded.

"What?" Larry asked.

"We belong together."

Larry slowed for a turn. "We're here. I can't believe the training's over, and we'll be starting our new life together."

I smiled. "We've been together for a long time. I can't imagine going through what we have with anyone except you. This is a big day for you. Let's do this."

Larry pointed. "Over there is your campground."

"That looks nice. It has shade and grass. Wait. Would you be hiding in the grass near my tent?"

Larry burst out laughing. "You know it."

He turned in front of a building. "I'll drop you off then park."

I soaked in his tall, lean body and untamable cowlick as he scanned the area on his way back to the building. He smiled at me with his lopsided grin, and I melted.

First, I'll slide off his tie, then his shirt... I fanned my face and snickered. *It's getting a little steamy out here.*

"Are you okay, Maggie?" he asked as we headed into the building. "You looked kind of flushed."

"I was leering at you." I tossed my hair as my crutches, and I swung into the air-conditioned building.

"Really?" Larry held the door for an older couple who came behind us then he caught up with me. "Can we follow up on that later?"

"Of course, honey."

We entered a small auditorium with a stage across the front. Larry picked up two programs from a small table at the back. A middle aisle separated the two sections of the old-style theater seats that flipped upright when a person stood.

"The first three rows are reserved for family. You and my folks are in the first row at the far right," he said. "Your folks will be in the second row behind you. After you are situated, I have to go check in."

People filed into the auditorium behind us, and Larry led me to the third seat from the end and gave me a program. After he left, I heard Mother's voice and turned and waved. Mother wore a hot pink pencil skirt, a pink and yellow flowered shirt with a pale green background, and a white jacket. She had piled her red hair on top of her head, but some curls had escaped and joined the tendrils around the back of her neck. Her high heels and purse matched the green in her shirt.

"There she is, Big D," Mother said. "Isn't she pretty?"

Sarge wore his dark blue dress uniform, and I smiled. *Sarge is a good-looking man.* He squinted at the drawing on the back of the program then led Mother to their seats. I rose when they were close; Mother rushed to me, and we hugged.

"Aren't you excited, Margaret? We're so proud of Larry. Aren't we, Big D?"

Sarge smiled. "Yes, we are." He pointed to the row behind me. "Our seats are at the end."

"You take the aisle seat, Big D." Mother sat at the seat next to his then reached forward and rubbed my shoulder, and I turned and smiled.

"Margaret, your dress is the perfect color for your porcelain skin and red hair. I absolutely love it, and I love that you've expanded your choices to new colors. I finally heard from Sylvia. She'll meet you tomorrow at ten at her office. If that's too early, you can call her. Here's all her contact information."

I copied Sylvia's contact information into my phone then as the auditorium filled, Lauren slipped in next to me. She greeted Mother and Sarge. She wore a pale blue linen suit, a white blouse with blue dots, and navy heels. Her sandy-brown hair brushed her shoulders, and her purse matched her shoes.

"Sean is still in the lobby talking with old friends. He'll find me." She hugged me. "I'm so proud of Kevin, and I'm excited that you're here. What a great beginning for your new life together."

As the program began, Sean and four other men rushed to their seats. Sean wore khaki pants, a blue shirt with a navy and blue striped tie and a navy sports coat. He shook hands with Sarge and nodded to Mother. He reached across Lauren and patted my hand.

When Larry and his classmates filed to their seats on the stage, my heart swelled. *He's worked so hard for this.*

Palace Guard wore his dress uniform and stood at the side of the stage close to Larry. Larry gave Palace Guard an upward nod and winked at me, and I smiled and placed my hand on my heart.

I didn't hear any of the speeches because my full attention was on Larry. When the speaker called out, "Kevin Ewing," everyone in the auditorium rose and applauded. Lauren helped me up, and I applauded through tears. Larry smiled and pointed to me on his way back to his seat, and my heart melted.

"That's a great honor. I know you're as proud as I am," Lauren whispered as we sat. I nodded then read my program and realized Larry was the outstanding recruit of the year besides being at the top of his class. *Of course he is. I'm not one bit surprised.*

After the remaining class members had received their certificates, the audience rose and applauded again as the class and dignitaries on the stage filed out.

Lauren said, "Kevin will need to go to the reception so everyone can congratulate him, but we won't stay long."

Sean and Sarge cut around on the outside aisle to hurry to the door while Lauren and Mother waited with me for the auditorium to clear.

"Those two know a lot of people here," Lauren said. "It's a great opportunity for them to see old friends. No reason for us to rush."

Mother and Lauren chatted about the trials and joys of traveling and camping while I daydreamed about Larry.

Lauren touched my arm. "We can go now, Maggie. You must be exhausted. I keep forgetting about your wreck and your ankle."

"I'm fine," I said.

Lauren led us to the reception. It was a relief to see it was indoors, so I didn't have to maneuver over uneven ground.

"We'll find Sean and Sarge." Lauren pointed to our right. "Kevin's headed this way."

Larry rushed to me and grabbed me in a big hug, and my crutches clattered to the floor. Mother picked up my crutches then she and Lauren congratulated Larry and left to join their husbands. As Heather and Moe approached us, I squealed then hugged Heather. Moe and Larry shook hands.

"Are the men here?" Heather asked.

"Palace Guard is," I said.

"Oh. I kind of miss Spike."

Palace Guard rolled his eyes, and I laughed.

"What?" she said. "Let's sit. You can catch me up. And you are stunning in the dress. I may borrow it sometime when I need to be a sexy spy." She wiggled her eyebrows then ushered me to the chairs against the wall. "What did Palace Guard say? And I need for you to catch me up on everything."

"Palace Guard rolled his eyes. We think Spike goes overboard when he sees you."

"Every girl should have someone who goes overboard," she said. "I've gone out a few times with this really cute middle-school teacher. He's great with the kids, and they're terrified to cross him. He reminds me of how you've described Spike. So, tell me what's going on. Who is setting all the fires in Harperville?"

"I'll tell you my theories if you promise to keep me updated on the cute teacher." I wiggled my eyebrows then caught her up on what I knew.

When I finished she said, "I'm sad you're leaving Harperville. My undercover job is dull compared to your real life. I'm inviting myself to visit you regularly for my updates. I'll bring tacos, beer, and maybe Todd. Are the real imaginary men going with you? And Lucy?"

"Yes, and yes."

She nodded. "I wonder if our chief has already sent a warning letter to the Columbus chief. I'll bet he has. Let me know if you can use my help with anything. I've got all kinds of vacation time saved up." She glanced at Moe. "He's getting antsy to leave. He doesn't go to big functions like this, but he didn't want to miss it, and I didn't either. I think he's in a rush to get back to his Ella too. Those two are getting serious. Have you been around them?"

"Only in small doses."

Heather snickered. "See you next week." Heather hugged me then she and Moe hurried out the door.

Lauren sat next to me. "Ready for me to round up the troops? Your mother and I decided against trying to go to a restaurant. We'll have lunch at the campground, and I have everything ready."

I laughed. "I'm ready for lunch. It'll be awhile before we can corral them."

"Watch this." She placed two fingers in her mouth and blew a loud, piercing whistle. Everyone in the room hushed and looked around.

Lauren spoke in a conversational tone. "Sean and Sarge. Time."

I snickered as Larry came to my side. The three of us headed to the door, and Sean, Sarge, and Mother joined us as we left.

Mother said, "Lauren, that was slick."

"Thank you. It's come in handy more than once."

"We'll meet you at the campground," Sean said. "You need directions, son?"

"No, I looked it up one time. We'll see you there."

After we were on the road, I said, "I am so proud of you, honey. I've always thought you were amazing. So, when did you look up the campground?"

"Well. It was…" Larry peered at his rear-view mirror and the side mirrors. "Is that a black car behind us?"

I glanced at Palace Guard who grinned.

"Nope. Was it when I made plans to camp at the training center?"

"Could have been." His mouth quivered in his effort to hide a smile, and his blue eyes twinkled.

"You keep flashing those baby blues at me, and I'll be distracted enough to forget that question, Mister."

He raised his eyebrows and chuckled. "That was my line. Kind of. Isn't that plagiarism?"

"You really want to pursue that literary path with me?" I narrowed my eyes, and he laughed.

I closed my eyes and leaned back in the seat. "Have you noticed we have some of the silliest conversations nobody else would understand?"

"Palace Guard agrees." Larry slowed the car, and I sat up as he turned at the campground entrance.

"This is pretty." I peered out my window. "They even have little cabins. I could have stayed here, except it would have been tragic if the bad guys had burned down the campground."

"Hadn't thought of that. You're right."

Larry lowered his speed as he passed the campground office. "Dad said they are on the fourth row, and the two RVs are parked at sites next to each other."

Midway down the fourth row, I pointed to the right ahead of us. "I see Mother and Lauren." Our mothers sat under a canopy in camp chairs, and Franklin's carrier was under the table. Larry parked between the two RVs.

After we stepped out of the car, Lauren rose. "Kevin, your dad and Sarge are inspecting Sarge's RV. You're welcome to join them or sit with us." She pointed to the four chairs that completed the semicircle facing the small dirt road. "I'll get two more glasses of tea."

"Congratulations on your awards, Larry," Mother said. "I know you're happy to have that training behind you."

"Thank you." Larry's ears reddened.

I sat next to Mother, and Larry moved a chair to sit next to me.

Sean and Sarge strolled toward us in deep discussion. Mother hurried to the RV door, and Lauren handed her a covered dish. Lauren stepped out of the RV with a large basket then emptied the basket while Mother arranged the food on the table.

"The Ewing buffet is open," Lauren smiled. "I'll bring out the pitcher of tea while y'all help yourselves."

Larry served our plates then sat next to me. "Eat what you want, sweetie. I tried not to overload your plate."

Sarge and Sean quizzed Larry about his classes and instructors then Sean launched into a story about one of the instructors. Before we finished eating, Sean had told two stories, and Sarge topped him with three.

Before Sean could start his third story, Lauren jumped in. "I know we're going to be out here all night with the stories, but we need to release these young people. It's been an exciting day, and they've got the trip to Columbus in the morning to find somewhere to live."

Larry smiled. "Thanks, Mom." Larry rose and helped me to my feet. "And thank you, everyone, for coming." After hugs and handshakes, we left.

When we reached my room, Larry said, "I need to catch up on my email. We got shorted on sleep last night, and you're still not quite up to par. Why don't you see if you can nap? Come down to the patio after you've rested, or I'll come get you for supper."

After I changed into jeans and a T-shirt, I sat on my comfortable chair and opened my book.

A buzz woke me, and I checked my phone then read the text from Glenn as Palace Guard peered over my shoulder.

"Confirmed Clara's grandson is Ross Walker. History of suspected blackmail, fraud, and murder but no prosecutions. Sleezy guy. Slick. Kicker: Your Maurice is Ross Walker."

I called Glenn.

"Thought I'd get your attention." Glenn chuckled. "Is Larry there?"

"You sure did. Larry's out on the patio, and I'll be on my way after we hang up. Are you gloating?" I asked.

"Paul's here. He did all the digging, but we're both gloating. How was graduation?"

I wandered to the window and gazed at the trees. "The training center grounds were beautiful, and graduation was awesome. Larry was at the top of his class and was named recruit of the year."

"That's great. Well deserved. Jennifer has invited Paul and Julie to dinner to celebrate Paul's success of the day. We'll toast Larry while we're at it."

After we hung up, I pulled on my boots. "I'd almost forgotten about Maurice. Glenn was right. Definitely a kicker."

Palace Guard nodded, and we headed to the patio. I peeked out as we neared the door. Larry had changed to jeans and a T-shirt. I sighed.

Larry glanced up then to hurried me. "What's wrong?"

No tie. "Nothing's wrong. I got a text from Glenn and called him."

"Come sit down. You're breathless." Larry helped me to a chair.

"I'm excited and couldn't get to the patio fast enough. Glenn and Paul confirmed Clara's grandson's name is Ross Walker, and, even more exciting, Maurice is Ross Walker."

I handed Larry my phone, and he dropped into his chair as he read. "Maurice? At the restaurant?"

Palace Guard nodded.

Larry stared at Palace Guard then me. "I have questions. Are we having Italian Sunday night or Monday night? Are you planning a shootout before or after we get the bill?"

My eyes widened, and Larry smirked. "Did I finally think of something before you did?"

I stuck my nose in the air then side-glanced him. "I'm not saying. Now you owe me a beer."

Larry cocked his head. "Why is that?"

I shrugged. "Because I saw Betsy setting out the hors d'oeuvres."

"On it." He snickered as he strode inside then returned with two bottles of beer.

"There's a line for hors d'oeuvres," he said. "From the way some of those plates are piled with food, that's their supper. They are missing out."

We sipped our beer.

"One of the guys told me Heather is seeing a schoolteacher. Did you know about that?" Larry asked.

"She mentioned a middle-school teacher, but she said they'd only gone out a few times."

"The guys are in awe of Heather. They're too scared to ask her out. Which reminds me, a couple of guys asked if I knew you. They wanted me to introduce them, and, to my credit, I only growled and didn't hurt them. Aren't you proud of my manners?" He chuckled, and I snorted as Betsy came out with two sacks of food and two glasses with ice.

"Tonight we have a special treat," Betsy said. "Indonesian food prepared by a talented chef from Java." She pointed to our empty bottles. "Thought you'd want iced tea with your spicy food." She left then returned with a large pitcher of iced tea and glasses.

When we opened our sacks, I inhaled the enticing aromas of jasmine rice, beef, coconut, and chili.

Betsy read from a card. "You have steamed jasmine rice with beef rendang. The beef is stewed in a brown sauce of coconut milk and special spices. On the side are sliced cucumbers and a dollop of sambal which is a hot chili paste that originated in Java." She peered at our plates. "Wow. Save me half of yours, Maggie. My partner and I want to try it."

"Get a plate, and we'll dish it up now," I said.

Betsy rushed into the B&B then returned with a plate. I dished up half of my rice, half of my beef rendang, a few cucumbers, and a third of the chili paste. Betsy shivered in excitement. "This is as good as Christmas. Thank you."

After she left, Larry said, "I've never had Indonesian food before. My loss, right?"

I paused long enough to nod then continued eating.

As I leaned back and placed my fork on the table, Larry drank the rest of his tea. "I couldn't have eaten your half too. I've learned from you to leave room for dessert."

"We finally found delicious food that was spicy enough for our tastes. My mouth still has a spicy buzz."

Betsy brought out two forks and two three-inch squares of chocolate cake on dessert plates. "Chef tried a new recipe she thought would go well with spicy food. See what you think. It's her version of a Texas sheet cake with a dark chocolate and mint frosting."

I ate a small bite of the dark sweetness. "This is outstanding, and I know I can't finish it."

Betsy chuckled. "Chef is counting on it. She wants to freeze what you have left so you can tell her how it compares after it thaws."

I ate three more bites then set my fork on my plate.

"Ready for us to wrap it for the freezer?" Betsy asked.

I handed her my plate, and Larry handed her his plate with half of his cake left.

After Betsy left, Larry said, "Do you feel like a short walk, sweetie?"

"Let's go. I need to move around."

As the three of us strolled on the walking trail with Palace Guard bringing up the rear, Larry asked, "Does knowing that Maurice is Clara's grandson clear anything up?"

"I'm not sure. I wonder if Ross Walker has replaced Vera in providing the talent and what could be the motive for all the attacks on me? I don't see the connection."

"Maybe the attacks are on Maggie Flanagan."

I frowned as we continued our walk. "That's an angle I hadn't thought about."

"Doesn't clear up anything, though, does it?" Larry asked.

"Not yet, but I think you might be on to something. Which reminds me, I have questions for Darren Martin when we go to Columbus tomorrow. I wonder..."

Larry was quiet as we strolled along.

"There's a bench," I said. "I need to sit a minute." I glanced at the concern on his face. "I need to check something on my phone."

Larry sat next to me, and Palace Guard peered over my shoulder as I scrolled. *I wonder where I ever got the idea spies work alone?*

"Here it is. Darren Martin. I'll send him a text.'

Larry scooted closer, and Palace Guard crowded me as I tapped my phone.

"This is Maggie Sloan. I'll be in Columbus tomorrow. Are you available?"

I rose. "Let's walk. I should have thought about arranging to meet him earlier, but maybe short notice is better."

"What time do we need to leave tomorrow?" Larry asked.

"After breakfast. We have a meeting with the real estate agent, Sylvia, at ten. Columbus is an hour and a half from here. It wouldn't hurt for us to have some time to find your office and drive around. It would work out best for us if we could meet with Darren Martin after lunch, but we'll see what he says."

We reached the end of the path and turned back. Halfway to the B&B, my phone buzzed.

CHAPTER EIGHTEEN

I read the text from Darren Martin. "Columbus Museum at two o'clock? I volunteer at the desk from noon until two on Sat."

I showed Larry my phone, and he nodded.

I sent my reply. "Perfect. See you at two."

"What do you want to talk to Darren Martin about?" Larry asked.

"I think he gave the Georgia map and the Isabella Stewart Gardner Museum brochure to the real courier who mailed the envelope to Glenn's post office box. I need Darren to confirm that, and I'd like to hear why, although my guess is Clara was trying to blackmail either Darren or Rebecca Martin. Mother said Rebecca Martin was still in Columbus. Now, I wonder if it was Rebecca Martin, not Darren, who sent the information to the real courier? She might have reached a breaking point with Clara."

When we reached the B&B, I said, "The best part of going to Columbus is we're going to find our first place together."

Larry lifted me off my feet into a hug, and my crutches clattered onto the porch floor. I was lost in his gaze then he eased my feet to the floor and picked up my crutches as Daisy padded to the far corner and flopped next to Palace Guard.

"I think Daisy just told us to get a room," Larry said.

I smiled and headed to my room, and Larry rushed ahead to open the door. After I sat on my soft chair, Larry removed the bandage with slow, flowing motions, and my heart rate increased as he undressed my foot then stroked my leg with a light touch.

I sighed. "My turn." I pulled his T-shirt up and over his head then rubbed his chest.

His eyes twinkled. "My turn."

He unbuttoned the top two buttons of my shirt. "I have wanted to see you and your lacy bra since before you even had one."

He touched the lace with his fingertips then unbuttoned my shirt and removed it. He sat back on his heels and gazed at me.

"I love you, Maggie."

I met his gaze and smiled. "I love you, Larry."

I leaned forward and kissed him lightly then pressed my open mouth against his. While I explored his mouth, he slipped down my bra straps and explored me. I unfastened my bra, and he removed my shirt then picked me up.

He grinned, and I laughed. "That's a wicked grin."

His blue eyes flashed. "You think?"

He dropped me onto the bed; after he tumbled in next to me, I snuggled against him.

"Early day tomorrow." My words were muffled by his chest.

"Yep." Larry rose, turned off the lights, and pulled off his jeans. I pulled off my jeans and threw back the bed covers.

Larry lay next to me and wrapped his arms around me as he kissed my forehead, eyes, nose, and chin.

"I'm sleeping here with you," he said.

"You always sleep in my room." I returned his kisses.

"I'm sleeping in this bed with you, Miss Literal."

"You win."

"Yes." He slipped off my panties.

The next morning, I opened my eyes when I heard whistling and the shower running. *I'm happy too.* I rolled to look at the clock. *Five-thirty.*

I opened the door to the bathroom, and Larry smiled as he turned off the water. He stepped out of the shower and wrapped a towel around his waist. "Good morning, my sweet, naked Maggie. I'll throw on some clothes and get us coffee. Four days."

I hugged his still-wet body and inhaled his soap and man smell. "Good morning, my sexy pants, Larry."

He groaned. "Dress then coffee. It's hard for me to stay focused when you're around; did you know that?"

I giggled as he left for his room. After I climbed into the shower, I heard the door shut. I lathered with the new girly-smell shower gel Jennifer had snuck into my bag then rinsed with the warm, soothing water. Larry returned as I rinsed my hair.

"You want your coffee in there or here in your room?" he asked.

"In there. I'll be right out."

I dried off then wrapped my head with my towel and hurried to my coffee.

Larry leered. "Still naked."

"Aha. I finally see your leer." I picked up my cup and gulped down the hot liquid then sashayed past Larry to the closet for clothes.

While I dressed, Larry stood at the closet door and sipped his coffee. "Do that walk-thing one more time, and we'll be late for our ten o'clock appointment."

I stopped in the middle of pulling up my jeans.

"Did I say something wrong?" Larry asked.

"Quiet. I'm trying to decide how important the appointment with the real estate agent is."

Larry laughed. "I love you, unpredictable Maggie."

After I dressed, I towel-dried my hair then combed out the tangles.

"I'm ready for more coffee, but would you wrap my foot first?" I asked.

"Good idea, then we can leave for Columbus right after breakfast."

Larry bandaged my foot then we left in search of coffee. When we stepped into the foyer, Betsy rose from her desk and pulled a folded note out of her pocket then handed it to me. "Chef made you a list of places in Columbus that she recommends. She said go to the first place on the list for lunch today. I just made a fresh pot of coffee. I'll bring your breakfast out when it's ready."

I unfolded the paper and read the list. "Tell Chef thank you. Barbeque for lunch sounds great."

"That was a terrible storm last night, wasn't it? Did you manage to sleep at all?" she asked. "It came up without warning. I went out to the patio earlier this morning and wiped down the chair seats, but there's a downed branch I couldn't drag away by myself. Just step around it, but don't fall. Here's another towel if your seats aren't dry enough yet." Betsy slung a small towel over my shoulder.

She shook her head. "You wouldn't believe the parade when the storm hit. Half of the guests came to the dining room. I enjoy my solitude and the chance to read uninterrupted, but they barged in on my private time in the middle of the night to tell me we were under a tornado warning. They wanted to know where the shelter was. Chef said I should have told them under their beds; that's why we don't let her out of the kitchen." Betsy cackled as she left the foyer for her office.

Larry poured two fresh cups. The door to the patio opened only part way because of the large branch that had fallen onto the walkway. Larry set our cups on our table then dragged the branch out of the way while I dried our chairs and wiped the table dry.

After we sat and scooted our chairs closer together, I asked, "Did we miss something last night? I didn't hear anything."

"Nope." Larry grinned. "We didn't miss a thing." He kissed me on the cheek.

I smiled. "You're right."

"I'm on a roll." Larry puffed out his chest and leaned back to sip his coffee.

Palace Guard stood at the edge of the patio. I rolled my eyes, and Palace Guard nodded.

Betsy brought us our breakfasts. "Chef made her special Georgia tornado omelet for y'all. Instead of rice, it's mounded on top of southern fried potatoes and has salsa on the side. The rest of the guests will have cheesy scrambled eggs with fried potatoes. Get it? Cheesy?" She snickered as she left.

I stared at my plate then lifted the tornado omelet to peek at the potatoes. "How did she do this swirl in the eggs?"

"Untapped talent." Larry dug into his tornado.

After I ate not quite half of my eggs and potatoes, Larry finished them off. While we relaxed with our coffee, he asked, "What do you need to pack for today?"

"My computer, go bag, and backpack. I can't think of anything else."

Betsy came out to the patio to pick up our plates. "Larry, thank you for moving the branch. Are you eating dinner in Columbus, Maggie?"

"We don't plan to, but it's hard to say," I said.

"I've ordered your dinners for tonight. Text me if your plans change or if you're on your way, but will be late. We'll put your meals in the refrigerator if you don't get back in time and warm up your food after you get here."

"That's nice. Thank you," I said.

"I'm just trying to bribe you to stay longer. Chef and Daisy will mope after you're gone, and so will I." Betsy smiled.

On our way to Columbus, I checked my list for our house requirements. "I have a fenced yard for Lucy, which, of course, means dogs allowed, two bedrooms, and two baths as our minimum."

"If we find the right yard and location, we could easily get by with one bedroom and one bath," Larry said.

I frowned at my list. "We've always had two bedrooms everywhere we've been. Two bedrooms have always been our minimum."

Larry nodded. "How many bedrooms do we have here?"

"Two." *Case closed.* I glanced at Palace Guard, and he shook his head.

Larry glanced in his rearview mirror. "Right. And how many do we use?"

"Two."

Palace Guard rolled his eyes.

"Yes, two. Because he keeps his clothes in his room."

"You're arguing with Palace Guard? Fine. I'll help," Larry said. "What if he moves his clothes to the closet in the one bedroom?"

Larry cocked his head. "Is one bedroom giving you cold feet?"

I raised my eyebrows. "If cold feet means anxiety that things might not stay the same, then yes, and you did say I could have cold feet first."

"Will you feel better if we leave two bedrooms on the list?" he asked.

"Yes, but only if we sleep together in one bedroom and put your clothes in the other bedroom closet." I wrinkled my nose. "That whole thing threw me, didn't it?"

Palace Guard nodded.

"All three of us," Larry said.

"Thank you, honey. I couldn't have worked through it by myself."

Larry smiled. "What else is on your list?"

"Next is the nice-to-have list. Fireplace, dishwasher, porch, washer and dryer." I tapped my notebook. "Do I need to put hook-ups for the washer and dryer on the must-have list?"

"I think the connections would be must-haves."

"I just realized the fire destroyed my grill and lawnmower. It would be smart to wait until we're in a more permanent location to replace them, but I'll start a purchase list."

"We're about twenty minutes from Midland," Larry said.

I peered at the passing farms and fields that transitioned to communities. "How far from your office are you thinking we should be?"

"No more than twenty minutes would be nice, but forty-five minutes for the right place would be okay."

Larry slowed then parked at the curb. "There it is. This is where I'll report next Monday." He stared at the building then pulled away. "I feel better seeing it, but I'm not sure why. Maybe because it's more real now that I've seen it. There's a park nearby. We can get out of the car and walk if you feel up to it."

Massive pecan trees dominated the park with their sweeping branches. The playground was empty, but runners and walkers were on the wide path that circled the park. While we strolled, my phone buzzed a text.

Glenn: "Call?"

"Glenn wants me to call. I'll put him on speakerphone."

"There's a bench." Larry pointed. "We can sit in the shade."

I called, and Glenn picked up after one ring. "I hope this isn't too early," he said.

"Not at all. We're near Columbus at a park."

"Paul just called me. He's on his way here. He found Rebecca Herkes Martin in a Senior Care Memory Unit in Phenix City, Alabama. It's just across the Chattahoochee River from Columbus. Phenix City isn't spelled like the Phoenix in Arizona. I'll bet there's a story there," Glenn chuckled. "We thought you'd see Darren Martin today and would like to know about his mother."

"Thanks, Glenn, and thank Paul for me. Very helpful."

After we hung up, Larry said, "This puts a new spin on your blackmail theory, doesn't it?"

"Sure does. I'm glad we're seeing Darren this afternoon."

Larry rose. "Let's find a place to live."

Sylvia smiled when we walked into the real estate office. "Maggie and Larry," she said. "Nice to meet you. I'm Sylvia. Let's go into the conference room. I have five possibilities for you then you can pick which ones we want to look at more closely."

We followed her into a small office with a table and four chairs. "Please sit and tell me what you're looking for. Your mother gave me a rough idea, but we can narrow it down."

"We have a must-have list and a nice-to-have list. We have a dog, so dogs must be allowed," I said.

"And a fenced yard," Sylvia added.

"Yes. We need a month-to-month lease. We'll be in Columbus for only two or three months then we'll leave for four or five months while Larry goes to training. One or two bedrooms. Two would be nice. We need washer and dryer connections, but a washer and dryer included would be better. As far as location, no more than thirty minutes away from Midland."

"What else is on your nice-to-have list?"

"A porch, fireplace, and a second bathroom," Larry said.

"Will you be coming back to Columbus?" Sylvia asked.

"We don't know," Larry said. "It's a possibility, but we won't know until my training is completed."

"What about cost? Is your budget tight?"

"Yes," Larry said.

"We're flexible," I added, and Larry raised an eyebrow.

Sylvia nodded. "I picked out six, but two of them are too far away. I'll get the folder I prepared for you, and we'll look at those four. Any of them would work for a young couple's budget."

After she left the room, Larry asked, "Flexible?"

"I have the inheritance from Olivia. We can be flexible. Remember, we decided I'd be in charge of the bills?"

"I don't want to be a kept man," he glared.

"Your paycheck will go towards bills, too. Isn't that what we said?"

"Yes, but I don't know about being flexible."

"It'll work."

Sylvia returned with two folders. "Here you go. Let's go through them. I can tell you how far each one is from Midland."

After we discussed all four houses, Sylvia said, "Let's look at these three first. The fourth one might be a little pricey. You can follow me to each house or ride with me."

"We'll follow you," Larry said.

"We'll see the one bedroom first. It's thirty minutes from Midland."

After we parked in front of the house, Larry said, "It's not fenced on all sides. Do you want to check it out since we're here?"

"We could."

While Sylvia unlocked the door, Larry circled the house. When he returned, he said, "Sylvia, the yard's not completely fenced."

"Oh, really." She read the listing. "It says it is. I'll follow up if you decide this works for you other than the fence."

"It does have a washer and dryer and a dishwasher," I said.

"Bedroom is large, and so is the bathroom. Two large closets in the bedroom," Larry said.

"Let's look at the other two," Sylvia said. "Both of them have two bedrooms. One is ten minutes from your Midland office, Larry, and the other is fifteen."

As we followed her to the next house, I jotted down notes on the one we just looked at. When we parked in the driveway, Larry said, "I'll check around the outside."

Sylvia unlocked the door when Larry returned.

"Fenced all the way around," he said.

"Good. This one is fifteen minutes away from Midland," Sylvia said. "Let's go inside."

"It has a dishwasher," I said. "Is there a washer and dryer?"

"No, and I'm not sure about connections. We'll have to check."

Larry strode down the hallway. "Connections for a washer and dryer in the bathroom. Maggie, come look at the bedrooms. One would be a perfect office for you since the living area is so small. There's no master bath."

"One more," Sylvia said, "unless we decide to look at the fourth one while we're out."

The gutters on the front of the third house sagged. I pointed with my pen before we got out of the car. "The owner may not be responsive to maintenance calls."

"Good point," Larry said. "We can tell Sylvia we'd like to see the fourth house if this one is iffy."

When we were inside, I said, "The corner ceiling tile is stained and bulging. The house may have a leak in the roof. I noticed the gutters need work too. Does the owner have plans for the repairs?"

Sylvia read the sheet, and her face reddened. "We're leaving. It appears the owner's plan is that the tenant is responsible for all repairs, and I don't see where it exempts existing issues."

After Sylvia locked the door, she said, "I apologize. This was a new listing, and I didn't realize it had unacceptable conditions. Some certain agent will get an earful about this. Let's visit the fourth house. It's fifteen minutes to Midland, so it's in our favorable driving time for Larry's work."

When we parked in the driveway of the fourth house, Larry said, "I'm glad you didn't decide to climb up on the roof to inspect it. Thought about it, didn't you?"

I snickered. "You know me too well."

Larry made his rounds of the outside and returned. "Fenced on all sides, and there's a porch in the back."

When we walked into the house, Sylvia said, "This is still two bedrooms with two baths, but it's larger than the others."

"Dishwasher," I said.

"Washer and dryer in the main bathroom," Larry said.

When we checked the master bedroom and bath, I said, "Shower, no tub, but that's fine."

"Second bedroom's perfect for an office."

Sylvia read her sheet. "This house must be leased for three months then it goes month to month after that. What do you think?"

"It might work, but we need to talk it over first," I said. "Shall we meet you at your office?"

"Perfect," Sylvia said.

On the way to the real estate office, Larry asked, "You'd be willing to sign a three-month lease?"

"Ignoring the lease, what did you think about the house?"

"It met all of our requirements, and it's a nice house."

"I agree. I think it's worth it to have a home that is what we want, even if we end up leaving two or three weeks before the lease is up. The next closest to meeting our needs was the second house, but we'd have to buy a washer and dryer."

Larry nodded. "You're right." He glanced in his rearview mirror. "Don't gloat, Palace Guard. I'm being flexible."

Sylvia waited for us out front and ushered us into the conference room.

"The fourth house is the best one for us," Larry said.

"I thought so too, after we looked at the other three. Give me just a minute to pull together the paperwork. The owner suggested we may want to change the locks. Do you want to do that? I'd recommend it."

"Isn't that unusual?" I asked.

"In some markets, yes," she said, "but many law enforcement and military people are security-aware and prefer to change the locks before they move in. Some owners don't allow it, but that is sometimes a deal-breaker since we're so close to a military base."

We signed the paperwork, and I gave Sylvia a check for our deposit, the locksmith, and the first three months' rent.

"I'll have the locks changed for you on Monday. Do you want to pick up your keys, or do you want me to mail them to you?"

"Could you mail us a key? Then we'll pick up the rest probably Friday. Maggie, mail them to Glenn?"

"Yes. I'll give you the address, Sylvia."

"Text it to me; then I won't lose it." Sylvia smiled. "Welcome to our neck of the woods. It was a pleasure to work with you two, and all my best with your upcoming wedding. Call or text me if you need me."

"Ready for lunch?" Larry asked after he pulled away from the real estate office.

"Sounds good." I sent Glenn's name and address to Sylvia with my name in parentheses.

I read our paperwork on our way to the restaurant.

"She filled out the paperwork for Larry and Maggie Ewing," I said.

"Awesome," Larry said.

"But I didn't notice and signed it *Maggie Sloan*."

"Then both of you are liable." Larry grinned. "I notice you didn't say anything about Larry Ewing."

"Why would I?"

Larry and Palace Guard laughed.

I don't understand men sometimes.

After we ate lunch, we climbed into the car. "We've got an hour before we meet with Darren Martin. What would you like to do?" Larry asked.

"We could stalk the house. You know, drive past it a few dozen times and explore the neighborhood."

He chuckled then started the car. "Sounds like exactly what we'd do."

"I forgot to ask about utilities," I said. "I'll text Sylvia."

I read her reply. "She'll send the contact information."

We found the nearest grocery store, gas station, and hardware store then cruised past the house again.

"Ready to talk to Darren Martin?" Larry turned away from our new neighborhood and headed to Columbus. When he pulled into the museum parking lot, he asked, "Shall I come inside with you or wait out here?"

"Come in."

I dug into my backpack and pulled out my sling purse then the three of us went inside. Darren was in conversation with an eight-year-old girl at the Information Desk. The girl's mother beamed as Darren and the girl continued their animated discussion.

Larry leaned close to me and whispered, "Seems like a nice guy."

I nodded. "He is. He and the little girl are having an intense discussion, aren't they?"

They came to an agreement of sorts. The little girl held out her hand, and Darren shook it.

Aww. That's sweet.

Palace Guard nodded and laid his hand on his heart.

A middle-aged woman, whose eyeglasses were attached to a beaded strap by clips and rested on her ample bosom, relieved Darren from his desk duty, and he rushed to me.

"Ms. Sloan, it's so nice to see you again. What did you think of the paintings you bought?"

"I love Americana folk art. Please call me Maggie. This is Larry Ewing."

"Darren Martin." Darren held out his hand, and the two men shook hands. "Come into the conference room. I assume this isn't a casual visit."

When we were inside, Darren closed the door. "Please sit. Now, what can I do for you today?"

I gazed at him. "I wanted to talk to you about the brochure and map you sent to the FBI."

Darren's shoulders slumped. "I suppose it was only a matter of time. I did my research, Ms. Sloan, Maggie. Or should I say Gray Lady? Are you with the FBI?"

"No." I glanced at the door then whispered, "Independent."

He nodded. "Is it Mr. Ewing?"

Smart way to ask if he's Agent or Officer Ewing.

Larry scanned the room. "Larry. I work with the Gray Lady."

Palace Guard blew on his finger, and I smiled then shifted in my seat and spoke to Darren. "I know you sent the brochure and map to the FBI so we would investigate Clara Hayden, and you may be relieved to know you've revived an active investigation. I think I know why too, but I wonder if you'd tell me off the record."

His eyes widened. "You're okay with off the record? I can deny ever talking to you?"

I smiled. "Of course."

He gazed at me, and I met his gaze.

"My mama was involved with Clara Hayden and Vera Willis Siddall during the late eighties and early nineties until Mama had her fill. She knew Clara had cheated her more than once, especially when Mama purchased art. Do you know about the Isabella Stewart Gardner Museum theft? Clara masterminded that. I don't have any proof, but Mama told me Clara had at least five of the paintings. When she discovered the extent of Clara's criminal activities, Mama disassociated herself from her."

"That couldn't have been easy," I said.

"No, it wasn't, and Mama's health suffered from it. Clara has grumbled about Mama and insinuated Mama committed fraud and other crimes over the years, but Clara turned more vindictive this past year. She threatened to expose Mama and turn her in for all of Clara's vile schemes. Of course, Clara had proof because she was the mastermind of the crimes. My mama is ill and not able to defend herself."

Believable? I glanced at Palace Guard, and he nodded.

"I'm sorry to hear she isn't well," I said.

"Thank you. Her good days are rare." He glanced away, but his face revealed his ongoing grief.

"When Clara sent Mama the stamp-sized sketch, I intercepted it and realized it was time to stop Clara. She is all about money and would not have given up Rembrandt's self-portrait except to feed her diabolical desire to ruin Mama's reputation."

Chapter Nineteen

"Do you still have it?" I asked. "I can give it to the FBI task force working on the museum theft, and they don't have to know where it came from."

His eyes widened as his disbelief was driven out by hope. "You can do that?"

I smiled. "I'm the Gray Lady."

He matched my smile. "That you are."

He strode to the far end of the room and tugged on the side of a painting. The false door opened and exposed a wall safe. After he opened the safe, he pulled out an envelope and closed the safe then handed me the unsealed envelope. I opened the envelope and the enclosed card, and the small sketch, less than two inches square, was nestled inside the card.

"I can get this to the FBI task force before tomorrow," I said.

"Do you live alone, Darren?" Larry asked.

"Yes, but I'm rarely home. I stay with Mama at the facility in case she has a moment of lucidity and asks for me. I sleep on a bed in her room and use the staff facilities to shower."

As I slipped the envelope into my purse, Larry said, "Stay close to people until Clara Hayden is stopped."

"I will. Thank you, Larry," Darren said. "Maggie, you are relieving me of a terrible burden."

"I understand. I'm glad I can help. Please call or text me if you'd like to talk or need any help at all."

I rose, and Larry handed me my crutches and waited for me at the door.

"I've enjoyed getting to know you, Darren." I hugged him.

Darren and Larry shook hands. When we left, Darren had tears welling up, and so did I.

When we got into the car, I said, "I'll text Della."

"Grandma D. I have another present for you. I'll be at the B&B this evening. Love, Maggie."

Della: "What time?"

"When will we be back to the B&B?" I asked.

He peered at the car clock. "Before five."

I texted: "After five."

Della: "Happy hour. I'll buy."

I laughed, and Larry asked, "What did she say, Crazy Lady?"

I read the string of texts aloud. Larry laughed, and Palace Guard smiled.

"Do you believe Darren?" Larry asked.

"I do. Three things: he was sincere, it all fit, and Palace Guard said he was believable."

"Is that what the exchange was between you? Explain how that works sometime."

I frowned. "I'm not sure if I can; it's like I kind of think something, and he hears me."

Larry shook his head. "It was astounding seeing your green-eyed magic at work. You have a lifelong friend in Darren Martin."

"He needed somebody he could trust." I gazed at Larry. "I am so grateful for you, Larry Ewing."

"You too, Maggie almost Ewing. He trusted the Gray Lady and shared his secret burden." He shook his head. "I still say it was your green eyes. Are you sure you don't have fairies sitting on your shoulder?"

Palace Guard smacked the back of Larry's head.

"Ow. I'm not talking about you. No way could you fit on her shoulder." Larry rubbed the back of his head and glared at his rearview mirror, and Palace Guard grinned.

"I'll let Betsy know we'll be there in plenty of time for dinner." I texted. "Will be back a little after five."

"Are you surprised we found a house?" Larry asked.

"I'm excited we did. I was afraid we'd be scrambling next week."

"Thanks to your mother."

"You're right." I popped my forehead with my palm. "I need to let her know. I'm trying to be more social. Thank you."

"You're welcome, and I don't mind all the texting you're doing in case you're worried. I couldn't do all this alone, sweetheart."

"Or me without you."

I sent Mother a text. "Found a great house not too far from Larry's work. Thank you for your help."

"Maybe that's the last one. I should catch Jennifer up to date, but I'll pretend she's too busy. So what we do tomorrow is go back to Harperville and relax before the weekend explodes, right?"

"Unless you're willing to help me go through what I haven't packed yet. I'm at the keep or pack point, and we might see what we'll need after we get to Midland."

"Our version of relaxing. Sounds good."

"Let's talk about bills and finances. I don't think I knew what I agreed to."

I shrugged. "I don't mind doing a recap. Olivia had amassed a sizeable fortune through shrewd investments over the years. I feel guilty that I never realized how sharp she was. Remember all the boxes in her office? I thought she was an eccentric librarian who hoarded useless documents. According to her lawyer, she had no family other than her brother, who was a thug. Remember Donnie? I didn't know she considered me her younger sister or cousin, but I guess I met her need for family. My lawyer set up a foundation in her name, and my lawyer's assistant and my financial advisors vet organizations, so I can select the charities for that year. I have an allowance that I live on that is very generous. I put at least half of it into stocks every month. Any time you want to hear my stock strategy, ask. It's very simple. And I think that's it."

"My turn," Larry said. "My salary is low, and most of it goes to living expenses. Most officers with families have a side job. I don't have any debt, and I don't spend a lot of money. You're right that we talked about money when we went over our questions, but I didn't know or didn't remember about Olivia. Thank you for catching me up."

I leaned back and closed my eyes.

"We could talk about babies next, but we're almost at the B&B," Larry said.

"What?" I opened my eyes and sat up, and Larry grinned.

I glared. "Don't you dare mention babies to our parents or Jennifer and Glenn. We'd be inundated with baby furniture, clothes, and names."

"You're right. How does going for a walk then relaxing on the patio sound?"

"Sounds lazy. I like it."

When we headed to the porch, Daisy spotted us, and her tail went into overdrive.

"We were missed, but I bet she's watching for you, Palace Guard," Larry said. "I'll carry our things to our room then we can go for a walk."

"I'll go with you. I want my bandage off for the rest of the day, but I'll still use my crutches."

Larry set our things in my room while I sat in my chair and began unwinding my bandage.

"Hey. That's my job." Larry knelt next to me and unwrapped my ankle. "I don't get to do a lot for the Gray Lady. Don't steal my one opportunity to touch your leg."

I raised an eyebrow and peered at him. "One?"

He snickered. "I should have said *every*."

"Ahh. That feels so good." I wiggled my toes.

"Want me to put a sock on your foot so it won't get cold?"

"In Georgia?"

"On the patio tile."

I nodded. "I need a sock."

He returned with a hot pink sock and put it on my foot. "I found it in the back corner of your drawer." He inspected my socked foot then rose. "Looks great. Let's go. I'll bring beer to the patio and snacks. I hear Betsy rolling the cart to the dining room."

I helped Larry pick out crackers and cheese to go with our beer then we settled in at our table on the patio. As we nibbled on our snacks and sipped our beer, the rattle of an old truck interrupted the birds' songs.

"Della's here," I said.

"I'll tell her where you are." Larry strode to the foyer then Della came out to the patio. She wore her brown leather work boots, jeans, a fringed pearl-button shirt and her signature Western hat.

"Maggie, girl. Good to see you. Larry's getting me a sweet tea. Can't drink and drive a fine truck like mine." She chuckled as she sat next to me and dropped her hat on the table. "So, Larry said you had a surprise for me. Whatcha got for me, hon?"

I pulled out the envelope and handed it to her. She inspected it then removed the envelope with the card and opened the card.

"Aww. This is so sweet of you to remember. Thank you," she said.

The other couple who was on the patio and the older woman who accompanied them smiled at us.

Della hugged me and whispered. "Amazing, Maggie. This is Rembrandt's pencil sketch. *Portrait of the Artist as a Young Man.*"

She leaned back and held the card to her chest with care. "You're such a sweetheart to spoil your old grandma. I love the detail, darling. So rare."

"I thought of you the instant I saw it." I attempted a sweet smile, but it may have turned into a smirk when I rolled my eyes.

Della brushed away an imaginary tear. "You do an old woman proud. Bless you, child."

Larry brought her a glass of tea, and she sipped her tea. "I hate that I have to run off, but I can't see so good after dark anymore. You be careful, sweet girl, and you too, honey boy."

When she leaned to give me a peck on the cheek, she whispered, "Good job. Be safe, Maggie."

Larry pulled out her chair as she rose, and I blinked as the older woman at the table with the couple raised her hands to applaud. When the younger woman shook her head, she stopped midair and placed her hands in her lap then winked at me.

Larry offered his arm and walked Della to the foyer.

When he returned, Larry held up his bottle to see how much was left. "Another beer?"

"With dinner. Let's visit Daisy."

"Good idea."

When we sat on our rockers on the front porch, Daisy padded to us. After we rubbed, cooed, and scratched appropriately, she trotted back to Palace Guard and resumed her guard dog stance.

Betsy came out to the porch. "Chef canceled your dinner order. She's preparing a special Saturday night dinner to commemorate your last night with us for a while. She said to get ready for a Western treat."

After she left, I said, "Do you mind getting my Texas Tech cap out of my backpack? Seems like it will be appropriate for dinner."

"Be right back."

Larry wore his Texas Tech ball cap when he returned with my cap. "Here ya go, ma'am."

My phone buzzed as I put on my cap. "It's a text from Darren."

I read to Larry, "Mama had a good night. She said my name. I told her the Gray Lady had everything under control, and she said, *Bless you, Gray Lady.*"

My eyes overflowed and tears ran down my face.

Larry rose and returned with a tissue. "Touched me too," he said.

Palace Guard nodded and pointed to his heart.

Betsy appeared in the doorway. "Ready for dinner? I'll meet you on the patio after I finish carrying plates to the dining room. All the rest of our guests prefer to eat indoors."

Larry picked up two beers on our way then we relaxed at our patio table.

"Do you suppose it's barbeque?" I asked.

"No, because that's where Chef sent us for lunch." Larry opened our bottles.

Betsy came out with our plates. Chef stood at the window and beamed. She was shorter than Betsy, but taller than me, and as wide as she was tall. She wore a black do-rag with skull faces and a black chef jacket. Wispy gray hair escaped from her head covering, but her brown face had no wrinkles. *Advantage of years of working in a steamy kitchen?*

"Ever have venison backstrap? It's the most tender cut of meat and much prized by hunters. Chef grilled your venison backstrap after she marinated it all afternoon in apple cider and spices. You have mashed potatoes, and a tossed salad with crumbly blue cheese, Georgia blueberries, and roasted Georgia pecans. I made a cobbler with Georgia wild blackberries for dessert. Enjoy!"

Larry rose and saluted Chef, and I golf-clapped. Chef's smile broke out even wider, and Betsy hugged her. Betsy tugged Chef's arm, but Chef shook her head.

Larry cut into his venison. "Grilled to perfection."

I cut a much smaller piece. "Mmm. This is outstanding. I don't think I've ever had venison."

Chef smiled then allowed Betsy to lead her away from the window.

"Really? You're in for a treat," Larry said. "Dad and I hunt every year. Mom has lots of venison recipes."

"Remind me to add a standalone freezer for our after-Tennessee shopping list."

I ate only half of my venison because Larry kept side-eyeing it. I ate half of my potatoes and all of my salad.

"Care for the rest of my backstrap?" I pushed my plate toward Larry, and he grinned.

"Thanks." He finished off my venison in two bites, then said, "I'll pass on the potatoes. I'm saving room for cobbler."

Betsy carried out bowls of steaming cobbler with vanilla ice cream that oozed as it melted down the sides of the pastry and fruit. "Blackberries and beer complement each other." She whisked away our plates and giggled.

"Might want to give the cobbler a minute to cool," I said.

"It's fine." Larry scooped up a bite and popped it in then opened his mouth to blow on the hot cobbler as it burned his tongue and the roof of his mouth.

I will not snicker. I snickered.

As Betsy cleared our bowls, the darkening sky crept toward the sliver of orange on the horizon.

"I'd never had venison before, Betsy. Please tell Chef I loved it, and your blackberry cobbler was awesome."

Betsy grinned. "I'll tell her. She harvested it on her first hunt last fall and filled our freezer. I picked the wild blackberries this morning. I've made your reservation for next year for your first anniversary and have a note to follow up the month before to remind you."

"Thanks, Betsy. We love it here, and what better place to be for our first anniversary?" Larry said.

After Betsy left, Larry asked, "Another beer? Evening stroll? Front porch? What's next on the agenda?"

I tilted my head and fluttered my eyelashes, and he laughed. "Was that a come-hither look?"

"I think I need to work on it. Evening stroll does sound nice."

As we made our way to the trail, Larry asked, "What's our minimum furnishings we'll need? Do we have a must-have and a nice-to-have list?"

"Not yet, but it's a good time to start one. I think must-haves are a bed that is long enough so that your feet don't dangle off the end, a sofa, and a kitchen table and two chairs. We'll need pots, pans, cooking utensils, dishes, silverware, bed sheets, and towels. I want to buy a new broom because an old broom brings old worries and sweeps away new luck. We may load up what you have then buy whatever we need in Columbus."

"I have a double bed and sheets, and my feet dangle off the end. I never thought there was an option."

"We could use your bed in the second bedroom for a night or two until we buy a longer bed in Columbus. The second bedroom is spacious enough for a bed and a computer desk, although furnishing the second bedroom is not a must-have."

"Why did I not know about longer beds earlier? Don't answer. Our plan for next week is to get our marriage license on Monday and my truck on Tuesday."

"And wedding rings on Monday or Tuesday. I think the Mom Force will insist on rings at the wedding."

"You're right. Is there something I need to stress about? I keep feeling like I'm missing something."

"We could think of something."

We continued in silence until we reached the end of the trail and turned around.

"Think of anything yet?" Larry asked.

"We'll need a dog bed and dishes for Lucy."

"You'll just put that on your list. I just thought of something. What if you lose your list? What do we do then?"

"Maybe it's your turn to breathe. Decide what gives you cold feet, and we'll check it off our list."

"That's a novel idea." Larry chuckled.

As we neared the B&B, Larry stopped. "What if I need a new hunting rifle, and you won't let me buy it?"

"That doesn't work because you'll have your generous allowance just like I do. You can spend it all or part and save the rest. It's completely up to you. Sorry, but you'll have to think of something else."

We continued to the porch. "What if I never get cold feet?" he asked.

"I'll give you a back rub, and you can mourn your lack of cold feet."

He grinned. "Okay then."

When we reached the porch, Daisy slept at Palace Guard's feet and didn't budge. Palace Guard nodded his greeting, and we went inside.

"Are you stressed?" I asked as we went into my room that had become our room.

Larry's brow furrowed. "No. Should I be?"

I unbuttoned his shirt. "You're supposed to be, so I can rub the tightness out of your back muscles."

He raised his eyebrows. "Oh, right. Yes, I'm stressed."

He unbuttoned my blouse and grinned. "Can you breathe better now? Because you seemed to be a little breathless."

I unfastened my bra. "Ahh. Much better."

Larry removed his shirt then my blouse, and I snickered as my bra straps slid off with my blouse. He pulled me close and kissed me gently then unbuttoned and unzipped my jeans.

I gazed at his face while I unbuttoned and unzipped his jeans.

"You're beautiful." Larry stroked my face. "You know that?"

"If you remove your sexy pants, I can rub your back." I ran my finger from his neck down his chest to his belly and waist.

"Why do my pants have to come off for you to rub my back?"

I shrugged. "Are you sure this is an argument you want to start? Because I can tell you right now, you lose."

I giggled as I moved to the bed, pulled back the covers, and lay across the bed on my back.

As he stepped out of his jeans, he said, "I may need to work on picking my battles." He grabbed the bottom of my jeans and pulled them off with a sweeping flourish as we laughed.

I scooted around and patted the bed, and he lay on his stomach and scrunched a pillow with his arms to support his head. I straddled him and massaged his back. His muscles relaxed to my touch, and he moaned. "I was tense and didn't realize it. I think I've been tense and waiting for you my entire life."

I applied more pressure and worked out each muscle knot as I found it. When every knot was gone, I lay on top of him.

"Are you holding me down?"

"Yes." I nibbled on his neck.

He flipped me onto my back, and I giggled.

"That was a brave move on my part, wasn't it?" he chuckled. "I have more moves for you." He reached up and turned off the light.

I awoke to birds singing outside the window and Larry whistling in the shower. I opened my eyes and bathed in the joyful sounds then padded to the bathroom and opened the door. The steam of the shower rolled over my head, and Larry grinned as he dried with his towel.

"Good morning, sweetie. Three more days."

I stumbled past Larry and turned on the shower.

"Dress. Coffee. Dress. Coffee," he mumbled as he headed to the extra bedroom for his clothes.

I snickered and jumped into the shower. I was dressed and towel-drying my hair when Larry returned with coffee.

"I have our coffee." He stopped after he'd closed the door. "Dang. I missed the floor show."

"There will be plenty of those. Don't worry."

He handed me my coffee after I sat.

Larry tossed down his coffee before my second sip. "When do we leave?"

"We can pack now and leave after breakfast."

"Great." Larry strode to the extra bedroom, and before I finished half of my coffee, returned with his bags.

"I have to drink all my coffee before I can move as fast as you do." I rose and went to my closet.

Larry came in behind me and wrapped his arms around me. "I could pack for you."

I leaned back against him and closed my eyes then turned and hugged him.

"Why don't you load your things into the car? I'll pack while you aren't hovering."

"Oh. Am I hovering? Never mind." He grabbed up his bags. "I won't run. How's that?"

I emptied the drawers into my bag and pulled pants off their hangers and rolled them then stuck them into my bag. I rolled each shirt and packed it then jammed my dirty clothes on top and zipped up my bag.

I dumped my toiletries from the bathroom into the plastic laundry sack from the closet and stuck it into my backpack. Larry opened the door. "Okay to come in?"

"I'm ready for breakfast," I said.

"You're packed?"

"My bags are on the bed. We can go to breakfast then pick up my things on the way out."

"You'll have to show me how you do that sometime."

"While you hover?" I raised my eyebrows.

"Oh."

I grabbed my crutches, opened the door, and cocked my head. "You coming?"

When we reached the dining room, Larry filled two cups.

Betsy said, "I'll bring out a carafe and your breakfast."

We sat at our patio table, and I sipped my coffee after it cooled. Larry drained his cup before I had my second sip.

Betsy brought out the carafe and our breakfast burritos with a side of salsa then refilled Larry's cup.

"Want a warm-up?" Larry asked.

"Not quite yet. I just got it to the drinkable stage."

I cut my burrito in half and spooned salsa onto my half then picked it up and ate my first bite.

"Yum. Egg, cheese, and bacon. It's good."

Larry nodded and bit into his half-gone burrito. I sipped my coffee and ate small bites of my burrito. Larry chomped down on his burrito and tossed down his coffee.

"Did you always eat fast or is that an occupational-induced behavior?"

Larry laughed. "I always ate slow until I became a cop. I learned to eat fast while I had the food and before the next call came in. It's an occupational habit of law enforcement, fire, EMS, and probably anyone else who is on call."

"I wonder if undercover cops have ever been inadvertently identified by their characteristic fast eating?"

Larry finished off his burrito. "Never thought of it before. It would be hard to break too."

"I'm eating only this half. Help yourself."

"Thanks. I'll have to think about eating fast when we're out in public. I'm not undercover, but I don't need to announce *cop here* to everyone who happens to be in the restaurant. You are really smart, sweetie."

My face warmed, and I touched my cheek.

"I know I'm smart, but why does it sound so sexy when you say it?"

He kissed the edge of my mouth and whispered, "Because of my sexy pants?"

I snickered, and he winked.

Betsy collected our dishes. "You two walked in as strangers and are leaving as our dear friends. Godspeed." She hugged me then Larry and hurried back into the B&B.

"Ready?" Larry asked, and I nodded.

I headed to the front porch, and Larry diverted to pick up my bags. When I opened the door to the front porch, Palace Guard sat on the steps with his arm around Daisy.

I sat on the other side of Daisy. "She'll miss you."

Palace Guard's mouth drooped as he nodded and hugged her.

Tears dripped onto my arm. *Did you want to stay with her?*

CHAPTER TWENTY

My question swirled and echoed in my head. *Stay?*

Palace Guard shook his head, and Daisy leaned against him. I rubbed her face, and she leaned her head against my hand.

Larry dropped my bags on the porch and squatted behind Daisy. He rubbed an ear the way she liked. "We'll miss you, Daisy. Guard Betsy and Chef and think of us when you're guarding the porch."

I hugged her neck then rose and headed to the car. Larry followed me. After he loaded my bags and backpack, he helped me into the car and handed me my purse.

"Is Palace Guard staying?" he asked.

"No. He's going with us."

"Do we wait?" Larry peered at the B&B.

I glanced in the back. "He's here."

We rode in silence for two hours. I stared at the passing landscape and thought about how hard it is to leave friends. *Even harder when we can't reassure each other with empty promises to write or call or see them again.*

I snorted. *Except Betsy and Chef. We're on their calendar.*

"A real friend puts you on their calendar."

Palace Guard nodded, and Larry blinked. "I think I missed the first part."

"I was thinking about how hard it is to leave friends even though we say the polite lies like I'll write or see you soon. It's even harder when we can't repeat those polite social lies to a friend like Daisy. But Betsy and Chef are the exception. No empty, polite promises there. Betsy put us on her calendar."

Palace Guard poked me on my back and pointed to the field on his side. *Cows.*

"You're on, bud." I stared out my window. After two miles, I said, "Cows."

Palace Guard poked me. *Cows.*

"Cows this side too."

Palace Guard tapped my shoulder and shook his head.

"Fine. They're goats. They count as half-cows."

Larry snorted. As we approached a small town, Larry slowed. "Well, look what's ahead."

When we came to an ice cream shop on Palace Guard's side, Larry stopped, and he and Palace Guard high-fived.

"Doesn't count." I stuck my nose in the air. "It's closed."

Larry cleared his throat, and a man and two boys came out of the shop. The boys held ice cream cones with two scoops of chocolate ice cream heaped high. They licked the melting ice cream that dripped onto their hands, and the man laughed.

"It's a conspiracy. Men sticking together." I crossed my arms, and Larry chuckled.

I love his laugh.

I glanced at Palace Guard, and he winked.

My frown morphed into a smile. "How long until we're in Harperville?"

"Little over a half hour. What's our plan of attack?"

"Let's go to Olivia's apartment first to drop off our stuff then we can go to your apartment to pack."

I leaned back and closed my eyes.

Larry slowed to the lower speed limits. "Do you still have your key to Olivia's apartment?"

"It's on my keyring in my backpack."

Larry nodded. "I'm not surprised."

He turned at the apartment complex entrance and drove around the traffic circle with the three bubbling fountains in the middle. When we pulled into the parking area, I smiled at the picture-perfect separate biking and walking paths around the lake. *Still has its magazine cover ambiance.*

After we parked, Larry handed me my backpack, and I pulled out the key.

"I'll carry your backpack," Larry said. "If the apartment is okay for this week, I'll come back for the rest of our things."

As we passed the L-shaped Olympic-sized pool on our way to the elevator, Larry asked, "Did you bring your swimsuit? Not that it matters. Relaxing in the pool somehow isn't on our list, is it?"

I handed Larry the key during our slow-moving ride to the third floor. "I don't think I've ever been on this elevator. I've always run up and down the three flights of stairs."

Larry unlocked the apartment door, and my eyes widened as we walked inside. An oversized emerald green sofa with three multicolored overstuffed throw pillows and two overstuffed deep purple recliners replaced Olivia's austere, white furnishings. Hardwood floors and a sage-green area rug completed the transformation away from all-white.

Larry snickered. "Your mother was here."

Palace Guard smiled.

I sat on the sofa then tried out a chair. "At least they're comfortable. Huge improvement. The colors explode in my head, but I grew up with them. It's almost like old home week."

Larry checked the fridge. "We have ice cream in the freezer, beer in the refrigerator, and we're stocked for breakfast. Mom Force."

After Larry left for the rest of our things, I sent a text to Jennifer. "Here. Thanks for stocking fridge. Sofa & chairs are comfortable, thanks to Mother. Please pass on info to all."

Jennifer: "Good. Will share."

I checked the first bedroom; when I gasped, Palace Guard rushed to my side. The walls were painted light, cool gray, and the bed cover and drapes were a medium-cool gray. The floor was hardwood, and the area rug was charcoal with tiny red stripes. I hurried to the second bedroom, and its walls were painted pale tan and the furnishings' color scheme was rustic red with zig-zag brown and gold stripes.

"Harriet gave Mother the living room, and she decorated the bedrooms."

Palace Guard nodded.

Larry came into the apartment. "Where do I put our things?"

"I'll let you decide. Check the bedrooms."

"Will they hurt my eyes?" he asked.

I shrugged. Larry carried our things into the first bedroom then checked the second. "Maggie," he shouted. "Somebody kidnapped your mother."

I snickered.

"That is the only plausible explanation for the bedrooms, isn't it?" I asked when he strode into the living room and grinned as he dropped onto the sofa next to me. "Which one did you choose?"

"The one that has the view of the courtyard. It was a hard choice: Gray Lady or Crazy Lady."

I snorted. "Let's have lunch then go see your apartment, Fashion Man."

"Made a mistake, didn't I?" Larry asked as he followed me to the kitchen.

Larry's apartment building was old. His apartment was on the second floor, and there was no elevator.

"Are you going to be okay?" he asked.

"I'll be fine going up, but I need you in front of me when I come down in case I stumble."

By the second floor, I was breathing hard. "I'm out of shape." I leaned against the banister to catch my breath. "Good workout. Where's your apartment?"

"Two doors down. This needs to be good because you aren't making that trip again."

My breathing slowed. "Let's see what we've got."

We went into Larry's apartment. I expected a bachelor pad with cheap aluminum chairs and piles of clothes, papers, and junk, but his apartment was spotless. The wooden floors were stained with burns and scrapes from years of renters, but the large, oval, green and cream braided rug and the rolled arm, olive-green sofa gave the room class.

"This is perfect, Larry." I sat on the sofa and leaned back. "So comfortable. I love it."

I rose to examine the kitchen table and chairs. "This looks hand-crafted." I rubbed my fingers across the table. "We won't need to buy any furniture at all, and Lucy will love the braided rug."

He frowned. "Really? You aren't just being polite, are you?"

Palace Guard rolled his eyes, and I snorted.

"Never mind," Larry said. "I had a lapse in memory or judgment or both."

I opened the kitchen cabinets and drawers. "We can use everything here. I can't think of anything else we'd need to buy."

"Bedroom next," Larry said.

The only furniture in his bedroom was the double bed and a tall six-drawer dresser. He had made his bed, and it was covered with a handmade quilt.

"Your double bed is perfect for the guest bedroom." I ran my fingers across the headboard. "I love the smoothness of the wood. We'll want your dresser in our bedroom. It's beautiful."

We returned to the kitchen, and I surveyed the cabinets. "If you'll pick up boxes at the hardware store, we can pack the kitchen. While you're gone, I'll pack your clothes into your duffle bag. What do you think?"

"Sounds like a plan."

When Larry returned with boxes, I had packed his clothes and organized the kitchen. After forty-five minutes, we had packed everything in his apartment.

I dropped onto the sofa. "We're an unbeatable team."

Larry sat next to me, and I snuggled against him.

"We already knew that. What's next?" he asked.

"We should gather our laundry, and I'll pick up the rest of my clothes from Jennifer's. We need to do laundry this evening. I was surprised there wasn't a washer and dryer in the apartment. There must be a laundry somewhere at the apartment complex, but I don't remember one. I know Olivia sent her clothes to the cleaners. I thought she was just particular. Do you suppose everyone else sends their clothes out too? I'll let Jennifer know we'll come by to pick up clothes."

Larry brushed my hair off my face and traced my jaw with a light touch of his finger. "Stop a second and breathe." He lifted my chin and kissed me. "Jennifer wants to hear about graduation. Glenn wants to talk to you, and we would enjoy a visit with Lucy and Spike. When you call, Jennifer will invite us for dinner. What do you say?"

"We can't stay for dinner; we have too much to do, and we planned pizza tonight."

"We can have our pizza on Wednesday or Thursday. Honeymoon on the balcony."

I snickered. "I'm not sure if that would sound romantic to anyone else, but it sounds wonderful to me. You're right. If she invites us, I'll say yes." I kissed his chin. "You're very smart."

I texted Jennifer. "Will be by later to pick up my clothes."

Jennifer: "Bring laundry, and stay for supper."

I laughed and showed my phone to Larry.

"Told you," he said, and I poked him in the ribs with my elbow.

Me: "Sounds great. Be there in about an hour."

"I'll carry my clothes and my gear down to the car then we'll go to Olivia's and collect our laundry."

He rose, and I put up my feet and leaned back then closed my eyes.

"Maggie?" Larry sat next to me on the sofa, and I blinked as I opened my eyes. "Did you know you have two speeds: go full speed and stop when you slam into a wall? You do them very well."

"I was resting my eyes." I yawned.

"I'm all loaded. Ready to go?"

I tried going down the stairs with my crutches. "This doesn't work. Hold my crutches, and I'll hang onto the banister."

"Why don't you hold on to the banister on your good side and onto me on your left, then you can hop down one step at a time."

After the first flight down, I stopped to catch my breath then I hopped, and Larry supported me.

When Larry parked in the driveway at Jennifer and Glenn's house, Spike and Lucy were in the front yard, and Glenn waited on the front porch.

"You know they've been out here for at least two days, don't you?" Larry smiled as Lucy yipped and ran tight circles in her excitement.

Larry helped me out of the car, and I sat on the grass with Lucy. She yipped and danced around me, and we snuggled.

When Larry helped me up, I said, "Thanks for taking care of her, Spike. I know she was happy to be with you and Glenn. I missed her and missed you too."

Spike hung his head then panda-smiled as he poked my arm and punched Larry's.

Jennifer came to the door. "Come inside, everybody, where it's cooler."

Larry carried our laundry to the utility room, and I loaded then started the washer.

When we returned to the kitchen, Jennifer said, "Maggie, I packed all your clothes and added the packet of documents from your mother to the suitcase."

"Thank you. Mother told me she left the paperwork with you, but I wouldn't have thought about it until tomorrow."

During dinner, Jennifer grilled Larry about graduation and me about the B&B. Glenn repeated everything he'd told me by phone. *It's nice to be with family.*

Palace Guard nodded, and Spike did his wacky dance. When Larry and I laughed, Glenn asked, "Spike's wacky dance? When this dang knee heals, I might need wacky dance lessons. I'll ask Kate to teach me."

I told them about the visit with Darren Martin and his follow up text.

Jennifer brushed tears off her cheek. "What a caring man."

"What's your theory about Christopher's document?" Glenn asked.

"I'm convinced he was hired by Clara Hayden. She always relied on Vera to hire the talent. Clara probably went for the cheapest, not the best, and I think she created the document to throw the suspicion away from herself and onto Darren Martin. Clara might have been the mastermind who planned one of the most successful thefts in history, but she relied on her team to carry through with the details. I think whoever killed Christopher orchestrated the attacks on me. I'm not sure why, but it has something to do with Clara Hayden."

"As far as the wedding is concerned, be here Wednesday at eight for breakfast then the wedding is at ten. There. That's all you need to know." Jennifer beamed.

"What do I wear?" Larry asked.

"That's on Lauren's list. Be here Wednesday morning at eight and bring Maggie."

"You have the toughest assignment, son." Glenn clapped his hand on Larry's shoulder then chuckled.

Jennifer glared at Glenn then turned to me. "Ready for dessert? We have cherry pie and ice cream."

"Oh, yes."

After we finished dessert, Jennifer asked, "Want to sit on the patio while the dryer's still running?"

Glenn and I moved to the patio while Jennifer brought out our tea glasses, and Larry carried the pitcher of sweet tea.

"I still don't understand why you're the target, Maggie. Am I missing something?" Jennifer asked.

"Whatever it is, I'm missing it too," Larry said. "Dryer's done. I'll empty it."

I rose. "We're going to go, if we're not rushing out on you. Is there anything you need us to do?"

"Let's see," Glenn said. "First, stay safe. Second, don't get shot this week. Or wrecked, caught in a fire, or blown up. Anything else, Jennifer?"

"Let your foot finish healing. I'm sure there's more. I'll text you."

Larry chuckled as he stood in the doorway with our clean laundry. "That's what I've been telling her all along. Thanks for the backup."

After we were at Olivia's apartment, Larry dumped our laundry on the spare bed then we folded, sorted, and put away our clothes.

"Ready for a beer and the balcony?" he asked.

I pointed to my ear, and he chuckled. "The apartment is clean. No bugs, but we should write notes on the balcony just in case."

I nodded. "It's what we do."

I carried a pad and a pen to the balcony, and Larry brought our beer. We wrote suggestive, sexy notes then left our half-full bottles on the balcony when we rushed to the bedroom.

I woke and listened. *Shower running; Larry whistling. My life is complete.*

I hurried to the bathroom and grabbed Larry's towel. "If you'll get the coffee perking, I'll cook breakfast after my shower, Mr. Sexy Pants."

Larry stepped out of the shower. "Deal."

I handed him his towel, and he hugged me then grinned. "Good morning, naked Maggie. Two days."

He dried then wrapped the towel around his waist and mumbled as he left for the bedroom, "Get Dressed. Coffee."

While we were eating breakfast, my phone buzzed. *Della?*

"Authentic. Gray Lady will receive a notice from the museum. Correction. Rich Gray Lady. Love you, Grandma D."

"Wow," Larry said when I showed him the text, and Palace Guard nodded.

I shuddered. "We'll talk to Ms. Rodriquez when we go to the office to discuss wedding rings with Shantelle this afternoon."

"We have almost two hours until our appointment to get our marriage licenses. We have all our paperwork. Want to go look at trailers? We can check sizes, availability, and costs."

"That sounds interesting." My phone rang.

"Hello, Darren. Everything okay?"

"You might not have heard, but it's a big deal in the art circle here. Clara Hayden's house burned down in the middle of the night. It was too far gone before the fire department got there, and they could not go into the house until the fire was out. They've been sifting through the rubble and ashes, but they haven't found her yet."

"That's terrible."

"It is. You know I didn't care for her at all, but it's still tragic. I thought you'd want to know."

"Thank you, Darren. I appreciate it."

After we hung up, Larry asked, "What's wrong? You're pale."

"Clara's house burned down in the middle of the night, and they can't find her. She must have hidden in the basement. I need to tell somebody to search the basement. She must be trapped."

"If debris fell across that narrow opening to the old root cellar, they wouldn't have seen it," Larry said. "I'll call Lieutenant Baker. He'll contact the Fire Marshall's office, and they'll get someone there immediately."

Larry made his call then put his arms around me. "Lieutenant Baker is on it. He says he'll get back to me as soon as he hears back." He kissed my forehead. "Do you still want to look at trailers?"

"There's nothing I can do to save Clara or find her. I'd only stew. Let's look at trailers."

After Larry parked at the trailer lot, a man came out of the rental office and shook Larry's hand. "You here to pick out a trailer? When do you want it?"

"It would be ideal if we could pick it up Wednesday afternoon."

The man nodded. "Check what's here at the lot. Go look around and come find me. I'm Cecil." He pointed to the embroidered name on his shirt and chuckled. "That was my high-pressure sales pitch."

We walked through the lot and peeked inside the cargo trailers.

"We have three large items: the bed, your dresser, and the kitchen table. I don't think we could go any smaller than the six by twelve," I said.

"Let's go find Cecil."

When we reached the office, Cecil was waiting for us. "You'll need the six by twelve for large items, not weight. Am I right? Come in where it's cool, and let's talk."

The office was clean and cool, as he promised. He pointed to the round table near the corner. "Let's sit. Now, what kind of vehicle do you have to pull your trailer?"

"We plan to buy a truck tomorrow," Larry said.

Cecil shook his head. "If you have the time, you might want to buy it today. You'll need them to set up the truck to haul. Let me give you a spec sheet. If you give this to the dealer, they can set you up exactly right."

"Thank you." Larry stared at the sheet. "I guess I thought any truck comes trailer-ready."

"You want a truck with a towing package that has the differential gear and sturdy transmission, brakes, and frame for towing and the electrical and cooling upgrades to handle a heavy load. There are a few extras you'll want for towing, and the dealership will need a half day or so for the installation."

"I'm glad we came here first."

"It's what we do. Let's fill out the paperwork for your trailer, and I'll reserve a six-by-twelve for you. If you change your mind, call me and I'll release it."

"How much do you want for a deposit?" I asked.

"No deposit until you pick it up. I'll give you an estimate sheet that will help you with your budget. We're talking one-way, right?"

I nodded, and he went behind the counter and set a multi-part form on the counter. "Fill this out, and I'll print your spec sheet and the estimate. Where are you going?"

"Columbus." Larry strode to the counter to fill out the form.

Cecil typed on a computer then printed two sheets of paper. He handed the papers to me while Larry completed the form and signed it. Cecil gave Larry his card. "Call me if you change your mind or have any questions. You have all your boxes?"

Larry nodded. "Already packed."

On our way to the county building, I said, "Shall I tell Mother we want to buy the truck later this afternoon?"

"Yes. Do you think we'd be done at the lawyer's office by three?"

"I would think so. I'll text her."

My phone rang after I sent the text.

"I'm on it, Margaret. Big D taught me that."

She hung up, and I laughed.

"What did she say?" Larry asked.

"I don't know why she didn't just text me, but she said she's on it."

Larry parked at the county building and grinned. "We're really here."

He opened my door then hugged me after I climbed out. Palace Guard scanned the area then nodded.

After a half-hour, we came out of the building and walked across the parking lot in stunned silence. When we reached the car, Larry hugged me again. "I expected to be there until at least noon."

"They were impressive, weren't they?" I showed him my phone while Palace Guard peeked over my shoulder. "Mother texted me the name, address, and phone number of a truck salesman that Sarge recommended. Shall I call him?"

Larry's phone rang. "Just a sec. It's Lieutenant Baker."

Larry listened, and I frowned. *Can't tell what he's saying.* "Understood."

One-sided calls with no speaker phone are now against the rules.

"Yes sir, what do we do?"

Larry listened and nodded. "Yes sir, thank you."

Larry hung up then cleared his throat. "Call the truck dealer then we can talk."

Only because I trust you. I asked for Jim, the man Sarge recommended.

A man interrupted the maddening hold music. "Ms. Sloan, soon to be Mrs. Ewing, I understand. When would you and Mr. Ewing like to look at a truck?"

"When are you available?"

"If you come now, you'll catch me before my lunch at one."

"Perfect. We're on our way."

After we hung up, Larry said, "I heard. He has Sarge's booming voice."

"Your turn."

"Let's get in the car and get the air conditioning going. We can talk while we head to the dealership."

When we were on the road, Larry said, "They found Clara Hayden's body in the root cellar. They're going to do an autopsy because the house had all the earmarks of arson. She had no visible injuries or burns, and while she could have died from a heart attack, especially at her age, it would still be murder because of the arson."

"I have so many questions, but I know you can't answer them."

"There's more." The fierceness in Larry's voice startled me, and I stared at him. "The police in Athens got an anonymous tip on their tip line with no real credibility, but somehow the media got wind and decided the police had a person of interest. Unfortunately, the internet has gone into a frenzy and is clamoring for an arrest. It's turning ugly."

"I don't like the sound of this. They aren't targeting Darren, are they?"

CHAPTER TWENTY-ONE

Larry narrowed his eyes, and his jaw tightened. "No. The person of interest is you."

"What?"

Palace Guard sat upright and moved behind me to cover my back.

"This isn't real. What do we do?"

"Lieutenant said to talk to your lawyer and let the family know what's going on, so they don't get blindsided."

"I'll call Shantelle so she can give Ms. Rodriquez a heads up then I'll call Jennifer. She has the coolest head; no, Glenn does. I'll call Glenn."

"After you talk to Glenn, call Sarge. I'll call my dad."

Larry turned at a park and parked in the shade. He left the car running and climbed out to call his dad.

I called Shantelle and gave her a quick rundown then called Glenn.

"Glenn, is Jennifer there?"

"Both of us are here, and the speakerphone is on. What's up?" Glenn asked.

"Clara Hayden died in a house fire last night or early this morning. The fire was most likely arson. The Athens police got a tip on their anonymous line, and the news media announced the authorities have a person of interest and is calling for an arrest. Social media jumped on it, and it's turned ugly. The person of interest is me."

"What?" Glenn roared. "That's bull..."

Jennifer jumped in. "Yes, it is. What can we do, Maggie?"

"I don't know. Lay low. Don't engage in any online discussions. We needed for you to be aware in case you get any media calls. I need to call Sarge."

"Okay, honey," Jennifer said. "We'll circle the wagons. Let us know if we can do anything. Is it okay if I tell Ella, and Glenn tells Paul?"

"Yes. Just caution them to stay out of it. Any attempt to defend me will only make it worse."

"Got it," Glenn said. "I still say it's bull, and it stinks of a set up."

After we hung up, I called Sarge.

"I just heard, Maggie. Utter nonsense. What can we do?"

"It will be hard on Mother. Please tell her the best way she can help me right now is to stay quiet. Any of her efforts to defend me will hurt me. We all have to stay low."

"You're right. Have you heard from anyone official?"

"Not yet."

"See your lawyer and don't agree to meet or talk with anyone without your lawyer. This smells like a railroad job to me. Stay off the tracks, and call me if you need any help."

My heart melted. "Thanks, Sarge."

Larry joined me in the car. "Are you okay?"

"Yes. How did your dad react to the news?"

"Fine. He's good. He said he'd call Sarge, Glenn, and all of his friends to find the root of the internet and storm it then rip out its wires."

I rolled my eyes, and Larry smiled. "Dad paints a strange picture with his words when he gets angry, but I'm glad you knew it might be a joke." Larry shook his head. "He was mad. He'll do whatever he can to help. What about Glenn and Sarge?"

"The same. Sarge said it sounded like a railroad job to him, and I should stay off the tracks. Interpret, please."

"A railroad job is when someone is falsely accused by false evidence. When he said stay off the tracks, he was staying keep as clear as you can."

"Let's buy a truck and stay away from the tracks."

When Larry parked at the dealership, a man rushed to meet us. "I'm Jim, but they call me Jimbo. Mr. and Mrs. Ewing?"

Jim was two inches shorter than Larry, but he was so thin and leggy, he looked taller.

"Yes." Larry and Jimbo shook hands, and I smiled.

"Do you know what you want?"

Jimbo and Larry talked engines and under the hood details, and Jimbo jotted in his pocket-sized notebook then nodded. "Think I know what you want. Mrs. Ewing?"

"We need a crew cab with four doors. A topper would be nice if it's on the lot and doesn't require extra time to install. We'll need a towing package because we'll be hauling a trailer. We have the specs as far as what we need to be sure we can tow a cargo trailer."

Jimbo added to his notes while I talked. "Color?"

"Not black. Tinted windows would be nice," I said.

"Four-wheel drive?"

"I don't want four-wheel drive," Larry said, "but if a truck has everything else and has four-wheel drive, it's okay."

Jimbo looked over his notes. "I have three trucks for you. They're last year's models, but new. Do you have your spec sheet, Mrs. Ewing?"

I gave Jimbo the sheet, and he nodded as he read it. "Standard. Can I give this to my service guy to look over? I'd like to be sure he has what we need or can get it by tomorrow morning. When did you want your truck?"

"Wednesday at the latest," Larry said before Jimbo bounded away in his long, easy stride.

"Are you okay, Mrs. Ewing?" Larry's eyes twinkled.

"I'm getting used to it, Mr. Ewing." I smiled.

Jimbo grinned as he loped back. "Good news. We either have what we need in stock or can get it by the end of today. One of our trucks has a topper. Let's look at it first."

Jimbo was right. The truck with the topper was what we wanted, and Jimbo handed Larry the keys for a test drive. I rode in the backseat to be sure the air-conditioning cooled the back. When we returned, Larry and I compared notes, then he said, "We're happy with this truck. We're ready to buy, Jimbo."

"Done. Let's get moving on the paperwork. Will you need financing?"

"No, we can write a check or move the funds, whatever the dealership prefers," I said.

"I'll let you talk to our accounting guy."

"We have an appointment at one. Can we get all of our end completed before then?" I asked.

"Will do. I'm a hunt and peck kind of guy. Would you be offended if one of our interns sat in on our session and handled all the computer work to speed us up?"

"Sounds brilliant," I said.

"Good. We'll have you out of here by noon, so you can have lunch before your one o'clock appointment."

Jimbo was true to his word. I completed an online transfer of funds, and we signed the last document at eleven forty-five.

Jimbo shook Larry's hand then mine. "It was a pleasure to work with you two. I'll call you in the morning, Mr. Ewing. If you don't hear from me by nine, feel free to call me."

"I know the perfect place to grab a fast lunch," Larry said as we left the dealership.

When we pulled into the drive-up order line, my eyes widened as I stared at the rest of the cars in line. "Are we hiding in plain sight? We're surrounded by patrol and undercover cars here."

Larry side-glanced at me. "How do you know they're undercover?"

I raised my eyebrows and peered at him over my sunglasses, and Palace Guard rolled his eyes.

"I sure do ask dumb questions sometimes."

"Yep." I scoped out the waiting customers while they examined us and turned away. "We don't look like criminals."

"Good. Do you know what you want?"

"Yes. Whatever you order."

Larry placed our order then after the transaction for our sandwiches and sweet tea was completed at the window, we headed to the nearest park and sat at a picnic bench in the shade.

While we ate, Larry asked, "What all are we doing at the lawyer's office?"

I pulled out my list. "Shantelle will help us with wedding rings then we'll talk to Ms. Rodriquez about Clara's death and me being the person of interest, the art award, and wills. What else?"

Larry's phone rang. "It's Lieutenant Baker." He answered, and his eyes grew wide as he listened.

"Yes, we do. Thanks."

He listened and nodded.

"Yes, I understand."

When he hung up, he closed his eyes. "We can do this." He leaned over and kissed my mustardy mouth. "Yum. Spicy. We've got more for Ms. Rodriquez. Clara Hayden's lawyer called the police and said Clara had him draw up a new will last week. She cut out her grandson and left everything to you. She told her lawyer you were Bruce Hayden's great-granddaughter. It won't be long before the lawyer contacts the media because the police didn't panic enough to suit his public ego. This is all unofficial."

I opened my notebook and added Clara's will to my list for Ms. Rodriquez then tapped the pad with my pen. "On the list. Are you sure you don't want a prenup?"

Larry burst out laughing. "You are awesome. Who else would laugh with me with all this mess? Our life isn't a railroad job. It's a train wreck."

I snickered. "Perfect way to start a marriage." I pointed to my sandwich. "I've eaten what I want."

Larry dropped my sandwich into the sack and gathered our trash. "I'm too hyper to eat any more. Let's see the lawyer and argue like normal people over wedding rings."

Larry opened my car door after he parked at the lawyer's small house that served as her office near the courthouse. "Are you okay?"

"It is overwhelming, but I'm fine. What about you?"

"Peachy," he grinned.

When we went inside, the old parquet floors and rich woodwork gleamed as the sunlight streamed through the windows. Shantelle's old wooden desk and the overstuffed armchair and square mission-style table had switched positions in the room. Shantelle came out of the small conference room and rushed to greet us at the door. Her skin was dark, her eyes were black, and her short, tight curls hugged her scalp. She had a ring piercing below her lower lip and a small scar in the middle of her chin.

"Hey, Maggie. This is Larry?" Shantelle held out her hand, and Larry smiled and shook hands. "Come into the conference room. I've got some samples for you to look at. Too bad you're allergic to gold, Maggie, but there are some beautiful rings that aren't gold. I forgot to ask you, did you want a set? You know, an engagement ring and a wedding ring?"

"Not at all," I said.

The sleek, modern table in the conference room was a stark contrast to the soft welcoming style of the main room. The conference room décor announced Business is Conducted Here.

"Sit wherever you like. I'll move the rings so you can examine them."

Larry sat at the head of the table with his back to the wall; I sat next to him in the seat that faced the door, and Palace Guard maintained a position near the windows.

"I didn't think you'd want a set, so there aren't any here. We have platinum and silver. Platinum is more durable, in my opinion. There's a ring with platinum on the inside and gold on the outside, which gives you the look of a gold band without the itch. I'll leave you to choose maybe three or four that you both like. Come get me when you're ready to talk. I'll be at my desk."

"What are your thoughts, Maggie?" Larry scanned the rings.

"I don't want diamonds. The simple, plain band is nice, and I like the carved ones. I think Shantelle called them scrolled."

Larry slid all the ring boxes with diamonds on the rings to one side. "Did you want our rings to match?"

"Of course."

Larry moved the plain ring and two of the carved scrolled rings together, and I pointed to one of the rings. "That one's too carved. It's trying too hard."

Larry moved it to join the diamond rings.

"Now what?" he asked.

I tried on both rings. "The plain one doesn't have the rolled edges like the carved one and isn't as comfortable."

"Carved, scrolled, and rolled it is. I'll get Shantelle."

When Larry opened the door, Shantelle hurried in. "You two aren't afraid of decisions are you? Don't tell me. You found the ring with rolled edges."

She checked the table. "I win. I'm so proud of myself." She sat with us at the table. "This ring is custom made. I'll measure your fingers, and you can pick them up tomorrow morning. I ordered both of your rings as soon as we got the call that y'all were going to be married because I have total confidence in my talent to match jewelry with its owner. The artisan is waiting to hear from me for the final size."

She measured our ring fingers. "Ms. Rodriquez will be here in a few minutes. Care for coffee or water?"

I shook my head, and Larry said, "No, thanks."

Shantelle bustled out of the conference room and closed the door.

"Another check mark for our list?" Larry asked.

Ms. Rodriquez opened the door. She was Mother's age, and her coal-black hair had a streak of silver near her temple. Her single braid hung down her back. She wore black flats, a gray flared skirt, and a loose black and red checked shirt. *No court today.*

She hugged me and shook hands with Larry. "Larry, I'm Amy Rodriquez. I've been looking forward to meeting you. I am so glad you two are here. I'm not sure Shantelle can survive any more exciting Maggie calls today."

Larry and Palace Guard nodded.

She chuckled as she sat, and we joined her.

"I've set the entire afternoon aside for you. Let's get started so I can release you and get my real Maggie work going. Let's start with money. We need to set Larry up with an annuity, just like yours, Maggie, and start-up money for both of you. Larry, do you have your checkbook with you? Can you give me a voided check?"

"Yes." He opened his backpack and pulled out his checkbook, wrote *Void* across the top check, and gave it to Ms. Rodriquez.

Shantelle came into the conference room. "The rings are on order."

"Annuity for Larry, and startup money for both." Ms. Rodriquez handed her Larry's voided check, and Shantelle swooped up the check, whirled around, and left.

"You should see your startup money in your checking accounts by Thursday. The annuity will start the first of the month, Larry. After you move and get new drivers' licenses, open a joint account somewhere and send us a voided check. We'll put seed money into it then start up another annuity to go to the joint account."

"I don't want a bunch of Maggie's money." Larry crossed his arms and scowled.

"Oh." Ms. Rodriquez said. "Do you have cold feet? I understand. If you want to call off the wedding, we may sue you for breach of contract."

Larry's eyes widened, and Ms. Rodriquez guffawed. "You can be mad at me if you want, but that was fun." She wiped her eyes. "The deal is, everything you have is hers, and everything she has is yours. Am I wrong? The amounts don't matter. If either of you change your mind later about what we do today, come see me, and I'll respect your wishes. No questions asked. How's that?"

"Okay," Larry said. "Sorry my bad attitude slowed us down."

"You're not doing bad at all, Larry. One money thing that I am postponing is the potential reward money. We'll wait until we see it and how much it is before we decide what we want to do. Is that it for money? Let's move to wills."

Shantelle returned with two folders. "Will time?" she asked.

Ms. Rodriquez nodded. "Perfect timing, as always. I drew up simple wills for both of you. Larry, you leave everything to Maggie, and Maggie, you leave everything to Larry. You'll need to decide what your wills need to say when you're both gone, but for now, if you're both gone, your four parents inherit. Maggie, I named Sarge and your mother. Do you want that to change? I used your legal names for the will, so they'd be legal." She snickered. "I never get to joke in court. Y'all get to suffer for that. Maggie, you are listed as Margaret Ewing with Maggie in parentheses; Larry, you are listed as Kevin Ewing with Larry in parentheses. If you'd rather have something different, let me know, but these names are perfectly legal as of Wednesday. Any questions? Complaints?"

We glanced at each other, then Larry shook his head.

"Fine. Over to you, Shantelle."

Shantelle said, "I'll run you through the wills and point out where you sign. Notice I said run, not walk. After you read through them at your leisure, call me with your corrections. First, the blue tab. Initial, initial, sign."

Shantelle ran us through each section, as promised, and we initialed, initialed, and signed. Then Shantelle dropped two more folders on the desk. "Again. This is your original. You keep a set. We keep a set."

We initialed, initialed, and signed at each tab.

"Not everyone gets this much handholding." Ms. Rodriquez wiggled her eyebrows, and we laughed.

"Remember, we expect questions later because there is a lot of legal language," she said. "What's next?"

"Person of interest and Clara's new will," I said.

"Yes. I sent notices to several news organizations on your behalf. They'll include an apology and correction in tiny print with no headline and claim it as a retraction, but I can't stop the internet monster. It will blow over in a week or two when another shiny object grabs the social media herd. I am sorry you have this when you should be focusing on your wedding. Call me if law enforcement or any attorneys call you. All communication goes through me. We won't worry about this supposed new Clara will. Her lawyer will call me if he has any brains. If he calls you, tell him to call me. What else?" She waited. "Fine. Neither one of you has mentioned a prenup. Have you already discussed it?"

Larry glared at me. "Yes."

"Well, good. The prenups I write are one sentence. *Go read your wedding vows*. What else?"

Palace Guard smiled, and Larry burst out laughing.

Ms. Rodriquez smiled. "You've got yourself a keeper there, Maggie. I like this man. We're done, right?"

"We are, Ms. Rodriquez. Thank you and Shantelle for everything."

Shantelle carried our folders and walked with us to the car. "I'll call you in the morning and let you know what time y'all can pick up the rings. It was great seeing you again, Maggie. Nice to meet you, Larry." She handed the folders to Larry and strode back to the office.

"What a day. I wish I could go for a run." I stared at the runners as we headed to Olivia's apartment. "Everybody in town is running except me."

"We managed to cram two days of work into one day. Let's grab a beer then go swimming. Or go swimming and grab a beer. See if our pizza place delivers. We need a relaxing evening."

I checked. "They deliver. We're set."

We raced in the swim lanes while Palace Guard scanned the area. When I was winded, I moved to the smaller pool and floated. Larry called out, "Cannon ball!" and swamped me. I swam after him, and he swam away. We played our version of tag until I climbed out and dropped onto a lounging chair. I lay back and closed my eyes. Larry kissed me, and I opened my eyes and scooted over so he could sit.

"Do you think Clara set her own fire but didn't plan a heart attack?" I asked.

Larry chuckled. "Love you too, sweetie. No. What are you thinking?"

"I don't either. I think the Real Bad Guy's original purpose was to kill me because he knew about Margarite Flanagan. I don't think it was the will he was worried about. I think he knew Clara might give me the stolen art before he could get it. I'll bet the reward far exceeds Clara's estate."

"That does explain all the attacks that appeared to be targeted at you, doesn't it? What about Clara's house fire?"

"I think he decided or Clara told him the art wasn't at her house, and I think he didn't know about the will change. Maybe her estate was good enough after all, which points to the grandson as the Real Bad Guy."

"Are you back to Maurice?"

"Maybe. Can we go out to dinner?"

"One condition. We go tomorrow night, not tonight. We've had a full day, and you need your rest before you put on your Gray Lady cape."

I furrowed my brow. "I don't have a cape."

Larry smirked. "Text Jennifer."

When I reached for my phone, Larry stopped me for a kiss. "I was kidding."

"I still need a cape." I sent the text to Jennifer.

On our way to the elevator, Jennifer replied to my text.

"LOL. Tell Larry to stop teasing you."

I bit my lip and showed my phone to Larry, and he chuckled. "You're good, Crazy Lady. Now I'm in trouble with Jennifer."

While I showered, Larry ordered the pizza then showered. We sat on the patio while we drank beer, ate pizza, and wrote notes to each other that were sexy and hilarious until they evolved to just sexy.

I opened my eyes before dawn and smiled at the music of whistling and running water. As I opened the bathroom door, Larry turned off the shower and reached for his towel.

"One more day, sweetheart." He stepped out of the shower, and I hugged him and closed my eyes as I inhaled his man smell. When he rushed to dress, I hopped into the shower; after I was dressed, I hurried to the kitchen and joined him at the bar for coffee.

After my second cup, I pulled out a skillet and eggs and sausage to cook our breakfast. While I cooked, Larry asked, "What's our plan for today? Jimbo is supposed to call by nine, and Shantelle will call this morning sometime. What else?"

"As soon as we know what time we can pick up the truck, we can call Cecil at the trailer place to arrange picking up the trailer. We might be able to leave on Thursday if we load the trailer tomorrow."

Palace Guard rolled his eyes, and Larry cleared his throat. "The Mom Force might complain if they hear about spending our wedding day loading the trailer."

"Oh. This social stuff is hard." I frowned. "I'll come up with something else."

"I'm sure you will, sweetie."

Larry's phone rang, and he sighed. "Lieutenant Baker." He answered and listened.

He nodded. "She works fast."

He listened then glanced at me and snorted. "Pretty much."

"Thanks."

After he hung up, he said, "Ms. Rodriquez is amazing. Lieutenant Baker said he had to call me because he knew I'd appreciate knowing."

I stopped buttering our toast and glared.

"You are so cute when you're about to slice me up with a butter knife." Larry smiled.

I narrowed my eyes.

"Okay." Larry held up his hands. "Clara Hayden's lawyer is scrambling to tell the world that he never said anything about you or Clara Hayden's will, and the fact that he has been reported to the bar for a breach in client confidentiality has nothing to do with you, Clara Hayden or any will. Social media is all over him. Nothing like a lawyer to draw the ire of the thundering herd. Lieutenant Baker said our lawyer was on the ball."

"Wow. Ms. Rodriquez is sharp, isn't she? What else?"

"Not much. More coffee?" He grabbed the coffee pot.

"After I hear what else."

Larry stared at the pot then poured himself a splash. "Lieutenant said this is all hearsay, but he knew I'd be interested."

He sipped his coffee and stared into his cup. "He wished me the best of luck. Not much, like I said."

Palace Guard rolled his eyes, and I said, "Thank you, Palace Guard. My thoughts exactly. You skipped most of the conversation, didn't you, Mr. Kevin Larry Ewing?"

While I cooked our breakfast, Larry whistled. After we ate, Larry said, "I've got the dishes. You cooked."

"Doesn't make up for whatever you and the lieutenant really said." I flounced to the sofa and put up my feet then crossed my arms. *I am not speaking to Larry.* Palace Guard dropped to the sofa and copied me, and I snickered.

Larry's phone rang, and he answered.

"Thanks, Jimbo. We'll be there."

"Truck's ready?" I asked. *Dang. I forgot I wasn't talking to him.* Palace Guard smirked.

"Ready at eleven. I'll call Cecil."

While Larry talked to Cecil, my phone rang. *Mother?*

"Hello, Margaret. Tomorrow's the wedding, but I guess you knew that. We're really excited. Jennifer and Ella made wonderful plans, but they won't tell me because Jennifer said I'd forget and tell you. That's true, isn't it? Have you been able to get everything done you wanted so far? Anything I can do to help? We'll be back in town later today, but the reason I called is that Big D got a call from the host at Vecchia Nonna. Big D won the dinner for two. He didn't remember entering, but he must have. We thought you might like to go out to dinner at a nice place this evening. Just the two of you. If you already have other plans, that's fine. Big D told them to put them in your name. I thought that was cute. You can go any time after six and no need for reservations. Oh. Big D said how are you?"

"Hi, Mother. Thank you for tonight's dinner. It sounds nice. We're fine."

"That's good. See you tomorrow." She hung up.

"Bye, Mother," I whispered then smiled.

Larry was bent over the dishwasher and stretched his back as he rose. "I think that's your tiger smile, Maggie. What did your Mother say?"

"Sarge supposedly won two dinners at Vecchia Nonna for tonight, and he put them in my name. Isn't that a coincidence?"

Larry's eyes widened. "Maurice wants to see you, but how could he have known Sarge would ask for them to be in your name?"

"I'm sure everyone who has been around Mother in the past few weeks knows we're getting married and that Sarge and Mother are traveling. It would be natural for Sarge to offer the free meals to us."

Larry nodded. "What are you going to wear?"

"Good point. I'll have to think about that. What's appropriate to wear to an ambush?"

"An armored tank." Larry narrowed his eyes.

"I could wear jeans and the flowery shirt that doesn't have to be tucked in. It's kind of low cut, though."

Larry pursed his lips.

"Well, what are you thinking?"

"Let's stay here and talk about your low-cut shirt and cleavage." Larry leered, and I laughed.

"Changing the subject, how were you planning on loading the trailer?" I asked.

"I have a couple of friends whose shifts are over at three. They'll help." He started the dish washer then sat next to me on the sofa.

"I'm squished between you two." I put out my elbows, and they both moved less than a quarter of an inch. "If we get a padlock, couldn't you load it this afternoon? I don't see where there is that much to load after the large items are in the trailer. We could always ask Ella to supervise the loading."

He nodded. "With Ella's warehouse experience, that's a great idea. Of course, you know that means Moe will come too. Bonus."

I called Ella. "We're picking up Larry's new truck at eleven then the trailer after that. Some of Larry's friends can help load after three. Would you be available to supervise loading the trailer this afternoon? It's a cargo trailer, and we can park it at the trailer spot at the apartment complex."

"Honey, that's a great idea, and I would love to. If they bring the big things down first, we'll load them in the trailer's front then fill in with the boxes. I left out some quilts and blankets to cover the furniture. Larry has some nice pieces there. I love the dresser and the dining table. I think we could have everything in the trailer in less than an hour. My Les will come with me, of course, and I'll bring your things from Jennifer's. What time?"

"Larry's friends get off at three, so we could probably plan on three thirty." I rubbed my forehead. "What things?"

"You've had a lot on your mind. Jennifer and I packed your things after your crash and put the boxes in Jennifer's garage. Three thirty is great. See you then. Bye."

"Bye, Ella. Thank you."

I shook my head. "I'd forgotten that Jennifer and Ella packed my things after the crash because I was staying at Jennifer's. The boxes are in Jennifer's garage, and Ella will bring them with her."

"You've been distracted, sweetheart." Larry rubbed my neck. "I'll text a couple of guys."

I received a text from Shantelle. "Pick up rings at ten."

"Rings at ten," I said after Larry finished his text. "Can you imagine doing all this if Cecil hadn't told us to buy the truck yesterday?"

Larry peered at me. "I haven't had time to get you a wedding present. Let's pick out a grill and a lawn mower this weekend. Grill for you and a lawnmower for me. Maybe they could match."

"That's a great idea. You aren't joking, are you?"

"Only about the matching part. I've been trying to think of what we'd like and decided a grill and a lawnmower were perfect, nontraditional fits for us."

"You are brilliant." I grabbed my backpack and crutches. "I've got my holstered gun and my knife in its holster in my boot. I'm ready."

On the way to the lawyer's office, I sent Jennifer a text. "Picking up rings at ten."

Jennifer: "Bring them here, but don't come in."

I read the text to Larry, and he laughed. "You won't ever get another text like that from Jennifer."

When we reached the office, Shantelle opened the door before we reached the end of the sidewalk, and her hands flapped. "Come in. Have a seat in the conference room, and I'll bring you your rings. Ms. Rodriquez has something for you too." She bounced on her toes as we headed to the conference room.

"Why is she so excited about the rings?" I asked.

Larry shrugged. "There's something else, but it must be good."

Palace Guard nodded.

CHAPTER TWENTY-TWO

Shantelle brought us two royal blue ring boxes. "See what you think." She clasped her hands to hold them still.

After we put on our rings, Larry held out his hand and inspected his. "Looks nice, and I see what you're talking about as far as the rolled band is concerned. Very comfortable. Perfect fit. Yours?"

"The same. Outstanding work, Shantelle." We put our rings back into their boxes.

She blushed then hurried out of the conference room and returned with Ms. Rodriquez who grinned as she entered. "You won't believe this."

Ms. Rodriquez placed the dirty, faded rose fabric ring box on the conference room table, and I gasped. "That's the ring box from Clara Hayden's house. How did it survive the fire?"

Ms. Rodriquez smiled. "Clara's lawyer and I had a chat last evening, and he got up early this morning to deliver this. Clara Hayden gave him the box the day that she signed her new will. She told him it wasn't her style, but she was keeping it for a friend. She asked him to give it to Maggie Flanagan, and he claimed he didn't know who she was talking about. This is for you, Maggie."

I opened the box, and the tiny piece of paper slid out. Margarite's ring, the heirloom emerald set in the gold Celtic knot, was nestled in its slot. When I picked it up, the stone sparkled in the sunlight, and Shantelle gasped. "What a beautiful ring."

"The inscription says *BH & MF*," Ms. Rodriquez said.

I handed the ring to Shantelle, and she inspected it. Larry read the slip of paper aloud. "For my Maggie. BH."

My eyes widened. "Margarite was Maggie Flanagan?"

"You must look like Margarite did at your age, and that's how Clara remembered her," Larry said.

"The ring belongs to Mother. Clara told me that phony letter she wrote needed to go to Maggie Flanagan's mother. Do you think she was giving me a hint about the ring?"

"That very well could be. The lawyer said Clara never said or did anything that didn't mean something. He was afraid, actually, to keep the ring because Clara Hayden had told him about her grandson being hexed. He said he didn't believe in that kind of stuff, but he didn't want to ignore an old woman's wishes." Ms. Rodriquez snorted.

"Try it on," Shantelle said. "I want to see it on your hand."

I put on the ring, and its soft rolled edges nestled against my finger.

"Ooh. That's beautiful," Shantelle said. "Does it feel hexed?"

Ms. Rodriquez glowered, and I laughed.

"Not at all; it's comforting. Now that I know what rolled edges are, I could never wear a ring that didn't have rolled edges. Mother will love this. You'll give it to her?" I put the ring back into the box.

"We can do that. It's an exquisite ring. I'm glad Clara Hayden decided to get it to its rightful owner," Ms. Rodriquez rose and picked up the ring then stopped. "Maggie, you should have the note. Do you want the box? We can swap it with your wedding ring box."

I glanced at Larry, and he and Palace Guard nodded. "I think that would be nice. Mother wouldn't understand the note, and I love the box."

Shantelle removed the emerald ring and placed my wedding ring in the old, frayed box then placed the emerald ring in the new ring box. "Done." She handed me the note, and Shantelle gave us a small sack for our rings.

On our way to Jennifer's, Larry said, "Keeping it for a friend? More like stolen from Maggie Flanagan."

Palace Guard nodded, and I snorted as I sent Jennifer a text. "Be there soon."

When Larry pulled into Jennifer's driveway, she stood on the porch. Glenn and Spike were at the window. I waved, and they waved. Larry ran the sack with the rings to the porch, and Jennifer snatched it from him and dashed into the house.

As he backed out, Larry asked, "Did we just do a drug drop?"

We laughed, and Palace Guard rolled his eyes.

"Sorry, Palace Guard. Let's get my truck," Larry said.

"And I get to drive my new car. I need my own key, Larry. You keep yours as backup. I'll add locksmith to our list of things to do next week."

On our way to the dealership, Sylvia sent a text.

"Sylvia sent me the contact information for the utilities. I'll work on that after we get back to Olivia's apartment. Oh wow. Sylvia put the house key in the mail yesterday morning, and we might get it today. I'll ask Jennifer about it."

I texted Jennifer. "Agent dropped our key into the mail yesterday. We expect it today at your house."

Jennifer: "Mail at noon. Will watch for it."

Larry parked in front of the dealership office, and Jimbo came out of the door before Larry opened my door.

"Truck's ready. It's in back. Let's go check it out."

"Maggie, you can stay here or go along."

"I'll stay here and fix the seat and mirrors. Text me if you need me to join you."

Larry grabbed his backpack, and he and Jimbo matched stride for stride as they headed to the back.

"No way could I have kept up with those two."

Palace Guard nodded.

While I adjusted the seat then the mirrors, Palace Guard stood outside the driver's door and scanned the parking lot. Palace Guard nudged my shoulder and pointed to a black car with dark-tinted windows that pulled into the dealership and crept from aisle to aisle. I crammed on my Texas Tech hat and sunglasses then lowered the seat so that only the top of my head was visible. I put my chin down as the black car rolled past me.

"Maurice?" I asked.

Palace Guard nodded.

The black car cruised the last aisle then drove away.

I readjusted my seat. "Wonder if he's checking all the dealerships because he knows I have to replace my car?"

Larry drove his new truck from the back and parked next to me. He hopped out and swaggered to my door. *I'm surprised he doesn't have his thumbs hooked in his belt.*

Palace Guard swatted my shoulder. *Fine. I'll behave.*

"Whaddaya think, Maggie? She's a beauty, isn't she?"

"Perfect," I said.

"You want to follow me to the trailer rental place or go on back to Olivia's?"

"I'll follow you."

He saluted then swaggered back to his truck. I narrowed my eyes. *Did he suddenly become bow-legged?*

Palace Guard grinned and shook his head.

Larry pulled out in front of oncoming traffic and sped away. I waited until it was clear then headed to the trailer rental. When I parked at the rental office, the trailer was hitched to the truck, and Cecil pointed while Larry nodded.

Last-minute instructions. That's good.

As I parked in front of the office, my phone buzzed a text.

Jennifer: "Key to your Columbus house is here. Pick up in the morning."

Larry and Cecil shook hands, and Cecil smiled and waved to me as he went inside the air-conditioned office.

Larry strode to my car, and I lowered my window.

"The house key from Sylvia is here. Jennifer said we can pick it up tomorrow morning."

"Perfect." He beamed and pointed to his truck. "She rides like a dream."

"Lots of power too."

"She's a beast. I'll meet you at Olivia's."

Larry drove away, and the trailer bounced along behind him. I caught up with him at a light then followed him to Olivia's. He turned to park in the trailer lot, and I parked in the closer car parking.

"He may spend some time becoming more familiar with his truck and trailer. I'm going to the apartment."

Palace Guard swaggered to the trailer parking, and I snorted. The elevator crept to the second floor. When I stepped off the elevator, I saw him as he turned the corner to my apartment. *Maurice.*

I reached into my backpack and pulled out my backup pistol and stuck it into the back of my pants. I set my backpack and crutches in the breezeway in full view of the elevator, and as I watched the corner for Maurice, I sent a quick text to Larry. "Need backup." And pressed the record button on my phone and jammed it in my belt. *Body cam, Maggie style.*

As I eased along the breezeway, Palace Guard stepped in front of me and stepped to the corner then held up his hand. I stopped. I heard quiet footsteps on the stairs behind me. Palace Guard's eyes widened, and he motioned for me to retreat, but I assumed a stance that was perfect for me to draw and shoot, despite its casual appearance.

Maurice rounded the corner. "Hello, Maurice, or should I say Ross? Looking for me?"

He froze, and his eyes were filled with hate. "She told you, didn't she?"

I sensed Larry was around the corner behind me and out of Maurice's sight. *He understands. He's my backup.*

"What was the purpose of burning down Clara Hayden's house?"

Maurice clenched his hands. "I inherit everything she has, but she clammed up when I asked her about those paintings she and her friends stole from that museum. She should have died fifteen or twenty years ago, but her friend hexed me and kept her alive. I did the old thief a favor when I burned her house down around her."

I nodded. "So why the attacks on me?"

He narrowed his eyes. "She told me you would get those paintings before I did. I needed to stop you." His twisted grin broadcast the depth of his hatred. "Nothing personal."

He twitched his right hand, and his eyes glanced to the right. *I see you, Maurice. Three, two, one.*

Maurice reached for his gun and fired as I flicked my knife at his hand with my left hand. My knife sliced into his wrist and quivered. The bullet lodged in the ceiling, and his gun flew over the railing. I pointed my gun at his chest. "Stop. Don't move."

"Why you..." He fumbled a gun out of his belt with his left hand and pulled the trigger, but his poorly aimed shot went wide. Mine didn't. I flattened against the wall as the circle of red at the left of his sternum pulsed and grew, and Larry shot Maurice square in the middle of his forehead. Maurice collapsed, and Palace Guard stood next to his body.

Larry rushed to me but kept his gun pointed at Maurice, and I pulled my cell phone out of my pants and turned off the recording

Larry hugged me, and I snuggled my face into his chest. "You okay?"

"I expected Maurice to ambush me this evening."

Larry's voice was hard. "I should never have let you come up here by yourself."

I leaned back and gazed at him. "But he talked only because he thought I was alone."

"I hate it when you're right." Larry growled as footsteps thundered up the stairway. Palace Guard rounded the corner from the stairs and nodded, and we set our guns down on the breezeway. Larry turned to shield me, and we raised our hands. I peeked around Larry and smiled when the first face I saw come around the corner was Moe's.

"Everything under control? Maggie okay?" Moe asked. "I heard four shots."

"Sure is. Maggie's fine." Larry released his tight hold on me, and I stepped next to him. "Two shots were Maurice's, one was Maggie's, and one was mine."

Moe exhaled and spoke into his radio then his eyes twinkled. "Of course she is. That Maurice?"

"I think I recorded most of it," I said as more officers stormed the breezeway. Larry, Moe, and Palace Guard crowded around me as I played the video. I glanced at the two men next to me, and Palace Guard who stood behind me. *Just like old times.* The video was sometimes jerky and off-kilter, but the sound was clear.

"Send me the video," Moe said, then he whispered, "Well done, Maggie."

"I'd like for Maggie to get off her feet. We'll be at the apartment," Larry said. "She left her crutches and backpack near the elevator."

"Go right ahead. I'll bring her things and be there in a few minutes."

Larry put his arm around me and lifted me off my feet. He strode, and I floated to the apartment. After he set me down on the sofa, I asked, "Will we be able to be at your apartment by three-thirty?"

He grinned. "Sure will."

While Moe asked questions and wrote in his notebook, Larry made sandwiches.

Before I finished my half-sandwich, Moe left.

While Larry loaded our dishes into the dishwasher, my phone rang. *Sarge.*

"Just heard," he growled. "You okay? And Larry?"

"We're fine."

"Good. Just needed to hear it from you." His voice softened. "We love you, Maggie. See you tomorrow."

"Love you both."

After he hung up, I said. "We won't have to call anyone. Sarge checked in, and Mother will pass the word."

I checked my backpack and put my spare gun back into its compartment then rose. "Ready when you are."

As we headed to the parking lot, Larry said, "This will be your first real ride in the truck. Wish I could figure out a way that you could ride with me to Columbus. I should have gotten a bigger trailer so we could put the car inside the trailer."

Larry helped me into the truck, and we clattered out of the apartment complex. On the way to Larry's apartment, I glanced at the surrounding cars. "There's a much better view of traffic in the higher truck, isn't there?"

Larry explained the advantages of having a truck and how much he loved finally having a truck that could tow. I leaned back and listened to the excitement in his voice.

When we reached his apartment, Larry backed into a parking spot near his building. I was pleased that it was easier to get up the stairs. "I'm finally getting better."

Larry smiled. "Good."

While we examined the boxes, Ella burst into the apartment. "I heard. You're amazing, as always. You too, Larry."

She scanned the boxes then rearranged a few. "After we get your large items in the trailer, we'll pack the boxes so that your most-needed items are first off. I'll explain the order to you, Maggie, and leave you up here to point. I'll be down at the trailer barking orders."

I entered my notes while she waved her hands and pointed.

When the first two helpers bounded into the apartment, Ella said, "Show time."

She bustled to the trailer with the padlock key, and Larry introduced me then explained the process to the helpers. The young men stared at me while he spoke. As they strode to the bedroom, one of the guys asked, "She's really The Maggie Sloan?"

Larry growled an answer that I couldn't understand, and I snickered.

I followed them into the bedroom and consulted my notes. "The dresser, then the mattress, box springs, and headboard. Dining table and chairs after that."

Two more men and Moe came into the apartment, and Moe introduced the two men to me. "Ella said you'd tell us what goes down next, Maggie."

I pointed and checked off items as they went out the door, and the apartment was empty in twenty minutes.

Moe came to the door. "Ella wanted me to check. Is that everything?"

"I think we got it all, but I'd appreciate it if you would check behind me."

Moe checked all the rooms, closets, and cabinets then strode to the door and called down. "Empty."

Moe smiled, and Palace Guard raised his eyebrows. "Maggie, you are the most amazing woman I have ever met. Congratulations to you and Kevin. Thank goodness he knows what he's getting into." He laughed as he left, and Larry came into the apartment.

"What's wrong with Moe? He was laughing as I passed him on the stairs. Are you ready? I'll lock up."

Larry locked the door and carried my crutches as he helped me down the stairs. Everyone had left except Ella.

She hugged me and winked. "See you later, Gray Lady."

"Ready for a swim and a beer while we argue over where to call for takeout?" Larry helped me into the truck. After he started the engine, he said, "It's a different ride with the loaded trailer, but Ella has the load balanced and tight so it won't shift."

On our way to the apartment, Larry praised the ease of driving his truck, explained how to back a trailer, and the advantages of a trailer brake and how to use it. I nodded and smiled.

After he parked at the apartment complex, he helped me out.

"If we can't think of anything else, I'm fine with pizza," I said as we entered the elevator. "Maybe we can find an old movie or two to watch. I'd like to see what it's like to do the regular stuff people do."

Larry unlocked the door. "I need a shower. Maybe we could binge-watch a series."

"I'll see what I can find."

I relaxed on the sofa with my feet up and searched for restaurants and diners in Harperville. My phone rang. *Heather?*

"Glad you're okay, Gray Lady. Don't plan anything for this evening. There's a surprise bachelor and bachelorette party at your place. It starts at six. See you." She giggled as she hung up.

When Larry joined me on the sofa, he asked, "Did you find anything?"

"Yep. We're going to a party; actually, a party is coming to us."

He nodded. "That's nice. Now explain."

I snickered. "Heather called to tell me there's a party here at six. It's a surprise party."

"A surprise party for us? And she called to tell us about it?"

"Of course. Isn't that the way it works? My turn for a shower."

I breathed in the warm, moist air then scrubbed, rinsed, and dried then dried my hair. At five forty-five, Larry opened the door, and Heather came inside accompanied by a man who was a young, slightly taller version of Spike. The three of us stared at him.

"This is Todd Murphy." Heather set the three sacks that she carried on the counter, and Todd placed the twelve-packs of beer next to the sacks. His grin was panda-style as he shook hands with Larry then hugged me. Palace Guard elbowed Larry.

"Welcome, Todd. It's nice to meet you." Larry elbowed me.

"We've looked forward to meeting you," I said.

Heather put the beer in the refrigerator and turned on the oven. "We brought tacos. I'll put them on low to keep them warm. Although there's nothing wrong with cold tacos."

Ella and Moe knocked on the door then were followed by Sierra, Toby, and Officer Perry.

Ella hugged me. "Told you I'd see you later. We brought chicken livers."

"Thank you for inviting me to your party, Ms. Maggie." Toby stuck out his hand, and we shook hands.

"Thank you for coming, Toby. It's nice to see you."

Officer Perry stuck close to Sierra, and I hid my smile.

More officers came with their wives or girlfriends. Ella and Heather organized the food buffet-style on the counter, and the apartment was filled with laughter and stories. At eight thirty, people drifted out. Ella, Moe, Heather, and Todd stayed behind.

"Sit," Ella said. "We invited you to this party; we'll have everything cleaned up in two shakes."

After they left, we collapsed on the sofa. "Did you know about this?" he asked.

"Not until Heather called. You?"

He shook his head. "First time the department ever kept a secret. Amazing."

He drew me close to him, and I gazed at him. He met my gaze and kissed me so lightly it felt like our first kiss. I turned and leaned against him then wrapped my arms around his neck and teased his mouth open then kissed him. He unbuttoned my shirt and stroked the lace on top of my bra.

I moaned. "I love you, Kevin Larry Ewing."

He nibbled on my neck. "I love you, Maggie Flanagan Sloan almost Ewing."

"Skip the balcony?"

He picked me up and carried me to the bedroom. "You got it, sweetie."

I rolled over and checked the clock. *Five thirty. Shower and whistling.* I smiled and stumbled to the bathroom. Larry grinned as he turned off the water. "Zero! Our wedding is this morning."

I hugged him then handed him his towel and smiled. "Happy zero anniversary, honey."

He grinned then patted my bare bottom as he headed out of the bathroom. "Get dressed. Coffee. Kiss the bride."

After I showered, dried my hair, and dressed, I hurried to the kitchen, and Larry poured me a cup. "It's six thirty. We can leave in an hour," he said.

"I need coffee time then we can pack our things and put them into the car. After the wedding, we can come back for the truck and leave."

"Perfect."

At seven forty-five, we put my crutches in the back seat of the car.

"You drive," Larry said. "The car seat's set up for you."

I parked across the street from the Coyles'. Spike and Lucy waited in the front yard. Lucy yipped and danced as we headed to the house. I rushed to the house and smiled at Spike. "I'm so happy to see you. Thank you for taking care of Lucy."

Spike nodded. When I sat on the steps, Lucy wiggled to me, and I hugged her. She rolled over, and Larry rubbed her belly. When we headed to the front door, she bumped into the back of my leg.

"She's going to stay close to you for a while," Larry chuckled.

My eyes widened as we went into the house. The house was decorated with blue and green streamers and flowers. "It's beautiful, Jennifer," I said.

Jennifer smiled. "Ella and I are a great team. Come see the patio then we'll have breakfast. Your folks will be here soon."

On our way through the den, Jennifer said, "Ella and Les are in the kitchen. I'll send them out."

When Larry and I stepped to the patio door, Glenn grinned. "I am so glad to see you. Come on out."

A large tent covered the backyard. An arch with flowers and greenery was at the end of the yard, and folding chairs decorated with gray, red, blue, and green streamers faced the arch. I said, "Wow. It looks like a classy wedding chapel."

Palace Guard walked with me as I touched the chairs and inspected the arch. Ella and Moe joined us, and Moe and Larry shook hands.

"We couldn't decide on the colors, so we went with all of them," Ella said.

"It's perfect."

Ella hugged me. "Good."

Sarge, Mother, Lauren, and Sean came out to the patio.

"This is beautiful, Ella," Lauren said.

"I'm glad I didn't know," Mother said as she touched the chairs. "I could never have kept this quiet."

Sarge nodded.

"Come to the dining table," Jennifer said.

We filed inside, and she pointed. "Look for your name. We decided we'd save a lot of time if we didn't have to work out seating after everyone got here."

Larry and I sat next to each other. On the other side of me, the name card said *Special Guest*. I nudged Larry and pointed to the card.

"Who's the special guest?" I asked.

"Oh, you know." Jennifer and Ella exchanged glances.

I glanced at Spike, and he made a fierce face. I elbowed Larry, and he looked at Spike. Palace Guard wiggled his eyebrows. Larry smirked.

"I'll have to be ready," I mumbled. Larry leaned to give me a kiss and whispered, "Yes."

Ella and Jennifer served our plates; after they joined us at the table, we ate, laughed, and talked. I finished eating before everyone else.

"Happy?" Sarge asked.

"Oh, yes."

I heard a scrape at the front door, and Larry placed his hand on the back of my seat. He smiled. "Ready when you are."

The front door opened slowly but not quite silently. I pressed my napkin to my mouth then rose as Larry eased away my chair. When Kate tiptoed into the house, I ambushed her as she stepped into the dining room. I tossed her to the floor, and when she sprang to her feet and reached for my foot, I bent down and grabbed her arm then tossed her over my back onto the floor. I scampered to hide between Mother and Sarge.

Kate laughed as she rolled on the floor. Larry and Glenn applauded. Moe rolled his eyes, and Sean and Lauren stared.

Jennifer said, "Okay, girls. That's enough."

Kate and I laughed even harder. "Come help me up, Gray Lady," Kate said.

"No way."

"Fine. You win. Truce." She sat up and shook her head. "I thought I'd give you a break. I won't repeat that mistake."

"Do they do this all the time?" Lauren asked.

"Oh, yes," Glenn said.

"They aren't supposed to," Jennifer grumbled.

I returned to my seat, and Kate sat at the table. Neither of us turned our back to the other.

"Hey, Spike. Missed you," she said.

Spike smiled.

"Kate, you need to meet Heather's new boyfriend, Todd Murphy," I said.

Spike cocked his head then stared at Palace Guard who nodded.

Jennifer said, "Maggie, if you're finished eating, come see your dress. The minister will be here soon."

I stuck my tongue out at Kate and followed Jennifer.

Jennifer pulled a dress out of the closet. It was shimmery blue at the top that blended into green at the bottom.

"This is beautiful, Jennifer."

"We wanted blue for Larry's blue eyes and green for yours. It will go fine with your boots. I'm glad you like it. Try it on. I'm going to braid your long hair into a single braid. What do you think?"

"That would be great."

There was a knock at the front door. "I'll be back. That's the minister. Lauren bought a suit for Larry. We'll clear the table in no time and be ready for the wedding. Are you excited? I can't remember when I've had more fun." Jennifer hugged me then left.

I put on the dress and frowned at the cleavage then shrugged. *Larry will like it.*

Jennifer braided my hair and placed a few flowers in the braid then said, "Kate is your maid of honor. She's under orders to behave. You too." Jennifer chuckled then left.

Kate came into the bedroom. She wore a pale green dress and her boots. She held a bride's corsage with white flowers and blue and green ribbons. "You look bride-y."

"You look strange."

We giggled.

Jennifer tapped on the door. "We're ready to start. Maggie, Lucy is your flower dog. I think the imaginary men are standing with Larry. It looks like he's standing by himself to me." Jennifer wore a blue eyelet dress and navy high heels. *Where's your cowgirl boots, Jennifer?*

We followed Jennifer to the patio door. Music came from somewhere, and Kate pushed me.

I stared at Larry with wonder, and he smiled. Palace Guard and Spike were next to Larry, and they smiled too. While we stood at the arch, I was so lost in Larry's gaze that I didn't hear any of the service.

Kate held my elbow and pinched me then mouthed what I was supposed to say. She handed me his ring and pushed my elbow toward Larry. My heart melted when he held my hand and slipped my ring onto my finger. He smiled as I slid his ring onto his finger. He didn't release my hands and met my gaze as we were suspended in time.

When Larry grinned then kissed me, everyone applauded, and I blinked. He hugged me. "Did you hear any of the service?"

"No."

"Good. Neither did I. You are so beautiful." We snickered and kissed again.

Kate elbowed me and whispered. "Go into the den, so everybody can congratulate you. I'll whisk you away before you panic."

I nodded, and Larry and I walked to the den amid smiles and whistles. We were hugged and congratulated, and our mothers, Ella, and Jennifer cried. Sarge, Glenn, and Moe shook hands with Larry, and Sean gave Larry a dad-hug. We answered questions about our plans and thanked Jennifer and Ella for all their hard work.

When Kate announced we needed to leave, she escorted us to our bedrooms to change. "Mom said leave your clothes here. She'll have them cleaned, and you can get them later."

After we changed, Kate hugged us. "I'll see you soon. Good teamwork on that Maurice guy. I'm proud of you."

Ella brought out baskets of flower petals, and everyone threw petals as we left. Lucy, Spike, and Palace Guard stood by my car, and we all climbed in.

Larry kissed me when he slid into the passenger's seat then turned to our backseat passengers. "I'm glad we're all together."

Lucy yipped, and the car dragged clanging cans as I drove away.

Are you ready for the next Maggie story?
ONE EYE ON THE KILLER, BOOK 4
MAGGIE SLOAN THRILLER

Maggie uses her uncanny skills and talents to navigate through the conflicting lies, half-truths, and clues to piece together the seemingly unrelated deaths at a senior center's staff and residents, real and fake jewelry, a fire, and a near-fatal attack on her. Maggie counts on the killer to underestimate her skills as she narrows her suspect list. The killer intends for her to die.

Find ONE EYE ON THE KILLER and all the other Judith A. Barrett Books
BARRETT BOOK SHOP! BarrettBookShop.com
Browse, Shop, Read, Enjoy!
Subscribe: to the newsletter!
Look for the Subscribe button on www.judithabarrett.com

ABOUT THE AUTHOR

Judith A. Barrett is an award-winning author of mystery, crime, and survival science fiction novels with action, adventure, and a touch of the supernatural to spark the reader's imagination. Her unusual main characters are brilliant, talented, and down-to-earth folks who solve difficult problems and stop killers. Her novels are based in small towns and rural areas in south Georgia and north Florida with sojourns to other southern US states.

Judith lives in rural Georgia on a small farm with her husband and two dogs. When she's not busy writing, Judith is still busy working on the farm, hiking with her husband and dogs, or watching the beautiful sunsets from her porch.

You keep reading; I'll keep writing!

Barrett Book Shop barrettbookshop.com

Website judithabarrett.com

Subscribe to the eNewsletter via her website

judithabarrett.com/newsletter

Let's keep in touch!

Made in the USA
Columbia, SC
20 August 2024